"Maybe _____ _____ eed to make sure the ____ _____ fall apart around us." He turned his attention to the science station. "Soloman, do we have internal sensors? Can you give us a damage report?"

The Bynar keyed commands to the science console as his face was bathed in the soft blue light of the station's viewfinder. Several moments passed as he reviewed the information supplied by the *Defiant's* limited sensors.

"There are . . . hull breaches on decks eight, thirteen, and . . . fifteen," he reported. "There is also some buckling . . . in the port warp nacelle." As he turned away from the viewfinder, the Bynar added, "The damage is minor, given the . . . intensity of the attack, Captain. We were . . . most fortunate."

Gomez sighed in relief. "I'll say. If that's the extent of the damage, then we should be okay even under the pull of the *da Vinci's* tractor beam."

"If she's still there," Gold said. "She may have been disabled or destroyed by the Tholians, or Mr. Duffy has obeyed my orders and taken her out of the area. Either way, we may not be able to rely on the *da Vinci* to get us out of here."

STAR TREK

S.C.E.

BOOK TWO

MIRACLE WORKERS

Keith R.A. DeCandido, Kevin Dilmore,
David Mack, & Dayton Ward

Based upon STAR TREK® and
STAR TREK: THE NEXT GENERATION®
created by Gene Roddenberry,
and STAR TREK: DEEP SPACE NINE®
created by Rick Berman & Michael Piller

POCKET BOOKS
New York London Toronto Sydney Singapore Sarindar

POCKET BOOKS, a division of Simon & Schuster, Inc.
1230 Avenue of the Americas, New York, NY 10020

Star Trek® S.C.E. #5: Interphase: Book 2 copyright © 2001 by Paramount Pictures. All Rights Reserved.
Star Trek® S.C.E. #6: Cold Fusion copyright © 2001 by Paramount Pictures. All Rights Reserved.
Star Trek® S.C.E. #7: Invincible: Book 1 copyright © 2001 by Paramount Pictures. All Rights Reserved.
Star Trek® S.C.E. #8: Invincible: Book 2 copyright © 2001 by Paramount Pictures. All Rights Reserved.

 STAR TREK is a Registered Trademark of Paramount Pictures.

This book is published by Pocket Books, a division of Simon & Schuster, Inc., under exclusive license from Paramount Pictures.

ISBN: 0-7434-4412-4

First Pocket Books paperback printing February 2002

10 9 8 7 6 5 4 3 2 1

POCKET and colophon are registered trademarks of Simon & Schuster, Inc.

For information regarding special discounts for bulk purchases, please contact Simon & Schuster Special Sales at 1-800-456-6798 or business@simonandschuster.com

Printed in the U.S.A.

These titles were previously published individually in eBook format by Pocket Books.

CONTENTS

INTERPHASE: BOOK TWO

Dayton Ward
&
Kevin Dilmore

CHAPTER 1

On more than one occasion, mostly during the early years of her career, Commander Sonya Gomez had experienced feelings of helplessness in the midst of a crisis. As she stood on the bridge of the *U.S.S. Defiant* and studied the surreal image displayed on its main viewer, such feelings once again taunted her and dared her to submit to their stifling embrace.

Along with Captain David Gold and Soloman, she watched as the interdimensional rift continued to mend itself, sealing the *Defiant* inside this pocket of chaos ambiguously known as "interphase" and separating them from the *U.S.S. da Vinci* and their entire universe. At the moment, helplessness seemed almost appropriate.

The mission, like so many others Gomez had undertaken since joining the Starfleet Corps of Engineers, had started out easily enough. Daunting and compelling from both technical and historical perspectives, the task of retrieving the *Defiant* had energized the entire *da Vinci* crew, from Captain Gold on down. The recovery of the fabled ship, lost for more than a century after becoming trapped in an interspatial pocket connecting this universe with another, presented a unique engineering challenge. When the ship disappeared in 2268, most scientific minds throughout the Federation believed that it had been lost in the other universe with no hope of being recovered.

That belief had held true until two weeks ago, when a Tholian vessel had discovered the *Defiant*, still trapped in the interdimensional rift but now visible again for the first time in more than a century. The circumstances leading to the ship's reappearance after so long remained a mystery and the Tholians, in their typical fashion, had not been forthcoming with any potentially helpful information.

And we could sure use that info now, Gomez mused.

She had led an away team to the *Defiant* with the task of restoring minimal power to the derelict vessel. Working with Kieran Duffy, the *da Vinci*'s propulsion specialist, she had decided that the *Defiant*'s maneuvering thrusters could be used to help extract the ship from the rift, with the help of the *da Vinci*'s tractor beam. Duffy and his team had also modified the *da Vinci*'s navigational deflector to stabilize the *Defiant*'s hull and make it easier for the tractor beam to lock onto the trapped ship.

Of course, it wouldn't have been an S.C.E. mission if the *Defiant* hadn't yielded a few surprises of its own.

First had been the condition of the ship itself. Drained of power, the *Defiant* was a lifeless hulk, dark and foreboding as the away team materialized in the depths of its engineering section. Then there were the remains of the ship's crew, drifting free throughout the vessel's interior in the absence of gravity. The nightmarish scene had caught Gomez off guard and caused her no small amount of anxiety. Her reaction to the situation troubled her, but she had managed to keep her unease at bay to this point by concentrating on the tasks at hand.

But then the Tholians had inexplicably fired on the *Defiant*, disrupting the *da Vinci*'s attempt to pull the century-old ship from the interspatial void and instead throwing the *Defiant* back into the rift. The action had the further effect of collapsing the pocket around the ship, trapping it and the *da Vinci* away team within the confines of interspace.

"The weapons fire could have disturbed the fabric of space near the rift," Gomez said as she studied the viewscreen. "The area is already so unstable, any kind of disruption would probably be enough to affect it."

Turning away from the viewscreen, Gold said, "Something similar was reported in the old *Enterprise* logs when they discovered the *Defiant*. It had the effect of throwing off the interphase timetable. The *Defiant* still continued to appear and reappear, but they had to recalculate the intervals."

"That means the *da Vinci* can probably still get us out," Gomez said.

"Maybe," Gold replied as he stepped toward the

starboard side of the command well. "But first we need to make sure the ship won't fall apart around us." He turned his attention to the science station. "Soloman, do we have internal sensors? Can you give us a damage report?"

The Bynar keyed commands to the science console as his face was bathed in the soft blue light of the station's viewfinder. Several moments passed as he reviewed the information supplied by the *Defiant*'s limited sensors.

"There are . . . hull breaches on decks eight, thirteen and . . . fifteen," he reported. "There is also some buckling . . . in the port warp nacelle." As he turned away from the viewfinder, the Bynar added, "The damage is minor, given the . . . intensity of the attack, Captain. We were . . . most fortunate."

Gomez sighed in relief. "I'll say. If that's the extent of the damage, then we should be okay even under the pull of the *da Vinci*'s tractor beam."

"If she's still there," Gold said, drawing shocked expressions from Gomez and Soloman. The *da Vinci*'s commanding officer didn't acknowledge the looks, however, instead adding, "She may have been disabled or destroyed by the Tholians, or Mr. Duffy has obeyed my orders and taken her out of the area. Either way, we may not be able to rely on the *da Vinci* to get us out of here."

"Even if the rift was open," Gomez said, "the *Defiant*'s maneuvering thrusters aren't enough to push us out on their own." The generators they had brought with them from the *da Vinci* would never be enough to power the ship's massive

I'll get there through the Jefferies tubes." She knew that navigating the crawlspaces and maintenance throughways connecting nearly every point on the starship would be difficult while wearing her environment suit, but that would be offset somewhat by the absence of the ship's artificial gravity field.

"Sounds like a plan," Gold said, nodding his approval. "In the meantime, Soloman and I are going to do some more detective work. It's pretty obvious that whatever set the Tholians off has something to do with that little *tchotchke* that Pattie and the doctor found in the cargo bay."

CHAPTER
2

Today was the last day Kieran Duffy wanted an excuse to lie down on the job.

Yet mere minutes after his first space battle as the commanding officer of a Starfleet vessel, he was sprawled across the deck plates in the main engineering room of the *U.S.S. da Vinci*. Scattered to his side were a number of isolinear chips, once translucent and operational but now charred black and useless. He fumbled a few more of the chips in one hand, eyeing them for telltale signs of burnout, then double-checking his visual survey with the diagnostic reader he grasped in his other hand. Next to his head was an open panel, glowing from within and sporting about a dozen empty sockets waiting for working chips to be inserted.

Duffy let all but a pair of the chips slip from his grasp before craning his head to peer inside the console. The bright control panels with glowing chips appeared clean and new, belying the fact that they, key components in the starship's warp-drive system, were about as functional as a wet match.

One hit.

That's all it had taken from the Tholian ship to disable the *da Vinci*'s warp drive. It had been bad enough only a few hours before, when Captain Gold had tasked him with keeping the warp core's intermix ratios in balance as the starship set about her mission of extracting the *U.S.S. Defiant* from the interspatial rift. The unusual, tenuous connection that the rift had created between the two universes had been known to wreak havoc on the warp engines of ships venturing close to it, and Captain Gold wanted no such surprises during their recovery operation.

Thanks to the Tholians, though, all of Duffy's calculating of formulas and finessing of the magnetic fields that prevented matter from blending too freely with antimatter was wasted.

How does that wisecrack go? The fight was two hits long: The Klingon hit the Cardassian and the Cardassian hit the floor. Who's the one on the floor now?

Duffy shoved his hand into the depths of the console to seat the pair of replacement chips. Straining, he slipped one chip into place, then maneuvered himself to another open slot, gripping the very edge of the remaining chip with the tips of two fingers.

But just as the chip found a purchase on the rim of the slot, a sharp blow to the bottom of his right foot rocked his entire body.

"Yaa!" he shouted, dropping the chip and smacking his head against the edge of the console's cavity. Worming his way out of the opening, he looked up to see Domenica Corsi towering over him, her jaw clenched and the toe of her boot next to where she had just kicked him.

"Just perfect," Corsi said. "Ostriches stick their heads in the sand. You stick yours into a bulkhead."

"Oh, excuse me," he fired back as he felt himself starting to heat up. "I had the foolish idea that warp drive might be a nice thing to have before the Tholians get back. That is, unless you'd like to get out and push."

Corsi's scowl darkened. "A ship full of engineers, and you're the only one who can fix it?"

The question made Duffy pause, giving him a moment to catch his tongue rather than launch another barb. Yes, he was the *da Vinci*'s top mind on matters of propulsion, and he acted as the ship's warp-core watchdog above and beyond even the chief engineer.

But now he was in command of the *da Vinci*. This was not the time for him to nursemaid a warp-drive problem, and it had taken Corsi to remind him of it.

Again.

As if to emphasize the point, she said, "You need to be on the bridge, Commander. Order someone else to repair the warp drive."

Duffy nodded. "You're right." With a mischievous smile he added, "You're getting to like keeping me in check, aren't you?" He was satisfied to see the security chief's expression soften a little as her jaw muscles loosened.

Not much, but it's a start.

After detailing the top-priority repair assignment to the small army of engineers tending to various tasks here within the heart of the ship, Duffy smiled at Corsi again and headed for the door. She followed him, and the pair made their way quickly down the corridor.

As they walked, Duffy said, "I need to know exactly where we are on repairs before Captain Scott tells us Starfleet's official response to our situation. I'd like some ideas on reopening the rift, too."

He tried not to dwell on his last conversation with the seasoned engineer who served as the figurehead for the Starfleet Corps of Engineers. It was Captain Montgomery Scott who had dispatched the *da Vinci* and her crew to Tholian space in the first place, charging them with the challenge of retrieving the *Defiant* from the rift, while at the same time entrusting them with the delicate task of working with the temperamental Tholians. It was he whose face had fallen as Duffy relayed the events that had erupted just when the mission seemed to be going so well, and it was he who was likely getting his aft shields chewed right now by Starfleet brass as a result.

Corsi's voice brought Duffy to attention. "I assumed as much, Commander. The team is already waiting for us in the briefing room."

Duffy couldn't help the small laugh that escaped his lips, feeling more at ease with the idea that "Core Breach" Corsi was acting as a safety net for his first tightrope walk of a command. With her at his side, he might just survive this mission yet.

They entered the briefing room and Duffy took note of who was at the table, while at the same time trying not to think about who was noticeably absent. Scattered about in their usual seats were other members of the team: Carol Abramowitz, their chief liaison with the Tholian Assembly; Fabian Stevens, the ship's expert on tactical systems; and Bartholomew Faulwell, the team's cryptography and language specialist, who had stepped in to help brainstorm options for salvaging their mission, given the current void of command officers. Duffy mulled taking the head seat at the table, the one typically occupied by Captain Gold, but settled instead for the comfort of his usual chair next to Abramowitz.

"Okay," Duffy began, placing his elbows on the table before him and lacing his fingers. "Warp drive is almost operational again. Everything else is good to go, right?"

Stevens was quick to answer. "We didn't take it on the chin too hard, Duff. Weapons are fine. Communications, shields, the deflector array, life support, everything checks right on down the line. I'd bet the warp drive would have been fine, too, if it wasn't for this space we're in."

Duffy wondered whether that was the rule and not the exception here. Tholian ships' disruptors could wreak havoc on unshielded vessels, he was certain, but it seemed that Federation starships with fully charged deflector shields usually could shrug off the initial volleys of such an attack.

"Maybe so, Fabian," Duffy replied, "but here, all bets are off. Right now I want to dig into the deflector modifications and see whether we can open the rift again without waiting for it." He knew that time was a precious commodity right now. The Tholians had to know how much damage they had inflicted on the *da Vinci*, and they most likely also knew that the starship wouldn't leave the area unless forced to, so long as there was a chance to recover the *Defiant* and the away team. The chronometer was ticking for those aboard both ships, however, so he wasn't willing to be patient.

Corsi leaned forward in her seat. "Shield harmonics need to be monitored closely as well, Mr. Stevens, in case that rift has the same degenerative effect on them as it does on our warp capability. We need to be prepared for an all-out attack once that Tholian ship returns with reinforcements."

Duffy was ready to answer, but instead was cut off by Carol Abramowitz.

"Prepare all you want," she said, "but we're not going into battle." The cultural specialist was met with Corsi's perturbed expression but continued unheeded. "You can bet that our next orders will be to head home without the *Defiant*. No one is going to throw away the trust that diplomats and ambassadors have earned with the Tholians during the Dominion War. Unfortunately, an antique ship and a few engineers will be considered expendable."

Abramowitz's assessment matched his own, Duffy realized as he hung his head a bit. Captain Gold had told them all up front that the mission would be scuttled should any signs of eroding relations with the Tholians appear, and an exchange of fire definitely seemed to qualify as erosion to him. Diplomats were sure to exercise their influence to pull the *da Vinci* from the mission, whether or not her crew was intact.

He had to be ready to say good-bye to his captain, his friends, and his . . . his . . .

Oh, Sonnie.

But Corsi did not appear content to keep her views to herself. "What, we're going to abandon the away team? The Tholians fired first! We didn't start this fight, but we damn well better finish it." Duffy watched as Corsi narrowed her eyes and scanned the others seated at the table for a sign of support before adding, "Let them say what they want back on Earth. Regardless of whether we bring the *Defiant* home, we're getting our away team back."

"It is a bold stand you hope to take," Abramowitz replied, "but I don't think you're being realistic." Her tone was clipped and polite, and Duffy knew it was a signal that she was already beginning to lose patience with the security chief. The women's dueling edginess would quickly become as volatile as a mix of matter and antimatter.

"Realistic is a quantum torpedo," Corsi snapped. "You think sweet-talking a Tholian at this point is—"

"*People!*"

Duffy was as surprised as everyone else when the word exploded from his mouth with such force and volume. All eyes turned to him, and no one said anything for several seconds, the only sounds audible in the room being that of the ventilation system and the omnipresent hum of the ship's engines.

Taking a moment to clear his throat, he began again in a more reserved tone. "People, don't think for a minute that Captain Scott isn't doing everything he can on his end to keep us here. Don't stop believing that Captain Gold isn't working to get the *Defiant* to our side of the rift."

He paused, focusing on Corsi as she sat crossarmed in her chair. "But we're not disobeying any order that comes from Starfleet. For now, though, we'll focus on doing everything we can until that order comes down."

Silence hung in the briefing room as Duffy asserted his command over his fellow officers and friends. He racked his mind for some words of support and confidence, the kind of statements that seemed to roll off Captain Gold's tongue in tough situations. Now was the time to be a captain, but all he felt like was a babysitter trying to quell a squabble between sisters while Mom and Dad were at the holotheater.

I can't very well send them to their rooms.

A flash of amber light caught Duffy's eye as it glowed on the tabletop near Faulwell's hand. The linguist tapped a control on the keypad near his arm, then looked up at Duffy with sympathetic eyes.

"It's an incoming message from Starfleet Command. Do you want to take it in private?"

Duffy shook his head. "No. Put it on the viewer."

As Captain Scott's wizened face filled the screen on the briefing room's wall, Duffy felt some of the group's tension seep away. The engineer's creased visage, his friendly eyes, and the hint of a smile were just what everyone needed at that very moment.

"It's not the worst news I'll be bringin' ye, Mr. Duffy," the face on the viewer began, "but the situation isn't good."

Steeling himself for the report, Duffy nodded. "We're ready."

Scott drew a breath before continuing. "Our ambassador to the Tholians is recommending that we scrap the mission. He wants the Federation to formally apologize to the commander of the ship ye fired on, and to the Magistrates of the Assembly. He says we're on the brink of losin' it all as far as relations are concerned, and that the *Defiant* isn't worth it."

Duffy's mind was numbed by Scott's words, which echoed those of Abramowitz moments before. Rather than lose his focus, though, Duffy fell back on his ready wit. "And exactly how is this not the worst news, Captain?"

Scott allowed a small smile before replying. "We've got the support of Admiral Ross, and that carries a lot of weight with the Federation Council. The admiral is arguing for the *da Vinci* to hold its position, saying that it was poor frame of mind and the effects of interspace, not a botched cooperative effort, that led us to this point. He says that it just might be the Tholians who do the apologizin' once this is all over."

Releasing a breath, Duffy relaxed a bit. "So what do we do in the meantime?"

"Tell me how your repairs are farin'."

It was a question Duffy hadn't expected, as he had explained to the S.C.E. leader in detail during their earlier conversation just what damage the starship had suffered. "All systems are operational except for the warp drive, just like—"

"Ah," Scott said with a sigh that was almost too dramatic. "And that's givin' ye lots of trouble to fix so close to the point of interphase, ye say."

"No, sir," Duffy replied, his puzzlement growing by the second. "We're almost—"

"It may take hours to repair before ye can even head back to Federation space."

Realization finally dawned, and a smile spread across Duffy's face as he began to pick up on Captain Scott's lead. It was a look that was shared by everyone else at the table.

"Oh, yes, sir. I'd say at least three—"

"Twelve hours to repair, ye say? I'll let Admiral Ross know right away." Scott nodded grimly and twitched a cheek. Duffy almost laughed aloud.

Did he just wink *at me?*

"Set your team to work, Mr. Duffy," Scott said, then adjusted his tone to a more serious timbre. "But I'll be needin' a word alone with ye now."

Here it comes, Duffy thought as everyone else rose from their seats, moving with only slightly less speed than they might exhibit during an emergency evacuation of the ship. Only Stevens paused just long enough to offer a "thumbs-up" gesture and to mouth the words "Good luck" before he, too, was gone. In seconds Duffy was alone in the room, leaving him to look squarely at the viewer and ready to get called down by the chief of the S.C.E. himself.

Well, it was fun while it lasted. So long, and thanks for all the . . .

"Mr. Duffy," the seasoned engineer said, "did I ever tell ye what the most frightenin' words I ever heard spoken on the bridge of a starship were?" Duffy shook his head as the veteran engineer continued. "Well, here they are: 'Mr. Scott, you have the conn.'"

Duffy laughed in spite of himself, realizing now that the captain understood his plight all too well. He didn't know many engineers who had risen through the ranks of command, at least not the engineers he perceived as being cut from the same cloth as he was. After all, why would an engineer want to command a starship rather than spend that time tearing it apart and putting it back together?

"An engineer's job isn't just to keep a starship runnin'. It's to keep her crew safe," said Scott. "Some of the best years I had in Starfleet were when I was third in command of the *Enterprise*. Keepin' the crew safe; that's what I kept in mind every time I had to sit in the center seat.

"Mr. Duffy, I'm gonna level with ye. That diplomat Marshall wants to hang this whole mess on you. He thinks that an immature officer, a mere *engineer* unfit for command caused the whole thing." Scott leaned forward, his eyes fixing on the younger man. "I know he's wrong. We'll show him he's wrong, Mr. Duffy."

Pride. That's what shone in Captain Scott's eyes as he spoke. Pride in the Starfleet Corps of Engineers, pride in the crew of the *da Vinci*, pride in the engineer who stepped from third in command to leading a ship in a mission that now was so much more than salvaging a relic from a bygone era.

I can do this.

"Yes, we will, Captain," said Duffy, now rising from his chair. "Just buy me the time."

Scott nodded a few times, forcing his lips together tightly in a small frown. To Kieran Duffy, the old engineer appeared lost in his thoughts.

"Laddie, once I thought I was leavin' my captain in that same damnable place. I'll push like hell to keep ye from thinkin' the same. Scott out."

CHAPTER
3

With only the light from her helmet lamps to guide the way and the sound of her own breathing to keep her company, Gomez pulled herself through the Jefferies tube and deeper into the bowels of the *Defiant*. Despite there being no gravity to impede her progress or to grab her and send her plunging headlong down a maintenance shaft, it was still difficult going. Her environment suit, designed for use in open space or on the exposed surface of an otherwise inhospitable planet, only seemed to hamper her movements here. Junctions and intersections were particularly challenging, as she had to be aware of snagging her suit on exposed controls or anything else sticking out from the sides of the crawlway.

And on top of it all, the walls were closing in on her. She was sure of it.

The thought came unbidden, surging to the front of her consciousness. She knew it was an odd notion and completely baseless, but she couldn't shake it. The Jefferies tube was contracting around her. The walls threatened to crush the life out of her, chased back only when she shone her light at them.

"The tube is *not* getting smaller," Gomez scolded herself. "It's your imagination, so get over it and keep moving." And so she did, pulling her weightless body through the crawlspace as quickly as she could, and doing her best to ignore the oppressive advance of the walls around her.

Movement ahead caught her attention, along with a swath of color contrasting with the dull gray dominating the rest of the tunnel. Gomez paused in her crawling, orienting herself so that her helmet lamps could illuminate the section of tube ahead of her. Her eyes focused on the source of the movement, and she felt a shiver travel the entire length of her body.

It was the skeleton of yet another *Defiant* crewmember, dressed in a red jumpsuit and floating freely in the confines of the Jefferies tube. The bones of the feet were bare, and there was no sign of the boots the man had once worn.

Man? Woman? Gomez had no idea what gender the crewmember might have been. She was only reasonably sure that the skeleton was even human. Had this person been an engineer, toiling away in the depths of the starship, only to be overcome by the effects of interspace? He or she had been isolated here, cut off from the rest of the ship's crew. A maintenance crawlway seemed to Gomez to be a particularly lonely place to die.

However, that thought didn't bother her nearly

as much as the realization that the skeleton of the hapless victim was blocking her path through the Jefferies tube. She would have to maneuver past the dead crewman in order to continue forward.

"Dear God . . . " she whispered, noticing the shake in her voice as the words escaped her lips. There was no way she could allow herself to touch the skeleton. The very idea of coming into contact with the crewman's remains revolted her.

What the hell's the matter with me? Her mind screamed the question at her. She had to press forward, of course. It was the only way to get to Lense and Blue. That's what she needed to focus on, not the tightness of the crawlspace or the lifeless body floating before her or . . .

"Stop it!" she shouted, her voice echoing in the confines of her helmet. Then she remained in place for the additional couple of minutes it took to bring her rapid breathing down to something approaching normal. "You can do this," she told herself. "You have to. Pattie and Elizabeth need you."

Yes, that was it. She needed to concentrate on Pattie and Elizabeth and the fact that they were trapped outside the ship and needed her help to get back inside.

"Gomez to Lense," she called out as she activated her communicator, painfully aware of the detectable nervousness in her voice. "How are you making out? How's Pattie?"

"I'm at the airlock, Sonya," the doctor replied. "Pattie is still unconscious, but her readings are stable." She, too, had apparently noticed Gomez's anxiety. "Are you okay? Is something wrong?"

Gomez forced herself to take several deep breaths before replying. It would do no good to display any false bravado, she knew, as Lense would see through the façade with little effort. Better to be open about what was troubling her.

"I'm feeling a bit claustrophobic, Elizabeth," she admitted. "I've spent my fair share of time crawling around Jefferies tubes, but I've never felt like this before. And there's something else." In halting, hushed tones, Gomez described the body blocking her path in the crawlway.

Enough of this! It was time to move, she decided. Lense and Blue didn't have all day to wait for her to get her act together. With a final, cleansing breath, she reached for a handhold and began to pull herself forward once more.

"I'm moving again, Elizabeth," she said, hoping her voice sounded more confident to the doctor than it did to her.

"Good," Lense replied. "Sonya, just talk to me if you start to feel nervous or uneasy again."

"Okay," Gomez said, nodding though there was no one around to see the action. She didn't care, her attention instead riveted on the task at hand. She closed her eyes and focused on the technical schematic Soloman had shown her, displaying the memorized route to the airlock in her mind's eye.

Her concentration faltered, though, when she felt her hand brush across something that was most definitely *not* part of the Jefferies tube. It was soft, yielding to her touch, and it moved slightly at her approach.

The crewman.

Almost immediately Gomez felt her pulse begin to quicken and her breathing accelerate. Still, she kept pushing forward, gritting her teeth and clenching her eyes closed even tighter as she felt the skeleton of the dead crewmember begin to pass down the length of her environment suit. Her mind tortured her with images of bones shifting beneath the material of the crewman's jumpsuit. Could she actually hear the sound of those bones rubbing against one another?

And then, the one thing she feared most happened.

She stopped moving.

Still gripping a handhold, Gomez tried to pull herself forward again but failed. She was stuck. Without thinking, she opened her eyes, only to see the skull of the doomed crewman plastered against the faceplate of her helmet.

The scream that tore itself from her throat echoed in the narrow width of the crawlway.

"Sonya!" Lense's voice called out over her communicator. "What is it?"

Gomez didn't respond. She tuned out her stranded teammate as she thrashed about, flailing her arms and kicking her legs against the sides of the tunnel in a frantic effort to free herself. One hand swiped at the skull still leering at her, forcing it away and up toward the ceiling of the tube. She felt something snap like brittle wood splintering and then she was free, pulling herself once more through the tunnel with no thought as to getting snagged on some projection or slamming head-first into a wall or maintenance hatch.

Suddenly the cramped walls of the Jefferies tube fell away, and Gomez spilled into one of the *Defiant*'s corridors. She barely managed to throw her arms out ahead of her, preventing herself from careening into the passageway's far bulkhead. As her hands touched the wall, instinct and training took over, orienting her body so that her magnetized boots could rest once again on the cold, dusty deck.

"Sonya?" Lense repeated. "Answer me. Are you all right?"

Taking a moment to gather herself, Gomez forced away the lingering images of the crewman's body and the way the skeleton's fragile remains had given way under her panicked assault as she fought to extricate herself from the crawlway.

"I'm . . . I'm fine, Elizabeth. Now, at least. But we're going to have Soloman find us another way back to the bridge, if it's all the same to you."

"Right now," the doctor replied, "I'd just be happy to be inside the ship."

A small chuckle broke through Gomez's remaining anxiety, bringing a much-needed smile to her face as she started down the corridor, examining directional signs on the bulkheads as she went. It didn't take long to find the room containing the maintenance airlock, as well as a collection of lockers holding environment suits and assorted engineering tools. If time hadn't been an issue, Gomez might have taken a few minutes to examine the century-old equipment and marvel at how well it had been preserved by the lack of atmosphere on the ship.

Instead, she turned her attention to the airlock itself. A moment's work with her manual door opener succeeded in coaxing the airlock hatch open and revealing the welcome sight of Elizabeth Lense. The doctor was still cradling the unconscious Pattie in her arms.

"How is she?" Gomez asked as she helped lower the Nasat to the deck. She held Pattie's still form down as Lense reached for her tricorder, but to Gomez's surprise, she was the first object of the doctor's scrutiny rather than Pattie.

"Just as I suspected," Lense said as she snapped the tricorder closed and reached for the medical kit on her belt. "The theragen I gave you has begun to wear off. You've started to feel the effects of interspace."

Gomez's sigh was a mixture of relief and apprehension as she allowed herself to relax somewhat and sag against the nearby bulkhead. At least now she knew that the feelings of panic and uncertainty she'd been experiencing had an external cause, and weren't due to her own failings. On the other hand, she hadn't expected the inoculations Lense had given them all to lose their effectiveness so quickly.

As if anticipating Gomez's question, Lense said, "Being in the rift might be having a more intense effect on us than merely being in proximity to it. I should give the entire away team another dose as soon as possible."

With hypospray in hand, the doctor reached for Gomez's right shoulder and placed the injector into the pressurized receptacle located there. The connection was designed expressly for the purpose of allowing injections into a suit's occupant when circumstances didn't allow for the removal of the helmet, making it easy to provide medical treatment in almost any environment. Once she had administered the theragen to Gomez, she repeated the process on herself.

"I didn't expect to have to give booster shots so soon, if at all," Lense said. "If we can't get out of the rift before my supply of theragen is exhausted, we could be in serious trouble."

Gomez thought about the near hysteria she had endured in the Jefferies tube. Knowing that those feelings were nothing compared to what she might experience should the away team be exposed to the full effects of the rift now filled her with a pronounced sense of dread.

CHAPTER 4

His thoughts concentrated somewhere beyond the image displayed on the *da Vinci*'s main viewer, Duffy sat in the captain's chair, staring into the reaches of starry space. His eyes followed a glowing ribbon of energy projecting from the starship's deflector dish as it lanced outward, then narrowed to a point near the center of the viewscreen. Somewhere out there, he hoped, the beam would find a crack or seam, anything that could be seized upon and forced open and give the *da Vinci* access to the interdimensional rift that had reclaimed the *Defiant*, along with their own away team.

As a young boy on Earth, Duffy had sometimes entertained himself with thoughts of contacting a passing ship of alien spacefarers. Armed with the biggest portable beacon his father owned, he would slip from his home in the dark of night and settle himself on a grassy rise in the backyard. There he would activate the beacon and point it into the night sky. Sometimes his fingers fiddled with the beacon's switch, making the beam of light pulse at random. Other times he would allow it to burn steadily for what seemed to him like hours. He would sprawl in the grass, paying little mind to the closely shorn blades prickling the back of his neck as he looked skyward and hoped that maybe this would be the night that the captain of a Vulcan science ship or a curious Pygorian trader would stop by for a visit.

Duffy's posture slumped a bit in the center seat as he recalled the night he had told his father that he wouldn't need the beacon anymore. His father had patted him on the shoulder and encouraged him to keep it at his bedside, should he ever change his mind. The response of his young voice rang in Duffy's memory.

That's okay, Dad. You can keep it. I'm tired of just watching the light. No one ever comes.

He tried to fend off the ironic ring of his memories as the deflector beam pierced the blackness. He continued to watch it for a few seconds longer, then turned reluctantly from the viewscreen toward the science station.

"Anything?"

"No detectable changes," Fabian Stevens replied. When he volunteered for a duty shift on the bridge, he typically had his eye on the tactician's seat. Now he had taken the post of the ship's science officer, monitoring the area of the rift for any effect from the deflector beam's attempt to influence it. "I've got nothing, Duff, but the rift is hard enough to read when it's open."

"I'm not asking for much here," said Duffy to no

one in particular, letting his frustration saturate his words.

It was their third attempt at massaging the area of interphase into a premature opening, and Duffy's hopes for success were fading. With the Tholians bound to return to the area at any time, he knew that merely idling here for three more hours and awaiting the rift's next predicted opening was not the most prudent course of action.

"I don't want the fabric of space torn wide open," he said. "I'm just looking for a little rip. Even a snag."

Stevens smirked at Duffy. "Maybe we could send in a torpedo loaded with a batch of P-38s?"

An unexpected yet quite welcome laugh burst from Duffy's mouth. Despite the seriousness of their current situation, he couldn't help but recall their recent and memorable mission involving the "fabled" P-38s.

It had happened a few months before, when the *da Vinci* had come across a drifting Pakled craft. At first the vessel appeared to have been disabled after an attack of unknown origin. Duffy, Stevens, and a few *da Vinci* technicians had beamed over to lend a hand, only to learn that the Pakled crew was trying to repair practically every onboard system. Their ship, Duffy quickly learned, had suffered a cascading circuitry overload following the crew's attempt at adapting an "official Romulan cloaking device" to their ship's computer defense systems.

Both Duffy and Stevens had then been forced to exercise every scrap of self-control they possessed so as not to fall over laughing when the captain of the

Pakled vessel told them that a Ferengi businessman was the source of the supposed cloaking device.

The electromagnetic pulse that resulted from engaging their new contraption had fried practically everything connected to a power source, including life-support systems, distress beacons, and even handheld devices hooked to charging ports. It was fortunate happenstance that the *da Vinci* had stumbled upon the dying craft at all, and the S.C.E. team had been viewed by the Pakleds as a mixture of magicians and divine agents.

What dazzled the stranded crew the most, Duffy and Stevens noted, seemed to be the team's use of what Starfleet personnel called a P-38. When gripped between thumb and forefinger, the small device could, at the press of a button, emit focused frequencies of light and sound that were perfect for freeing the covers of circuit panels fused shut from the electric backlash of the contraband "cloaking device."

Neither of the officers had the heart to tell the Pakleds that their wondrous P-38s were basically glorified Starfleet-issue can openers.

Duffy brought his smile under control long enough to mimic the Pakled captain's words to Stevens. "'You make things open. That is good.'"

The two laughed again. "That's us," Duffy said, curbing his laughter. "The Starfleet Corps of Engineers: Miracle Workers for the Alpha Quadrant and beyond."

Duffy's face sobered a bit as he looked to the viewscreen again.

Nothing.

If anything qualifies as "beyond" right about now, it's the Defiant.

"It's not working," he said, his words tinged with disgust. "Shut it down, Fabian." Duffy paused as he watched the golden-hued ray snap out of existence with not a shimmer of the rift he had hoped against hope to see. "Analyze the latest set of sensor readings and let me know when you're ready to try it again."

"Sure, Duff," Stevens replied as he turned back to his console. "Fourth one makes the charm, right?"

"That's what the Andorians always say."

Duffy's attention was drawn by the opening of the turbolift doors, from which emerged another reminder of the masked dangers awaiting those who merely occupied this area of space. Armed with a hypospray, Nurse Sandy Wetzel stepped onto the bridge and cut a path directly to Duffy.

"Commander," she said, "I need to administer theragen boosters to everyone. Dr. Lense's orders were for the shots to be given out if she wasn't back by 1600 hours."

Duffy nodded, remembering Lense's report from her earlier briefing. The effectiveness of the theragen treatment received by the entire crew would weaken over time and require bolstering through additional inoculations.

"Fire away," he said, craning his neck to allow the nurse access. As the spray hissed below his ear, he had a momentary pang of concern as he thought once more about the substance being pumped into his bloodstream.

Actually a Klingon nerve gas that was instantly lethal in its purest form, the theragen derivative was also the *da Vinci* crew's best defense against slipping into the same space madness that had gripped those aboard the *Defiant* a century ago. Duffy, for one, was thankful for the medicine. The last thing he needed right now, on top of everything else, was to have to cope with a mentally unstable crew.

As Wetzel finished inoculating him, Duffy said, "Thanks, Sandy. How's Songmin doing?"

Wetzel had been the first of the medical team to report to the bridge during the Tholian attack that had interrupted the *da Vinci*'s recovery operation and sent the *Defiant* plunging back into the interspatial rift. She had arrived to find the usual assortment of bumps, cuts, and bruises except for the more seriously injured helmsman, Ensign Songmin Wong.

"We're treating him for a concussion," she replied. "He'll be released for duty after a night's rest."

Duffy nodded thankfully as Wetzel moved to the helmsman now seated at Wong's usual position. Then his attention was drawn to the communications station, where an animated discussion looked to be taking place between Carol Abramowitz and Bart Faulwell. The two had been hard at work since Duffy had returned from his private conversation with Captain Scott. He'd been too busy to wonder what they'd been up to before now, but as he watched their exchange for several more seconds, he decided that this was the time to find out.

He walked toward them, trying to be obvious about his approach, but the two didn't flinch. Abramowitz leaned forward in her seat, occasionally keying commands as the tall, lean Faulwell stood beside her, both remaining intently focused on their work. Then Duffy noticed that they were both straining to listen to small Feinberg audio receivers plugged into their ears. Who were they talking to? What in the hell was going on?

Speaking softly, he said, "Hello? Heh-*lo*-oh."

The best comparison Duffy could make to the sound that came out of Abramowitz's mouth was that of a tribble freshly tossed into a Klingon's lap. The cultural specialist's eyes widened in momentary shock as she registered Duffy's presence, her surprise nearly jerking her against the back of her chair. Duffy chuckled at her response, but neither she nor Faulwell seemed amused at the interruption.

"I'm sorry, Commander," she said, regaining some of her composure. "I guess we were somewhere else."

"Where?"

Faulwell couldn't seem to help the hint of a proud smile starting to creep onto his face. "Truth be told, Mr. Duffy, I was giving Carol here a lesson in Tholian cryptography. We've been reviewing some of the coded messages between the commander of the Tholian ship and his contact on their homeworld. You may find this interesting."

Duffy didn't try to hide his surprise as he looked to Abramowitz. "Coded messages? You mean you tapped into their communications?" He couldn't help but be amused when Abramowitz didn't reply immediately, but instead actually shuffled her feet, as if uncertain how to answer his question.

"Um, I kind of intercepted and recorded all of the transmissions to and from the Tholian ship while we were maintaining contact." She shrugged her shoulders and widened her eyes, the very picture of innocence. "Maybe I hit the wrong button?"

For nearly every moment since the attack, Duffy had been gripped with apprehension that he had somehow unwittingly prompted the Tholians' actions, and that something he had done or ordered had resulted in the *Defiant* and his teammates being lost in the rift. He saw now that his friends had probably harbored similar concerns, and had channeled that anxiety toward finding an answer. Maybe the true motivation behind the attack was somewhere in these transmissions, just waiting to be discovered.

"That's very, um . . . damn, Carol. You're good."

Abramowitz smiled. "I listened in once or twice, but I couldn't make sense of any of it. Tholian speech sounds like someone grinding glass, let alone whatever scrambling protocols they add. I thought it would be useless to us, until I talked to Bart."

Aside from being a master linguist, Bartholomew Faulwell had been steadily carving a reputation for himself in Starfleet circles as a crack cryptographer. One of the oldest members of the *da Vinci* crew, Faulwell had been one of a legion of minds tapped by Starfleet brass during the Dominion War to aid in sifting through enemy communications. His quick and accurate translations of garbled or encrypted transmissions had proved vital to admirals planning strategic moves for the allied forces. Had the war still been waging, Duffy knew that the S.C.E. would most certainly not be reaping the benefits of Faulwell's skills.

Faulwell let his smile grow a bit as he patted Abramowitz on the shoulder. "We don't know much, but it's a start. Tholian communiqués are typically brief, probably out of fear that somebody will try to do just what we're doing. We can tell you one thing for certain, though. Our escort ship was ordered to fire on the *Defiant*, and on us, by the Assembly."

Duffy's brow knit in confusion. "So they didn't just go space-happy, then. Any clues as to why they attacked us?"

"Absolutely," Faulwell replied. "The last thing sent to the Assembly before returning the order to fire was the same tricorder information that Captain Gold sent to us from the *Defiant* about whatever it was the away team found."

Of course, Duffy thought. The away team had found a mechanism of Tholian design stored in one of the *Defiant*'s cargo bays. After recording detailed scans of the device, Captain Gold had notified the commander of the Tholian ship, Nostrene, about their discovery.

And naturally, things had gone to hell shortly afterward.

"So what is it about that gadget that has the Tholians all worked up?" he asked. Based on the information P8 Blue had gathered and on the theory she had put forth, Duffy and Stevens had figured out that the strange device found by the away team was some sort of power emitter. Using that as a starting point, they had scoured the *da Vinci*'s databanks for all references to Tholian encounters by Starfleet ships. Sensor scans recorded by various vessels during those engagements supported Pattie's hypothesis that the mechanism she had found was similar in design to those employed by Tholian ships to generate their infamous energy webs. But what was so secret about that? The Federation had known about the Tholian's web technology for more than a century. What was so special about this particular piece of equipment?

Duffy shook his head in growing frustration. He wasn't used to not having all the pieces to a puzzle within easy reach. As an engineer, he prided himself on being able to see to the heart of any problem based solely on the evidence available to him at the time. The answers were here, he knew, somewhere in the midst of the data gathered by the *da Vinci*'s sensors or by the away team. It would simply require more time to sift through it. Time, however, was something he was quickly running out of.

Still, he did have enough time to show his gratitude to a pair of specialists willing to take the mugato by the horn. It was just such initiative that made Duffy appreciate the rewards of command.

"This is great, you two," he said, returning his attention to Faulwell. "I'll make sure to report this to Captain Gold after I buy you both dinner at the best restaurant aboard this ship." He smiled again. "Once this is all over, Bart, you'll have plenty of new material to write Anthony about."

"Commander Duffy!"

It was Lieutenant David McAllan. More so than the words themselves, the sound of alarm coming from the *da Vinci's* typically reserved tactical officer caught the entire bridge crew off guard and made Duffy jerk his head in the direction of the tactical station.

"You need to see this," McAllan said, his face not turning from his console viewer. As Duffy started in that direction, he was followed not only by Stevens but also by Domenica Corsi, whom Duffy knew was just waiting for any sign of trouble. Duffy hoped this would end up disappointing her.

Looking up from his console, the tactical officer's face was pale as he said, "It's the Tholians, Commander. Long-range sensors have just picked up six ships heading this way at maximum warp, and . . ."

"And what, Lieutenant?" Duffy looked down at the console's tactical viewer, which depicted six solid blips, representations of Tholian ships, flying in a hexagonal configuration. Amid the configuration was something that Duffy had a hard time discerning from the viewer.

"Sensors read it as pure energy," McAllan reported. "It's fluctuating slightly in intensity, but keeping pace with the Tholian ships."

Judging from the readings, Duffy saw that the energy output was intense, incorporating the power of a dozen photon torpedo explosions in a stable field or cloud. . . .

Or a web.

Stevens elbowed his way past Duffy to get a look for himself, tapping a few commands on the console's smooth surface and pausing to read the streams of data now scrolling next to the tactical image. He laughed in spite of his assessment of it all.

"Now that's pretty clever!" Stevens looked back up at Duffy, his smile evident but quickly fading. "Clever strictly from a tactical point of view, I mean. Sorry, Duff."

Duffy decided not to dampen Stevens's enthusiasm. It was just that kind of appreciation for the enemy that would motivate the tactical expert to calculate the appropriate defense against them. "Fabian, is that what I think it is?"

"It is, if you think it's an energy field capable of frying the systems of several starships at once." Stevens studied the tactical viewer once more and nodded. "Those ships are generating a net of power that's a thousand meters in diameter, Duff. Think of it as a massive butterfly net, and guess who the butterfly is."

Duffy weighed his options for the *da Vinci*: Hold the ship's position and become ensnared in the Tholians' deadly web, or retreat and lose their fix on the interspatial rift, as well as their away team, for good.

"How much time do we have, Fabian?"

Stevens's expression was grave as he consulted his console one last time. "If they maintain their speed, the Tholians will be here in about an hour."

CHAPTER
5

"*Captain's log: stardate 5683.9. My engineer and science officer have spent the past twelve hours examining the alien object recovered from the destroyed Klingon colony on Traelus II. They theorize that, when combined with other similar devices we found deployed at equidistant positions around the colony's perimeter, it generated an energy field enshrouding the entire settlement. Residual energy traces recorded by the landing party indicate the field was lethal to any living being within its sphere of influence. Judging by the condition of the Klingon bodies we found, it wasn't a particularly pleasant way to die, either.*"

David Gold could almost feel his blood chill as he once again regarded the image of Thomas Blair, the late captain of the *Defiant*. Unlike the log entries they had reviewed earlier, the Blair in this excerpt didn't possess the haunted, exhausted expression that would dominate his features in those later recordings.

Then again, Gold mused soberly, *he didn't know he was going to die at this point.*

"Well," he said, "this would certainly go a long way toward explaining why the Tholians were so upset earlier."

Gomez replied, "So the *Defiant* crew found the colony, took the web generator for study, and then fell into the rift while evading Tholian vessels and trying to get the evidence back to Starfleet Command."

At the science station, Soloman said, "There is no evidence to . . . suggest that the Tholians had knowledge of the *Defiant*'s actions before it became . . . trapped in the rift."

Gold shrugged but nodded in agreement. "Perhaps. It's never been discussed in an open forum, that's for sure."

"It would not be a . . . wise course of action," the Bynar replied. "According to sensor data I have examined . . . along with reports filed by the . . . landing party, the colony was defenseless, particularly by . . . Klingon standards. The Tholians attacked a . . . group of unarmed civilians."

From where she knelt next to a seated and now conscious P8 Blue, Dr. Lense looked up from tending the Nasat's head injury. "Why would they do that? I mean, the Tholians are aggressive, but isn't that a bit extreme?"

Gold shook his head. "We know that the Tholians have always been fiercely protective of their space. I guess we just didn't realize at the time to what lengths they would go in the interests of that protection."

"All this time," Gomez said, "the *Defiant* held the key to a terrible secret."

"It still does," Gold replied. "The Klingons never found out what happened at Traelus II, and by all reports they were more than a bit upset over the incident. If word of the Tholians' involvement reaches the Klingons now, some in the Empire may well want vengeance."

"So the Tholians try to destroy us, only we get pulled back into the rift," Lense said. "Lucky us."

"What about the *da Vinci*?" Pattie asked, her voice weak and tired.

Gold strolled around the bridge's upper deck in the Nasat's direction, talking as he went. "Well, either Mr. Duffy followed orders and evacuated the area, or he was forced to fight. In that case, the *da Vinci* disabled the Tholian vessel . . . or she didn't."

The statement hung in the air for several seconds, with no one on the bridge wanting to respond. Realizing the somber mood he had inflicted on his people, Gold rallied quickly.

"At any rate, I'm afraid we have more pressing concerns." Turning his attention to P8 Blue, he asked, "Pattie? How are you feeling?"

Pattie nodded slowly. "I will recover, Captain." Turning to Lense, she added, "Many pardons for the trouble I caused you, Doctor."

Lense patted the Nasat on the nearest of her eight limbs, then rose to her feet to face Gold. She ran a hand through her matted hair, thankful for finally being able to remove her environment suit's helmet.

"I've treated her concussion, Captain. She'll

have a headache for a bit, but it's the best I can do until we get her back to the *da Vinci*."

Gold nodded. "We'll see to that as best we can, Doctor."

The attention of everyone on the bridge was caught as the overhead lighting dimmed and the displays on the various consoles flickered. Gold could even hear the mild hiss of the air-circulation system fade momentarily.

"What's that about?" he asked.

Soloman was already examining the sensor data being relayed to the science station. "We are experiencing . . . a power fall-off. It is affecting all . . . of the generators we brought with us from the *da Vinci*."

"How bad is it?" Gomez asked as she moved to the bridge's engineering station.

"At the current rate of drop-off," the Bynar replied, "the generators will be completely drained . . . of power in less than two hours."

"Damn," Gomez spat, drawing a questioning look from Gold and the others. With an embarrassed expression on her face, she said, "Kieran suggested that we bring along backup power supplies for the generators, but I decided against that." She shook her head in disgust. "The generators can normally operate for days without interruption, and I figured we'd be here for eight to ten hours at most. By then, the *da Vinci* would have pulled us out of the rift."

"Something tells me that Mr. Duffy will have plenty of colorful observations about all of this when we get back," Lense said. Looking at the viewscreen and the matte of darkness that had once been the opening to the rift, she added, "That is, *if* we get back."

"Enough of that," Gold snapped. "We've just been given a deadline for getting out of here, people, and we can't afford to waste time with defeatist gabbing." Turning to the science station, he asked, "Soloman, can you calculate the time until the next interphase?"

The Bynar spent several moments peering into the console's viewfinder before turning back to the group with a troubled expression on his face.

"According to the data I have . . . at my disposal, the next interphase should occur in . . . three hours and twelve minutes."

Gold absorbed the report. It was simple to understand, really. The power supplies of the generators would be exhausted more than an hour before the next interphase.

"Why didn't we register the power drain before?" he asked.

It was Gomez who replied. "Up until the attack, the *Defiant* was always on the threshold of the rift. Now that we're completely enveloped in interspace, the negative effects associated with it must be intensified."

"What about the power cells in our suits?" Pattie asked. "They should be affected as well."

Gomez activated her tricorder and quickly scanned her suit's control panel, located on her left sleeve. "There is a minor power drain, but it's not alarming." She frowned at the tricorder readings. "They should be fine at least until the next interphase, but I'm not sure I'd bet on them."

"Well, it's all we have for now," Gold said. "So rather than worry about it, I think we'd be better served by finding a way out of here." Looking over at Soloman, he said, "Give me a scan of the rift opening, or at least the area where it used to be."

Soloman turned to the sensor displays once more, his small hands playing over the controls of the science station. Gold noted with satisfaction that the Bynar had become so fluent with the antiquated control panels that one would think he had been born to serve on this ship. Soloman seemed quite at home there, the *da Vinci* captain thought, toiling away at the science station with the viewfinder's tell-tale blue glow washing over his face. It was in stark contrast to the rest of the bridge illumination that reflected off the back of his pale, bald head.

The Bynar's head . . . so small and fragile. Gold imagined he could feel the smooth texture of Soloman's skin beneath his fingers, could almost feel the curve of his skull as he at first caressed, then pressed harder, yearning to hear the final satisfying crack of the slim neck supporting—

What?

Gold wasn't aware that he'd fallen until his tailbone struck the deck and the back of his head smacked against the side of the captain's chair. The dull ache from the dual impacts had barely begun to assert itself before he felt a hand on his arm.

"Captain, are you all right?" Lense asked, already waving her tricorder near the area of his head that had struck the chair.

Reaching up to wipe his brow, Gold blinked several times in an attempt to reorient himself. He looked up to see the entire away team staring down at him, nearly identical expressions of concern etched on their faces.

"Am I? I . . . I don't know," he said, his voice unsteady. "One minute I was watching Soloman working, and the next I was . . . I was imagining . . ." The murderous anxiety he had felt only seconds before threatened to wash over him again, and he bit down on the rest of the sentence, leaving the remaining words unspoken.

Lense lowered her tricorder. "The theragen in your system has begun to lose its effectiveness." She retrieved a hypospray from her medical kit and checked its setting. "It's as if we're all building up a tolerance for the drug." Shaking her head, she added, "I'm going to increase the dosage for all of us, but at this rate, my supply won't last more than a few hours."

Gold cast a final, guilty look at Soloman as he drew a deep breath to calm himself. The horrid vision that had filled his mind only moments before continued to burn in his memory. Even as the theragen took hold in his bloodstream and he felt the anxiety that had gripped him begin to dissipate, he knew that the image of his hands closing around the Bynar's head would haunt him long after this mission was over.

"Soloman," he said in a subdued voice, "what did your sensor scans reveal?"

"There are . . . residual energy traces indicating the rift's entrance, sir," Soloman replied. "I am able to determine the boundaries of the opening."

"If we can detect it," Gomez said, "then maybe we can find a way to force it open."

Rising from his seat, Soloman said, "Opening the rift may not present . . . much difficulty, Commander. A great deal of force may not . . . be required."

"How so?" Gold asked.

"I see what he means," Gomez cut in. "When the *da Vinci*'s deflector and tractor beams were locked onto us, the interspatial pocket seemed to react in the opposite direction, exerting more and more force to hold us here. But we might be able to overcome that resistance by pushing ourselves through the rift from within."

Gold frowned, not entirely convinced. "With what? The *Defiant*'s maneuvering thrusters couldn't possibly be strong enough to push us out."

It was Pattie who provided one possible solution. "Perhaps the warp drive could be used."

Gomez made no effort to hide the skepticism on her face as she regarded the Nasat. "The warp engines are as cold as ice, Pattie. The dilithium crystals have decayed to nothing, and even if we had one, we'd still have to find the right intermix formula. It would take at least thirty minutes to initiate a restart of the warp core. And then there's always the possibility that the engines won't stand the strain of restarting and will buckle completely."

Pattie shook her head as she rose from her seat at the bridge's communications console. "No, no. My apologies for not explaining myself. I was thinking that we could use the generators we brought with us to provide a quick start to the warp drive. The action would almost certainly drain the generators within seconds, but it should be enough to provide a short-duration warp pulse that could push us through the rift."

"Why does that sound as crazy as I think it does?" Lense asked.

But Gomez was nodding at the Nasat's idea. "No, it's not crazy. I've seen something like it done before, when I was on the *Enterprise*." She quickly relayed the story of the time that Geordi La Forge, the *Enterprise*'s chief engineer, and the son of the ship's doctor had devised a scheme to jump-start the warp engines of an eighty-year-old starship. They had used a minute amount of dilithium and some antimatter that the boy had retrieved from one of his ongoing science experiments. The "warp pulse" had lasted only two seconds, but it was enough to get the old ship out of harm's way when a Ferengi marauder showed up and attempted to hijack the vessel.

"The generators might be able to provide the necessary power for such a pulse," she said. "But even if we can manage that, is there any antimatter down in engineering?"

"Anything in the warp core itself would have been automatically ejected from the ship once power was lost," Pattie replied. "But there may still be some in magnetic storage bottles."

Gold had until this point stood silently, observing with unabashed admiration as his engineering specialists talked out their makeshift plan. Watching his people in their element always gave him the feeling that there was no problem they couldn't solve, no obstacle they couldn't overcome.

"What do you think, Commander?" he asked Gomez. "Can we do it?"

Gomez rubbed her chin thoughtfully. "We'll need to use at least three of the generators to trigger the warp engine restart. That will leave two to provide power for the thrusters and the bridge systems."

"We can use the thrusters to maneuver closer to the edge of the rift," Pattie added. "The effect of the warp field's abrupt activation should provide enough disruption to open the rift and push us through."

Gomez shook her head slowly. "We'll only get one shot at this, though. If the restart is successful and doesn't shred the warp engines, it will drain the power from the generators within seconds."

Gold liked the bold plan being presented by his officers. Given a choice between actively seeking a way out of their predicament or simply waiting for their power systems to deplete themselves, he preferred the more aggressive option. He had never been one to sit idly by and wait for fate or luck to visit him, not when he had the opportunity to fashion his own course of action.

Besides, he wasn't ready to abandon the *Defiant* just yet, not while any chance of salvaging her still remained. He knew that the ship held a political powder keg in its cargo hold, but he refused to accept that, after all they had ultimately sacrificed, the deaths of the men and women aboard the *Defiant* would amount to nothing more than the spark to ignite an interstellar war.

Maybe it doesn't have to be that way.

The thought came unbidden, catching Gold by surprise. Did it mean what he thought it meant? Could he bring himself to destroy the evidence the *Defiant*'s crew had recovered and tried to bring home when fate had cruelly intervened?

It would be so easy to do, ordering the ship to travel deeper into the rift. Maybe they'd tumble into the other universe, forever lost to any recovery attempts from their own side of interspace. He could give the necessary orders, and he was confident that his crew would understand his reasoning. The greater political good would be served.

But not Captain Blair and his people, Gold reminded himself. *They wouldn't be served at all*.

No matter the consequences, it would do the *Defiant* crew a tremendous disservice to cover up the details of their last mission for the sake of political expediency. Therefore, he would do everything in his power to see the vessel, and its crew, returned safely home.

Dismissing the troubling thoughts, Gold said, "Let's get started, then. Gomez, take Blue and Lense to assist you. Soloman and I will remain here and guide the ship to the edge of the rift." He smiled grimly at his team. "Work quickly, people. Time is most definitely not our ally today."

"Like it ever is," Lense said as she donned her helmet in preparation for the journey down to engineering.

Gomez smiled to herself as she added, "It just wouldn't be an S.C.E. mission without a time crunch."

CHAPTER 6

The last time Duffy had sat in the *da Vinci*'s briefing room, he had been thankful for Captain Scott's words of advice. He'd also been buoyed by the captain's attempts to buy them the time they needed to salvage their mission and come home from Tholian space with a lost starship, or at least with every member of the *da Vinci*'s crew. Now all Duffy could think was that the veteran leader of the engineering troubleshooters had wasted his efforts.

Within half an hour the six Tholian ships they had detected would be here, bringing with them their massive energy net and looking to snare anything in their collective path, most notably the *da Vinci*.

It wouldn't have mattered now if ol' Scotty had bought us a year. If we're not out of here before long, we're done for.

He shook off the thought and focused his eyes once again on the briefing room's main viewer and its projection of the tactical image that had burned itself into his mind not more than thirty minutes earlier. "Okay, let's go over it one more time. Run it again, Fabian."

Stevens entered a series of commands into the keypad next to the viewer and the image reset itself. Six cones representing Tholian ships en route to the *da Vinci*'s current position now glowed a threatening red in the screen's upper-left corner.

Amid the cones was an amber-colored grid, seemingly innocuous on the screen but representing the potential to destroy the *da Vinci* in one fell swoop. Just below and to the right of the screen's center was a soft blue dot for the *da Vinci*, which Duffy's ever-wicked mind underscored with the caption "You are here," just to lighten his mental load. To the virtual *da Vinci*'s right was a field of blue, a computer-simulated haze marking the area of interphase that, up until now, had drawn the bulk of Duffy's attention.

Stevens tapped once more and the tactical image sprang to life. The six cones bore down on the *da Vinci* in formation.

"This variety of the Tholian web has never been observed in the field by anyone from Starfleet," he said as he pointed to the configuration of red and amber shapes. "It differs from the web employed by Tholian ships for more than a hundred years, which was literally spun around a craft, then constricted. Once the energy field made contact, the trapped ship was powerless at best, or destroyed."

"That seems like a lot of energy to maintain

among those ships," Domenica Corsi said, her brow knitting in confusion as she studied the computer model. "Why did they engage the web so far from our position?"

Stevens shrugged. "Who can tell? Maybe they hoped it would act as a deterrent. If I were in a Tholian ship, I'd rather scare an enemy away than engage one in combat. Even with the web drawing its energy from their ships' warp fields, as I'm guessing it does, flying around at high warp with that thing glowing hot is still a safer alternative for the Tholians than getting shot at."

That made sense to Duffy. The Tholians probably charged their energy web many more times than they actually used it. Even theories on the widespread damage such a web would be capable of wreaking on a snared craft would shoo away the most wizened combat veteran.

"Deterrent? They obviously don't know what kind of thickheaded people they're dealing with today," he said in a deadpan voice.

Stevens laughed in response as Corsi scowled. Duffy couldn't help but smirk a little himself. There was nothing like knowing your audience.

Corsi studied the screen for another moment before saying, "It's pretty obvious that we either fight or run. How do we fight it?"

Stevens reached for the keypad once again, the image on the screen responding to his commands. "I don't know how many ships we really need to disable in order to shut the web down. I recommend targeting no less than three of them, but I'm hoping that getting two might be enough for us to slip through their fingers. That is, if Tholians have fingers."

On the viewer, the image's perspective jumped as the distance tightened between the Tholian cluster of ships and the *da Vinci*. Suddenly a line of white lanced from the Federation ship's position, connecting to one of the red cones. Two more lines quickly followed it, each one homing in on a ship directly adjacent to the first target. As the animation played out, the Tholian ships broke from their hexagonal formation and swooped past the dot representing the *da Vinci*.

"Looks good in theory, Fabian," Duffy said as Corsi nodded her approval.

Stevens's expression was appreciative, yet he maintained his attitude of concern. "That's not to say, though, that the remaining ships can't just regroup and come back at us with a smaller web." He paused for the others to digest his assessment. "What we really need is another ship on *our* side."

Yeah. Wouldn't that be nice, Duffy mused.

He had an idea of what to expect, should things not go in their favor, but he voiced the question nonetheless. "And when, uh, *if* we're hit by the web?"

Stevens entered the command to freeze the tactical animation on the viewer. "Again, Duff, I'm just guessing. It might smoke all of our systems, and that could just shut us down, or it might force us into a warp-core breach. Hell, that thing might cut through us like an exoscalpel."

To Duffy, it was obvious from the silence that suddenly descended upon the room that his two companions were envisioning their own worst-case scenarios for the *da Vinci*'s entrapment. Before Duffy had much of a chance to mentally unspool his fate for himself, however, Stevens took a step toward the briefing room's door.

"As much as I hate to break up this party, Duff, I need just a couple of minutes to run the last check on my deflector equation."

Duffy nodded his head. "Sure. Hey, Fabian, try not to blow us up before the Tholians get here. They'll be upset if we take all the fun out of it for them."

Stevens just smiled and left the room, leaving Duffy with Corsi and the still-illuminated tactical display. The security chief visibly stiffened in her seat, and Duffy knew that she was about to unload her true feelings about their current situation to him. He held up his hand to her, cutting her off just as she opened her mouth.

"Okay, it's not as bad as it sounds," he said.

Corsi didn't ease up. "What is Stevens planning to do?"

"Fabian says he's thrown just about every combination of stimuli he can channel through the deflector dish at the rift. Everything except a warp field." Duffy paused, noting the frown on Corsi's face. "I know you're not an engineer, and most times you could give two bloodworms about tech talk, but bear with me here. Fabian thinks that maybe the rift shows some of the same characteristics as a wormhole. He's going to siphon off some plasma from the warp nacelles, mix it with some artificial verteron particles, and channel it all through the deflector dish. It's risky, but the upside is that the rift could flash open like a Bolian skyfire."

Corsi seemed unconvinced. "And the downside?"

Duffy's gaze faltered, and he looked away before replying. "We could blow out the deflector and short out the warp drive."

"Commander, that *is* as bad as it sounds."

Despite her response, Corsi's expression wasn't nearly as fierce as Duffy had anticipated it would be. Of all the unexpected twists that this mission had thrown at him so far, one thing he never, ever would have bet on was that he'd find a supportive ally in Domenica Corsi. He had to admit that heading into battle against the Tholians didn't seem as fearsome a prospect with her at his side. Corsi had kept a level head when he himself had come close to losing all composure. In her eyes, Duffy saw the desire to believe in the plan, to try one last time to pull the *Defiant*, and more importantly their friends, from a fate even worse than death at the hands of the Tholians.

"Nah, it's no big deal," Duffy lied. "You'd understand it all with a little more training in warp theory. And you know, I could steer you toward some good texts on the subject if you need a little night reading."

"That would not be the way I'd choose to spend my nights, Mr. Duffy." Corsi cracked a hint of a smile as the ship's intercom sounded its hailing chime. In the moment before the chime was followed by a voice, Duffy chastised himself for wondering just how Corsi did spend her nights.

"Duff? I'm ready to go out here and time's a wastin'."

The two rose from the oval table without answering Stevens's invitation. As they moved to take their posts on the bridge, Duffy noticed himself crossing almost too naturally to the center seat. However, as he settled into the chair, he gripped its armrests a little too tightly, feeling as though it was he who would be fired into the rift instead of the deflector's delicate intermix.

Boy, will I be glad when this is over.

"Mr. Stevens, engage the deflector beam," he said, hoping that the trembling he thought he heard in his voice was strictly in his imagination. Duffy's eyes did not leave the main viewer as Stevens activated the deflector.

He saw no beam.

What he did see was a shower of sparks and fire erupting from the science console, and Stevens throwing himself away from the billowing smoke and hungry flames.

"Fabian!" Duffy shouted, leaping from his seat and bolting to where his friend had landed on the deck.

"I'm all right," Stevens said, rolling onto his side and grimacing slightly from the abrupt impact.

Looking at Corsi, Duffy called out, "Damage report!"

The security officer's fingers were almost a blur as she fed commands to her console. "I can't get any diagnostics from the deflector relay system. The dish is either damaged or destroyed. I'm routing a damage-control team there now." After another few seconds she looked up from her station. "The warp drive is off-line. There was feedback from the deflector to the plasma conduits from the warp nacelles and it caused an overload. Engineering reports they may have to shut down the warp core."

Everyone on the bridge knew what Corsi's words really meant. With the Tholian ships only minutes away, the *da Vinci* was, for all intents and purposes, a sitting duck. There was no way they would be able to outrun the enemy vessels without warp drive.

"Dammit, dammit, *dammit!*" Duffy launched himself from where he had knelt next to Stevens and raced to the turbolift's doors. He was carried at first by instinct, but his sense of duty to the *da Vinci*'s crew kicked him into an even higher gear. As it was, he had to brake himself so as to avoid slamming bodily into Corsi, who had materialized between him and the turbolift with the efficiency of a transporter.

"Where the hell are you going?" she demanded, her eyes boring into Duffy's.

"I can have warp back on-line in three minutes," he said, moving to push past her. The turbolift doors hissed open at his approach, but he was halted by Corsi's hand clamping down on his arm with the strength of a vise.

"You can't leave this bridge," she said, her icy-calm voice belying the force she was exerting to keep him in place. "The Tholians will be here any minute."

Duffy wrenched his arm free from Corsi's grip

and backpedaled into the waiting turbolift. As he stepped into the car, he met the gazes of the bridge crew and at that instant felt certain that he was doing the right thing. Captain Scott had said it himself: An engineer's job was to keep his crew safe.

Well, that was a captain's job as well, Duffy decided. The *da Vinci* was hardly safe from the Tholians without the power to jump to warp speed, and no one knew those engines better than he did. Acting as captain or engineer, Duffy knew there was only one place for him to be right now.

"Three minutes!" he said to Corsi, hoping the urgent volume in his voice would slow her down. When it didn't, he finally resorted to the words that would stop her dead in her tracks.

"Commander Corsi, you have the conn."

And stop she did.

With a grim smile on his lips, he called out "Engineering!" and the turbolift's doors slammed shut. He felt the customary lurch in the pit of his stomach as the car dropped him from the bridge into the bowels of the ship.

CHAPTER
7

Sonya Gomez regarded the master systems display panel in the *Defiant*'s engineering section and marveled once again at the antiquated controls. Though the systems she was used to overseeing were vastly more advanced, she still perceived the echoes of function and purpose in the consoles around her. The admiration she felt for the engineers of this vessel and the bygone era it represented grew with every hour she spent here. More than once during this mission, she had imagined a younger Montgomery Scott, more than a century before he would come to lead the Starfleet Corps of Engineers, proudly riding herd on massive engines like the ones that had once powered the *Defiant*. The thought brought with it a momentary twinge of envy.

The 23rd century, Gomez decided, had to have been a more challenging time to be an engineer. With ships out of contact with command bases for weeks and sometimes months at a time, no

SpaceDock facilities or starbases could be relied upon for repairs. Ships' engineers were the ultimate masters of their vessels' fates. The crews of ships like the *Defiant* had pushed back the frontiers of unknown space and expanded the storehouse of knowledge that she and many modern-day Starfleet officers took for granted.

"The modifications to the generators are complete," Pattie reported, moving from the main engineering area to stand next to Gomez. "They are tied into the warp drive, and I have programmed a new start-up sequence into the main computer."

Gomez nodded in satisfaction. Their preparations were finished, and with any luck they would all be back on the *da Vinci* within thirty minutes. She, for one, would be glad for that. Despite what she might feel for this ship and the 23rd century, she had grown weary of traipsing around the derelict ship in near darkness and chancing upon the scattered remains of the *Defiant*'s crew. She had also grown tired of being forced to listen to the echo of her own breathing inside her helmet. If she were granted one wish, she decided it would be to never wear an environment suit again for the rest of her life.

"Thanks, Pattie," she replied, turning to smile at her Nasat companion. Despite having what must surely be a splitting headache, thanks to her concussion, Pattie had plunged into preparing the generators for the unorthodox task they would shortly undertake. It hadn't been a simple proposition, either. Tying the modern-day components to the century-old power distribution systems had required even more finessing than Gomez had used to install the generators to begin with.

And assuming they succeeded in pushing the *Defiant* out of the rift, what was waiting for them on the other side? Was the *da Vinci* . . . was Kieran standing by to help them? To help her? What had happened after the *Defiant* had been forced back into interspace? Had Kieran made a stand and tried to protect the away team, or had he been forced to retreat? Had he managed to disable or destroy the Tholian ship, or . . . ?

Gomez couldn't bring herself to complete the thought. It was probably just as well, she decided. The coming minutes would require her complete attention. She couldn't afford distractions, especially now.

The telltale sounds of a tricorder made her turn around to see Dr. Lense waving the device over Pattie's head.

"Problem, Doctor?" Gomez asked.

Lense shook her head. "Just checking for signs that Pattie might be starting to feel the effects of interphase. So far, she's fine." She smiled at the diminutive engineer. "Must be that sturdy Nasat constitution."

"Too bad she can't share any of that," Gomez said with a grim smile of her own. Her mood turned serious again, however, when she asked, "Elizabeth, how much longer do you think your supply of theragen will hold out?"

"I really don't know," the doctor replied. "The inoculations are continuing to lose their potency and the effective period for each successive dose is decreasing rapidly. I'd give us another couple of hours before it loses its effectiveness altogether."

Gomez had no intention of being around when that happened. She had no desire to revisit the panic and sheer terror she'd experienced earlier in the Jefferies tube. So long as there remained options that would let her fight to avoid it, she refused to consign herself to such a fate.

"Well, I'm ready to see about getting us out of here," she said as she activated her communicator.

"Gomez to Captain Gold. We're all set down here, sir."

On the *Defiant's* bridge, David Gold smiled in satisfaction to himself. As good as her word, Sonya Gomez and her team had completed their modifications well within the time remaining to them before their power supplies succumbed to the effects of interphase. They would indeed get their one chance to push the *Defiant* from the rift.

"Excellent work, Commander," he said. "Stand by." Stepping down into the bridge's command well, the *da Vinci* captain moved to stand next to Soloman, who was seated at the ship's helm. Putting a hand on the Bynar's shoulder, Gold asked, "Are we ready?"

Soloman nodded. "Thrusters are continuing to . . . function normally, Captain. They should provide sufficient power to . . . maneuver us out of the rift once . . . Commander Gomez triggers the warp pulse."

"Fine," Gold replied. Of course, he couldn't stop from asking himself what they might expect to find on the other side of the rift. If they were successful, would they be greeted by the welcome sight of the *da Vinci*, or the ominous presence of a Tholian battle fleet?

As if hearing the unspoken thought, Gomez said, "We might not be able to see what's waiting for us, Captain, but I might be able to give us a bit of insurance. I can divert power from our remaining generators to the shields and maybe one phaser bank. We'd have to sacrifice access to the main computer and life support to the bridge, though."

Gold needed no time to consider his options. "Take whatever power you need, Gomez, but make sure we retain sensor control and the thrusters." As he spoke, he indicated for Soloman to don his helmet. Moments later, both of them were once again ensconced in their environment suits.

"Let's do this, Commander," Gold said. "Throw the switch."

"Aye, sir," Gomez replied. "Brace yourselves up there. This might get a bit bumpy."

No sooner had Gold moved to the *Defiant*'s command chair than he was thrown bodily into it as the mighty starship suddenly surged forward. There was only the briefest of rumblings from the deck plates as the ship's massive warp engines received the single concentrated burst of power from the away team's portable generators.

In his mind's eye, the *da Vinci* captain pictured the spike of energy instantaneously traveling the conduits that connected the generators to the ship's warp drive, improvising an intermix reaction in the absence of dilithium. Gold didn't pretend to understand the mind-numbing complexity that enshrouded the concept of warp propulsion, but he was content in the knowledge that he commanded people who did. He knew he could best serve the specialists comprising the rest of the away team by staying out of their way and allowing them to do what they did best.

The main viewer registered the *Defiant*'s sudden explosive acceleration as crackling, multihued energy playing across the screen. It was felt in the ship's hull as well, as deck plates and bulkheads groaned in protest at the vessel's abrupt movements.

"Look at that," Gold said. "The rift is reacting to the warp pulse."

Just as quickly as it had begun, the sounds of the ship's struggling warp engines died out. Their effects on the peculiar interspatial pocket surrounding the *Defiant* were still being felt, however. The frenzied collision of energy continued on the main viewer, its intensity increasing as the ship hurtled closer to the edge of the rift.

Gold moved to the science station and activated the sensor controls. "It's working," he said after consulting the viewfinder. "The rift is beginning to open. Hold us on course, Soloman, steady as she goes."

At the helm, Soloman said, "Guiding the ship is . . . proving much easier than anticipated. It seems that . . . our theory about the rift's resistance was correct."

The relative quiet of the bridge was abruptly

shattered as the engineering station erupted in a shower of sparks and flame. A deafening explosion echoed in the confines of the ship's nerve center, throwing metal shrapnel and shards of plastic composites across the bridge. Both Soloman and Gold instinctively ducked, throwing their arms up and turning away from the explosion to protect their helmet faceplates. Gold felt the outside of his suit peppered by debris and prayed its rugged construction would withstand the bombardment.

"Soloman! Are you all right?" Gold called out as another console near the front of the bridge blew apart, sending both officers scrambling for cover yet again.

"Captain Gold!" Gomez's voice called out over his communicator. "We're getting massive feedback from the warp pulse. It's overloading our circuits."

Gold's reply was cut off as sparks burst from the helm, causing the lights and indicators on the panel to flicker wildly as the systems contained within the console fought to retain control.

"Get away from there!" he yelled to Soloman, but the Bynar needed no such prodding as he bolted from his seat and jumped out of the command well. An instant later the helm console was enveloped in a vicious ball of flame and exploding circuitry.

"We've lost helm control up here," Gold said into his communicator. "We can't steer the ship."

"Captain," Soloman called out, drawing Gold's attention. "Look!"

Gold turned in the indicated direction, and his

mouth fell open. Beyond the bulkheads flanking the main viewer, the hull was losing its solidity and he could see stars and the roiling energy streams comprising the rift.

"We're shifting out of interphase," he said. Without thinking, he looked to the deck at his feet and saw that the plating had begun to lose its cohesion there as well. Wiring and conduits were already clearly visible.

"It's getting too dangerous to stay here," he said.

Soloman nodded. "Phase shifts will be occurring . . . throughout the ship, sir."

Gold moved to the turbolift, pulling his manual door opener from a suit pocket as he went. "We can't do anything more from here, so we might as well move. Gomez, are you listening?"

"Yes, Captain," Gomez replied.

Forcing the turbolift doors apart with the opener revealed the darkened walls of the turboshaft. Leaning in, Gold directed the lights of his helmet downward and they illuminated nothing except more of the vertical conduit. Only a pair of narrow maintenance ladders, one on both the front and rear walls of the shaft, interrupted its smooth texture.

"Where's the auxiliary control center?" he asked.

Gomez's response was immediate. "Deck seven, sir. I've already begun routing power to that location. All you have to do is get there. We can . . ."

The rest of the engineer's report was drowned out by the sounds of rushing air. Even muffled as it was through his helmet, Gold immediately recognized the source of the sound.

Decompression!

Spinning around, he saw that a section of bulkhead near the main viewer no bigger than a desktop LCARS terminal had disappeared entirely. The area was expanding rapidly and the sounds of escaping atmosphere were growing louder.

"That's it," he shouted over the rush of departing air. "Time to go!"

Grabbing Soloman by the arm, Gold pulled the Bynar close to him and hurled them both into the yawning darkness of the turboshaft.

Sonya Gomez and P8 Blue worked feverishly at the master systems console in main engineering, trying to divert power from damaged or unresponsive areas of the ship to those that could still be useful. Alarm indicators illuminated across the board, bearing mute testimony to the severity of the situation.

"Bridge systems have gone totally inoperative," Pattie reported as she consulted one display. "I am seeing power fluctuations in the remaining generators."

"Cut the feed," Gomez ordered. "Stand by to route whatever's left to deck seven, section 21-Alpha." With three of the away team's five generators committed to the ship's warp engines, the remaining units were being tasked with providing power for the other systems Gomez had determined were necessary to control the ship and complete their mission. Now more than ever, the vessel's design was working against her. Though well-constructed and possessing a performance record nearly unmatched in the annals of Starfleet history, *Constitution*-class starships had never been intended to rely on small, localized power distribution schemes. The huge power plants normally used to drive the ship and its multitude of onboard systems were, of course, unavailable to her, so she would simply have to make do with what she had.

"Sonya," Elizabeth Lense called out from the other end of the bank of consoles, "I'm reading a massive feedback in the other generators."

It had been a gamble, Gomez knew, tying the generators directly into the warp drive. Forcing the momentary burst of energy required to jump-start the ship's mighty engines was definitely not something the power units were designed to do.

A massive explosion rocked the engineering room, slamming Gomez and the others into consoles and bulkheads. The concussion wave was still washing over them when two more blasts erupted in the chamber, sending flame and shrapnel in all directions. Gomez could hear it burrowing into the walls and the control panels around them, but they were partially protected from the explosions by a wall separating the master console from the rest of the engineering area.

"Is everybody all right?" she called out as she regained her feet. No one reported any injuries as Gomez tentatively stepped around the wall and peered into the main engineering area. A scene of utter destruction greeted her.

The overloaded generators ultimately had succumbed to the tremendous energy impulses forced back into them from the *Defiant*'s warp engines, unleashing a sizable portion of their considerable power into the room. The resulting explosions had decimated the chamber, destroying consoles, power distribution nodes, even hurling debris into the ship's impulse engines. Gomez doubted that more damage could have been inflicted had the room been subjected to the detonation of a photon torpedo. It was saddening to see the once-vibrant heart of the starship reduced to near ruin.

At the master console, Pattie had already shaken off the effects of the explosions and had returned to work. "Power has been rerouted to auxiliary control, Commander."

Gomez acknowledged the report, knowing that the two remaining generators were the only things preventing the *Defiant* from reverting to the lifeless hulk they had originally discovered. Already burdened with the requirements of supplying power to essential systems, the surviving units might also be needed to deal with whatever awaited them on the other side of the rift.

As if sensing her troubled thoughts, Lense said, "You've done all you can, Sonya. It's up to the captain and Soloman now."

The sentiment, well-intentioned as it was, did little to ease Gomez's mounting frustration. What she really heard was: *There is absolutely nothing more you can do about it.*

CHAPTER
8

Okay, so it's taking more than three minutes.

A bead of perspiration rolled into Duffy's right eye as he lay on his back, his head once again shoved through a bulkhead opening and into the mesmerizing glow of the *da Vinci*'s warp-drive control system. He squinted and blinked the sweat from his eye, trying to refocus his sight on rerouting circuitry paths.

When he first stormed into main engineering and tore open an access panel seemingly at random, other engineers looked at Duffy as if the space madness had finally caught up with the young commanding officer. He now chuckled to himself as he thumbed the controls of his handheld nanopulse laser and sealed the last of the shorted connections. Even a seasoned engineer might have needed precious minutes simply to track down the problems keeping the *da Vinci*'s warp engines from functioning. But Duffy had suspected just where to start looking in the system for effects from the deflector dish feedback loop, and his instincts had been correct.

He squirmed his way out of the bulkhead and pushed himself to his feet. Pointing to one of the engineers standing nearby, he called out, "Conlon! Finish up here!" The ensign rushed to work as Duffy sped out of engineering, calling over his shoulder, "And let me know the instant it's ready!"

Though his work in engineering wasn't complete, Duffy knew he had to be elsewhere. Never in his life had he wanted to be on the bridge of a starship as badly as he wanted to be now, he realized as he sprinted down the corridor. His momentum nearly carried him into the nearby turbolift's doors before they could whisk open with their signature pneumatic hiss.

"Bridge!"

Come on, come ON!

The car began to move and he stared at the ceiling, as though he could urge the turbolift to travel faster through sheer force of will. After a handful of seconds that seemed to last an eternity, the doors finally parted and he didn't so much step onto the bridge as he hurled himself onto it. Panting, he looked at the main viewscreen, ready for anything.

Nothing was there but black, empty space.

His breathing slowed somewhat as he whirled to face Corsi, who stood almost where he had left her just . . .

"Six minutes, thirty-seven seconds," said the security officer after a glance at her console. "Welcome back, Commander."

He gasped at her, trying to regain his composure. "We still don't have warp, but we will." He moved to the center seat and plopped himself into it. "Fabian, keep working. I'm playing a hunch that we'll have time for one more shot at this."

McAllan spoke up from his tactical station. "Commander, the Tholians are approaching. They're in viewing and communications range."

The final grains of sand were falling through the hourglass, and the crew of the *da Vinci* was out of options. Duffy wanted to get a real look at the threat that had hung in his mind's eye for what seemed like forever.

"Put them on screen."

The dark of space vanished in a flash as an amber glow radiated from the main viewer. There it was: A deadly hexagon of Tholian ships linked by the powerful energy web, burning with what seemed to be a life of its own. The formation did not waver from its course as it bore down on the *da Vinci*.

Duffy didn't blink. He stared at the viewer, refusing to let the web scare him from saving his crew.

His crew.

"Hail them," he ordered. "And get ready for a fight."

The *Defiant*'s auxiliary control center was a room pulsing with life, energy, and purpose as its doors parted to admit David Gold and Soloman.

"Bless you, Gomez," the *da Vinci* captain said as the pair moved to the room's central control console. A quick glance of the display readouts there showed that they would be able to control all available systems from this point.

That's good, Gold thought, *because we're running out of places to go*.

The journey from the bridge had been an interesting one, with Gold and Soloman using their suits' small maneuvering thrusters to control their descent into the turboshaft. By comparison, forcing the doors to deck seven had been easy, after which Soloman's tricorder had guided them here.

Intended for use only in the event of the main bridge being destroyed or otherwise compromised, this room harbored none of the aesthetic niceties that so characterized the ship's primary nerve center. It was designed solely with function in mind, and at that moment such efficiency suited David Gold just fine.

"Activate the viewscreen," he said. Soloman found the necessary controls and seconds later the screen on the far bulkhead flickered to life, its blank slate replaced with the now-familiar chaos that was the rift. But it wasn't all that was visible.

"Stars," Gold whispered. Indeed, the fabric of space, with its millions of stars, was growing more distinct with each passing second. The bold plan put into motion by Gomez and her team had worked, and the *Defiant* was emerging from the rift.

"Captain," Soloman said, "sensors are detecting the *da Vinci*. She is holding station . . . just within transporter range." Continuing to consult the limited information provided by the ship's scanners, the Bynar added, "I am also reading six Tholian vessels . . . on an approach vector."

Looking at the displays himself, Gold pointed to one that displayed a large, undefined energy reading. "What's that?"

"It is similar in configuration to . . . the energy webs normally created by . . . Tholian vessels," Soloman replied. "Though it is not a deployment . . . I am familiar with."

"They're pulling it like a big fishing net," Gold said, experience and instinct giving him the answer. "They mean to snare the *da Vinci* with it."

Soloman nodded. "It is of sufficient strength to . . . overcome the *da Vinci*'s shields."

"Stand by on the thrusters," Gold said before tapping his communicator. "Gold to Gomez. I need whatever power you have left for the deflector shields, and that phaser bank if you have it."

The engineer's reply was most definitely lacking in enthusiasm. "I was really hoping you wouldn't say that, Captain. This ship can't go into combat."

Gold was well aware of what he had at his disposal. One hundred years ago, this vessel was the match of just about anything the Federation's known enemies could throw at her. Now, however, she was a shell of what she had once been, barely able to move at a limp and with no real weaponry. Realistically, the *Defiant* stood no chance of withstanding any sort of prolonged battle.

But that wasn't what he was after. He knew his team of engineers wouldn't understand immediately, but that was only natural. After all, he was out of his element in the midst of most engineering problems. But now they were on his turf, playing a game he had more experience at than he liked to readily admit.

"I know, Commander, but hopefully we won't have to. I just need the old girl to come through one more time."

CHAPTER
9

As he studied the bank of tactical displays dominating the forward bulkhead of his ship's command center, Nostrene could not help but be amused at the readings they conveyed. Scans showed that the Federation ship was still maintaining station near the last known position of the derelict vessel that had led Starfleet into Tholian space. It now hung broadside and vulnerable to the energy net.

The human in command of the rescue ship had to know that any attack against a Tholian ship would not go unanswered. Further, if he had paid any attention to the intelligence briefings Starfleet had surely provided regarding the Assembly, the human would also know that when attacked, Tholian vessels always retaliated without mercy. Any competent commander would almost certainly realize that a single ship stood no chance of survival when faced with such a situation. The prudent course of action would be to flee rather than risk capture or destruction.

And yet, the Federation ship remained.

"Are they damaged?" Nostrene asked.

Overseeing the subordinates at the sensor and weapons stations, Taghrex replied, "Not severely, Commander. Their hyperlight drive appears non-functional, but they have full use of weapons and defensive systems."

"Can they outrun us at sublight speeds?"

The second-in-command turned to study the sensor displays once more before replying. "For a time, but ultimately we can overtake them, and then the energy net will do the rest."

Nostrene nodded at the report. Even though their six ships could deploy only weakened defensive shields while generating the energy net, he was not concerned. Once ensnared in its confines, the force of the mesh would quickly deplete the power reserves of the enemy ship and leave it helpless against Tholian weapons. The Starfleet crew would be at the mercy of their captors within moments.

Taking another look at the scanner readings for himself, Nostrene shook his head and tried to understand the thought processes of the Federation ship's commander. Even without hyperlight capability, the human surely must know that being a moving target was more desirable than being a stationary one. Nostrene decided that he must either be a reckless maverick or a naïve fool.

"We will attack and disable them," he said. "The Magistrates want prisoners, but if necessary we will destroy them." Taking captives from enemy vessels was not standard procedure, nor was it something Nostrene himself preferred to be involved with. Prisoners were troublesome, even discounting such things as providing sustenance and environmental conditions when other races were involved. He would rather just destroy the Federation vessel and be done with it, but he knew there were larger concerns here.

The Starfleet crew undoubtedly would have contacted their parent command about their current situation. There was also the possibility that they had passed on information regarding the web generator that the salvage team had discovered aboard the derelict. Though it was doubtful that the crew of the recovery ship had learned the true nature of their find, Nostrene had to proceed as if that were the case.

There was also the matter of obtaining or destroying the web generator itself. Once he had taken prisoners from the rescue ship, Nostrene merely needed to wait until the vessel trapped in the interdimensional pocket reappeared. If, at that time, the generator could not be retrieved via transporter, then he would simply order the entire ship destroyed, along with any Starfleet personnel still aboard it.

"Commander," called out the subordinate manning the communications station, "the Starfleet ship is hailing us. Its commander wishes to speak with you."

Nostrene waved the report away. "No response. I am not interested in anything a human would have to say."

"We are entering weapons range," Taghrex

called out. After a moment he added, "The Federation ship has energized its defense shields and weapons."

Studying the central tactical display before him, Nostrene noted the Starfleet ship's movement, orienting itself to face the incoming attack.

Apparently, the human commander is going to make a fight of it.

Nostrene was pleased at that thought. He had heard of the tenacity displayed by Starfleet in combat situations and had seen reports of their actions during the Dominion War. Those who fought aboard Federation ships showed remarkable resolve, even in the face of certain defeat. It was a trait Nostrene could admire even in nonTholians. He knew that the brief skirmish he had experienced earlier with the Starfleet recovery vessel had not been a true test of its crew's mettle, so it was with great anticipation that he greeted the coming battle.

The subordinate overseeing the tactical scanners suddenly turned from his station. "Commander, I am detecting a fluctuation in background radiation readings. The interspatial pocket is opening."

"How is that possible?" Nostrene demanded. According to the readings obtained by his science advisor, the rift was not expected to reopen for some time yet. "Put it on screen."

The image on the command deck's main viewer shifted in time for Nostrene and everyone else to see the mysterious black void appear once more, a gaping hole in the fabric of space. Seconds later, part of the rift was itself blocked out as a blue-green shape erupted from its center.

"The other ship," Taghrex exclaimed. "It has returned." Turning to Nostrene, he said, "Should we alter our attack course? It would be powerless to defend itself against us."

Indeed, Nostrene thought. Even as it emerged from the rift and shed the multihued cocoon of energy enshrouding it, the *Defiant* appeared to be nothing more than a powerless hulk. Its warp nacelles were dark, as were the numerous portholes that pockmarked its surface. It was inconceivable for it to be capable of mounting any kind of defense.

"Negative," he decided. "It poses no threat. We will dispatch the other vessel first. The derelict will still be there when that task is complete." Turning back to the row of tactical scanners, he said, "Target the rescue ship's weapons banks. Stand by to attack."

That was when the derelict opened fire.

CHAPTER
10

Alarms wailed on the bridge of the *da Vinci* as an electric-blue phaser blast sliced through the viewscreen's image of the Tholian attack formation and connected with the ship anchoring the lower-left corner of the pulsating, hexagonal web.

Kieran Duffy watched in awe as the stricken enemy ship reeled from the blow of raw energy and wavered in its flight. He couldn't believe his eyes as he found himself in his second battle at the helm of the *da Vinci*.

But I know damn well I didn't give any order to fire.

"Who the hell is shooting?" Duffy shouted as he saw the web flicker in intensity. It quickly resolidified as the five remaining ships moved into a pentagon of offensive power, leaving the injured craft to drift away from the group.

Stevens's answer was awash with excitement. "Duff! She's back! The *Defiant*'s back!"

The news shocked Duffy, then the thrill of it

immediately infused his body. The center seat felt electrified to the young commander as he spat order after order to the bridge crew.

"McAllan! Fire a spread on your predetermined targets! Helm, angle us toward the rift! And put the *Defiant* on the viewer, for God's sake!"

As Duffy tried to regain his perspective of the battle with its new participant, the viewscreen's angle now assisted him with a view of the newly configured Tholian force and the glowing *U.S.S. Defiant*. The century-old starship was moving through the doorway of its interspatial cage under what appeared to be its own power. Duffy gasped as the ship's secondary hull and finally its twin nacelles cleared the rending of space just in time to be called back to active duty with a vengeance. He squirmed in his seat as he felt the tide of the battle turning more in their favor.

Oh, Sonnie! You and your timing!

"Direct hit!" Gold called out from the sensor console in the *Defiant*'s auxiliary control center. "Nice shooting, Soloman." Peering into the viewfinder mounted against the room's rear bulkhead, the *da Vinci* captain could see that, although the antiquated ship had managed to produce a mere half-strength phaser blast, it had proven enough to pierce the defensive screens of the Tholian vessel.

After studying the Tholians' odd formation, Gold played a hunch that spoiling the trajectory of one or more of the ships might have the effect of disrupting the energy net generated by the group.

Watching the sensor readings on the net flicker and readjust as it compensated for the spoiled flight path of the ship the *Defiant* had just fired on, he was pleased to see his instincts proven right.

"The damaged ship is . . . breaking formation, Captain," Soloman reported from the auxiliary helm controls. "The remaining vessels are . . . maintaining their attack vector toward the *da Vinci*."

His eyes not moving from the viewfinder, Gold said, "Then we'll have to do it again. Target another of the ships and stand by to fire."

"Engineering to Captain Gold," Gomez's voice filtered through his communicator. "Sir, I need a moment to reroute power. The generator's overloading, and I can't feed power to the phasers without sacrificing something else."

"Route power from the shields, Sonya," Gold said without hesitation. "Take whatever you need for the phasers, then put everything you have left into the forward screens."

"Captain," Soloman said as he turned from the helm, "with only thrusters to . . . maneuver the ship, we will be at a distinct . . . tactical disadvantage."

Shrugging as if he was used to taking a vastly outclassed ship into combat on a daily basis, Gold replied, "If the Tholians finish the *da Vinci* off, our defenses won't matter."

During a career of nearly fifty years, Gold had served aboard and even commanded some of the most advanced vessels the Federation had to offer. It therefore seemed ironic to him that his last assignment would be going into combat aboard a dilapidated, hundred-year-old starship that had spent its entire lifetime confined to the pages of history.

Lifting his face from the viewfinder, Gold took an extra second to look around the auxiliary control room, taking in its archaic design and yet once again admiring how vibrant and full of life it seemed to be. After so many years locked away from the rest of the universe, all but forgotten, the *Defiant* had emerged proudly from its prison. Even though it limped and struggled to overcome its decades of captivity, the once-mighty starship would still head valiantly toward its one final mission.

Only in Starfleet, he decided. *I guess weird really is part of the job.*

"Come on, people! We're not going to let Captain Gold take the lead here!" Duffy pitched forward in his seat as a thought struck him.

The Tholians are going to turn on the Defiant!

The irony of being so close to saving the away team, only to see them die as the Tholian web savaged the woefully outmatched vessel ripped at Duffy's brain. Time narrowed for the commander as he tapped into every resource of strategy he could recall: every old Starfleet Academy course, every holographic simulation, every past conversation with Gold or anybody who ever steered a starship into battle.

"Keep after those targets! We have to kill the power to that web!" Duffy studied the Tholian formation and it became clear that the enemy ships had no intention of engaging the practically defenseless *Defiant*. They were bearing down on the *da Vinci*, and this moment was their last to act.

And suddenly, he knew what to do.

"Helm, full power to aft-Z axis thrusters, now!"

To her credit, the ensign manning the helm didn't hesitate in the face of the unusual order. Instead, she quickly fed the string of commands into her console, and the *da Vinci* responded with comparable speed.

Though the ship's inertial dampeners protected the crew from feeling its effects, the result of Duffy's order was evident on the main viewer. The stars on the screen spiraled dizzyingly as the *da Vinci*'s thrusters fired, pushing the ship on a perpendicular trajectory from the direction it had been facing.

"Bring us about, helm," Duffy called out. "Port thrusters only."

The ensign responded, and Duffy imagined he could feel the ship rotating as it pivoted on its axis. On the viewscreen, he saw the Tholian battle group hurtling past the point where the *da Vinci* had been an instant before. Then the image shifted as the ship reoriented itself, and instead of sitting in the path of the menacing energy net, Duffy now had his best shot at the Tholian ships as they overshot their mark.

"Fire!"

Phasers blasted from the *da Vinci*, catching a Tholian ship square in its propulsion unit. A second ship took a fresh blast from the *Defiant*, and the energy web sparked once before fading entirely from view.

"That's it, Duff," Stevens called out from the science station. "The formation is scattering and the web has deteriorated completely. It looks like the Tholians are retreating."

Duffy rose from the command chair, his expression one of unmasked pride. They had done it! "Looks like it's all over except for the bragging. Nice work, people. Open a channel to the *Defiant*, and let's see about—"

"Commander," McAllan said, "one of the Tholian ships has lost all power. It's heading directly for the rift." Turning his attention back to the viewer, Duffy saw the lone enemy vessel spinning without control toward the dark area and the chaotic area of space behind it.

"Helm, intercept course," he ordered. "Mr. McAllan, ready the tractor beam. Lock onto that ship."

At her station, Corsi made no effort to disguise the shock in her voice. "Commander?"

His attention focused on the viewscreen, Duffy ignored her as the tractor beam enveloped the Tholian ship, instantly stopping its tumbling descent into the rift.

"Got her, Commander," McAllan reported.

"Pull them out of there, McAllan, nice and slow." Looking over at Corsi, Duffy added, "And let's hope somebody's paying attention."

Corsi nodded in agreement, the corners of her mouth turning upward as she realized what Duffy was after. No matter what action the Tholians might take against the two Federation ships, it didn't justify consigning the disabled Tholian ship to the unpleasant fate awaiting them in the depths of interphase.

McAllan looked up from his tactical console. "We're clear of the rift, sir. We can release her without danger."

Shaking his head, Duffy instead asked, "What's the status of the other Tholian ships?"

"The undamaged ships are moving to assist the others," McAllan replied. "They have broken off their attack."

"Well, then let's extend an olive branch," Duffy said. "Angle the tractor beam to send that ship in their direction. Helm, lay in a course that will back us away from the Tholians and toward the *Defiant*." Taking one last look at the viewscreen, he added, "And Mr. McAllan, deactivate all weapons."

"What?" The single word exploded from Corsi's mouth, but she must have realized her grievous lapse in protocol because she drew a deep breath before continuing. "Commander, that may not be our best course of action right now."

Duffy nodded. "I understand your concerns, but somebody has to take a chance here." On the viewer, he watched as the Tholian ship they had rescued, still guided by the *da Vinci*'s tractor beam, moved toward its companion vessels. After a moment the beam faded, leaving the damaged ship to move forward under its own momentum.

"One of the other ships is moving toward it, Commander," McAllan said. "No sign of a regroup for another attack."

At the communications console, Abramowitz turned in her seat. "Mr. Duffy, we are being hailed by Commander Nostrene."

Still wary that the Tholian ships might attempt to resume their offensive, Duffy nevertheless knew that he was obligated to pursue a peaceful resolution here. He'd already initiated such an attempt by rescuing the drifting Tholian ship. He wondered now what that action had purchased for them.

"On screen, Carol. Let's see what the commander has to say."

The now-familiar image of the Tholian leader appeared on the viewer, the reddish hue of his crystalline body dominating the roiling spectrum of color that filled the picture.

"Federation vessel," Nostrene said, "your presence in Tholian space is no longer welcome. Retrieve the derelict you came for and depart our territory immediately. This concludes our cooperative effort." With that, the image faded and was replaced by the starfield once more.

Stevens was the first to react. "That has to be one of the most heart-wrenching apologies ever offered by a Tholian."

"Any bets on how much that hurt him to say?" Corsi asked. Turning her attention to Duffy, she said, "Well done, Commander."

Duffy's first impulse was to respond with one of his usual flippant comments, but he checked himself. Domenica Corsi didn't hand out compliments lightly, and coming from her, the simple statement was high praise indeed. He decided not to undercut the moment and instead accept her words in the spirit he was sure they were intended.

Indicating McAllan with a nod of his head, he said, "Keep your eyes on the Tholians until we're out of range. In the meantime, contact the *Defiant*. I think it's high time we got the hell out of here." He paused, then added, "Oh, and someone ask Captain Gold which big chair he wants to sit in for the ride home."

CHAPTER
11

Normally a hive of activity, as it had been since first entering service more than two centuries ago, operations aboard the primary SpaceDock facility orbiting Earth had come to a virtual standstill. Observation galleries overlooking the station's interior docking areas were crammed to overflowing with spectators, and every available viewscreen had been tied into the bays' visual feeds. A similar image was also being transmitted on subspace frequencies throughout the Federation, offering a view of history to anyone who might be interested.

And Admiral William Ross couldn't imagine anyone not being interested.

For years it had been a common complaint among the older, more seasoned members of Starfleet that respect for tradition and history seemed to be waning among younger officers and enlisted personnel. The explorers and defenders of peace from those bygone eras had supposedly exhausted all that they could offer to those who now wore the uniform. It had been said that many outside Starfleet had also outgrown the need to honor and appreciate those who had forged trails through the cosmos in the Federation's early days.

However, looking down at the throng of people gathered in SpaceDock's main observers' gallery, Ross smiled in satisfaction at the fervor he saw. He could almost feel the energy washing over the room in the anticipation of the next few moments. Maybe the arrival of the *Defiant* would engender only momentary fascination among the masses before they all returned to their regular lives, he decided. Then again, perhaps respect and interest in the past would be reclaimed here today, if indeed it had been lost at all.

"Mighty flashy party we've got here today, wouldn't you say, Admiral?"

The voice was gravelly and weathered, much like its owner, Ross discovered as he turned to face the speaker. His expression brightened at the new arrival, nodding with enthusiasm of his own. On a day that would play host to legends, it seemed only fitting that he be visited by one of their living representatives.

At nearly one hundred fifty years of age, Admiral Leonard McCoy still presented an imposing figure, though his shoulders slumped and his skin was little more than a waxy film covering the bones and muscles of his withered body. None of that seemed to matter, however, as Ross could still see the fiery determination in the admiral's eyes that had been captured countless times in biographical databases and historical narratives. The former chief medical officer of the original *U.S.S. Enterprise* represented the same history as the ship approaching Space-Dock, and Ross felt it more than appropriate that he should be here on this day.

"Admiral," Ross said, extending his hand to the aged McCoy, "it's good to see you. Couldn't resist coming out to see the *Defiant*'s homecoming?"

Taking Ross's proffered hand in his own frail grasp, McCoy nodded in greeting. "Wouldn't have missed it for anything. Not a whole lot excites me anymore, you know, but this is somethin' special. I'll bet Scotty is champin' at the bit to get into the *Defiant*'s engine room. He'll be like a newborn Horta in a rock quarry once he starts diggin' around in there."

Ross smiled at the thought of Captain Scott contentedly pulling himself through the depths of the antiquated starship. "Well, I'd imagine you're anxious to take a tour yourself, aren't you?"

His face taking on a somber expression, McCoy replied, "Maybe after all the work is done." He nodded in the direction of open space beyond the plexi-steel viewing port. "I've volunteered to lead the forensic detail going aboard the *Defiant*. It'll take several weeks to identify all of the crewmembers, based on what I've read of Captain Gold's report. It's a sad duty, but one I couldn't in all good conscience leave to someone else." Ross saw McCoy's eyes begin to water as the admiral cast a glance downward before continuing. "I've always felt a bit guilty that I was able to figure out how to counteract the effects of that interspatial nonsense where the *Defiant*'s doctor couldn't. Maybe if she'd had more time, she would've come up with something like the theragen cure eventually. We were lucky we only had to deal with the effects of that space from outside the rift, but they were stuck right in the middle of it. They never really had a chance."

He paused for a moment before returning his attention to Ross. "The least we can do now is make sure the crew gets to their final rest as best we can."

Ross nodded quietly in agreement before the SpaceDock intercom system attracted their attention, along with that of everyone in the observers' gallery and, in all likelihood, the rest of the station.

"Attention, all personnel: Incoming starship on approach vector. Stand by for docking."

"Ye've done a fine job, Captain. My compliments to your crew."

In his ready room aboard the *da Vinci*, David Gold absorbed the praise from Captain Montgomery Scott, noting a glint of satisfaction in the legendary engineer's eyes that he hadn't seen in quite a while. Like himself, Scott had only barely been able to contain his enthusiasm at the idea of stepping aboard the *Defiant* to revel in the history it represented. Of course, Gold knew that his friend's desire to examine the fabled starship was more personal, more deeply ingrained from life experience than he himself would ever know.

"All the credit goes to Commander Gomez and her team," Gold said. "In addition to her figuring out a way to get the *Defiant* out of the rift, Commander Duffy played a large part in straightening out the rest of the mess we managed to get ourselves into."

"Ah, Commander Gomez," Scott replied. "Yes, I've read her report, and I mean to have a conversation with the lass once she's finished aboard the *Defiant*. Of all the areas of that ship to blow to hell, did it have to be engineering? I was so lookin' forward to gettin' in there and pokin' around." Gold could see that Scott was joking, naturally, though he couldn't help but wonder how much truth lay behind the playful words.

"As for Mr. Duffy," the S.C.E. commander continued, "I must tell ye, Captain, I know somethin' about bein' thrust into a command situation when ye don't feel qualified to do the job. Your Mr. Duffy comported himself remarkably well for a lad who's not lookin' for a command of his own. His quick thinkin' to save that Tholian ship went a long way toward avoidin' severe damage to our relations with the Assembly. The bloody politicians are still foamin' at the mouth over the whole thing, but I suspect they'll eventually get over it."

Gold couldn't resist a small chuckle at that. "Well, they need something to keep them busy. On that note, though, what's the word on bringing the Tholians and the Klingons to the negotiating table?"

Shrugging his shoulders, Scott replied, "There's no tellin' what those popinjay diplomats are plannin'. Ye'd think that with the information your team discovered aboard the *Defiant* that the Diplomatic Corps would want to get everyone into negotiations now, while the situation can be contained. From what I hear, that's exactly what Ambassador Worf is pushin' for."

Gold nodded in agreement. Revealing the secret of the web generator and its use on the Traelus II colony to the Klingons would have to be handled with utmost delicacy if any good were to come from it. While the Federation could not continue to allow negative feelings to dominate their relations with the Tholians, they could ill afford to lose the valuable alliance they had cultivated with the Klingon Empire after decades of tension and mistrust. He hoped that Worf, the Federation ambassador to Qo'noS could pull it off.

"Perhaps something positive can come from all of this," Gold mused. "If the Federation can get the Tholians and Klingons past a very dark chapter in their history, and if we gain new allies in the bargain, then the sacrifice made by the *Defiant*'s crew won't have been for nothing." Not many people could claim that their actions would have such far-reaching ramifications more than a century after their deaths, after all. Gold mentally saluted Captain Thomas Blair and the men and women who had served under him.

The whistle of the *da Vinci*'s intraship communications system and the voice of Domenica Corsi interrupted their conversation.

"Bridge to Captain Gold. Sir, the *Defiant* is approaching SpaceDock."

"Thank you, Commander," Gold replied as he rose from behind his desk. He indicated the door to Scott. "Well, Captain, shall we play witness to one more bit of history?"

With her main power plants restored to partial operation, the *Defiant* no longer resembled a ship of the dead. Instead, the majority of her portholes were brilliantly illuminated, and her running lights shone brightly against the scarred and pitted surface of her tritanium hull. Her warp nacelles remained inactive, though, the Bussard ramscoops still dark rather than the vibrant crimson they had once pulsed. Except for that detail, the *Defiant* looked as though she might be an active ship of the line.

Space traffic controllers throughout the solar system had found themselves burdened with the demands of tracking thousands of Starfleet and civilian spacecraft converging on Earth, their crews all clamoring to see the return of the legendary starship. A swarm of smaller vessels shadowed the course being followed by the *Defiant*, many carrying journalists from worlds spanning the Federation and all working diligently for impressive visual images of the ship to transmit to their home planets.

Sitting in the command chair on the bridge of the *Defiant*, Sonya Gomez could not shake completely the temptation to be overwhelmed by what she was seeing. At first the crowd of vessels bearing curious spectators and well-wishers had unnerved her, but that had quickly faded. Now she allowed herself to give in to the enormity of the moment. After all, how often did something like this happen?

With partial power restored throughout the ship, the *da Vinci*'s crew had spent the past several days carefully transferring the bodies of *Defiant* personnel into portable stasis containers, where they would remain until Starfleet forensic teams completed the arduous task of identifying each crewmember. Automatic atmosphere scrubbers had removed the worst of the dust and pulverized remains of the *Defiant*'s crew, though Gomez doubted she would ever forget the dank smell that had greeted her the first time she had removed her suit helmet.

She had suggested that Captain Gold guide the *Defiant* into SpaceDock, but he had declined the honor, deferring it to her instead.

It was your team that got her out of that hellhole, he had said. *It's only fitting that you finish the job you started.*

Gomez was grateful he had made the offer. With its brightly lit consoles and assortment of background noises, she could easily lose herself in the ambiance of the bridge and believe that she was serving on a ship of the line in the 23rd century.

"It really is something else, isn't it?" Duffy said from where he sat at the communications console. More *da Vinci* crewmembers staffed other bridge stations as well, providing Gomez with navigational, sensor, and engineering information. Below decks, other engineers were nursemaiding the *Defiant*'s engines on their final cruise.

Though the ship had been towed by the *da Vinci* back from Tholian space to the edge of the Terran system, Gomez had requested that the *Defiant* travel the last leg of its journey under its own power. She and Duffy, along with Pattie and several other S.C.E. specialists, had toiled for two days to ensure the ship's ability to make the trip. Seeing the response from onlookers as they traversed the solar system, Gomez was glad she had pushed the idea.

"It's something, all right," she replied. "And it should be. The men and women who served on this ship deserve nothing less." Turning the command chair to face Duffy, she said, "I haven't had the chance to say this before now, Kieran, but I wanted to thank you for all you did. We couldn't have completed the mission by ourselves."

Duffy attempted to wave the praise away. "Thank Fabian, or even Corsi for that matter. They had as much to do with it as anyone." His features took on an odd quality, one that Gomez couldn't remember seeing before as he added, "They helped get me through the tough spots."

At the helm where he was trying, without success, not to enjoy this occasion too much, Fabian Stevens turned in his seat. "Don't listen to him, Commander. Ol' Duff there is on the verge of becoming a real 'lead-from-the-front' kind of guy. Captain Gold might have to watch out for his job." With a mischievous smile he added, "Or maybe you should."

Gomez laughed, happy that her friend had performed so well under such trying circumstances. More than instilling added confidence in his shipmates, as well as Captain Gold and even herself, she knew that the experience would do much toward allowing Kieran to eventually realize his ultimate potential.

Still, she couldn't let Stevens's crack go uncontested. Her response was cut off, however, by a hail whistle from the communications console, followed by a female voice full of enthusiasm.

"*U.S.S. Defiant*, this is SpaceDock Approach Control. Stand by for docking maneuver."

It was a straightforward message, Gomez knew, conveying nothing behind the magnitude of the occasion. But she also knew that the time for reflection would come later. For now, there were the simple yet necessary obligations to tend to.

Nodding to Stevens, Gomez waited until he entered the necessary commands to transfer the ship's maneuvering control to SpaceDock, then reported, "Approach Control, this is *Defiant*. We have transferred guidance to you. She's all yours."

"Affirmative, *Defiant*. SpaceDock confirms control. Welcome home."

Her duties aboard the legendary ship finally at an end, Gomez replied, "*Defiant* confirms. Thank you, SpaceDock."

Under the guidance of automated maneuvering systems, the resurrected starship aligned itself with SpaceDock's main entryway. With thousands of spectators looking on in the station's observation areas and billions more watching over sub-space video feeds, the ship quietly entered the orbital facility, sinking into the welcoming embrace that it hadn't known for far too long.

After more than a century, the *U.S.S. Defiant* had finally come home.

COLD FUSION

Keith R.A. DeCandido

Historian's Note

Cold Fusion takes place between the *Star Trek: Deep Space 9*® novels *Avatar* Book 2 and *Section 31: Abyss*. It also takes place simultaneously with *Invincible*.

CHAPTER
1

"Commander, I humbly request permission to feed Abramowitz to the larvae."

Kieran Duffy sighed, rolled his eyes, took a sip of his coffee, then looked up at the Nasat standing before him in the mess hall. "What is it *this* time, Pattie?"

P8 Blue, presently standing upright on her two rear legs, was tossing a padd back and forth among four of her arms. "Oh, it's nothing different. She simply will not stop playing that music."

"Have you asked her to stop?"

"Repeatedly. Endlessly. Constantly."

"Well, at least your grasp of adverbs is improving."

"Commander—"

Holding up a hand, Duffy said, "Look, I'll talk to her, okay? I have to be on the bridge in five, and—"

"That's the other thing, we're always on and off duty at the same time. I cannot avoid her. I would like to renew my request for a new roommate."

"I've asked around, but nobody—"

"Of *course* nobody wants to room with her!" Pattie said. Her voice raised several octaves—a range Duffy hadn't known her to be capable of—and she was now tossing the padd around so fast, it was blurry. "Nobody can stand that music of hers!"

Sonnie, come home, was all Duffy could think. Especially since this was mostly her fault. Kind of.

In addition to her duties as commanding officer of the Starfleet Corps of Engineers team on the *U.S.S. da Vinci,* Commander Sonya Gomez was also the *da Vinci*'s first officer, and was therefore responsible for making up the duty assignments. Of course, the last time she'd done so was before Carol Abramowitz, the S.C.E. team's cultural specialist, got her hands on a new recording of Sinnravian *drad* music, specifically the newest from Blee Luu, the founder of *drad*'s "atonal minimalist" subgenre.

Unfortunately, Gomez was presently on a special assignment to the planet Sarindar, helping the Nalori Republic to get a subspace accelerator working. This left Duffy, normally the ship's second officer, pulling double duty as the ship's XO. Which meant that personnel issues like this, that he had been more than happy to dump on Sonnie's lap, were now his problem.

In all his years in Starfleet, Kieran Duffy had heard many different types of music, and many more reactions to same. He'd heard Klingon opera that could put a spring in one person's step and stop others dead in their tracks from the headache. He'd once seen a Vulcan ambassador moved to tears by the same Mozart piece that, years later, moved a Tellarite engineer to throw up.

But pretty much everyone who wasn't from Sinnrav (and many who were) found Luu's music to be completely unlistenable—except for Carol Abramowitz.

Gulping down the last of his coffee, Duffy got up. After swallowing, he said, "Pattie, I'm not really sure what I can do, except—"

Except maybe change the duty roster, he thought suddenly. *You're first officer until Sonnie comes back. You can do that.*

"Except maybe change the duty roster," he said after his moment of clarity. "I'll fix it so that you're on gamma shift when Carol's off. Okay?"

Now holding the padd in only one hand, Pattie made a tinkling noise. Most non-Nasats couldn't distinguish one such noise from another, but Duffy had been serving with Pattie long enough to be able to do so. This one—high-pitched, with the higher notes about a second and a half apart—was the equivalent of a sigh of relief. "Thank you, sir."

"You're welcome. And no feeding her to the larvae." Duffy hesitated. "Do your larvae really eat people?"

Another tinkly noise, this one lower-pitched—a shrug. "Only when they can get them. They'll eat anything. Well, I must take this report to Lieutenant Barnak. Thank you again, sir."

With that, Pattie got down on all eights and skittered out of the mess hall. Duffy wondered how much of Carol's insistence on playing Luu's music was personal preference, and how much was a defense mechanism triggered by living with an insect.

Two security guards, Drew and Hawkins, were sitting at one of the far tables. Hawkins said, "I think she was kidding, sir. About the larvae."

"Definitely," Drew said. "They're actually very picky eaters."

Sighing and shaking his head, Duffy left the mess hall, wondering if Sonnie had ever had to put up with this.

CHAPTER
2

David Gold had been listening to the latest letter from his granddaughter Ruth for the fifteenth time when the call from the bridge came.

"Message from Deep Space 9, sir," said Lieutenant McAllan's voice.

Gold frowned. They were en route to DS9 already. "On screen."

Ruth's pretty, glowing face was replaced on the viewscreen in Gold's quarters by the Starfleet logo, and then by the image of a woman wearing the uniform of a Bajoran Militia colonel. Though he had never met her, Gold instantly recognized her as DS9's commanding officer, Kira Nerys.

"Colonel Kira," he said. "This is Captain Gold. Is everything all right?"

"Hello, Captain. Yes, everything's fine. Don't worry, this is a simple diversion call."

"So the last dispatch we got *was* accurate? Those Jem'Hadar who attacked the station were renegades?" For some time, the whole quadrant was on yellow alert and many were convinced that the Dominion War, over for less than four months, was going to start right back up again. Gold was worried that this call was going to be bad news—unexpected calls from high-ranking officers almost always were.

"Yes, the dispatch was accurate. Unfortunately, part of the process of stopping them involved ejecting our fusion core."

"Oy."

Kira looked almost amused. *"'Oy' pretty much sums it up, Captain. We still need your help putting the station back together, just not here at the station. You're to rendezvous with one of our runabouts, the* Rio Grande, *in the Trivas system. We're forwarding the exact coordinates to you now. You'll meet up with Lieutenant Nog, our chief operations officer."*

Gold recalled that the Trivas system was in unclaimed space near the Cardassian border. "And this is going to help the station?"

"Let's hope so. We need to get this place operational before we run out of emergency power. The lieutenant will have all the details."

"Whatever you say, Colonel. We're happy to be of service however you need us."

At that, Kira actually smiled, though it didn't extend to her entire face. *This is a woman under a lot of pressure,* Gold thought, being all too familiar with that look from his own years in the center seat.

"Actually, Captain, the S.C.E. has already been a great help to us. And, honestly, if you could accompany the Rio Grande *back to DS9, we could probably use some more of that service."*

"That should be do-able, Colonel. I've heard a lot of good things about your station—in fact, one of my engineers used to serve there. It'll be a privilege to visit—and to help out."

"The privilege will be all ours, Captain. And I wouldn't worry about the mission, either. Nog's a pro. I'm sure it'll all go completely smoothly."

CHAPTER
3

Fabian Stevens stared at the sleeping form of Domenica Corsi in the bed with him, wondering how, exactly, this had happened. He had gone into the mess hall when he had come off shift the night before, figuring to do a little reading over a synthale before going to bed. To his surprise, Lt. Commander Corsi had been there. It was the first time Stevens could ever remember seeing the *da Vinci*'s chief of security in the mess hall. She generally preferred to eat in her quarters. Even more surprising was her request for him to join her. He'd conversed with her while off duty about as often as he'd seen her in the mess hall, and yet here she was inviting him over.

Intrigued by the novelty as much as anything, he had agreed.

"Senior staff and S.C.E. team, report to the observation lounge immediately."

It was Lieutenant McAllan's voice, and the beep that had preceded it had an immediate effect. In repose, Corsi's features were unusually soft—like a porcelain doll sitting under lights in a glass case. The effect was magnified by her blond hair, normally tied severely back, cascading loosely about the pillow.

As soon as the beep sounded, though, the hard edges returned, and the porcelain became duranium as she awakened.

"Let's go," she said, getting up from the bed without hesitating. She went from dead asleep to wide awake in less than a second, an ability that Fabian Stevens envied, to say the least.

The previous night, Corsi had moved toward the bed with a lithe elegance and softness that Stevens would not have previously credited her with. Now, though, *soft* was the last word he'd use to describe how she moved away from it.

Efficient, though, that he'd use. Though he'd been awake for almost half an hour, it took Stevens several seconds to drag himself out of bed, grab the various parts of his uniform (he hadn't really been paying attention to where he'd dropped them last night), and put them on. By the time Corsi was in uniform and had tied her hair neatly back, Stevens was still struggling with his pants.

"Mr. Stevens," she said formally, "I'd appreciate it if you didn't speak of this to anyone, and I hope you won't think that it was the beginning of anything."

Stevens let out a bark of laughter. "To be honest, I hadn't thought that far ahead. I just—"

"I appreciate what you did," she said, still talking like an officer, which Stevens supposed was inevitable, "and I am grateful, but I'm not in the habit—"

Holding up a hand, Stevens said, "Say no more, Commander. This stays between us."

"Good. I'm going ahead to the meeting. I'll see you there."

She turned on her heel and left. Stevens watched the door for several seconds before putting on his shirt.

When he arrived at the observation lounge, most of the usual suspects were seated. Captain Gold was at the head, of course, with Duffy at his left. Duff was holding a mostly full cup of quinine water, so he'd already had his morning coffee. Soloman, Corsi, and Dr. Lense sat next to him— Corsi seemed to be pointedly not making eye contact with Stevens as he entered.

Pattie Blue was in her special chair opposite the captain. Abramowitz was, Stevens noticed, sitting next to Gold on his right, which put her as far from Pattie as possible. *Guess the* drad *music battles haven't concluded yet,* he thought with a smile. Of course, Abramowitz could only sit there because Gomez—the one missing S.C.E. member—was still off-ship.

Faulwell was seated next to Abramowitz, which left two chairs free—one opposite Lense, one opposite Corsi. Deciding that discretion was the best he could do, Stevens sat opposite Lense. Corsi didn't seem to notice.

"Now that Stevens has deigned to join us," Gold said dryly, "here's the story. We're not going to Deep Space 9 to help them with repairs, though

we are going to their aid. We've been diverted to
rendezvous with one of their runabouts and then
proceed to an abandoned Cardassian station in
the Trivas system known as Empok Nor."

Stevens muttered, "Quoth the Empok, 'Never
Nor.'"

"Excuse me?" Gold said, one of his bushy eye-
brows raised.

Shifting in his seat, Stevens said, "Sorry, sir.
That's something one of the engineers at DS9
came up with after the first time we—Well, see,
when I was assigned to DS9, our chief of operations, Miles O'Brien, went over there to get some
spare parts. Unfortunately, half the team didn't
make it back—there was some kind of Cardassian
booby trap left behind. We never really wanted to
go back after that, and one of the engineers was a
fan of old poetry, so she made that joke. It kinda
stuck."

"Edgar Allan Poe's 'The Raven,'" Abramowitz
said helpfully. "The line is really 'Quoth the raven,
"Nevermore".'"

Nodding, Gold said, "Well, these ravens are flying back. DS9 had to eject their fusion core, and
their new chief of operations—a lieutenant named
Nog—is meeting us in the Trivas system in order
to obtain a replacement."

Stevens looked up in surprise at that. "Nog's
chief now?"

"You know him?" Gold asked.

"Yeah, he was a cadet when I was there. In fact,
come to think of it, he was part of the team that
went to Empok Nor."

With a small smile, Duffy said, "Obviously he was one of the ones who survived."

"Good guess," Stevens said, also smiling. "He's a *lieutenant* now?"

"That's what the mission profile says," Duffy said, punching up a display. It showed the familiar features of the nervous young Ferengi Stevens remembered, but now wearing a junior-grade lieutenant's uniform.

First Corsi and I wind up in bed together, then I find out that Nog's got a commission and is doing the chief's job. This is a very weird day.

"The plan," Duffy continued, "is to detach the fusion core and bring it back to DS9."

"The whole core?" Stevens asked.

"Yup. Apparently they had to eject it during that little brouhaha with the Jem'Hadar."

Stevens started scratching his chin. "Geez, the emergency power wouldn't last five minutes—we'd have to link together a bunch of emergency generators, maybe six or seven to get them running."

"Way ahead of you, Stevens," Gold said with that avuncular smile of his that meant he was being indulgent of the silly engineers and their endless ramblings. "They don't need our help with that—there's already a passel of S.C.E. folks on-station. What they do need help with is getting Empok Nor's fusion core from Trivas to DS9."

Faulwell spoke up. "Are we sure there's anything there to take? I mean, if the station's just sitting there . . ."

Duffy shrugged. "The lieutenant seemed to think there was."

"Uh, sir?" Corsi said as she stared down at a padd. "I'm looking over the records of the station right now. From the looks of it, it's a security nightmare."

"Oh, c'mon, Corsi," Duffy said with an incredulous look. "The station's in the middle of nowhere. The Cardassians didn't just abandon the station, they abandoned that whole star system—and it's *still* unclaimed. It's got to be the least strategically valuable piece of real estate in the sector."

"Maybe, but besides the mission Stevens mentioned, there've been a bunch of incidents on the station. It's been used as a 'neutral territory' meeting place on more than one occasion, and a group of Bajoran cultists used it as their base of operations last year. Last reports do have it being abandoned, though."

"So what's the problem?" Duffy asked.

Corsi finally looked up from her padd and fixed Duffy with a withering look. Stevens found he couldn't help but contrast it with the expression on her face not fifteen minutes earlier when she was asleep. "The problem is that anybody can just waltz in. The station has no defenses worth mentioning, but plenty of equipment that might attract salvagers. I can easily see Ferengi, Yridian, Orion, or Cardassian pirates—not to mention someone like the Androssi—gutting the place. We need to be on alert for *anything*. Whatever or whoever you send over there, I want a security detail of at least five."

Duffy nodded. "Fine." He looked around the table. "This is a straight-up nuts-and-bolts operation, so it'll be me, Stevens, Blue, and Soloman. Fabe, you'll be especially useful, since your time on DS9 means you actually know these systems."

"Well, mostly," Stevens said. "I mean, I spent most of my time on the *Defiant,* and the station had been pretty thoroughly modified by the time I got there. Empok Nor's still pure Cardassian. I'm not saying I can't do anything, but I don't want anyone getting raised expectations or anything."

Smiling, Duffy said, "Don't worry about it, Fabe—we always have low expectations for you."

A chuckle passed around the table. "Gee, thanks," Stevens said sardonically, and he considered throwing something at the second officer.

"Anyhow," Duffy said, turning back to Corsi, "counting this Nog guy, that's five—one security guard for each of us."

"We may want to double the security detail." Corsi's lips were pursed.

Duffy frowned. "We've already got a ten-person away team, Commander. I think making it fifteen is excessive."

"I don't. Those cultists I mentioned? I just noticed who led them." She held up her padd, the display of which now showed a familiar Cardassian face. "Dukat. You remember, the guy who brought the Dominion to this quadrant in the first place? And before that, the station crawled with Jem'Hadar, Vorta, Ferengi—not to mention that mission that Fabe mentioned with the Cardassian booby trap."

Stevens looked up sharply. *She called me "Fabe."*

While on duty. *In a meeting, for crying out loud.*
What the hell—?

If Corsi or anyone else noticed the slip, they
didn't show it.

"A ten-person team is enough," Duffy said.

"Good," Gold said, cutting off Corsi's protest.
"We're set to rendezvous with the *Rio Grande* at
0830. Make sure the team's ready, Commander."

Duffy got up. "Yes, sir."

A buzz started to sound in the room as people
got up from their chairs. Corsi, Stevens noticed,
shot a venomous look at Duffy before turning and
leaving the observation lounge. Pattie also didn't
get up from her chair until after Abramowitz had
left the room. Stevens went to the replicator and
got himself a cup of coffee. By the time it materialized, only he and Bart Faulwell were left in the
lounge.

"So," Bart said, "when did this thing between
you and Corsi develop?"

Stevens sputtered his coffee.

Chuckling, Bart said, "Computer, napkin." One
materialized in the replicator, and Stevens snatched
it and wiped the stains off his uniform jacket.

"How the hell did you—?"

"Deductive reasoning," Bart said with a grin.
"You two were the last ones in, you spent the
entire meeting pointedly not looking at each other,
and you didn't come back to our cabin last night."

Trying to sound dismissive, Stevens said,
"That's it?"

"Plus, she called you 'Fabe' during the meeting.
That pretty much clinched it for me."

Stevens sighed. *I suppose if anyone was going to catch that, it'd be the linguist.* "Look, Bart, this can't get out. We—"

"Easy," Bart said, holding up a hand. "The only reason I figured it out is because I know you didn't come home last night. If you two want to have an affair and keep it secret—"

"Hell, it isn't even an affair. Just a one-nighter, really. And I still haven't got the first clue as to what brought it on."

"What happened?"

Stevens told Bart about seeing her uncharacteristic appearance in the mess hall and her equally uncharacteristic invitation to join him. "We talked for *hours*. She moved around a lot when she was a kid—her family lived on about twelve different planets. That got me going about planet-hopping around the Rigel colonies with my parents' shuttle service. Then it was Starfleet stories."

He took a sip of coffee, managing to actually swallow it this time, and then continued. "Next thing I knew, she's inviting me back to her cabin. Lense was on duty, so we had the place to ourselves."

"Now there's a pairing," Bart said. "What on Earth do you think our security chief and chief medical officer talk about in their downtime?"

Chuckling, Stevens said, "Bart, until last night, I wouldn't have believed that Domenica ever *was* off duty."

"Now *you're* doing it."

"Doing what?"

"You called her 'Domenica.' I don't think *anyone*

on this ship has *ever* referred to her as anything other than 'Corsi,' 'Commander,' or 'Core Breach'— at least in the four months I've been here."

Stevens thought back. "She asked me to. I was actually calling her 'Commander' for the first hour or so, then she said to call her 'Domenica.'" He laughed. "Come to think of it, she also said if I called her 'Dom,' she'd kill me."

"Well, they teach you that stuff at the Academy."

Another sip of coffee. "She was amazingly— well, gentle. And warm. Bart, I did not spend the night with a woman who deserves to be nick-named 'Core Breach.'"

"And you don't know what prompted it?"

Stevens shook his head. "No clue."

"Well, do yourself a favor. Try not to think about it until after the mission. Neither of you needs the distraction."

Grinning, Stevens said, "What, you're ship's counselor now?"

"No, but you don't need a linguist for this mission, so I thought I'd moonlight," Bart said, returning the grin. "Seriously, before I met Anthony I had my share of one-nighters. They have this tendency to linger in the brain—more so, if you have to interact with the person." He put an encouraging hand on Stevens's shoulder. "Just be careful, okay?"

Stevens took a sip of coffee, then nodded. "I will. Thanks, Bart."

"Hey, that's what roommates are for."

CHAPTER
4

Nog hated being alone.

The fact that he spent most of his formative years in Uncle Quark's bar probably had a lot to do with that. Most of his life had been spent in either the bustle of Deep Space 9, the crowded confines of the *U.S.S. Defiant,* or at Starfleet Academy. Indeed, the only time he could ever truly be alone was during his convalescence after losing his left leg at AR-558—hardly a fond memory.

So he popped a tube grub into his mouth, took a sip of root beer, and tried to will the *da Vinci* to hurry up and arrive here in the Trivas system already.

Ideally, of course, he would've had a team of engineers with him in the *Rio Grande.* But if DS9 could have spared the engineers, he wouldn't have needed the *da Vinci*'s help in the first place. The entire engineering staff and the other S.C.E. personnel that Starfleet had assigned *and* the Bajoran engineers were all too busy keeping DS9 from falling to pieces without a fusion core, and also preparing the station for the insertion of a new one.

I just hope this plan works.

Of course it'll work. Shar and I ran the numbers a hundred times. Both Colonel Kira and Commander Vaughn approved it. It will work.

So why don't I feel confident?

"Computer," he finally said after swallowing the last of his tube grubs, "play some music."

"Please specify."

Nog thought for a moment. *Since I am alone, may as well take advantage.* "Play the third movement from Blee Luu's *Endless Dream.*"

The *drad* music cascaded over Nog's ears, and he immediately felt more relaxed. Nog could never understand why so many people reacted so badly to this lovely sound, but everyone from Jake Sisko and Uncle Quark to his roommates at the Academy had practically run screaming from the room every time he tried to play it. *One of these days, I need to get my hands on a copy of her new recording.*

Naturally, the *da Vinci* showed up just as he was getting into it.

With two quick stabs at the console, Nog opened a channel and cut off the music. *"Rio Grande to da Vinci, this is Lieutenant Nog. It's good to see you."*

The face of an older human with wispy white hair on his head and four pips on his collar appeared on the viewscreen. *"This is Captain Gold of the* da Vinci *at your service, Lieutenant.*

We're ready to head to Empok Nor whenever you are."

"Thank you, sir. Please set course 187 mark 9 and proceed at full impulse. We'll be there in twenty minutes."

"Good. Lieutenant Commander Duffy has a full away team ready to go."

"I'm transmitting beam-over coordinates now," Nog said, and he suited action to words on his console. "That'll put us right at the access to the core."

"Good," the captain repeated. Then he smiled a friendly smile. *"Let's get moving."*

Nog nodded and cut the connection. He took an instant liking to Captain Gold, and it gave him a good feeling about the mission in general. He had a plan, it would save the station, and the *da Vinci* crew would help him to implement it.

In ten minutes, Empok Nor was close enough for visual range. He called it up on the main screen.

His left leg started to itch. He didn't bother to scratch his prosthetic—besides, he knew it was just a psychosomatic reaction to this place. After all, he'd been here twice before, and each time he'd almost been killed—once by a drug-crazed Garak, once by a squadron of Jem'Hadar during a prisoner exchange. *Let's hope that I keep the not-dying streak going.*

The first time he came here, he thought it looked exactly the same as the Bajoran station. And on the face of it, it was: the classic Cardassian design of a circle with pointed protrusions that looked like limbs trying to claw themselves out of

dirt. One of Nog's classmates at the Academy theorized that it was an architectural metaphor for
how Cardassian culture managed to claw its way
up from being a resource-poor planet to a major
player in Alpha Quadrant politics.

Now he looked at it with a more professional
eye, and he could see all the differences. Empok
Nor had been abandoned for four years, after all,
and hadn't had the benefit of the Starfleet
upgrades that had been going on on Deep Space 9
for the last seven-plus years. Empok Nor had none
of the weapons or sensor upgrades, the improved
structural supports, or any of the other dozens of
improvements—some of which Nog had been
involved in himself.

Of course, Empok Nor right now had one very
critical thing that DS9 didn't, and it presently sat
enticingly in the lower portion of the station.

A working fusion core.

The core was still active, too, and the quick scan
Nog did showed that life support and artificial
gravity were still functioning, as they were last
year when the *Defiant* rescued Colonel Kira from
the Pah-wraith cultists. However, some of the
readings, Nog noticed, didn't jibe with the readings the *Defiant* took back then.

"Rio Grande, *this is the* da Vinci," said a voice
that wasn't Gold's over the runabout speakers.
"We're ready to beam over."

Nog settled the *Rio Grande* into a parking
orbit—the pylons were too unstable to risk docking there, especially with nobody in ops to check
on the station end—and then responded. "So'm I,

sir," he said, hoping that "sir" was the right thing to say, since whoever this person was didn't identify himself. It was probably the Lt. Commander Duffy person Gold mentioned, assuming Duffy was also a male, as the voice was. He'd been so busy quadruple-checking his calculations, he hadn't had the chance to familiarize himself with the names of any of the *da Vinci* crew.

Setting the runabout on standby, he programmed the transporter to beam him to the core access.

Within moments, he was present on the eerily familiar catwalk. An access panel was at his right, as were nine Starfleet personnel—all, Nog noticed, in gold-trimmed uniforms, with the exception of the Nasat, who simply wore a combadge. Nog assumed the four humans and one Bolian holding very large phaser rifles were security and the two humans, the Nasat, and the Bynar were the actual S.C.E. team. He was surprised to see a single Bynar—*I thought they all came in pairs*—and one of the human engineers looked familiar. He also noted that only two of those present were officers. Though an officer himself, his years studying under Chief O'Brien had made Nog appreciate the importance of enlisted personnel, especially in engineering.

The human female security officer started directing her people to take up positions at various parts of the catwalk. Nog caught the names of each of the guards: the dark-skinned human male was Hawkins, the pale human male was Drew, the olive-skinned human female was Lipinski, and the Bolian was called Frnats.

The other human engineer—the officer—walked up to Nog and offered his hand. "I'm Lieutenant Commander Duffy. I'm in charge here."

Taking the hand, Nog said, "A pleasure, sir. If you don't mind, I need to check something."

Duffy shrugged. "Check whatever you want. We'll get started now."

Blinking, Nog said, "Excuse me?"

"Don't worry," Duffy said, putting a hand on Nog's shoulder, "we'll get your core for you before you can eat a tube grub."

Sputtering, Nog said, "But—sir, with all due respect, I've already—"

"Don't worry about it, kid."

Kid? "Commander Duffy, I'm not a 'kid,' I'm the chief operations officer of—"

"Hey Duff, you'd better take a look at this. You too, Nog."

Nog looked over to see that the other human engineer was at the console. Duffy moved to join them, as did Nog. Once he got a good look at his face, Nog finally recognized him. "Stevens, right?"

Fabian Stevens smiled down at Nog. "Yup. Good to see you again, Nog. And congrats." Then he turned to Duffy. "Take a look."

"All the reaction chambers are online," Duffy said after a moment.

Nog said, "What!?" He looked at the console. Sure enough, all six of the fusion reaction chambers were active. "That's incredible! We don't—didn't even keep all six active on DS9."

"I thought this place was dead," the female security officer said to Nog. "The reports from your first trip here said that it was just running on emergency battery power."

"Well, one of the chambers was brought online by the Pah-wraith cultists who squatted here," Nog said. "But all six—it doesn't make sense."

"Someone's been here," the security woman said, hefting her rifle. "We need to bring more people over."

Duffy shook his head. "Corsi, that isn't necessary."

The Corsi woman moved almost eye to eye with Duffy. "Commander, there's a very good chance that we're not alone on this station."

"Actually, there's no chance that we aren't. We checked—there're no life signs here."

"Excuse me," Nog said.

"Right now, maybe," Corsi said, ignoring him, "but somebody had to bring those reactors online, and I doubt it was Pah-wraith cultists."

"Excuse me," Nog repeated.

Also ignoring him, Duffy said, "Keep your people on alert, and I'll let Captain Gold know, but we don't need more security down here." He smiled. "There's too many people on this catwalk as it is."

"*Excuse* me," Nog almost shouted.

"What is it, Lieutenant?" Duffy asked.

"Sir, I have already laid out a plan for the extraction of the core and the transporting of it to DS9. If you'll just—"

Again, Duffy put his hand on Nog's shoulder. Nog was sorely tempted to brush it off. "Look,

Lieutenant, I appreciate you wanting to look good to your superiors, but don't worry about it. We're pros. We do this sort of thing every day. We'll have your core out before you know it. Just sit back and watch us go at it, okay?"

He then turned his back on Nog and went to talk to the Bynar.

I don't believe this. I spent days on this, and they're just blowing it off. Who do they think they are?

Before Nog could say anything, though, he heard a strange noise. It was fairly high-pitched, and seemed to be coming from behind him. "What's that noise?"

Duffy frowned. "I don't hear anything."

Nog closed his eyes and focused in on the sound. "It's over—*there!*"

He pointed right where Frnats was pacing on the catwalk. She walked a step closer to the edge of the catwalk—

—and then the noise grew louder, energy crackled around her, and suddenly what appeared to be a giant brown mesh appeared in the air.

The Bolian went flying across the catwalk toward Hawkins.

Nog peered at the mesh. It seemed to be covering the entire fusion core. The strands of the mesh were about twenty centimeters wide with small square holes. It was brown, and Nog noticed that it seemed to be—well, flowing. Almost as if it were a running body of water.

What was most fascinating was that the mesh didn't project out from a source, the way, say, a

Starfleet force field could be seen to emanate from emitters in bulkheads. It was simply *there,* as if it had always been.

"The Androssi." Corsi, Duffy, and Stevens all said it simultaneously—the security chief with a tone of anger, the engineers with more of an "oh-no-not-again" attitude.

Although Nog had heard of the Androssi, he couldn't recall much at the moment. There wasn't time to try to dredge the memory in any case, as another high-pitched sound came from the middle of the catwalk, and another form materialized there.

It was the same shade of brown, and shaped like a ball about a meter in diameter. Its surface also seemed to be flowing.

"Androssi Protocol 1, *now,*" Corsi said, and fired her own phaser. It fired at, of all things, level 2, which was a light stun setting. Nog stared incredulously at the security chief.

However, the other three standing guards followed suit and fired.

Amazingly enough, the ball seemed to disrupt for a moment, fading in and out. Then it came back into existence and arcs of electricity shot out at each of the guards.

Corsi, Drew, and Lipinski managed to duck out of the way, but Hawkins was still standing near Frnats's prone form, and so was unable to avoid the attack.

"They've upgraded," Drew said grimly.

"Protocol 2," Corsi said, without missing a beat. Nog ran over to where Hawkins and Frnats were now lying on the catwalk, the former twitching. He hadn't come armed, but the Bolian wasn't using her phaser rifle anymore, and Nog hadn't spent the Dominion War fighting—and losing his leg—in order to stand and watch a fight now.

The Nasat and the Bynar did likewise, the former grabbing Hawkins's phaser, the latter checking the two guards with his tricorder.

Protocol 2, based on what the Nasat did with Hawkins's phaser, involved putting the phaser on random mode. All phasers created after Starfleet's first encounter with the Borg a decade earlier were able to randomly change settings and frequencies.

Okay, so obviously these guys have faced this Androssi security device before, Nog deduced as he changed the settings on his phaser.

As Nog joined the others in firing at random settings on the device and ducking to avoid the bolts of electrical energy that shot around the catwalk, Duffy tapped his combadge.

"Duffy to *da Vinci*. We've got an Androssi security device here. Two guards are down, and the trick we used on Maeglin isn't working this time."

"Dammit," Gold said. *"So much for an uninhabited station."*

Nog ducked as another arc of electricity shot at him, then he fired two more shots, one at level 1, one at level 9, each at a different EM frequency. The ball seemed unimpressed.

"Duffy to transporter. Diego, *please* tell me you can punch through the interference this time."

"Sorry, Commander, but I lost the lock on you guys about a minute ago."

Gold said, *"Find a way this time, Feliciano."*

"Trying, sir."

One of Lipinski's shots disrupted the ball—its surface stopped flowing and it disappeared from view for a second. Unfortunately, when it came back into view it immediately zapped her, and she also fell to the catwalk.

Nog fired again, cursing the thing for its effectiveness—Lipinski hadn't had a chance to call out what setting she'd used, and there was no way anyone could risk moving over to her.

Or so he thought. The Nasat suddenly curled up into a ball—making her look like a chitinous counterpart to the security device—and rolled over to Lipinski. Two electrical bursts hit her, but they didn't seem to slow her down. She uncurled when she reached Lipinski and checked the setting.

"Level 4, low-frequency!" she said in a tinkly voice.

Nog quickly adjusted his phaser accordingly and fired.

So did the others.

The brown ball fizzled, and then disappeared. As soon as it did, the shots being fired continued through past where the ball had been. Drew, who had been standing opposite where Nog was crouched, barely ducked Nog's shot in time.

Letting out a very long breath, Nog tried to ignore the latest phantom itch on his leg. *The war's been over for months, and it seems like I'm fighting just as much since it ended as I did during it.*

"Good work, Pattie," Duffy said. "Soloman?"

The Bynar looked up at that. "All three guards are alive. But they will require immediate medical attention."

Duffy tapped his combadge. "Diego, any luck?"

"Sort of. The interference is still there, but I can actually get a lock on Lieutenant Nog's signal."

Stevens was looking at his tricorder. "I think I know why, Duff. Look at this." He showed his tricorder's display to the other human.

Corsi said, "Let's see if we can take out the mesh the same way."

Nog was about to take a look at Stevens's readings—it was odd that his combadge would penetrate the interference when no one else's would—when he heard Corsi's words. "No!" Nog cried. "If you disrupt it, the phaser shots will go through to the core!"

Nodding, Corsi said, "Fine, we'll try something else." Then she regarded Nog's phaser rifle. "Nice work with that, by the way."

"Experience," Nog said quickly, not wanting to dwell on it.

Again, Corsi nodded. "Right, DS9 was pretty much the front line for most of the war, wasn't it? Well, thanks for the assist."

"I don't believe this," Duffy said before Nog could reply.

"What is it, Duffy?" Gold asked.

"Captain, apparently these security devices are broadcasting a huge number of specific interference patterns—including ones keyed to our specific combadges. In fact, one of them is 111's combadge."

Nog noticed the Bynar wincing at that statement. *Sounds like 111 isn't around anymore. Is that the other Bynar? Is that why this one's alone and has such a weird name? It'd certainly explain why he speaks so hesitantly.*

He didn't ask, though, but simply said, "I don't get it."

"What it probably means," Gold said with a deep sigh, *"is that we're dealing with Overseer Biron again."*

Corsi fixed Stevens with an incredulous look. "Wait a minute. You mean to tell me that, when we were on Maeglin, the Androssi scanned and recorded the combadge frequencies of the entire complement of the *da Vinci* and programmed it into their security on the off chance that they'd meet up with us again?"

Duffy smiled grimly. "That's exactly what we're telling you, Corsi."

"Hey, Feliciano," Stevens said. "I got an idea. Can you use the signal you're getting from Nog as a booster on the overall signal?"

"If that doesn't work," Duffy said, "we might be able to just take turns beaming people back and forth with his combadge."

"We can make it work," Stevens said. "Just modulate the pattern enhancer to the upper ranges and increase the confinement beam's range."

Nog looked at them like they were insane. All they had to do was beam Nog himself up to the *da Vinci*, then beam him back with a pattern enhancer.

"Or," Feliciano said before Nog had a chance to voice this thought, *"I can just beam the lieutenant up, hand him a pattern enhancer, then beam him down."*

There was a dead silence.

Duffy and Stevens looked at each other.

"Yeah, okay," Stevens said.

"I mean," Duffy added, "if you want to actually do it the *sensible* way, sure."

Rolling his eyes, Nog thought, *These are the people I'm supposed to trust with extracting the core?*

"Can the comedy, you two," Gold said. *"Let's get the lieutenant up so we can get the wounded out of there. Once that's done, we're going to yellow alert— if I know Biron, he'll be back, and I want to be ready. Hell, if DS9 didn't need this core so badly, I'd call the whole damn thing off. I want reports every fifteen minutes, Duffy, clear?"*

"As a bell, sir," Duffy said.

Corsi said, "Sir, I recommend that new combadges be replicated for the entire crew as well, and I'll need three more security guards to replace Frnats, Lipinski, and Hawkins."

"Way ahead of you on the combadges, Corsi. Barnak's already on that. Nog, get ready to be beamed up."

"Yes, sir."

As the transporter effect started to form around Nog, he heard Duffy say, "We'll get to work on the—"

Then Nog found himself on a small transporter platform, only slightly larger than the one on the *Defiant.*

"—field surrounding the core in the meantime." That was the rest of Duffy's sentence, heard over the comm.

A human with olive skin and black hair stood behind the console. His eyes went wide, and he said, "You're a Ferengi."

"And you're a human," Nog snapped. He wasn't in the mood for the usual shock at seeing a Ferengi in a Starfleet uniform. He'd gotten more of it at the Academy than since he returned to Deep Space 9, but it still grated. "Can we get a move on, please?"

"Right. Sorry, just didn't realize." He grabbed something off the floor and then walked around to the platform. "I'm Chief Feliciano. These are the pattern enhancers." He set them down on the platform.

"Great," Nog said. "Let's get going."

"Hang on," Feliciano said, walking back to the console. "I'm supposed to wait on security." He hesitated. "Look, I'm sorry about that Ferengi comment. You probably get a lot of that. I just wasn't expecting it, is all."

Nog let out a breath. "It's okay. I'm sorry I snapped. Things have been a bit hectic."

The doors opened and three security guards walked in, all human females. One of them tossed a combadge to Feliciano. "New jewelry, Chief."

Feliciano caught it with a smile and looked at it. "I'm not into brooches."

The guard snorted, then looked at Nog. "I'm Robins. This is Eddy and Friesner. You must be Nog."

Nog just nodded. He wanted to get back to the station—for one thing, he wanted someone to tell him precisely what they were up against with the Androssi; for another, he still hadn't had a chance to check out that anomalous reading he'd gotten on the *Rio Grande*.

"Energize, Chief," Nog ordered as soon as the three guards were assembled on the platform.

CHAPTER 5

The chime alerted Overseer Biron to the fact that his shift was to begin shortly. He awakened instantaneously and immediately noticed that something was wrong with the engines. The vibration of the deck that he felt under his bare feet as he got down off his hammock deviated from the norm.

The Androssi overseer touched his ear with one hand. "Engineering."

"Engineering." It was one of the workers; Engine Master Claris would not be on duty for another hour.

"This is the overseer. The overdrive is not performing at maximum efficiency. Please check the eldrak consumption rates. It will be repaired in one hour."

"Yes, my overseer, it will," the worker said without hesitation or surprise. After all, he was the overseer. If he said it would be fixed in an hour, then it would be done. That was the way of things. If the worker somehow failed to bring the over-

drive back to proper efficiency within that time frame, Biron would instruct Claris to have the worker disposed of and replaced.

Within five minutes Biron had removed his sleeping clothes and put on his overseer's jumpsuit, tied his waist-length hair back, and put in the five nose rings that symbolized his position. This last he did in front of a small mirror; the reflection that gazed back at him was of a male Androssi with light sepia skin, slightly wavy golden hair with a full brown beard, and an unusually bulky build for one of his kind. The latter was due more to his weakness for anprat, a particularly fattening delicacy from the homeworld.

As he prepared himself, he went over the day's schedule in his head, and also thought of a better way to integrate the new weapons systems they had obtained with Cardassian technology.

He left his quarters—which were the same size as every other cabin on the ship—and went to the flight deck. Sub-Overseer Howwi stood up upon Biron's entrance, as did the other four workers. They remained standing until Biron took his place at the front left seat of the rectangular deck.

Biron turned his head slightly to look at the darker-skinned Howwi in the seat to his right. The sub-overseer had trimmed his golden beard down to almost the skin, an affectation that Biron had never understood. Such attention to irrelevancies tended to interfere with the work. Still, Howwi had proven to be competent at his job, and perhaps he would learn the uselessness of trying to groom himself as if he were a member of the Elite.

Like Biron, Howwi was of the officer class—which meant, if nothing else, that he was entitled to eye contact when Biron spoke to him.

"Have we heard from the client?"

Howwi blinked his eyes four times. "Negative. We will receive a communication via subspace within the hour."

"No more specific time than that?"

"Negative. The client is . . . elusive with regards to punctuality, as usual."

Biron sighed. He entered the idea he had earlier into the ship's vast database.

"Overseer," one of the workers said.

"Speak," Biron said without looking back. Those of the worker class were only worthy to be spoken to on duty-related issues, and then only when given leave.

"The security on the Cardassian station has been breached."

"Specifics?"

"The triovar field around the fusion core has been activated and the panshar has been disabled."

Frowning, Biron turned to Howwi. "Starfleet?"

"Possibly. They have proven to be most resourceful."

Again, Biron sighed. This was all the client's fault. Biron had not wanted to leave the Cardassian station, but the client had insisted on this face-to-face meeting, and also insisted it take place here in the Vlugta system. It left the Cardassian station exposed to other salvagers.

But the client needed to be kept happy, in this particular case. This client was providing the upgraded holo-emitters that Biron's sponsor among the Elite had been wanting for so long. As with every member of the officer class, Biron's sole purpose was to provide technology for the ship's Elite sponsors. He had been particularly skilled at doing so for his sponsor—it had led to his quick promotion to overseer. In fact, Biron had achieved that rank faster than anyone in recorded memory, mainly because he knew how to properly exploit the clients. In this case, it was best to give in to the client's peculiar whims.

However, now the security on the target had been breached.

"Set navigational course 44491," he said without looking up. "Set FTL at 7.2. Send a subspace communication to the client. Message to read: 'Must investigate security breach on target. Will reschedule rendezvous when difficulty is solved.'" He did not give the orders to anyone specific—he knew that someone would carry them out. If they did not, he would simply dispose of the four flight deck workers and bring in replacements.

Not that he expected that. His successes meant that the workers on his ship were particularly efficient. Sure enough, his status board indicated that all his orders were carried out with dispatch. The viewscreen showed the visual distortion of space brought about by the implementation of the faster-than-light drive. At 7.2×10^9 times the speed of light, they would arrive at the Cardassian station in under an hour.

"With respect, Overseer," Howwi said, "the client will not like this."

Biron looked at Howwi. "The client will like losing the station even less. If it truly is Starfleet, we cannot risk letting them run loose."

Howwi scratched his nose at the spot where, once he was promoted to full overseer, his fifth nose ring would go. "Might it be possible that the *da Vinci* is the ship we will face?"

"To speculate would be unproductive." Biron considered. "However, I would certainly welcome a chance to face them again." The defeat at Maeglin still grated on Biron. He had not failed often in his career.

"Overseer," said a different worker.

"Speak."

"Receiving telemetry from the triovar field now."

"Report."

"It has detected and interfered with the communication badge signals from nine members of the crew of the Starfleet vessel *U.S.S. da Vinci*, registry NCC-81623: Kieran Duffy, Domenica Corsi, Fabian Stevens, 110, P8 Blue, Vance Hawkins, Stephen Drew, Andrea Lipinski, and Frnats. It no longer detects those signals, however."

"Perhaps they left," Howwi said.

"Or perhaps they discovered the interference and adjusted their communication badges accordingly," Biron said. "Adjust FTL to 9.5."

That would bring them to the Cardassian station in fifteen minutes. To go faster would risk damage to the engines, which Biron was not willing to do. As it was, he was disappointed in his emotional response to the presence of the *da Vinci*. Such thoughts of revenge were inefficient.

But he wanted to get back at the humans David Gold and Sonya Gomez and the rest of their crew for the humiliation on Maeglin. The fact that he would get to do so while continuing to service the client that would get his sponsor the holo-emitters simply made it *more* efficient to do so.

CHAPTER
6

Fabian Stevens stared at the Androssi field that was now surrounding the fusion core. He had spent the last several months trying not to think about their last encounter with the Androssi—it had been Commander Gomez's first mission on the *da Vinci,* and more than once he had been convinced it was going to be her last.

As if it wasn't bad enough that they might have to deal with that Androssi overseer Biron again at any minute, there was also the fact that each second that they couldn't get at the fusion core was another second that DS9 was in serious danger. Stevens still had plenty of friends on the station, and he was seriously worried about them right now.

Then there was Corsi. Each time that damn brown ball shot at her, Stevens's heart skipped a beat. *Focus, Fabe, focus. Remember what Bart said—don't let this distract you.*

Looking over at that hard face—such a contrast from the peaceful woman who was sleeping next to him this morning—he knew that there was no chance of anything developing between them. Leaving aside any other considerations, he doubted that Domenica would allow herself to get involved in such an inappropriate dalliance.

Not "Domenica." She's Corsi. Or Core-Breach. Just keep it professional.

He heard the familiar sound of a transporter—in fact, Stevens could tell just from the level of noise that it was four people materializing—and turned to see Nog, Eddy, Friesner, and Robins appear on the catwalk. Nog had three pattern enhancers, which he wasted no time in placing in a triangle, with one point at Lipinski's twitching form, the other two around the heap that Hawkins and Frnats had fallen into on the opposite side of the catwalk.

Robins, meanwhile, started distributing new combadges to everyone. Stevens had to admire the thoroughness of Biron and his people, despite himself—that had proven a remarkably effective tactic. *If Nog hadn't been here, we might've had serious problems.* They probably still would have been able to get the casualties off-station, using the *da Vinci*'s shuttlecraft, but who knew what other security was floating around here?

After the three guards dematerialized, Nog said, "Can someone please explain to me what it is, precisely, that we are up against?"

"Simple," Duffy said. "The Androssi. They first showed up in the Demilitarized Zone a few years back, trying to convince the Maquis to accept their help."

"Help?"

Duffy sighed. "In a lot of ways, the Androssi are like the S.C.E.—they offer to fix technical problems. The difference is, they always have a price."

Nog seemed confused. "What's wrong with that?"

Stevens grinned. *Once a Ferengi* . . .

"There tends to be a big difference," Duffy said, "between what they ask for and what they actually take. They've also been known to cause the problem in order to come in and solve it. Most of the places they claim to have helped out are usually worse off than when they started—mainly because what they ask for is technology. They're *constantly* looking for new tech."

"What about adjusting existing technology?" Nog asked.

Stevens frowned. "What do you mean?"

Nog walked over to a console. "When I got here, I picked up some strange readings." He started entering commands into the console. "Look at this."

Stevens and Duffy both walked up to join the young Ferengi at the console. *That's Lieutenant Young Ferengi to you, Fabe,* he admonished himself. He still had trouble wrapping his mind around Nog as an officer—hell, it had taken him a while to get used to the idea of Quark's nephew as a cadet. . . .

Looking at the console, Stevens saw that Nog had called up the station specs and put them alongside an internal scan of the station.

Duffy spoke before Stevens could. "They've made modifications."

Corsi stepped forward. "What kind of modifications?"

"Not sure," Duffy said. "The Androssi use dimensional shifts in their technology. It's why their stuff will sometimes not be visible until you interact with it."

"Okay, here's a question," Corsi said. "Let's say they've modified the station. Do we have any reason to stop them?"

Nog whirled on her. "We need the fusion core."

"So the hell what? I remind you, Lieutenant, that we're on an unclaimed station in unclaimed space."

"Overseer Biron and his people are still wanted on Maeglin after what they pulled," Duffy said.

"That's assuming that this really is the work of Biron, which we don't know. Besides, we don't have the authority to act on behalf of the Maeglin government, and it doesn't change the fact that this station is in free space. They have as much a right to it as we do."

Stepping forward, Nog said, "We're not just abandoning the station to these people! We *have* to have that fusion core."

Corsi looked at Duffy. "Commander?"

Well, that's impressive, Stevens thought, *she's actually passing the buck to Duff*. But then, Corsi always deferred to whoever was in charge, once she got her complaint in. Normally that was Gomez or Gold, but with the commander off on Sarindar, that left Duff in charge—*just*, he remembered, *like it was against the Tholians*.

"I'm with Nog here, Corsi. You're right, the Androssi have as much right to the station as we do—but we have just as much a right to try to dismantle their net. Besides, we really do need this fusion core."

"Lieutenant Commander Duffy?" The hesitant voice belonged to Soloman.

"Talk to me, Soloman."

"I have done a preliminary investigation of the Androssi security device. As far as I can determine, the Androssi have upgraded their technology from the last time we encountered them. I do not believe that I can interface with their technology as 111 and I attempted the last time."

Stevens sighed. He had expected something like this—and honestly, he was grateful. Soloman had been through enough since 111 died on that big ship at Blossom IV. His and 111's attempt to interface with Androssi computers on Maeglin almost didn't work—he doubted that Soloman could handle it on his own now without his partner.

Duffy nodded. "Okay. Take a look at the station computer, see if you can figure out what they've done to it."

"Yes, sir."

Stevens thought about that incident on Blossom IV—the *Beast*, they'd nicknamed that massive ship that had fought the *Enterprise* to a standstill and whose uninvited insectoid inhabitants had killed 111. It had been a near thing that they weren't *all* decapitated by those things.

P8 Blue then skittered over on all eights. "I have an idea, sir."

"Good, we could use one," Duffy said dryly.

"The field was disrupted with a level-4, low-frequency phaser blast. The problem is, we can't just fire on it without risking hitting the core once it's disrupted."

"We know all that, Pattie."

Then something occurred to Stevens, and he went back to the console.

"Right," Pattie said, "but what I'm thinking is that we can set up one of the rifles to emit a pulse at that level and frequency that would dissipate on impact no matter what."

"It's certainly worth a shot—if you'll pardon the pun," Duffy added with a smile.

"That's it!" Stevens cried.

"What is it, Fabe?" Duffy asked.

"I was trying to figure out why these modifications look so familiar. The Androssi have added their own wrinkle to this stuff, but it looks like the same kind of tech that we found on the *Beast*."

"The *Beast*?" Nog asked.

"An alien ship the *Enterprise* came across," Duffy said quickly. "We crawled around its guts before we had to blow it up. It was huge, about a thousand times the size of a *Sovereign*-class ship—more like a planet. Had some pretty nasty weaponry, too, as I recall."

Pattie was looking at another console. "I think you're right, Stevens," she said. "Once you compensate for the dimensional shift the Androssi always use, the match is pretty close."

"Great, so the Androssi came across a *Beast* of their own," Duffy said with a sigh.

"Maybe it was even the same one," Stevens said, "and they just copied the tech."

Nog let out a small noise, then said, "It doesn't

matter! We need to find a way to get around it!"

The Ferengi seemed particularly anxious. Stevens remembered that the kid was always a bit high-strung. Then again, with Rom as his father and Quark as his uncle, he could hardly be otherwise. *And he's not a "kid," he's a lieutenant.*

"Easy, Nog," he said aloud, "we'll find a way through it."

Pattie had gone back to modifying Eddy's phaser rifle. The security guard, in turn, was pacing the catwalk with a hand phaser.

Stevens, meanwhile, started doing a more detailed scan of the modifications. Now that he knew what he was looking at, he was able to ask the computer the right questions—even this somewhat more limited Cardassian computer. It had been a couple of years since he had to deal with the eccentricities of Cardassian systems, and he hadn't missed it all that much.

"Modifications are done," Pattie said, clambering up onto her hind legs while hefting the phaser. She handed it to Eddy. "Would you like to do the honors, Claire?"

Eddy smiled. "Happy to do it."

Okay, Stevens thought as he ran through the scan, *the parts up on the pylons are in the same spot as where we put the weapons upgrades on DS9. No, wait, the ones on the lower pylons are different. Weird. But it looks like—*

Oh boy.

Eddy fired her phaser at the fusion core—or, more accurately, at the mesh surrounding it. Stevens noted that it looked like the *Defiant's* pulse weapons rather than the standard beam one got from a handheld phaser. It did, however, seem to have the desired effect—the mesh surrounding the fusion core disrupted and then disappeared, but the beam did not continue through to damage the core.

"Yes!" Nog cried, pumping his fist.

"Good work, Pattie," Duffy said with a grin.

"Uh, Duff?" Stevens said, hating to dampen everyone's enthusiasm with what he just figured out.

"Yeah, Fabe?"

"I think I know what they've done here. I'd kinda like you and Soloman to check it over, though."

Duffy went to the console to examine his findings. Soloman was still communing directly with the main computer in that weird way Bynars did. By the time he came out of his trance, Duffy was finished.

"I'd like to state for the record that this really, really sucks," Duffy said. He tapped his combadge. "Duffy to Gold."

"Go ahead, Commander."

"I've got good news and bad news, sir."

"Give me the good news."

"We've broken through the field around the fusion core, so now we can get at it."

"Good."

Duffy let out a very long breath. "The bad news is that the Androssi appear to have salvaged some tech from the same people who built the *Beast*. Based on what we've been able to determine, assuming that our reading of the *Beast* equipment is accurate, and without being a hundred percent sure *how* it works exactly—"

"*Spit it out, Duffy!*"

Duffy took a breath.

"The Androssi are turning Empok Nor into the mother of all mobile weapons platforms."

CHAPTER
7

Captain David Gold stared at the viewscreen, which presently showed him Empok Nor drifting in space. The station itself gave no clue as to its sinister new purpose.

"You sure about this, Duffy?"

"*Completely? No. To be honest, we'd need about a year, a full research team, and a starbase facility to dope most of this stuff out. But they've definitely put some upgraded thrusters onto the lower pylons and some very nasty weapons systems into the upper pylons. We're talking phasers at what I'd have to call level 30 or so.*"

"Damn," Gold muttered. That was enough to split a planet in half.

Stevens added, "*It also looks like they've got some kind of plasma-based directed-energy weapons. I've never seen anything like them, and I couldn't begin to figure out how powerful they are.*"

"*Sir, if I may?*" That was Nog's voice.

"Go ahead, Lieutenant."

"I just examined the fusion core itself. These Androssi have also made modifications to it. Only one of the reactor chambers is actually running the station. The rest of it is powering a massive propulsion system that's been integrated with the core itself. If I'm reading this right, it might well be capable of speeds up to warp 6."

"Captain," Soloman put in, *"I have communed with the station computer. It confirms what Mr. Stevens, Lieutenant Commander Duffy, and Lieutenant Nog have said. In addition, there are preparations under way, albeit incomplete, for the installation of quantum torpedo bays in the docking ring. Based on the specifications, the torpedoes would have a yield of approximately one thousand times that of the torpedoes on a Defiant-class ship."*

David Gold tried to figure out a way that this all could be translated into good news, but couldn't. A weapons platform the size and shape of Deep Space 9 capable of speeds up to warp 6 with enough weaponry to lay waste to a solar system in about half an hour, all in the hands of Biron.

"Gevalt," he muttered. "All right, people, listen up. I want a *full* analysis of what the Androssi have done to the station."

"Sir, what about extracting the core?" Nog asked.

Gold's instinct was to tell the young Ferengi that they had bigger problems—but, of course, they didn't. True, the Androssi were bad news—it would be decades before Maeglin fully recovered from what Biron and his crew did to the place—but Deep Space 9 was counting on that fusion core. They needed it, not just for the people on the station, but the billions of lives in the Bajoran sector that DS9 was responsible for.

"We can do both, sir," Duffy said before Gold could say anything. *"Soloman can handle the analysis. Stevens and the lieutenant both know these systems well enough that they should be able to handle the computer even without his help."*

"Good," Gold said. "Then—"

From ops, Lieutenant Ina interrupted. "Sir, long-range scans are picking up a vessel on direct approach to Empok Nor—traveling at warp 7.3."

"Identify." Gold gripped the arms of his command chair. If the queasy feeling in his gizzard was any indication, it would be the Androssi. To his chagrin, his queasy gizzard had proven to be depressingly reliable over the years.

"Configuration and power output matches that of the Androssi," the Bajoran ops officer said. "Sensors say it's a ninety percent match with the ship we encountered at Maeglin."

Gold muttered several curses in Yiddish. "Yellow alert."

"Transporter room to bridge."

"Go ahead, Feliciano."

"Sir, I've lost the lock on the away team."

"Da Vinci to Duffy," Gold said immediately.

When no response was forthcoming, he turned to McAllan at tactical, who was operating his console and shaking his head. "I've lost the away team's signals—all of them, even Lieutenant Nog's. Something's jamming them."

Gold muttered several more curses. "Engineering.

Barnak, punch a hole through that damn interference, pronto."

Jil Barnak, the Atrean chief engineer of the *da Vinci*, said, *"On it, sir."*

"Androssi ship coming out of warp and on an intercept course with us," Ina said.

McAllan added, "They're running weapons hot."

"Raise shields. Arm weapons, but don't lock on yet. Let's give them a chance to play nice."

Gold could feel McAllan's dubious look without bothering to turn around and see it. The tactical officer said, "Sir—do you really think they're going to?"

"No," Gold said with a grim smile. "But I like to live the life of a cockeyed optimist. Put 'em on screen."

The viewscreen's image changed from Empok Nor to that of a familiar-looking ship. The hull was brown—just like Androssi skin, and the jumpsuits that they seemed to favor. Gold's first impression of the Androssi had been that they had no aesthetic sense whatsoever, and their vessel design bore that out: the ship, which had no name as far as anyone knew, was basically a big box. Abramowitz's cultural profile on them, limited though it was, indicated that the Androssi had a preference for the practical that bordered on the utilitarian. That, their overriding interest in technology, and their rectangular ship construction had led some to make comparisons to the Borg, but the Androssi had a definite hierarchical structure and they were most definitely individuals.

"Hailing frequencies."

McAllan manipulated his console. "Open, sir."

Gold sat up straight in his command chair. He had a tendency to slouch, but he always made sure to sit up whenever he was sending a visual communication. "This is Captain Gold of the Federation Starship *U.S.S. da Vinci*. Identify yourselves."

"They're responding, sir, but audio only."

"Just like last time," Gold said with a nod. The Androssi never communicated visually. Abramowitz's theory was that they didn't want anyone to see any aspect of their technology, even if it was just in the background. "On speaker."

"This is Overseer Biron. You are once again interfering in a legitimate Androssi operation, Captain Gold. You will utilize your transporter to beam your away team off the station and warp out of the area immediately, or we will be forced to take hostile action."

"So, it is you, Biron. Don't insult my intelligence. You know damn well that I can't 'remove' the away team because you're jamming their combadges. In any case, this is unclaimed space. You have no jurisdiction over our actions, and no justification for taking any kind of action against us."

"Perhaps not, Captain Gold, but you have no jurisdiction over ours, either."

Smiling, Gold said, "Actually, we've been deputized by the planetary government on Maeglin. We have standing orders to place you under arrest and remand you to the Maeglin Law Enforcement Bureau." That was a complete fabrication, of course, but Biron didn't know that. "We therefore request that you lower shields and prepare to be boarded."

"Now it is you who insult my intelligence, Captain. Do you really expect me to accede to that request?"

Gold gave a half-smile. "Not really, no. But I thought it was worth a shot. Now the question is—"

"They're firing," McAllan interrupted.

"So much for cockeyed optimism," Gold muttered. "Red alert. Wong, evasive."

"Yes, sir," the conn officer said.

McAllan said, "It's a torpedo. If it's anything like the last time, our shields should hold."

Ina shook her head. "It's not a perfect match for that one, Mac," she said.

"Lock phasers and fire," Gold said.

"Firing." As McAllan spoke, Gold saw the image on the viewscreen of the amber beams from the *da Vinci*'s phaser banks strike the Androssi vessel. "Torpedo impact in ten seconds. Their shields are down to eighty percent. Torpedo impact in three . . . two . . . one . . ."

The torpedo struck with what felt to Gold's experienced self as a light blow. "Damage?"

"No damage at all," McAllan said, sounding rather surprised. "Maybe they— Oh, hell. Captain, shields are *completely* gone."

Gold was grateful that he had such an impressive lexicon of curses.

"They're firing again," Ina reported. "Phasers this time."

Which will cut us to pieces without shields, Gold

thought grimly. "Wong, get us the *hell* outta here, full impulse, pattern gamma."

"Pattern gamma, aye."

Under Songmin Wong's expert guidance, the *da Vinci* blasted away from Empok Nor at its fastest sublight speed.

Away from Empok Nor and, to Gold's annoyance, away from Duffy and his team.

But without shields, they were sitting ducks.

"Sir, whatever that torpedo did completely disrupted the shields," McAllan said. "I can't get them to reconstitute."

Wong said, "Androssi ship is not pursuing."

Gold leaned forward. "What?"

"They're taking up a position relative to one of Empok Nor's upper pylons."

The captain pounded his fist on the console. He had run out of Yiddish curses, and started muttering a few in Klingon.

"Bring us back, Wong. We can't leave the away team exposed. McAllan, as soon as we're in range, full spread of phasers."

The *da Vinci* arced back toward the box-shaped ship.

"Sir, they've lowered their shields," Ina said.

"In weapons range," McAllan said at almost the same time.

"Fire," Gold almost shouted. The only reason the Androssi could have had to lower shields was to transport someone to the station.

Phaser fire lanced out from the *da Vinci* once again, this time striking right on the Androssi's unprotected hull.

"They've raised shields," McAllan said.

"Barnak to bridge. Captain, I can't get the shields back up, and whatever's jamming communications has increased in intensity."

Ina said, "They're firing phasers."

"Evasive, Wong," Gold said. "Pattern epsilon."

McAllan added, "They've also raised shields again, still at eighty percent."

Wong's maneuvers were partly successful—there was an impact, but it was less than Gold had feared, though more than he'd hoped. "Damage report."

"Hull breach on Deck 6," Ina said. Gold noticed that the lieutenant put one hand to her left ear. Bajoran beliefs said that the *pagh*, or life force, resided in the left ear. "Force fields holding. Power systems rerouting." She turned around to look at Gold with a dismayed expression. "Sir, they were able to get a transporter beam off before we fired. Sensors are picking up five Androssi life forms on the station."

At this rate, I'm going to run out of curses, Gold thought.

CHAPTER
8

Duffy heard Ina Mar say, *"Sir, long-range scans are picking up a vessel on direct approach to Emp—"* before the signal started to degrade.

He tapped his combadge. "Duffy to *da Vinci*— you're breaking up."

"—figuration and po—the Androssi. Sens—ered— Maegli—"

"*Da Vinci*, come in!" Duffy shouted.

Corsi tapped her combadge. "Corsi to *da Vinci*, come in."

Duffy looked over at Pattie, but it was Nog who spoke. "There's some kind of jamming field—the combadges are useless."

"Which means we can't be transported even with these pattern enhancers," Pattie added with the tinkly noise that indicated that she was annoyed.

Corsi hefted her phaser rifle. "Ina identified them as Androssi. I think they came back to see who's been sleeping in their beds."

Duffy snorted. "Fairy tale references, Commander? That's new." He did notice that Stevens was particularly taken aback by the reference.

"Commander Duffy, this is serious. We need to—"

"Keep doing what we're doing—what the captain ordered us to do," he added quickly, hoping that it would cut off Corsi's inevitable objection. "Soloman, continue the analysis. I want to know everything the Androssi have done."

"It would be best if we . . . if I did that work in the central computer core, Commander."

Duffy winced at Soloman's slip. He'd done so well adjusting generally to living up to his new designation that the Bynar's occasional lapse into thinking himself as part of a two-person team was fairly jarring.

"We shouldn't split up," Corsi said sharply.

"Actually, we'll have to," Nog said. "If we're going to extract the core, I'll need to get deeper into the system in order to see what, exactly, the Androssi have done to the core."

"I *strongly* recommend against it, Commander," Corsi said to Duffy. "The Androssi might be boarding the station at any minute. We have to be ready for anything, and splitting us up will make us considerably more vulnerable."

Before Duffy could make a decision, he saw a bizarre transporter effect in the midst of the platform. It was one he'd seen before, on Maeglin—it was faster and quieter than Starfleet's transporters.

Five Androssi appeared in the midst of the catwalk. Like all Androssi, they had brown- or sepia-toned skin, with long hair of either blond, gold, or brown, and wearing beige jumpsuits; the men also all had thick beards. They were probably the most nondescript aliens Kieran Duffy had ever seen in his career. Two of them wore three nose rings, two wore none, and one wore four. Duffy recognized the last of those, who stood in the center: Sub-Overseer Howwi, Biron's second-in-command.

Corsi and her people moved as one—each of them stood between the Androssi and a member of the S.C.E. team, with Friesner standing beside Nog. Corsi herself stood by Stevens, which surprised Duffy—he had expected the chief to go to the second officer's side. Not that he cared one way or the other, but it was the kind of protocol thing that Corsi usually followed pretty religiously.

Duffy shot Corsi a look, and she gave a quick nod back—they wouldn't fire unless Duffy himself gave the order. They did, however, all point their weapons.

Okay, he thought, *let's see if we can get through this without trying to kill each other.* Duffy did not like the idea of a firefight breaking out on this ever-more-crowded catwalk, but it was looking inevitable.

"Lieutenant Commander Duffy," Howwi said upon sighting him. "This is the second time you've interfered in a legitimate Androssi operation." Duffy noticed that the Androssi appeared to be unarmed, but with their dimensional-shifting technology, those appearances were quite deceiving.

"That's your interpretation, Howwi," he said, trying to maintain an amiable tone. "We were the ones who were asked by the Maeglin authorities, and we have as much claim to Empok Nor as you do."

"Perhaps. But we have a mission to fulfill."

Duffy smiled grimly. "So do we. In fact, thousands of lives are counting on us to get this fusion core to one of our space stations."

"In fact," Nog said, to Duffy's surprise, "that's all we need. Can't we negotiate this? Most of your systems are tied into other parts of the station. Surely you can supply your own power source? We can extract the fusion core, and you're welcome to the rest of it!"

Duffy glowered at the little Ferengi. *Dammit, kid, we don't work like that!* But he didn't say that out loud—the last thing he could afford to do was show weakness of command in front of Howwi. Of course, Nog had never dealt with the Androssi, so he perhaps didn't know what, precisely, they were dealing with. But even a Ferengi should know that there was no possible way that a weapons platform of this magnitude could be used for any good purpose.

Howwi shrugged. "Why do these lives you wish to save concern us?"

Duffy blinked. "I beg your pardon?"

"We are performing a mission for the Elite. You wish us to hamper that mission in order to preserve the lives of irrelevant aliens. I'm afraid that this negotiation would serve no purpose. We have nothing to gain by allowing you to take the fusion core." He turned to his people. "Kill them."

Dammit, dammit, dammit, Duffy thought as he ducked to his knees behind Drew.

One of the Androssi wearing no nose rings pressed a button on her wrist and a force field that looked just like the flowing brown mesh that had surrounded the fusion core—and was, indeed, the signature of much Androssi tech—formed around the quintet of Androssi. Duffy noted that, just like that one, it did not appear to come from any particular source—one second it wasn't there, the next it was.

Like the security device, this thing shot out electrical bursts. As it did so, Corsi said, "Fire!"

All five security guards fired—at, Duffy noticed, Level 4, and on a low frequency. Eddy's was still in pulse-phaser mode; the other four were standard beams.

The mesh dispersed instantaneously, and Duffy found himself facing five very surprised-looking Androssi.

Duffy grinned. "You ain't the only ones with cute tricks, Howwi."

"On stun," Corsi said, "and fire!"

All five security guards fired, this time on the standard stun setting, and the five Androssi collapsed.

"You know," Duffy said, still grinning, "it's really nice for it to be *easy* every once in a while."

"We're not out of this yet," Corsi said.

Nodding, Duffy said, "I know." He looked at his people who, in turn, were all looking at him, waiting for orders. Part of him once again thought, *Sonnie, come home.* This should've been her job.

But, to his own surprise, that was only part of him. The rest of him felt relatively calm and confident. The cold sweat he broke out in when he was in command of the *da Vinci* and the old *Constitution*-class *Defiant* fell into interphase while the Tholians opened fire was nowhere to be seen. Kieran Duffy chose to view this as a good sign.

He took a deep breath through his nose and then breathed out through his mouth. "Okay, we need to figure out how to get the Androssi tech separated from the Cardassian tech, and we need to figure out how to extract the fusion core."

Nog spoke up. "Sir, I've already put together a plan for extracting the core—it's one that's already been approved by Colonel Kira and Commander Vaughn."

"And I'm sure it's a fine one, Lieutenant, but we prefer to do things our own way. Besides," he added with a smile, "I need you and Fabe here to do something more important."

Stevens raised an eyebrow. "Why do I always get nervous when you smile like that?"

Ignoring the comment, Duffy said, "Fabe, you've said before that the biggest problem on DS9 was always getting the Cardassian and Starfleet equipment to talk to each other."

"Yeah, the chief complained about it all the time. Like I said, I was mostly detailed to the *Defiant,* so I didn't have to deal with it much. . . ."

With a smile of his own, Nog said, "I certainly did. I think I know what you want us to do. Chief O'Brien showed me when I was assigned to the station as a cadet how he'd worked around the incompatibility issues. You want us to make the Cardassian systems reject the Androssi additions."

"If that's possible."

Stevens had what Duffy had come to recognize as his inspirational look. Fabian Stevens worked best when he was handed a problem and told to fix it somehow. He could improvise a solution with the best of them, and he had the feeling that Nog was cut from the same cloth—especially given that they both worked under Miles O'Brien. The former *Enterprise* transporter chief was one of the more creative engineering minds Duffy had ever encountered.

Nog and Stevens immediately started putting their heads together. Leaving them to it, Duffy turned to Pattie and Soloman. "You two get cracking on the fusion core. I'm going to try to punch through this interference so we can find out what's happening with the *da Vinci*."

The two aliens nodded, and went to work.

As Duffy turned to Corsi, Drew spoke up. "Sir, I think I've worked out a program that will recognize when the Androssi use that dimensional shift of theirs."

"Really?" Duffy asked, his eyes wide with surprise.

Drew shook his head. "What, you think you guys are the only ones who know how to use a tricorder on this ship?"

Putting up his hands, Duffy said, "I stand corrected. Good work, Drew. Between that and Nog's ears, we should have a good early-warning system in place if they come back."

"Not if," Corsi said, "when. Howwi's the sub-overseer, remember. As soon as Biron realizes his second hasn't reported in, he'll send a replacement."

Unholstering his tricorder, Duffy said, "Assuming that Captain Gold hasn't taken care of Biron on his own."

"We can't assume that."

Way to keep the morale up, Duffy thought sourly. "That's why I'm going to be working to punch through the interference. Let's get to it, folks. We may not have a lot of time before trouble comes back."

CHAPTER
9

Just once, David Gold thought, *I'd like to go on a mission where my ship doesn't have the crap kicked out of it.*

Damage reports were coming in at a constant clip. Much shorter and less impressive damage reports on the Androssi ship were also coming in, but it was a losing battle for as long as they didn't have shields.

They couldn't even get out a distress signal as long as Biron kept that interference up. Unfortunately, the ship's engineers were too busy keeping the ship from coming apart at the seams to focus properly on finding a way to cut through it to contact the away team. Sensors were still detecting five Androssi, seven humans, one Nasat, one Bynar, and one Ferengi on the station—all in the same general vicinity—but they couldn't determine anything more specific than that. All Gold knew for sure was that his team was alive—for the moment.

"Faulwell to bridge."

Gold frowned. The S.C.E. linguist/cryptographer should have been in his quarters. He had no engineering training—aside from what he might have picked up by osmosis from being on the *da Vinci*—and this particular mission didn't call for his talents.

But Gold also knew that he wouldn't have contacted the bridge without a damn good reason. "Go ahead."

"Sir, what about the runabout?"

"What about it?"

"We have its prefix codes, and I'm willing to bet that it has shields and weapons and other things like that."

Gold blinked. Then he blinked again. Then he turned to McAllan, whose look of annoyance combined with embarrassment more or less matched how Gold felt right now.

"He's, ah—he's right, sir," McAllan said. "We can remote-control the *Rio Grande* from here."

"You want an engraved invitation, man? Do it!"

The *da Vinci* took another hit. "Structural integrity field down to sixty percent," Ina said. "Another hit and we're going to start coming to pieces."

"Computer, prepare escape pods. McAllan, return fire and get that runabout over here."

"Sir, we're down to our last four torpedoes—and I now have control of the *Rio Grande*," McAllan added with a grim smile.

Ina whirled around to face Gold. "Sir, Androssi starboard shields are down!"

Gold leaned forward in his command chair. "McAllan, target the starboard shields with those last four torpedoes, but don't *touch* that fire control until I say so. Set the *Rio Grande*'s course to 189 mark 2 and have its phasers do a strafing run on the Androssi's port side."

"Yes, sir," McAllan said. Gold could hear the unasked question as to what the hell the captain was thinking implied in those two words, but the lieutenant was a good enough officer to keep that question unasked.

As soon as the *Rio Grande* started firing, the Androssi ship changed its position in order to keep its vulnerable side away from the runabout and also to put it at optimum position to return fire.

Which was exactly what Gold was hoping for. "Fire torpedoes!"

The torpedoes blasted away from the *da Vinci* just as the *Rio Grande* finished its run. Since torpedoes traveled slower than phasers, the Androssi ship actually had time to try to take an evasive course, but it was too little, too late.

"Multiple hull breaches on the Androssi ship," Ina said. "Their overall power levels are reading at fifty-five percent."

"Follow it up with dessert, McAllan," Gold said. "Fire phasers."

As the phasers fired, tearing more into the Androssi hull, Gold added, "Bring the *Rio Grande* about and prepare to extend its shields around us."

"Sir," Ina said, "if we do that—"

"We'll only get twenty percent effectiveness

from the runabout shields. I took basic engineering at the Academy too, Ina, even if it was before you were born—the old man's mind isn't *that* addled. It's still twenty percent more than we have now."

Ina turned contritely back around to her console.

"Overseer."

"Speak."

"There is a runabout moving toward our position with its impulse drive."

Biron actually looked at the worker who made this pronouncement. "Explain yourself!"

"The Starfleet runabout *U.S.S. Rio Grande*, registry NCC-72452, was in a standby position proximate to Upper Pylon 1 of the Cardassian station. It is now in motion and on an elliptical course toward us."

"I should have been informed of this sooner," Biron said. He pressed a button on his right cuff. An electrical charge surged through the chair on which the worker was sitting, vaporizing the worker instantly.

Another worker said, "Starfleet runabout is arming its phaser weapons and preparing to fire."

"Adjust position to present minimal aspect to runabout. Prepare another ladrion burst for the *da Vinci*."

"*Overseer, we can't fire the ladrion bursts,*" came the voice of Engine Master Claris over the communications system. "*We have sustained damage to that system from the Starfleet ship's phaser fire.*"

Biron thought. He had use of the remaining anril torpedo, but it was only effective against shields—it would have minimal impact on the *da Vinci's* hull, even as damaged as it was. Several of his ship's other weapons systems had been integrated into the Cardassian station at the request of the client, who had found Biron's original designs for the weapons platform to be insufficiently powerful.

His status board indicated that the runabout was firing on their still-shielded port side. *Good,* he thought. *Now we can—*

No. The board also indicated that four quantum torpedoes were being fired by the *da Vinci* at their vulnerable starboard side. *If we still had the ladrion burst or our other weapons . . .*

But recrimination was foolish. Instead, he barked orders. "Set an evasive course away from the quantum torpedoes and implement overdrive instantly!"

Instantly, as Biron could have predicted, was not fast enough.

"Overseer, our hull has been breached four times over," Claris said. *"Our power levels have been reduced to fifty-five percent of capacity and our tactical and defensive systems are off-line."*

Biron cursed. The mission was becoming less and less viable. "Open a subspace communication channel to Sub-Overseer Howwi."

Several seconds passed, and Howwi did not reply.

Overseer Biron considered his options. Scans showed Howwi and the officers he'd brought with him were still alive. Those same scans also showed that the workers and the Starfleet personnel were also alive. So Howwi's mission to secure the station from Starfleet must have failed. Starfleet's rather confusing predilection for preserving individual lives at the expense of the greater good was probably the only reason why Howwi and the others were still alive—even the workers.

His weapons capacity consisted of one anril torpedo. His shields were reduced to forty percent of capacity. His opponents now had two ships with which to fight.

Much as Biron's sponsor wanted the holo-emitters, the mission was now becoming too risky. As it was, he had several more risks to take in order to retrieve Howwi and the other two officers.

And the client's own actions were the reason why it had come to this. If Biron's ship had its full complement of weapons, he would be able to dispose of this tiresome Starfleet ship and its smaller compatriot with little difficulty. Instead, he was being forced into the position of fleeing the *da Vinci*—again.

I swear by the power of the Elite and the glory of the Leader, he thought at the entire crew complement of the Starfleet vessel, *you will pay for this effrontery.*

Still, the mission was not a total loss. They had obtained a certain amount of Cardassian technology on the station that would be worth something to another client.

"Lock matter-transferral device onto Sub-Overseer Howwi, Officer Dun, and Officer Huuk."

After a moment, one of the workers—one who hadn't been on the flight deck before; this was obviously the replacement for the one Biron had disposed of—said, "Lock achieved."

The status board showed another hit from the *da Vinci*. It would be several seconds before they fired again, if the usual Starfleet pattern held. "Power down the shields and engage matter-transferral device. Engage dimensional blockers on all equipment currently present on the Cardassian station."

Howwi, Dun, and Huuk appeared on the flight deck, unconscious. Biron remembered that Starfleet's weapons had a setting that could do that—one of many things about Starfleet that Biron did not comprehend. They were a strange conglomeration of beings, this Federation they represented—they did not exploit. It continually amazed Biron that such an inefficient government had managed to survive all these centuries.

Biron gave not a thought to the workers who had been left behind. They were, after all, only workers and easily replaced. But good sub-overseers and officers were hard to find—even ones who groomed themselves and allowed themselves to be rendered unconscious by Starfleet. Indeed, Biron felt that some kind of punishment was in order for Howwi.

That was for a later time, however. His status board indicated that the dimensional blockers had been engaged—Gold, Gomez, and the *da Vinci*'s other workers would not be able to make use of the technology they had used to improve the Cardassian station. Biron made a note to retrieve the technology from Dimension 7 when they returned to Androssi space.

He also noted that the Starfleet vessel's navigation systems were damaged, and could only accomplish an FTL of 1.02. "Set navigational course 76521. Set FTL at 15."

Within moments, Biron's ship left the Trivas system behind.

"They're leaving the system at warp 8.7, sir," McAllan said urgently.

"Wong?" Gold prompted the conn officer.

The young ensign shook his head. "Best we can manage is warp 4, sir."

Gold sighed. "No point in the tortoise chasing the hare if the hare's actually gonna go full bore."

"*Duf*—Vinc—*in. Duffy to* da Vinci, *can you hear me?*"

"We hear you, Duffy. Status report."

Duffy hesitated before giving the report. Gold suspected that the lieutenant commander wanted a status report of his own, but that would have to wait. Right now, Gold needed to know what was happening on Empok Nor more than Duffy needed to know the current situation on the *da Vinci*. "*Well, sir, we had an Androssi boarding party— including our old pal, Sub-Overseer Howwi—but we took care of 'em. Unfortunately, someone beamed him and his two officers out. The workers were left behind, though. I guess they're prisoners?*"

"I suppose." Gold rubbed his chin. "We'll turn them over to a starbase—maybe remand them to Maeglin. How about the station?"

"*That's the weird part. Soloman screamed right as the three Androssi were beaming out. Remember last time, when all their tech just disappeared?*"

"Let me guess."

"*Yes, sir, they did it again. It all fell into whatever dimension they hide it in when they don't want us to know it's there. As far as we can tell, they left Empok Nor the way they found it.*"

"Is Soloman okay?"

"*Yeah, he was more surprised than anything—the entire computer network hiccupped while he was in the middle of talking to it.*"

"Excuse me, sir," Nog said, "but Empok Nor hasn't been left exactly *the way the Androssi found it. There are several components from the original structure that are missing.*"

"Biron's people probably salvaged 'em," Gold said. "Hate to say it, but they've got as much right to it as we do to the fusion core. Anything else?"

"*Yes, sir.*" Nog hesitated. "*The structural integrity of the fusion core's been compromised. I don't think we can safely tow it back to Deep Space 9.*"

CHAPTER
10

Nog stood in Empok Nor's ops. It felt weird, sitting in a place that was so much like the ops he was used to, and yet so different. Half the consoles didn't work properly, and most of them looked different without the Starfleet upgrades.

Lt. Commander Duffy had ordered them all to come up here to evaluate their options. The catwalk by the fusion reactor was not ideal for that, and Duffy felt that they all needed a change of scene in any case. Nog found he couldn't argue, which numbered it among the few things Duffy had said for which that was the case. Nog used to think highly of the S.C.E.—and they certainly handled themselves decently against these Androssi saboteurs—but the Ferengi was well and truly sick of their condescending attitude toward him. As if somehow he wasn't worthy to be considered a *real* engineer because he wasn't part of the hallowed Corps.

Robins and Friesner had beamed back to the *da*

Vinci, along with the two Androssi prisoners. Corsi, Drew, and Eddy remained behind, and were presently standing at the upper level of ops. Stevens, P8 Blue, Soloman, and Duffy were seated around the table with Nog.

"All right, people," Duffy said, "I want options and I want them now, and I don't care how ridiculous they seem."

"Can we not fix the structural integrity field?" Soloman asked.

P8 Blue gave a low-pitched tinkling sound, which, Nog noted, differed from other, like sounds the Nasat made. He wondered what the differences among them were. "Not unless you have Cardassian emitters in your pocket, Soloman. We don't have replicator patterns for them, and I doubt we'd be able to get Cardassia to ship us some new ones."

"Even if they could," Stevens added, "it'd probably take over a week to get here, and several more days to get the thing up to snuff."

"We don't have that kind of time," Nog said anxiously. "Captain Gold just heard from DS9—we have ten days at the most before we'll have to abandon the station."

"We know that, Lieutenant," Duffy said in what the human probably thought was a soothing voice, but which only served to annoy Nog more.

"Can't you put it in a force field?" Corsi asked.

Duffy shook his head. "Not and tow it at warp, no. And if we stick with sublight, it'll take a helluva lot more than ten days to get there."

"Maybe," Stevens said, "if we use the runabout's

warp engines—create a static warp bubble around the core so it can handle the force field."

Blue repeated the low-pitched tinkle. "With the SIF in the shape it's in, the stresses of the warp bubble would rip it to pieces."

Nog watched as the four engineers threw ideas back and forth, each more incredible than the last. Each suggestion seemed to top the last in being overly complicated and difficult to engineer— almost as if they were taking Duffy's admonition about ridiculousness to heart—or would require considerably more than the ten days they had left to them.

Then, suddenly, it came to him. An idea more ridiculous than anything the S.C.E. crew had said.

". . . but there's no way we could construct a sub-quark resonator for that," Stevens was saying.

"Besides," Blue added, "those things only work about half the time anyhow. They're mostly untested."

"Okay, that's out," Duffy said.

Finally, Nog thought, *a lull.* "Why don't we just move the whole station?"

Everyone looked at Nog.

"I beg your pardon?" Duffy said after about five seconds of silence.

"Move the whole station. Get a bunch of ships to tractor it at warp to the Bajoran system." Already, Nog was imagining the possibilities in his head. In retrospect, he should have thought of this in the first place. Empok Nor was, after all, the perfect place for spare parts for Deep Space 9. They could stick it in orbit somewhere—maybe around Bajor or one of its moons—and have a permanent storage locker. Not to mention a testing place for new upgrades . . .

"Uh, Nog, if I'm remembering right," Stevens said, "DS9 is about fifteen hundred meters by three hundred seventy meters—and this place has the same dimensions, right?"

"Yes."

"And you want to tow it at warp?" Duffy asked, incredulous.

"Low warp, but it can be done." He thought for a moment. "We'd need twelve ships. One on each pylon and six around the docking ring."

"They'd all need to be the same general size and class," Blue said. "If not, the tractor beams will be incompatible."

"No, they won't," Nog said. "With that many ships, we can calibrate the tractor beams with each other. The *Rio Grande* can serve as the coordination point. It can take point and make sure the warp fields and the tractor beams stay aligned."

"Yeah, but you could only do that at warp 2," Duffy said, "and then you'd never make it."

"We can do it at warp 4," Stevens said before Nog could speak. Nog grinned. *Finally, one of them's on my side.*

"Fabe—"

"I'm serious, Duff, we could do it at warp 4. I mean, c'mon, warp 6 is the normal cruising speed for most ships anyhow. The *da Vinci* just took a major pounding from the Androssi and *it* can still do warp 4. It's baby steps. Think out of the box, for a change."

Duffy rolled his eyes. "Don't get cute on me, Fabe. Besides, there's another problem: think about what kind of subspace disruption you're going to cause. Communications will be spotty at best—how the hell're you going to coordinate everything when you won't even be able to stay in consistent contact?"

Nog deflated. "I'm not sure," he admitted reluctantly. "But there has to be—"

"Oh, that's easy," Blue said, this time making a much higher-pitched tinkling noise. "There's a new method of close-range ship-to-ship using tight-beam tachyon pulses. The Romulans developed it about twenty years ago, and finally decided to share it about a week before the Dominion War ended."

Blinking, Nog said, "I didn't know about that."

"Neither did I," Duffy said.

Another noise, this one of a medium pitch. "You people really need to keep up on the trades. It's all they've been talking about in the *Journal of the Federation Consortium of Engineers and Technicians* for the last two months."

"Can you build one of those?" Nog asked.

"Of course," Blue said. "I have the replicator pattern stored on the *da Vinci* computer."

Duffy had a few more objections, but either Nog or Stevens or Blue had an answer for it. Before long, even Duffy was sharing Nog's enthusiasm—he certainly seemed excited when they finally contacted Captain Gold on Empok Nor's viewscreen.

"There's only one problem," Duffy said after doing so. "We need twelve ships."

Gold's face broke into a smile. *"Oh, let me just make a call."*

CHAPTER
11

David Gold had been listening to the latest letter from his granddaughter for the sixteenth time when the call from the bridge came.

"*Message from Earth, sir,*" said Lieutenant McAllan.

"On screen," Gold said, once again removing the image of Ruth's face and replacing it with the Starfleet logo—which was, in turn, replaced by the familiar visage of Captain Montgomery Scott, the liaison between the S.C.E. and the admiralty.

"*I got your request, David, and I've got to ask you—have ye gone completely daft?*"

Scotty had a huge grin on his face, which was the only reason why Gold wasn't stunned. After all, Nog's plan was the type of thing that Scotty himself would have come up with during his days as a full-time engineer.

"No more than usual. The real question is, can you do it?"

"*Yes and no, lad. There are nine ships en route to*

*the Trivas system now. They should be there within
a few hours. I'm afraid that's the best I could do.
And even then, I can't promise that they'll do what
you're askin'. That'll be up to you an' your lot to
convince 'em of."*

"Fair enough."

*"By the way—which one o' that motley bunch
came up with this scheme? Duffy? P8 Blue?"*

"Actually, it was the Ferengi kid from DS9—
Nog. His idea, his specs for implementing it, and
his request for twelve ships."

With a twinkle in his eye, Scotty said, *"Well,
then, I think it's only appropriate for me to be the one
to break it to him that he only gets nine. Besides, I'd
like to meet the man who came up with this. 'Tis
only a pity I won't be able to shake his hand."*

Gold smiled and tapped his combadge. "Gold to
Nog. Report to the captain's quarters immediately."

Within a few minutes—which Gold spent giving
Scotty a quick verbal report on the entire Empok
Nor mission—the doorchime rang. "Come in,"
Gold said, and the doors parted to reveal the
young Ferengi lieutenant.

"Nog, there's a man here that you need to meet.
Captain Montgomery Scott, this is Lieutenant Nog."

The Ferengi's eyes went wide. "It is an honor to
meet you, sir."

*"Pleasure's all mine, lad. This is quite a little plan
ye've cooked up."*

"Thank you, sir. Coming from you, that means a
lot."

*"I'm afraid I have some bad news, though. I
could only rustle up nine ships—and as I told the*

captain, I canna guarantee that they'll go along."

Grinning, Nog said, "Leave that to me, sir. And don't worry about it—with the *da Vinci*, we'll have ten ships, and that's actually one more than we'll need."

Gold whirled toward the Ferengi. "Then why'd you say you needed twelve?"

Nervously, Nog said, "Fifth—Fifth Rule of Acquisition, sir: 'Always exaggerate your estimates.'"

Scotty laughed, which seemed to relieve Nog. *"That was an engineer's axiom long before you heathens took it on,"* he said. *"Well done, lad, well done."*

"Thank you, sir. I know that this plan doesn't exactly follow the established norms, but—"

Waving his left arm dismissively, Scotty said, *"Good God, lad, don't concern yourself. The established norms are just guidelines, and your job as an engineer is to find a better way around them. Always remember that."*

Smiling, Nog said, "I will, sir. Thank you, sir."

"Now be off with you—I've business to discuss with the captain."

"Yes, *sir.*"

Still smiling from ear to oversize ear, Nog left Gold's quarters.

"Back home, we call that a *mitzvah*," Gold said with a chuckle.

"Well, the lad deserved it. But I wanted to talk to you a bit more about the Androssi."

"What's the word, Doctor?" Domenica Corsi asked as she entered sickbay.

Seated behind her desk, Elizabeth Lense looked up from reading a padd and smiled. "The word is good, Commander. Frnats, Hawkins, and Lipinski all received serious shocks to their systems, but with some bed rest and CNS therapy, they should be able to report back to duty within a week. For Frnats, more like a week and a half."

Corsi frowned. "Why so long?"

"Commander, CNS is central nervous system. The weapons the Androssi used on them were like the effect of a phaser on stun magnified by a factor of about a thousand. In fact, I'm amazed it didn't kill them, though it came pretty close with Frnats. I want to do some bio-scans on our two prisoners, to see if this weapon is fatal to Androssi. If it is, we have to be aware of the fact that they might eventually upgrade the weapon to have a maximum impact on aliens."

"That's a good idea," Corsi said with a nod. Lense took a practical viewpoint that Corsi found refreshing on a ship full of engineers who tended to have their minds buried in isolinear chips. She was also a good roommate—quiet, considerate, and not given to irritating habits. Her people had been chatting endlessly about the feud between P8 Blue and Abramowitz, and Corsi was grateful to have been spared that.

Leaning back in her chair, Lense fixed Corsi with another smile. "So what's happening between you and Stevens?"

"What're you talking about?" Corsi felt her face flush.

"He spent the night in our quarters the other

day. I saw him coming out when that meeting was called yesterday morning."

Corsi clenched her fists.

Lense wasn't finished, though. "And when Drew was visiting Hawkins earlier, he was talking about how you were—how'd he put it?—'making goo-goo eyes' at him."

"What!?"

Corsi spoke loudly enough that Lense actually flinched. "I'm just telling you what he said."

"Right," Corsi said, forcing herself to calm down. It wasn't fair to the doctor, biting her head off like that. Though right now, Corsi wasn't all that interested in what was fair. What she was interested in was putting Fabian Stevens through a bulkhead.

What for, exactly? she thought, as she excused herself from Lense and exited sickbay. *For saying yes when I asked him back to my quarters?*

No, it was hardly Fabian's fault that he was there for her when she needed companionship. It was her own stupid fault for indulging herself on a ship the size of a toolbox.

Damn you, Dar, why did you have to do this to me? Why did you have to—

She cut the thought off, refusing to dwell on it. The anniversary had come and gone. What was done was done.

Nog was hunched over the *Rio Grande*'s controls, listening to his recording of Sinnravian *drad*, when the hail from the *Sugihara* came in. *Finally,* he thought. Captain Demitrijian was the only one of the nine ship captains who hadn't gotten back to him. The other eight had all agreed to go along with it—some enthusiastically, some with the greatest reluctance, but they all did agree in the end. Except for Captain Janna Demitrijian.

He put the captain's round face on the screen, then remembered to turn the music off.

"Lieutenant," she said, *"I've been thinking about your proposal. I've also gone over it with my chief engineer. For what it's worth, she thinks you're categorically insane and has said that if we go through with this, she refuses to accept any responsibility for it."*

Nog sighed. *Well, I've been lucky up until now. Besides, with the* da Vinci, *we'll be fine.*

"Well, thank you for taking the time to come here, Captain."

Demitrijian frowned. *"I haven't said we won't do it, Lieutenant. Last time I checked, I was in command of the* Sugihara, *not Lieutenant Barbanti, nor you."*

Feeling his lobes shrivel, Nog said, "I'm sorry, sir, I—"

"What I want to know is, what's in this for me if I do go along?"

His lobes perked back up. Now the captain was speaking his language. "As I said in my original communication, you'll have shore leave for your crew on Bajor, which is one of the loveliest planets in the quadrant—plus whatever maintenance your ship needs from my engineering staff."

"Both of which I can get from Starbase 96 which, if nothing else, has a working power source. I'll need more than that."

Nog spoke slowly. "I'm not sure what else I can offer—" He let the sentence hang—usually if you paused there, the customer would finish the sentence for you.

"*When you established the commlink,*" Demitrijian said, "*you had some kind of music on. It sounded like Blee Luu's* Endless Dream."

"Yes! Yes, it was! I can make a recording for you."

"*No, thank you, I can't stand that stuff. But my son is dating a Sinnravian, and she loves Luu. However, they've been living on the Canopus Planet, and she hasn't been able to get her hands on Luu's newest recording—I forget what it's called.*"

"It's yours," Nog said.

"*An original, not a copy,*" Demitrijian added. "*Sinnravians are fussy about that sort of thing. Something about their inner ears.*"

Shaking his head at the relative ignorance of such stunted-eared folk as humans, Nog said, "You'll have an original recording by the time we reach DS9."

"*In that case, Lieutenant, the* Sugihara *is at your disposal.*"

"Excellent! Thank you, Captain! *Rio Grande* out."

Nog cut the connection.

Now where am I supposed to get an original of Blee Luu's latest recording?

The runabout was currently docked at Empok Nor. P8 Blue was due back at any moment with a full structural report, after which point the Nasat would come on board, download the information to the runabout computer, and then beam back to the *da Vinci* while Nog took up position at the head of the convoy that would tow Empok Nor back.

Nog started *Endless Dream* up again as he went over the data. The computer models were all encouraging, and the S.C.E. were all sure that it would work. Of course, the report he'd gotten from DS9 was that everyone except Commander Vaughn thought he was insane, but nobody actually objected, either—probably because they'd seen the computer models also, and besides, nobody had a better idea.

The doors to the runabout opened, and P8 Blue came in—

—and immediately let out a screech that nearly punctured Nog's delicate eardrums.

"Lieutenant," Blue said as Nog gripped his oversize ears with his undersize hands, "if you do not shut that music off, Deep Space 9 will need to find a new chief operations officer, as the present one *will* be larvae food!"

"Computer, terminate music," Nog said quickly.

"First Abramowitz, now you," Blue said.

"Abramowitz?"

"She's our cultural specialist—also my roommate. She just got the latest recording of that fecal matter you call music by that Blee Luu person, and it's been driving me insane."

"Really?" Nog said. "Maybe we can help each other out."

Kieran Duffy was rather pleased as he sat in the center seat of the bridge for the *da Vinci*'s gamma shift. Everything was going smoothly. The ten ships were taking up positions, with one ship on each of the six pylons and the remaining four evenly spaced around the docking ring. The *Rio Grande* was taking up position nearby, ready to lead the convoy to Deep Space 9. Some last-minute figures needed to be gone over, of course, but they were on schedule to start at the beginning of alpha shift.

Closer to home, the Abramowitz-Pattie difficulty had been settled thanks to their Ferengi visitor. Nog had apparently convinced Carol to let him have her new *drad* recording for the *Sugihara*'s captain in exchange for—something. When Fabe Stevens shared this bit of intelligence, the engineer had been unclear as to what the something was that Nog had promised to Carol, but Duffy was sure he'd find out soon enough.

The gamma shift tactical officer—a young ensign named Piotrowski—said, "Commander, we're getting a priority-one distress call." She looked up, and gave Duffy a stricken look. "Sir, it's from Commander Gomez on Sarindar!"

Duffy felt a fist of ice clench his heart. *Oh no, Sonnie . . .*

It took him a moment to make his mouth work. "Confirm."

"The distress call is definitely coming from Nalori space, and was sent two days ago, sir."

"Engineering, this is Duffy. Are we back up to capacity yet?"

Nancy Conlon, the current duty officer, said, *"Yes, sir, Commander. Can give you warp 9.7 for twelve hours, just like the specs say—longer if we have to. Why? I thought this trip was going to be at warp 4."*

"We may be taking a different trip. Duffy out." He took another deep breath through his nose and exhaled through his mouth. "Captain Gold to the bridge."

It hadn't taken long for Nog to rearrange the convoy to accommodate the loss of the *da Vinci*. It simply meant that the three remaining ships on the docking ring would take up position halfway between each pylon.

Captain Gold was on the viewscreen as the *da Vinci* was preparing to warp away, apparently to respond to a distress call from the ship's first officer.

"I'm sorry I won't get to see the look on Colonel Kira's face when we tow the station in," Gold said. *"And tell her I'm sorry I won't get to see the station."*

"I will, sir."

"You did good work here today, Lieutenant. Any chance I can convince you to transfer here? I get the feeling you'd fit right in."

Standing next to Gold, Duffy added, *"He's right, Nog. I know we may not have seemed very hospitable at first, but—well, I was wrong to slap you down. I'm sorry for that. And I'd be honored if you'd join us."*

"I'm flattered by your offer, Captain—and I accept your apology, Commander—but I have to say no. I'm very happy where I am."

"It's our loss," Gold said with a smile. *"Good luck, son."*

"To you also, Captain."

The image of the *da Vinci* bridge winked out. Nog stared out the runabout porthole and watched the *Saber*-class ship go into warp toward the far-off Nalori Republic. Nog didn't know Commander Gomez, though he knew of her reputation after the trick she pulled on the *Sentinel* during the war. He hoped that Captain Gold and the others would get to her in time.

Nog activated P8 Blue's tachyon communications network. "Nog to convoy. Engage tractor beams."

Nine Starfleet ships emitted blue cones of light that tethered them to Empok Nor. Nog smiled.

"Prepare to go to warp on my mark."

He was truly flattered by Gold's offer. But in the S.C.E., he'd just be a cog in the wheel. On DS9, *he* was the chief.

"Engage."

INVINCIBLE

David Mack
&
Keith R.A. DeCandido

First officer's log, Commander Sonya Gomez,
U.S.S. da Vinci, Stardate 53270.2

I'm leaving the *da Vinci*.

Luckily, it's only a temporary assignment, to the planet Sarindar. Captain Scott gave me the assignment after we dropped the old *Defiant* off at Spacedock.

Sarindar's located in a fairly remote region—it'll take a week just to get out there from Earth—but it's in an area of space controlled by the Nalori. That area is pretty much all that stands between the Federation and exploration of Sector 969. I remember when I was on the *Enterprise*, Command had considered having us map that out, but ultimately decided against it. The Nalori would not permit a Starfleet vessel safe passage through their space, and going around would add several months to the journey.

I told Captain Scott that when we met in his office on Earth. He laughed. "Aye, lassie, the Nalori are a right unpleasant bunch. There was a border clash with 'em a couple hundred years ago—that was before even my time. We gave 'em a good punch to the nose, and they went back to their space with their tails between their legs. They haven't been too keen on the Federation ever since."

"So what's changed?" I asked him.

"The usual. They need our help."

The captain called up a holographic projection of Sarindar. As he spoke, the image rotated, then went in for a close view of a section of the surface. The entire planet appeared to be made of crystal. I can't wait to see what it looks like in person.

"Sarindar's completely scan- and transporter-proof, thanks to an element called chimerium."

That surprised me. "Really?"

"You know of it, then?"

I nodded. "It's a composite of magnesite and kelbonite. They've found minute traces here and there, but—"

"Well, Sarindar's loaded with it, and the Nalori are tryin' to make use of it."

"You'd need to refine it first, but how can they mine it? It's *much* too dense to move manually. I don't know of any ship that could achieve escape velocity with a significant amount on board. You can't transport it—you couldn't get a lock. I don't think even a dimensional shifter would work." I ran a bunch of possibilities in my head, then remembered a paper I'd done at the Academy. "Wait a minute, if you can put together a subspace accelerator to push it with a quick warp pulse—"

Captain Scott smiled that avuncular smile of his. "Congratulations, lassie—you've worked out in two minutes what it took those bloody Nalori a

couple centuries to figure out. In fact, they already
designed themselves a subspace accelerator. But
they're fallin' behind schedule, and there's a lotta
bugs in the system. So they asked for Starfleet's
help.

"Thing is, they still dinna like the Federation
very much, and they like Starfleet even less. So
they'll only let us send one person—in order, if
y'can believe it, to 'minimize cultural contamination.' As if contamination is what they're worried
about." He shook his head. "The good news is that
the one person'll be in charge of the whole kit and
kaboodle."

"And I'm supposed to be the one person?"

"Aye." Scott nodded. "And ye'll be in command.
The last supervisor quit in disgust, so that's where
there's a vacancy, an' they figured they'd be better
off with Starfleet's help at the very top. I've read
that paper y'wrote about subspace accelerators—
that's why I recommended you specifically."

That threw me for a loop. I never thought that
Montgomery Scott, of all people, would find some
old Academy paper of mine to be of the least interest. "Really, sir?"

Laughing, he said, "Aye, really. Thought it was
brilliant, actually. Why d'ye think I recommended
you to David back when he was trolling for someone to head up his S.C.E. team after poor
Commander Salek died in the war?"

He had not only read my Academy paper, it was
what led him to recommend me to Captain Gold
for the *da Vinci*. Wonders upon wonders. "I—I
didn't know that, sir."

"Well, now you do."

We went over the other details of the mission. In addition to the chimerium problem, Sarindar is also in a star system that is home to a quasar/pulsar pair that interferes with communications and navigation. "Ye'll only be able t'send messages from the surface once every fourteen hours or so. For that matter, ye'll only be able to do any useful testing during those windows."

The biggest annoyance, though, was the revelation that the Nalori are a bit—well, backward about gender roles. The engineering team consists of several civilians made up of numerous Nalori races, all male. Women don't do this sort of work in Nalori society.

"Wonderful," I said. "So you're asking me to lead a team that hates Starfleet, hates the Federation, and hates women?"

For the first time, Captain Scott sounded like a captain when he asked, "Is that a problem, Commander?"

"No, sir," I said with full confidence. "I can handle it."

The avuncular smile came back, and he sounded like an engineer again. "That's what I like to hear. You'll be headin' out with the *da Vinci* to Starbase 96, where you'll meet up with a civilian ship, the *Culloden*. It'll take ye the rest of the way."

Then Captain Scott put his hand on my shoulder. "I can't emphasize how important this mission is, lassie. The Nalori have been showin' us their backs for almost two centuries. This is the first time they've extended a hand. We may finally get the chance to explore Sector 969, *and* this is our first chance to study chimerium up close." The captain had that glint in his eye that Lt. Commander Duffy once described as the "new toy to play with" look. And he was right—chimerium has uncounted tactical uses, particularly against a technologically superior foe like the Borg or the Dominion.

"Don't worry, sir. I won't let you down."

"Of that, Commander, I have very little doubt. Now, be off with you. I've got an appointment."

We're now en route to Starbase 96. I've been studying everything there is to know about the Nalori in general and Sarindar in particular— which, unfortunately, isn't much. The latest updates on the Sarindar Project are two months old, and the information in the cultural database is sketchy at best. I'm going to have a talk with our cultural specialist, Carol Abramowitz, before we reach the starbase to go over some of this. One interesting thing—while the nation is called the Nalori Republic, the Nalori race is only one of the five members of that republic. And it looks like the work crew has representatives from all five.

The design of the SA is generally sound, but they've overdesigned it to an appalling degree, and some aspects of the engineering are, to be blunt, wrong and will need to be fixed posthaste.

It's going to be a challenge to get the project up to speed, but I'm looking forward to it.

I think I need to kill Kieran.

Before the mess with the *Defiant* and the
Tholians, we had hit the latest in a series of land
mines regarding our relationship.

If you can call it that.

What we had on the *Enterprise* was wonderful,
while it lasted. When I transferred off, though, we
weren't really able to keep it up, and since we got
thrown together on the *da Vinci* again, it's been
one awkward moment after another. When we're
on duty, everything's fine, but the minute we see
each other in the mess hall, it gets—well, messy.

But then he had command of the *da Vinci*
against the Tholians when Captain Gold and I
were on the *Defiant*, and he did great. I'm happy
for him—it's been a shot in the arm to his confidence, and one he really needed, to be honest.

The thing is—he's getting more aggressive with
me. Yesterday we went over the duty rosters for
when I'd be gone, and he sat closer to me than

usual—his hand brushed against mine more than
once, too. When some minor crisis in engineering
came up, he suggested finishing in his quarters
later—which he's never done before, not even
when we were actually dating on the *Enterprise*.
But then, it was easier to keep business and a personal life separate on a *Galaxy*-class ship. The *da
Vinci* is a much smaller—more intimate—ship.

I think he wants to start up what we had on the
Enterprise again, and I just don't know if I can
handle that. For one thing, I'm his CO. And look at
what we do. What if I'd been trapped in that
dimensional rift or on Eerlik's moon? What if the
da Vinci had been destroyed by the Tholians or the
Pevvni or Friend or the Androssi?

What if I had to order him to go to his death?

That's why I just can't give him an answer yet.

We'll be at Starbase 96 tomorrow, so at least I
can get away from him—and he'll be in charge of
the S.C.E. team while I'm gone, so he can put that
newfound confidence to good use.

Sooner or later, though, I'm going to have to
deal with this.

Later. Definitely later.

Personal log, Commander Sonya Gomez, S.S. Culloden, Stardate 53273.9

This may be the most beautiful sight I've ever seen.

We're just starting to descend into Sarindar's atmosphere on the *Culloden*. The ship is owned by Zilder, a Bolian who was hired by the Nalori to ferry people to and from the surface and perform various other technical and administrative tasks for the project. When I asked him how a Bolian contrived to get a ship named after a place on Earth, he just smiled and said, "Ho'nig will provide."

That's the really odd thing about Zilder. Ho'nig is the collective god of the Damiani, a humanoid three-gendered Federation species. I didn't think that anyone off of Damiano worshipped their god. It wouldn't bother me, except Zilder spent the first day of our trip trying to convert me. After over twenty hours of his missionary zeal, I'd convinced him that my religion was none of his business, and he let up. If he hadn't, he'd be easy enough to avoid: the *Culloden* is built to transport up to three hundred people, so with just the two of us, it's pretty roomy.

But I was talking about Sarindar.

From space, the planet looks mostly white, almost like it's a big snowball flying through the night. As you get into orbit, it starts to look more like a jewel—at the right time of day, from the right orbit, you can see glints and reflections. According to what I've read, the plant and animal life is all silicon-based, and the vast majority of it is crystalline.

We're descending now, and it's even more amazing than I could've believed. When you come out of the reddish-purple layer of clouds, you look up and see an orange sky. As expected, the delicate flora is photosynthetic living crystal. What I didn't realize is that the ground is also made up of similar substances: jagged plains of diamond spikes, quartz-and-topaz mountains, and forests of amethyst. The water of the streams and rivers that I can see from the *Culloden's* viewport are sparkling and crystal-clear—literally!

Now we're flying in closer, and I can see some animals that I recognize from the file—a shii drinking from a stream; a meir gliding through the air; a pack of kliyor running into the forest.

The suns are starting to set, so the shadows and the reflections are especially spectacular, with colors bursting from all the crystalline flora.

Intellectually, I expected this to be a lovely planet, but I had no idea it was going to be this beautiful.

Ah, now we're seeing something less beautiful: the work site for the SA. The prominent feature of the site is the perfectly circular, two-hundred-meter-diameter concave dish. In the center is an opening roughly four meters wide. The surface of the dish is incomplete, just an empty skeletal framework. Turning it into a full dish is part of what I need to accomplish here. The site's also dotted in many places by slender metallic towers that hold sensor palettes. The long shadows cast by the suns setting make it look *very* eerie.

We're about to land. I think I'm looking forward to this.

Supplemental, planet Sarindar

I'm now settled in my tent. That's right, *tent*. I'm in a canvas *tent*. Not even a proper Starfleet shelter, but a *tent*.

I don't even know where to start. The equipment that I've seen is old and horribly maintained. Old I can live with—since joining the S.C.E., I've dealt with everything ranging from three-thousand-year-old computers to hundred-year-old starships to state-of-the-art Androssi security devices—it's the badly maintained part that's going to cause headaches. The only weapons on the planet are sonic pistols and rifles that look like they're about a thousand years old. Light-based directed-energy weapons would be tantamount to suicide on a planet with so much crystalline flora and fauna— the beams would refract all over the place—so I didn't even take a phaser with me, though I did bring a Starfleet-issue sonic rifle as a backup. We're not likely to need weapons, but it's good to be prepared—especially given the unfortunate state of the Nalori's armament.

They don't have food replicators—the food is all cooked with these chemical stoves that don't work half the time. The food is stored in freezer units that also don't work half the time, so a lot of it is spoiled. In fact, Zilder had picked up some fresh food when he went to get me at the starbase—it got a much better reception than I did.

Which leads me to the workers themselves. As expected, they're a mix, but most of them are either Nalori or Osina. The Nalori are humanoid, with skin tones ranging from medium ash gray to almost charcoal. Their eyes, by contrast, are uniformly black, with no apparent pupils. They practice a form of ritual scarring of the forearms and face—according to the database, this marks rites of passage like adolescence, adulthood, marriage, birth of sons, veneration of elders, and so on, which Carol confirmed. Most of the men are bald, though I have no idea if that's biology or fashion, with long braided chin-beards of pale, violet hair.

And they hate my guts.

Okay, maybe that's a little harsh, but when Zilder introduced me to the foreperson—a large man named Kejahna—I could feel the disdain oozing out of his pores.

The only one who wasn't hostile was Razka. He showed me to my tent—my *tent!*—and said he'd be serving as liaison between me and the workers. He seems nice enough—at least he didn't glare at me—so maybe this won't be so bad. And, since

I'm both in charge and the only woman, I get my own tent. Every other tent has four people in it. Lucky me.

I'm going to try to get some sleep, then see what I can do in the morning. But I already miss the *da Vinci*.

First officer's log, Commander Sonya Gomez, planet Sarindar, Stardate 53274.1

My first day on Sarindar was spent being given a tour of the SA site by Razka, after a breakfast of cold oatmeal because the main cooking unit broke down, and I didn't think to bring my own stove.

The design flaws that I found in the specs for the SA are exacerbated by shoddy work and a backward method of implementation. The first thing I did was order the detail assigned to construct the tubing for the delivery system to stop that and help in the digging of the hole for the antimatter reactor. The warp pulse is going to require the most testing, and it needs to be in place long before the tubing has to be finished. Kejahna wasn't happy about this, and the workers even less so—digging is much harder work, after all—but they agreed.

Another problem are the antigrav units, which are slow and go off-line regularly, which slows the work down. After pointing this out to me, Razka said, "Welcome to Sarindar. This is the worst place in the galaxy. Nothing works here."

"That's going to change," I said, and proceeded to stop the tour, sit down, and look at one of the anti-gravs.

"It's pointless, you know," Razka said cheerfully. "We've poked and prodded that thing for days at a time. Everything's in working order, it just doesn't work. This planet is cursed, you see."

"I don't believe in curses. I do, however, believe in faulty diagnostic routines."

Razka frowned at that. "What?"

"The diagnostic routine's all messed up. It's in test mode." I put the diagnostic program into the right mode, and it started listing all the things that were wrong with the unit. "They're probably all like this."

I called the assistant foreperson, J'Roh, over. J'Roh was a member of the Osina, an insectoid race—nothing like the Nasats, though. They have large compound eyes, tentacles instead of the more arm-like extremities that P8 Blue has, and six rather than eight of those extremities. None of them have Pattie's sparkling personality, either. The one trait they share with Nasats, though, is the ability to stand upright on their hind legs.

"This antigrav's diagnostic program's in test mode. So, probably, are the others. Fix that, then you'll know how to fix the units themselves. I want a detail assigned to take care of this."

J'Roh's voice sounded like a bird's angry chirp after a predator attacked its nest. "It still won't work."

"Maybe not, but you're going to do it anyway."

"Why should I?"

Before I could reply, Razka said, "Because if you do what she says and it still doesn't work, you'll prove that you're right, and that you're the smart one."

Amazingly enough, that seemed to work. J'Roh didn't say anything, but did start working on the unit. He didn't actually pull a detail together, but I decided to take what I could get.

My next task was to streamline the construction of the magnetic containment unit, which should have been completed by now. The workers assigned to that task were about as receptive to my orders as J'Roh, but they went ahead and implemented the new duty schedule.

Finally, I went to the camp hospital to meet the doctor, a Gallamite man named Dolahn. Apparently he had been hired by the Nalori government because of his work with silicon-based life forms.

This assignment is proving to be much more challenging than I thought, but I'm confident that, with Razka's help, I can accomplish our goal.

Personal log, Commander Sonya Gomez,
planet Sarindar, Stardate 53274.1

Dolahn may be an expert on silicon-based life,
but he needs some work on the carbon-based variety. The hospital—which is a solid, if crudely built
structure—is full of people with either minor viral
ailments (inevitable in a cross-species environment like this, especially since the Nalori aren't up
to Federation medical standards) or work-related
injuries.

Annoyingly, half the injuries were sustained
thanks to the faulty antigrav units, which wouldn't
have happened if any of these idiots had the brains
to notice that the diagnostics were in the wrong
mode.

The first time I met a Gallamite was on the
Sentinel. I knew that they were basically
humanoid, but with much larger brains. What I
had not known until that day on the Sentinel was
that you could see that brain—their craniums are
transparent.

Dolahn was shorter than the other Gallamite

And they all look at me with contempt as I walk by. I wonder how much of it is because I'm Starfleet and how much is because I'm a woman.

Not that it matters. I'm going to do this job, dammit. I've never failed an assignment yet, I'm not about to start now.

**Personal log, Commander Sonya Gomez,
planet Sarindar, Stardate 53274.9**

It's amazing what you can accomplish by fixing an antigrav unit.

J'Roh skittered to my tent about ten minutes ago and said, "It works."

"What works?" I asked him.

"The load-lifter. I fixed everything the diagnostic program said was wrong with it. And it works."

"That's kind of how it goes, J'Roh—that's what diagnostic programs are *for.*"

"Maybe for you, but that's never happened here."

"Did you fix the other units?"

J'Roh chirped. "No. I only just finished repairing the one you told me to fix."

"It took all day?"

"There were a great many things wrong with it—and, to be honest, I'd never fixed one before. Usually we would just smack it on the side."

I put my head in my hands. "What about the rest of them?"

"I fixed all the diagnostic routines on them—that was pretty easy, actually—and I assigned a detail to fix them first thing in the morning."

Probably the same detail I wanted to fix the antigravs in the first place. The point is, they all should be functioning within the next twenty-eight hours.

I needed that boost after the day I had had, though. I went with Razka to check up on the detail I had reassigned from tubing construction to digging—turns out nine of them called in sick.

I went to Kejahna to ask him about this. He stands almost two meters tall, and has arms roughly the size of warp nacelles. He has more scars on his face and arms than any of the other Nalori in the workforce. Part of me is curious as to what led to that, but most of me thinks I'm better off not knowing.

In any case, when I asked him about all the sick people, he said, "Oh yes, they've all come down with Dakota's disease. It's been going around. They'll be out for at least a day or two."

Dakota's disease is a minor respiratory problem—not even a disease, really, more of a viral infection, but the doctor who discovered it was named Dakota, and the name stuck. It shouldn't even be enough to keep people off work. It is *very* easy, however, to fake the symptoms, especially with the substandard medical equipment in Dolahn's hospital.

In other words, the perfect thing for a "sick-out." The erstwhile tubing detail didn't want to dig, so they decided to pretend to be sick to get out of working at something they didn't like. It's a particularly immature form of protest, and it wasn't something I was going to stand for.

"Dakota's disease?" I said with as much shock as I could muster. "I'll need their names right away." I started inputting commands into my padd. "They'll each need to be isolated in separate tents for fifty-six hours."

"Excuse me?"

"Standard quarantine procedure," I said offhandedly. "We'll have to set aside nine tents for them each to stay in. Someone will have to be assigned to take them meals. Oh, and, of course, the tent assignments will have to be rearranged, but it should only discommode a few dozen people, and I'm *sure* they won't mind for the good of the project. I mean, we wouldn't want them *all* to come down with this, would we? Besides, those tents can *easily* accommodate seven or eight people each instead of the four they have now."

In fact, the tents can barely fit four, and Kejahna knew it.

"Oh," I added, "and they won't be able to take their personal items with them when they switch tents. Too much risk of spreading the infection."

"That won't be necessary," Kejahna said. "This happens all the time."

"So did inefficient work, bad design, and poor scheduling. That's all changing, and so's this. Now I want each of those nine to report to the hospital, and once Dr. Dolahn has verified that they have Dakota's, I want them each isolated in separate tents for fifty-six hours, as per Starfleet Quarantine

Regulation #471946A, Paragraph 9, Subsection C.
If they *don't* have Dakota's, I want them back at
work immediately. Are we clear, Kejahna?"

An interesting thing I've observed about a race
with no discernible pupils is that they're not
nearly as good at menacing stares as races with
them. Nevertheless, Kejahna's expression was not
a particularly pleasant one.

He finally said, "Very clear, Commander. I will
let you know what the doctor tells me about their
medical status."

"I'm sure you will."

Kejahna walked off. Razka looked at me with a
smile on his face. "You remembered that regulation number from memory. I'm impressed."

I smiled. "Don't be. I made it up."

Completely deadpan, Razka said, "I'm shocked
that you would do such a thing, Commander.
Simply shocked."

I laughed at that, and then went on with the
inspection.

Not surprisingly, by the end of the day all of the
digging detail had reported to work. Of course,
they were even more behind, but one takes what
one can get.

Personal log, Commander Sonya Gomez, planet Sarindar, Stardate 53277.1

J'Roh now thinks I'm the most amazing thing he's ever seen, and has been telling anyone who'll listen—and many who won't—about how I lifted the curse on this planet. He started calling me "Sañuul," which sounds similar to my given name and is Nalori for "curse-lifter."

It took his detail until noon yesterday to get all the antigravs fixed, but they did it. The units continued to work flawlessly all afternoon and all day today—which, as far as I can tell, is the longest they've gone so far without any one of them breaking down since the project started. I'm fairly confident that we'll be back on schedule within a day or two.

This has impressed some of the workers. Not all of them, mind you. The ones who tried the "sickout" still glare at me dolefully (though, at least they're almost done with the digging—it should be complete in time for tomorrow's test of the antimatter reactor). Kejahna also keeps glowering at me.

Many others, though, have joined J'Roh in calling me "Sañuul," and even smiling at me occasionally.

Of course, I didn't lift any curses, really, I just applied myself to the task. But the Nalori seem to believe in curses—and who knows? Maybe in some bizarre sort of way, I did actually lift a curse. Zilder keeps smiling and saying, "Ho'nig works in very bizarre ways," and who am I to argue?

But then, maybe I'm feeling whimsical after the story Razka told me tonight. We were sitting outside my tent (and no, I still can't get over the fact that I'm sleeping in a *tent*), sharing a particularly tepid supper of mashed vixpril—a root from the Nalori homeworld that's probably a delicacy when prepared right.

"There are legends of a monster, you see. There are animals here called the shii."

I told him I remembered reading about them in the mission briefing—and seeing them on the way down, for that matter. Four-legged creatures of solid crystal, they're predators, but not particularly harmful to carbon-based life, since they can only digest other silicon-based life. Kind of the local equivalent of lions or sharks.

"Ah, yes, but you see," Razka explained, "there is the monster shii."

"Monster," I said dubiously.

Razka's voice started taking on a singsong quality, and he set aside his own bowl of vixpril. "The monster comes after those who would dare to try to tame Sarindar. All those who have come have been slain by the great beast, who claims the heads of the invaders as its prize."

"You're kidding, right?" I said as I washed down the vixpril with some mineral water.

Shrugging, Razka said, "That is the story, anyhow. It is why there have been so few expeditions to this world."

"I thought it was because of the chimerium and the suns."

Again Razka shrugged. "Well, they complicated things—it makes the world hard to function in. The natural beauty attracted many, but they stayed away because of the stories of the monster shii."

"That's crazy."

Razka grinned. "Of course it's crazy. If it wasn't, you would not be here, Sañuul."

Groaning, I said, "Please don't call me that."

"But it's true. There may not be any monster shii, but this place *was* cursed until you arrived."

"It's nothing any competent engineer couldn't have done. I'm much more interested in getting the antimatter reactor on-line."

"A task for tomorrow, to be sure. Unless," he said with a mischievous smile, "the monster shii attacks us in our sleep."

"Ri-ight."

"Oh, come now, don't humans tell fanciful stories before going to sleep?"

"Actually, we do. Particularly around campfires. Or the equivalent," I added, pointing at the stove.

"My father often told me stories like that. I sometimes tell them to my children—including ones about the monster shii."

"How many children do you have?"

"Seventeen."

I almost dropped my spoon. He didn't seem to be old enough to have sired that many kids, and I said so.

"Well, it's much easier when you have five wives."

"Five."

"Yes."

"O-o-o-okay."

For some reason, the Nalori tradition of polygamy didn't come up in the cultural database I was given.

"It must be terrible for you to be so far away from them for so long," I said.

"Not really. In fact, it's something of a relief. I never really considered myself the marrying type."

"Then why'd you do it five times?"

"Oh, it has to do with one's status. The more important you are, the more wives you have—except, of course, it doesn't *really* work like that. You just accumulate wives to make yourself *look* more important. And besides, we have to propagate the species. Much easier to do that this way."

I put down my vixpril unfinished. "If you say so."

"I say so."

Zilder came over and joined us. "Commander, don't you like your vixpril?"

"I'm just not that hungry."

He smiled. "That's because your spirit is empty. You need to fill it with the love of Ho'nig."

Razka good-naturedly let loose with a couple of epithets in the Nalori language. Zilder just laughed it off. "You are impure, my friend, and that is a shame." He held up a small book with a cracked leather binding. The pages were dog-eared. "This is a copy of the *Se'rbeg*. There's a passage in particular I'd like to read to you, if I may." He opened up the book and flipped to a particular page.

I yawned and said, "Zilder, my religious beliefs are just that—mine, and none of your business. And while I'm sure the *Se'rbeg* is a fascinating read, I'm about ready for bed."

Undaunted, Zilder turned to Razka. "And what of you, my good friend?"

He yawned. "I also say that it is time for sleep. Good night, Sañuul."

I wished him a good night, and he went off to the tent he shared with several other workers.

Zilder put his book away and scratched the ridge that bisected his face. "You wait, Commander. I'll save your soul before this project is done, and Razka's as well, I promise you that."

"Good luck," I said with a laugh, wondering what Ho'nig's views on polygamy were. Given that the Damiani have three genders and tend toward trios rather than couples, I suspect that they might be lenient. Pity—it'd be an easy out for Razka.

In any case, after wishing Zilder good night, I climbed into my tent and started this personal log. Tomorrow, we'll tackle the antimatter reactor. I'm looking forward to it.

The test of the antimatter reactor was a qualified success. (Results appended.) The injectors are not at one hundred percent, and they need to be. If there's even the slightest imbalance, the warp pulse will be uneven and the chimerium will get shot sideways or back down into the planet's surface, which could cause incalculable damage.

I was hoping to do a test of the SA within the next two days, but until the reactor is at peak, we can't risk it.

The good news is that the dish should be completed within those two days, even if we aren't ready for the first test yet. Morale has been steadily improving—the fact that the antigravs function is the primary reason, I would say—although the crew that has been transferred to digging details has been slow and malingering. Despite these problems, I believe we can complete our mission in a timely fashion.

Zilder came to me first thing this morning and
didn't have a word to say about Ho'nig. He did, however, have a lot to say on the subject of the ability of
the antigravs to move the materials for the reactor.

"They can't do it?" I asked, incredulous.

"They can't do it on time," he said. "At least not
just two of them. There's no way we'll be able to
have the thing completely assembled in time for
the window."

All the testing is being done during the window
when the suns calm down enough to allow outside
contact. Sarindar has a twenty-eight-hour day—the
windows are at high noon and midnight, and they
only last from thirteen to twenty-two minutes.

I took out a padd and tried to see if there was
some way to juggle the antigravs so that I could
reassign one of them to Zilder, but they were all
needed for other tasks—now that they were all
actually working, every subsection had great use
for them, and I didn't want anyone to lose their

sudden enthusiasm for working. It was the only way to get anything significant accomplished.

Kejahna walked over then. "Is something wrong?" he asked.

"Zilder seems to think that you can't get the antimatter reactor on-line in time for the window to open at noon."

Kejahna looked down at Zilder. "Really?"

Zilder swallowed. "Not with only the two antigravs. See, we—"

"It'll get done," Kejahna interrupted. "If the load-lifters can't handle it, we'll use our hands. Don't worry, Commander." And, for the first time since I landed, Kejahna smiled.

I smiled back. "What, me worry?"

Zilder looked at both of us like we were crazy, and then said, "Ho'nig help us all."

Still smiling at me, Kejahna said, "Ho'nig helps those who help themselves."

I got distracted by other things until 1355 hours—five minutes to noon, local time, meaning it was almost time for the test—and then I went to the reactor. Zilder informed me that it was ready. With the suns at their apogee causing a cascade of colors in the trees, I ordered the test begun. The full results are attached to my officer's log.

I looked over at Kejahna, who just gave me a knowing smile that seemed to say, *We used our hands*.

Some work needs to be done on the reactor, but at least I'm making progress—both with the accelerator and with the workers. I'll whip these guys into shape yet.

Transcript of tricorder recording by Commander Sonya Gomez, camp hospital, planet Sarindar, Stardate 53277.5

GOMEZ: Okay, Rimlek, tell me exactly what happened.

RIMLEK: We were just—just sleeping. It—it all happened so—so fast. One minute, we're sleeping, the next, this—this—this *thing* is tearing us to shreds! We were—we were just lying there—sleeping, you know. Suddenly, I hear this noise, like something's tearing. Doesn't sound like anything you usually hear, so I wake up—and just then, this big, I don't know, *claw* thing was ripping through the tent. It was *terrible*, it—

GOMEZ: What did it look like?

RIMLEK: It was—it was—it was like a whole bunch of crystal triangles. The head, all four claws, body, tail—they were all pointed at the end and flat on top.

GOMEZ: A shii.

RIMLEK: No! I mean, yes, it was like a shii, but—Commander, this was twice the size of any shii I've seen. I've—I've been on this planet since the project s-started a year ago, and—and I'm telling you, this was no—no shii. I've *never* s-seen anything this—this *vicious*. It—it tore through Saolgud like he was nothing. *Nothing!* It was terrible! And—and then it went after Kani and smashed his skull like it was a piece of fruit and then it sliced Mokae's head clean off and then it turned to me and I've never been so scared in my life and it came after me and those claws and those claws and those claws and please don't hurt me, don't hurt me, *don't hurt me!*

DOLAHN: That's enough, Commander! He's going into shock—and Kani is already in a coma from blood loss.

GOMEZ: Report, Doctor.

DOLAHN: Well, Saolgud and Mokae are quite dead—assuming it *is* them, since they're missing their heads. I'm going to go out on a limb and list the cause of death as decapitation.

GOMEZ: What can you tell me about the wounds?

DOLAHN: Aside from the fact that they were vicious?

GOMEZ: Do they match what Rimlek said? Could a shii have caused this?

DOLAHN: One with a massive glandular disorder, perhaps.

GOMEZ: Doctor . . .

DOLAHN: I'm simply telling you what I saw. Yes, these wounds could have been made by a shii, but only one that was several times larger than any one that has *ever* been reported. I know whereof I speak, Commander. The shii and the other silicon-based life on this planet are my specialty, and I can assure you that this is *not* a shii found in nature.

KEJAHNA: It's a monster shii, then.

GOMEZ: Oh, come on.

KEJAHNA: That's what the legends say, yes?

DOLAHN: I wouldn't know. I don't pay attention to children's stories.

KEJAHNA: Obviously, *Doctor*, they are not stories. We need to kill this thing.

GOMEZ: Don't be ridiculous. Tell me, Doctor, are there shii on any other world besides this one?

DOLAHN: No.

GOMEZ: And when was the last time that anyone did an anthropological survey of this world, prior to the start of this project?

DOLAHN: Well, it's been about five hundred years—

GOMEZ: And how detailed was that survey?

DOLAHN: Well . . . Look, I'm telling you that—

GOMEZ: You're telling me that your "expertise" is at least five hundred years out of date. Which means it's quite possible that this is a normal evolutionary step for the shii.

KEJAHNA: We still need to hunt it down.

GOMEZ: Why?

KEJAHNA: It attacked for no reason!

GOMEZ: We don't know that. Rimlek was asleep when it attacked—and shii generally only attack when they're provoked. For all we know, Saolgud or Mokae or Kani did something to provoke it.

KEJAHNA: They also attack for sustenance.

DOLAHN: That wouldn't matter. They could no more consume carbon-based life for food than you or I could have a Spican flame gem for lunch.

KEJAHNA: So are you saying we do nothing?

GOMEZ: Of course not—but we don't need to hunt it down. We'll just improve our defenses. This encampment doesn't have any kind of protection against local fauna attacking—mainly because nobody expected it to. Have the rest of Saolgud's detail construct a fence around the perimeter.

KEJAHNA: That will put us behind schedule again.

GOMEZ: That detail's already lost four people, they were going to be behind schedule anyhow. And I'd rather play it safe, in case the shii decides it wants to finish the job. Make sure the fence is electrified.

KEJAHNA: This is a mistake, Commander.

DOLAHN: If you two are finished posturing at each other, would you mind getting out of my hospital and letting my patients rest? Thank you.

Letter from Kejahna on Sarindar to Revodro on Nalor, fifth day of Sendrak, twenty-third year of Togh

My son:

One of your mothers told me in her last letter that you are walking and talking now. This is good.

I am writing this letter to you so you know what it is that your father is doing away from you in this formative time of your life.

My work has taken me to the cursed planet of Sarindar. Perhaps your mothers have told you stories of Sarindar. Well, they are all true. This is an evil place. Or, at least, it was.

Our government did not think it was ever a cursed land, but that those were simply stories to frighten children such as yourself. They told us that we were to come to this home of evil and construct machines that will mine the planet. There is an element here that is called chimerium. Supposedly, harvesting this element will make our government rich.

I suppose that is so, but I doubt that I will see any of those riches. Our wages are above standard, but nothing compared to what the government will reap from our labors. That is, it seems, the way of things—and it is worth it, perhaps, to make sure that you and all your brothers and sisters have a better life.

It has been worth it for other reasons, too. I have seen things that I thought I would never live to see.

When I was your age, my father and mothers told me many stories to both frighten and excite me—no doubt your mothers are doing likewise. Perhaps they have told you of the monster shii, or of the sañuul that can lift curses and bring the light.

I have seen both these things.

In order to explain *how* I have seen these things, I must first tell you about Commander Gomez. She was sent by the Federation. I'm sure you've heard stories about them, too. The evil empire who fought us three ages ago and demolished our fleet. To be honest, my son, when I heard that they were sending someone from that foul nation, I almost quit. I only did not because I knew that I would be blacklisted from this kind of work—not only would the government never hire me, but neither would anyone else. I have my family to think of. So I stayed.

Our last supervisor was a good man by the name of Nalag. At least, he was a good man when we first came here. He had every intention of making this project work. He was a sensible man, who had a good plan for the machine we are building. He was also a calm, well-adjusted man, who always kept his beard short and neatly braided.

By the time he quit, he was a wreck. He screamed constantly. His beard had become a long, tangled mess that he didn't even bother to braid. He talked to himself.

Sarindar had destroyed him.

I feared that it would destroy all of us.

And then, then the government informed us that Nalag would be replaced by someone from the Federation.

Worse, a *woman* from the Federation.

For a woman to supervise a man's work is absurd. But I remembered you, my son, and the rest of the family, and I persevered.

When Commander Gomez arrived, she immediately set about destroying Nalag's work. This offended me even more than her presence. She spit on the work of a good man. It was not Nalag's fault that this place is cursed, and his methods were good and fair.

Then she did something truly astounding.

She fixed the load-lifters.

You see, my son, the load-lifters were the true embodiment of the curse of Sarindar. They would not work. We tried everything we could to fix them, but still they would not work.

The woman had not been here an entire

day before she solved the problem of the load-lifters. Since she worked her magic, they have consistently worked. My assistant, J'Roh, called her "Sañuul" after that, and I was half-tempted to go along with it.

But I could not. She was still a woman, still from the Federation, and still spitting on the memory of the noble Nalag. This was made worse when she tried to use her Federation trickery on the workers, who staged a simple protest.

All that, however, changed today.

I know what you are thinking right now. "When is he going to tell me about the monster shii?" Patience, my son.

Two days ago, four men were attacked in their sleep by a creature that one of them described as a monster shii.

Yes, that's right. It is real.

I can see your mothers now. They are all probably reading this and making disapproving sounds about how Kejahna is filling his son's head with insane stories.

And perhaps the two men who survived were telling absurd tales about the creature that wounded them and killed their comrades.

Yes, my son. The creature killed them.

I know this is harsh, but there is nothing to be gained by hiding behind euphemisms. Two of my men were dead, two others badly injured. And the injured ones claimed it was a monster shii.

In any case, I soon learned the truth.

Either way, though—whether it was truly a monster shii or simply some other vicious animal—I knew we had to hunt this creature down. Commander Gomez said no to that, said to simply construct an electrified fence—which we did. But I knew that it would not be enough. I assumed that Commander Gomez, being only a woman, did not understand these things.

Today, Commander Gomez and I were discussing some aspect of the work when we heard a loud noise. We ran to the source of the noise, which was on the perimeter near the electric fence we had built.

The first thing we saw was that the fence itself had been damaged—broken by something that had ripped through it. There were pieces of the fence's structure inside the encampment—meaning that whatever broke the fence, did so by coming in from the outside. Since no one was allowed outside the camp without permission (and they could not break this rule without electrocuting themselves, since only Commander Gomez and I held the keys to the fence) and since no one had asked for that permission, we knew that it was no member of the workforce who had done this—not that any of us could and live.

I told Commander Gomez that the monster had returned. She scoffed. At the time, I believed it was because she was only a woman and did not know better.

Then we saw it.

The monster shii is truly as the legends have said: it looks just like a shii, only bigger. It actually looks much like a man—smooth head and pointed chin, though its chin is natural rather than the result of a beard—only the top of the head is flatter. And, of course, it is made of crystal and walks on four legs. And those legs are remarkably similar in shape to the heads. The legs—and the chin—are razor-sharp.

The one we saw was also stained blue with the blood of a man.

We saw the man, too—or, at least, his body, which lay on the ground under the monster. After a moment, I saw his head—tucked in between the monster's hind leg and rear shoulder. It was Kelrek. He was only three scars old, a mere youth.

As foreman, I had been issued a sonic pistol. I did not hesitate to use it, but even as I unholstered the weapon, the monster turned to run away. I fired, but missed—the sonic beam ripped through one of the tents, instead.

However, as the creature turned, I saw that it was bleeding—a silvery substance dripped from a gash in its side. I tried to fire again, but it seemed to move at warp speed.

Commander Gomez ran after it, as if that would do some good. Where I had unholstered my weapon, she had taken out her scanning device. She ran, continuing to look down at her scanner.

We reached the fence, at which point she

stopped. The monster had gone through the same way it came, apparently unbothered by the electricity. We were not so fortunate—the charge from the fence was arcing all over, and we had to keep our distance.

Commander Gomez deactivated the fence, then turned to look at me.

She then said three words I never expected to hear her say to me: "You were right."

"About what?"

"Forming a search party. There's no way anyone could've provoked that thing in such a way that it would break through the fence and make a beeline for Kelrek like that. We've got to track it down." She put her scanner away. "I was hoping to get some readings on the thing, but the tricorder's useless with all this chimerium around."

"We have a trail to follow," I said, pointing at the creature's blood trail.

She looked down at the silvery blood in surprise, then smiled. "Good catch. Okay, put a detail together—but one thing, Kejahna. *I'm* in charge of this party. We'll issue weapons to everyone, but nobody fires without my *direct* order, understood?"

"Commander—"

"Understood?"

In fact, I did not understand, but I gave in and nodded my assent—if not my approval.

My opinion of her tactics did not improve when she spoke to the hastily assembled hunting party several minutes later.

"I want to make something very clear here—this is *not* a hunting party. It's a search party. We know very little about this thing. Federation history is replete with encounters with life-forms that we thought were utterly hostile and became good friends—ranging from the Klingons, whom we knew to be sentient, to the Horta, whom we had thought of as simple animals. Now it's possible that this, too, is just a nasty animal—it's also possible that we provoked it in some way. We will defend ourselves if we have to, but we are *not* going to hunt this creature down. For now, my main concern is to find the creature, retrieve the heads of the people it's killed, and learn more about it."

One of the party—an Osina named D'Ren—muttered under his breath, "And how is she supposed to do that?"

People from the Federation apparently have very good hearing, because she replied to that, even though she was not meant to hear. "We won't know until we make the attempt."

"Right," D'Ren said, louder this time, "I forgot. You're Starfleet. You can do *anything.*"

Commander Gomez looked up and down the line of men she was leading. "No one is to fire their weapons without my authorization. Anyone who does will be confined in the *Culloden* until the next window and shipped out of here. Is that understood?"

That surprised me. The threat was a very

serious one—to lose this work would mean sacrificing great wages, and also virtually guaranteeing that the person in question would never work for the government again. And only the government pays this well.

After her speech, we marched out of the camp, following the trail of silver blood. There were nine of us, for luck.

This is an ugly, unpleasant world. There is no shading here—it is all glare and blinding light. The plants all have sharp edges and the ground is difficult to walk on. Aside from the occasional burst if the suns reflect the right way, there is no color here. It is bland and lifeless—no less than one would expect from a place so evil.

The blood trail became harder to follow after a certain amount of time, but the animal seemed to be going in a straight line, which we followed.

Before long, the suns started to set. Commander Gomez led the way—her weapon had a lamp attached to it, which became our beacon. Our own lights were much poorer, and since I brought up the rear of our "search party," I got the least benefit from that light. Only Commander Gomez had her weapon unholstered, at her order— and no one was willing to contravene an order that came with such potentially disastrous consequences.

We saw many creatures on the way. Some of them were even normal shii. Once D'Ren started at the sight of one, thinking it was the monster, and reached for his weapon. Before he could, though, the shii itself ran off. I assured him that that was *not* it—it was far too small.

This did not stop D'Ren from panicking once again when we happened upon a pride of shii, but they ignored us. All of them were fairly diminutive—nothing at all like the monster I saw in the camp.

Then we came to the cave.

Commander Gomez shone her light into the cave—and then gasped. Thinking that we would never get a coherent answer out of her, I ran to the front to see what she saw.

What I saw were skulls.

The skulls of animals. The skulls of men. *Hundreds* of skulls.

As repellent as the sight was, the smell was worse.

In the camp every day are the mixed smells of food, the chemicals from the cooking units and the lamps, and the various materials used for the machines we construct. The smells of *life*.

When we left the camp, those smells dissipated to be replaced by nothing—for just as there is no color, there is no odor to this world, either. Nothing to indicate that anything worthwhile has ever come here. It is as sterile and antiseptic as that idiot Gallamite wishes his hospital was.

But the cave . . .

I hope, my son, that you live a long and fruitful life. And I hope you *never* have the smell of death invade your nostrils the way it did for me in that cave today.

Commander Gomez's lamp was insufficient to see all the way into the cave, so I could not begin to describe how many skulls were actually present. But I did know one thing: some of them were very old indeed.

There was one head I saw that was *not* a mere skull, but in fact a head with a face still attached, belonging to Kelrek. It had been placed unceremoniously in a pile of skulls, no more or less important than any of the other hundreds of trophies this abomination had collected.

Immediately, the talking began. Everyone in the party wanted the creature dead. Some even unholstered their weapons.

"Put those weapons away," Gomez barked. "I told you—"

I was about to interrupt her. I was going to tell her that she was a fool. I was going to tell her that we needed to destroy this creature *now*. I was going to tell her that if she did not authorize us to eliminate the monster, I would order the men to do it myself and damn the consequences. I was going to tell her that I didn't care what it took, I would see this abomination who would display the heads of men in such a manner eliminated. I was going to tell her that anyone who did not see things this way was a fool.

I did not get the chance to say any of those things.

Because that is when the monster attacked.

I cannot say where the creature came from. All I know is that one moment, I was standing before Commander Gomez preparing to speak my mind to her, and the next, I was diving for cover as a crystalline demon leapt into our midst.

After rolling on the ground for several moments, I looked up to see J'Roh flailing blindly at the monster, several other men running away from it—and Commander Gomez holding her ground.

The monster leapt into the air and then headed straight for Commander Gomez.

She still stood her ground, even as I cried out, "Commander, duck!"

Instead, she fired her weapon.

Then she ducked.

Unfortunately, she had only put the weapon on its lowest setting. Equally unfortunately, she did not duck fast enough. The creature sliced at her left arm, tearing her uniform and her skin.

To my amazement, Commander Gomez's blood was red. For some reason, I assumed that her blood would be a more normal blue color. Perhaps all her people have blood like that. Or perhaps she is special.

The creature came at her again. Though she lay on the ground, though one arm was injured, she managed to change the setting on her rifle and fire it.

Waves of sonic energy battered the monster in midair. It twirled around in midleap and spun like a head-ball being intercepted. It fell to the hard ground just as I had when it first attacked.

Unlike me, it did not get back up.

"Is it dead?" D'Ren asked.

"Looks like it is," Gomez said. "Dammit!"

J'Roh was chittering madly. "Did I not tell you all? Haven't I been saying all along that she is the sañuul? This proves it! She has destroyed the monster shii."

If I had not seen it with my own eyes, I would have called J'Roh a fool.

But I had seen it.

Commander Gomez *is* the sañuul. She has taken the curse of this evil place and removed it.

"Hail to Sañuul!" J'Roh cried, lifting his four front legs into the air.

The Nalori men did likewise with their arms, as did the Osina with their legs. Calwei, the lone Cabbi in the party, waved his flippers.

Regardless of their gestures, they all repeated J'Roh's cry.

"Hail to Sañuul!"

It took me a moment, but I joined in the cry.

Because, my son, I had seen it. In all the stories, there is one constant: none can kill the monster shii. Yet she did.

Sañuul killed it.

We marched triumphantly back to the camp. By the time we arrived it was completely dark, but a large number of men—including the Bolian zealot, Zilder—were waiting for us at the entryway.

Four of the men carried the body of the monster back. As soon as he saw that, the Bolian cried out, "They have killed it!"

Cheers erupted from the assembled men.

I wanted to display the monster's corpse on the fence as a testament to victory, and said so as we came in to the adulation of the other workers.

"No," Sañuul said. "Bring it to the hospital. I want Dr. Dolahn to conduct an autopsy."

"That fool wouldn't know which end to cut open!" Calwei said, at which many laughed.

Sañuul even smiled at that. "Maybe. But he's *supposed* to be an expert on silicon-based life, and I want to know where this thing came from."

I walked up to her as the four men continued toward the hospital and the remaining three told the others of our adventure. "We know where it came from, Sañuul."

"Oh, don't tell me *you're* going to start calling me that, too."

Bowing my head respectfully, I said, "If you do not wish to be called that—"

"I don't," she said quickly.

"In any case—*Commander*—it is a monster shii. It came, presumably, from other shii."

"Maybe. But Dolahn was right about one thing—it's a *lot* bigger than any of the other shii that we saw on the way out there. Or the ones I saw from orbit, for that matter. It might be some kind of mutation or something else. I want to know what." She took a deep breath. "In the meantime, I think we've all earned a night off. First thing in the morning, I want to work out a new schedule with you and J'Roh—with that thing dead, we should be able to get back on track."

"Of course, Sañ—Commander."

"Meanwhile, I'm going to follow the corpse to the hospital, get this looked at." She pointed at her injured arm.

As she walked toward the Gallamite's chamber of horrors, I called after her. "Commander, if you wish—would you join us?"

She stopped, turned, and frowned at me. "Join you where?"

"Outside my tent. I intend to celebrate our victory with a bottle of Saurian brandy that Entorr thinks he's been keeping secret. I would be honored if the sañuul would join us."

She sighed. "I'm *not* the sañuul!" Then she smiled. "But I'd be equally honored to join you. Thank you, Kejahna."

And she did join us. We drank long into the night. Mostly, Sañuul listened as we regaled each other with stories. Some of them were even true, though they were less so the more we drank. It was very good Saurian brandy, and Entorr only sulked for a little while when I told him to bring it out.

Ah, but your mothers are no doubt distressed at this drinking and carousing so soon after talking of fighting and death.

But a victory should be celebrated. So should a miracle. And Commander Sonya Gomez—the sañuul—is most definitely a miracle.

Thanks to her, I should be home to see you soon, my son. I look forward to it.

> With all the love I have,
> Your father,
> Kejahna

First officer's log, Commander Sonya Gomez, planet Sarindar, Stardate 53281.2

Today at noon we will be doing our first test of the annular confinement beam. This is the most important test we've done so far, as the ACB is an important component of the SA. The ACB is similar to the kind used in transporters, but much more powerful by several orders of magnitude. It will be used to clear a path of vacuum through the planet's atmosphere, through which the payloads of chimerium will be accelerated with an eight-nanosecond high-warp pulse that will drive them up to the refinery.

I've been a bit concerned about this particular aspect of the SA, as it's the most experimental, inasmuch as no one's ever (to the best of my knowledge) created an ACB on this scale. It's also a very good thing that I—or at least someone from Starfleet—was assigned to this project before this test was done. The power systems for the ACB were not sufficiently recalibrated for the increased power. The nature of the ACB is such that, as the beam increases in size, you have to increase the power output logarithmically, not exponentially. If they'd built this up to the original specs, as mandated by my predecessor, the best-case scenario would be that the ACB would burn out and shut down. Worst-case: the entire SA would've exploded in a fiery mess, people probably would die, and the project would have to start over from scratch.

The original schedule the project had been on when I arrived didn't have this test being attempted for another two weeks. My own revised schedule had it for two days from now. I would like to formally commend the foreperson Kejahna, my assistant Razka, and the assistant foreperson J'Roh for their exemplary work in putting the project ahead of schedule, despite the numerous impediments that have been placed in our path.

Morale has improved tremendously since the unfortunate incident with the so-called "monster shii." I am still awaiting an autopsy report from Dr. Dolahn on the nature of the creature. However, my killing the thing has elevated me in the eyes of the Nalori workers. Many have taken to following J'Roh's example and calling me "Sañuul." I have tried to discourage this, but to no avail. I'm also not entirely comfortable with the fact that it has taken me killing an animal to gain the respect of the workers.

On the other hand, I can't argue with the results. We've worked the bugs out of the antimatter reactor, the magnetic containment system is up and running, and we'll be ready to bring the antimatter pods on-line tomorrow. In addition, when I informed Kejahna and the workers assigned to the ACB that we'd have to so radically change the power systems output, his response to my criticism of the methods employed by my predecessor—for the first time since I arrived—was not hostile.

Now it is simply a question of waiting until noon, when we get our pulsar/quasar window.

**Personal log, Commander Sonya Gomez,
planet Sarindar, Stardate 53281.2**

I have learned several valuable lessons these last few days.

The first, and most depressing, is that if you want to gain the respect of a party of Nalori workers, kill a mutated animal (or whatever that overgrown shii was) that attacked your camp. All the sexism, all the anti-Federation sentiment, seems to have disappeared since we came back to the camp with the corpse of the "monster shii."

The second is that I'm no good at eulogies. We held a funeral service for Kelrek, Saolgud, and Mokae the day after I killed the shii. Nalori death rituals are fairly straightforward: the bodies are burned, and a person of authority—of any authority, it doesn't have to be someone religious—commends their souls to the afterlife. To be precise, according to the crash course Razka gave me prior to the funeral, their deaths must be announced to the *Shigemos* so they can welcome their *mazza* into the Endless Wind. (This was something else missing from the cultural database I read on the *da Vinci*.)

I tried suggesting the ever-evangelical Zilder as a substitute, but the Nalori would hear none of it. Zilder is an infidel, as far as they're concerned. (Zilder's predictable response was, "Give me time to convert you all.") Of course, I'm as much an infidel, but Razka said that I was the only person on the planet qualified. I'm just grateful that the ritual calls for burning—burial wouldn't be possible on the glassy surface of Sarindar.

Still, I did my best, which was pretty awful. I see no reason to commit the stumbling, awkward mess to the record—I pointedly turned my tricorder off before the funeral—but suffice it to say, the *Shigemos* were suitably, if not always intelligibly, informed of the incoming *mazza*.

The third is that I need to double-check everything. I made what could have been a huge mistake by assuming that the power output on the annular confinement beam was properly adjusted for the size of the ACB, and it wasn't. Since the diagnostic programs were created by the same people who got the ratios wrong, no error was detected—especially since there's no point of reference for an ACB this powerful. J'Roh expressed a concern that the nodes might not be able to handle the additional power, but I made sure the auto-shutdown features were up and running in case of such a difficulty.

The fourth is that I've gotten remarkably dependent on a tricorder. On a planet so loaded with chimerium, a tricorder is often little more than a glorified paperweight. That's not entirely fair—medical tricorders still function, certain data can still be examined, and I'm, of course, recording this log on it—but there's still a lot I can't do. Every time there's a problem—and there's *always* a problem, no matter how smoothly things might be going at any given point—my instinct is to whip out the tricorder. I did it when the shii attacked poor Kelrek, and I've done it any number of times with the equipment. I'm tempted to just leave the thing in my tent, but it doesn't feel right to walk around the surface of a planet without the familiar weight on my side. Still, I've spent more time opening up the guts of machinery than even I'm used to.

The fifth is that the best way to guarantee that Dr. Dolahn will never do something is to tell him that it isn't top priority. It's been several days since I told him I needed an autopsy of the monster shii, but he hasn't gotten to it yet. It was Zilder who explained my tactical error in saying that it wasn't top priority—apparently, the only way Dolahn ever does anything is if you emphasize that you need it right away. Even then, he may not get to it for days.

Of course, this really *isn't* a top priority. I'm curious as to how this creature evolved, especially since all the evidence does seem to point to it being an aberration. We saw plenty of other shii, all of a size commensurate with the anthropological reports. (And don't think Dolahn hasn't enjoyed reminding me of that.) I've decided to keep the electrified fence up as a precautionary measure, even though none of the other shii we encountered showed any interest in us.

Still, it's a side concern. The main thing is to get

the project finished. I'm happy with our progress, and even happier with the smoother working relations—whatever the reason. But mostly I just want this to be finished so I can get back to the *da Vinci*. It's gotten to the point where I'm not even impressed by the crystalline ecology. When I got here, it was a beautiful new world—every time the sun struck a tree or bush, resulting in a spectrum burst, I was captivated. I don't even notice them anymore.

Looking back over that, I'm getting depressed. Ten years ago, I came out of the Academy hell-bent to seek out the unknown, to experience what was out there in deep space. I wanted to see it all, and I didn't want to miss a thing. (Of course, what I got was the Borg and a rather brutal lesson in being careful what you wish for, but that didn't change my overall desire.)

Dammit, I'm not going to become one of those moldy officers who treats a new world as just another mission to go on instead of an adventure. I didn't join Starfleet to slog from one mission to the next.

Next time I see a spectrum burst, I *will* stop and stare at it. Dammit.

Supplemental

The test of the ACB was an unqualified success. The full results are appended to my main log, but suffice it to say, the power nodes were able to handle the additional input, the beam successfully shunted all the air out of the way and held its integrity for the entire time the window was open, and it shut down smoothly.

One thing I hadn't been expecting: the ACB's brightness is such that all the nearby trees give off some pretty amazing spectrum bursts. Even some of the Nalori—who never seemed to be in the least interested in or impressed with the local light-shows—gasped appreciatively at that.

When Razka announced that the window was closing and we shut down the beam, a huge cheer went up. They started crying, "Sañuul" again, and this time I just let them. It would've been churlish to deny them at this point.

The other good news is that we received assorted communiqués. Zilder and I went straight to the tent that held the comm equipment and went through what we had received during the window. Most were of a personal nature, and would be saved to individual padds by Zilder later. Two were for me: one from the *da Vinci*, and one from the Nalori government. I was eager to hear from Kieran and the rest of the S.C.E., but the other one was unexpected, so I told Zilder to put it on screen.

A particularly long male Nalori face appeared. He looked pretty sallow, and his beard had more gray than violet. I had spoken to this man—the senator in charge of the project—once on the *Culloden* en route to Sarindar, but I couldn't for the life of me remember his name.

Zilder, conveniently, came to my rescue. With as disdainful a tone as I'd ever heard him use, he said, "Senator Moyya. Everybody's favorite person. I wonder what pearls of wisdom he has to offer."

This message is to inform you, Commander Gomez, that we are less than impressed with your performance to date. The accelerator is still behind what we consider an acceptable schedule. When we asked Starfleet for assistance, we were assured that we would be getting the best. I have seen nothing in the preliminary reports to indicate that you could be given that description. We removed Nalag because he was behind schedule. While you have improved on his work, you are still performing your task at below par. Either you are incompetent or Starfleet's standards are lower than I was led to believe. If you have not brought the project to what we deem an acceptable level, we will have to consider having you replaced.

That was it. I stared in open-mouthed shock at the screen for several seconds.

"Ho'nig," Zilder muttered, shaking his head. "Nalag quit, they didn't 'remove' him. Can you believe that?"

Having dealt with enough bureaucrats in my time, I had to say, "Unfortunately, I can."

"Should I prepare a reply?"

I thought about several creative ways to respond to that particular message. Then I got an inspiration. Smiling, I said, "No. When the next window opens, send all the results and reports on the ACB test we have at that point as a reply."

"Any accompanying message?"

"None. Let the results speak for themselves."

Zilder also smiled. "Ho'nig is smiling on you today, Commander."

I laughed. "Whatever."

I downloaded the message from the *da Vinci* to a padd, then went back to the camp.

After finishing the day's work, I ate with the workers—something I've been doing every night since I killed that shii. It's been fun hearing the different stories.

Then I read the *da Vinci* message, which turned out to be from Kieran.

Hey, Sonnie. Well, things are business as usual here on the ol' homestead. Captain Gold got a nice message from his granddaughter— her child's going to be a girl, and she and his grandson-in-law are arguing over the name. I started a betting pool, which the captain is pretending not to know about. Right now, "Judith" is the favorite.

Let's see—Pattie went into a fit yesterday. Carol got another recording of that Sinnravian drad music she loves so much. It's the latest from that person who founded the "atonal minimalist" subgenre. She's been playing it over and over again. I really wish you were here—'cause then you'd get to listen to Pattie request a new roommate. I hate being the first officer, you do know that, don't you?

I miss you—and not just because I want you to be first officer again. We had to crawl inside the guts of a derelict Tellarite freighter yesterday, and you know more about those weird overpowered engines they insist on. Fabe nearly blew the thing up—it was pretty ridiculous. We got out of it okay, though.

There've been some nasty rumblings coming from the general direction of Deep Space 9—apparently they were attacked. There's a rumor going around that the Defiant *was destroyed. I'll let you know—I'm sure you don't get much Starfleet gossip out on that crystal ball of yours.*

Well, I gotta go—it's my turn to run engineering. Talk to you later, Sonnie, and try not to have too much fun.

Razka came in as Kieran was finishing up. "Is that your mate?" he asked.

I took a long enough pause that Razka probably thought I didn't hear him, and he repeated the question.

"I guess you could say that. Sort of."

"Do you like your mate?"

I smiled. Whatever else I could say about how I felt about Kieran, I could safely say that I liked him. "Yeah, I do."

Razka looked thoughtful. "I haven't liked *any* of mine."

At that, I couldn't help but laugh—which turned

out to be okay, because he laughed, too. Then he took out two mugs and started to pour some Saurian brandy.

Gazing askance at him, I said, "I thought we finished Entorr's stash."

"We did. You think Entorr's the only person who smuggled in brandy?"

"My mistake."

He handed me one mug, then raised his. "To mates. We cannot live with them, but we really cannot live without them, either."

I raised my mug as well, and decided not to tell Razka that he had just quoted a *very* old human cliché.

Another good day. The antimatter pods are on-line and working well, the tubing is almost finished, the dish *is* finished, the delivery system will be on-line in two more days—a week ahead of schedule—we seem to have finally gotten the bugs out of all the sensor palettes, and the mining mechanics are almost finished as well.

Best of all, I was distracted no less than four times by a spectrum burst. I'm very proud of my sense of wonder, and grateful for its return.

Right now I'm relaxing in my tent with a bowl of halfway decent vixpril and a mug of Saurian brandy, having just read the latest letter from Kieran. Apparently those rumors about DS9 were mostly true—a Jem'Hadar ship *did* attack the station, and now the entire Alpha Quadrant's at yellow alert. It wasn't the *Defiant* that was destroyed, it was the *Aldebaran*. The *da Vinci*'s still on its latest assignment—some three-hundred-year-old ship that they found in the event horizon of a black hole.

Kieran joked that they're going to try to tow it out with wires, as if *that* could possibly work. They're also ready to drop that at a moment's notice in case this really is a prelude to another war.

I hope that it isn't. I don't think I could deal with another war so soon after the last one. I still have nightmares about that time the *Sentinel* was trapped behind enemy lines. I know I got a commendation for that, and everyone talks about how heroic I was for getting the warp drive back on-line and then recalibrating our shields and warp signature so the Breen thought we were Cardassian—but the fact of the matter is, I was scared to death and running on pure adrenaline and instinct.

Then again, Geordi gave me a commendation for helping get the shields back up when the Borg attacked way back when. I still haven't the foggiest idea what he was thinking. I was the greenest of green ensigns, staring off into space at the drop of a hat because eighteen people died.

Not that I should be blasé about death, of course.

God, listen to me. I think I've been drinking synthehol too long—my system isn't used to the real stuff.

That does it. No more of this damn brandy.

I still haven't written a response to Kieran since the last letter. He's probably going to start worrying. But I just don't know what to say to him.

At least he isn't pushing in these letters. That's typical, really. He never pulled his goofy aw-shucks act or his c'mon-go-out-with-me-again routine while on duty, and he wouldn't do it on an open channel, either.

What really gets me is that Razka asked me if he was my mate, and I almost said yes.

And yet, I haven't really thought about him all that much since I got here. Part of that is just the grind of the project, and part of it is probably just my predilection for avoiding anything unpleasant in my personal life.

That's our Sonnie Gomez. She can field-strip a warp core, can fool a Breen into thinking an *Akira*-class starship is a Cardassian freighter, can get a subspace accelerator built with substandard equipment and cranky workers, can defeat the mighty monster shii—but can't get her love life straightened out to save her life. The last time things were in danger of getting really serious with Kieran, I was promoted and transferred off the *Enterprise*. I wonder if I could've fought to stay on the ship—I mean, there had to be *something* an antimatter specialist at the full lieutenant level could do on the *Enterprise*. On the other hand, I could hardly pass up that project on the *Oberth*. On the third hand . . .

On the third hand, I'm *definitely* giving up the brandy. It makes me *way* too philosophical. And maudlin.

I just heard a scream. Better go check it out.

Supplemental

Oh, my God.

Oh, my God.

Oh, my God.

Letter from Commander Sonya Gomez on Sarindar to the family of Kejahna on Nalor, tenth day of Sendrak, twenty-third year of Togh

Gentle beings:

You don't know me, but my name is Sonya Gomez. I was recently put in charge of the Sarindar Project, for which Kejahna, the head of your household, was the foreperson.

I regret to inform you that Kejahna is dead.

I am sure you have heard the legends of the monster shii on Sarindar. We had believed those legends to be false. It turns out that—like many legends—these have a basis in fact. A creature that fits the description in your culture's tales of the monster shii attacked the camp and killed three people last week. I had killed that creature myself, and thought that it was the last we'd seen of it.

However, yesterday, another creature attacked the camp. It is quite a bit larger than the animal that I killed. It went through our electrified fence like it was nothing and went after the nearest people.

Kejahna was very brave. He leapt into the monster's path in order to save the life of another of the workers. He gave his life so that others would live. You would be very proud of how he died, though I know that it is small comfort to you right now.

We are about to go out to hunt the creature down, but I wanted to take the time to compose this letter in case I don't make it back. I felt I owed it to Kejahna to tell you myself about what happened.

He was an excellent worker, and a good man. I will miss him, and I feel his loss deeply—though not, of course, as deeply as you. He spoke often of his family during evening meals, particularly how much he was looking forward to spending time with his son Revodro when this project ended.

I hope I get to convey my condolences in person, and again, I am very sorry for your loss.

Sincerely,
Commander Sonya Gomez

First officer's log, Commander Sonya Gomez, planet Sarindar, Stardate 53283.1

There is a second "monster shii" on Sarindar. At 2342 hours, it broke through the electrified fence that surrounds the work camp. Unlike the previous shii that I killed, and which murdered several workers, this one suffered no appreciable injury. It immediately ripped into the nearest tent, which belonged to Kejahna, the foreperson, and three other Nalori: Erobnos, Caargenne, and Houarner. The creature definitely killed Kejahna—who leapt in front of an attack that would have decapitated Caargenne, and was disemboweled—and gravely injured the other three.

The shii then carried all four bodies out of the camp.

I witnessed most of this, having come to investigate when I first heard the screams of the Nalori being attacked.

While I record this log entry, my assistant Razka is organizing a second hunting party. I have composed a hasty condolence letter to be sent to

Kejahna's family. If Erobnos, Caargenne, and Houarner wind up killed, as I suspect will be the case, I will do the same for their families—assuming I survive. I fear that this creature will not be as easy to stop.

Razka is calling me. The party is ready to go.

Second officer's log, Lt. Commander Kieran
Duffy, *U.S.S. da Vinci*, Stardate 53288.1

I'm worried about Sonnie. And I'm worried about
me, too.

The *da Vinci*'s still at yellow alert while we wait
to find out what's happening at Deep Space 9.
There's every possibility that another war with the
Dominion is in the offing. If that's true, we're all in
for a galaxy of trouble, especially since our first
officer's so far away.

Commander Sonya Gomez, first officer of the
da Vinci, my immediate superior, and a woman I
have grown *very* fond of over the years, is right
now in the very distant Nalori Republic. That
distance, combined with the Nalori's lack of
Federation relay stations, means that just a communication to her would take two days to arrive.

I've already sent her two messages, but haven't
heard anything back. I hope she's okay. The Nalori
don't like the Federation much, and only asked for
her because they needed her expertise to help

build a subspace accelerator, to help them get chimerium off the planet Sarindar.

A planet full of that super-dense ore is a great find, and I'm glad that we're getting to help mine it. I'm also glad that this will probably mean improved relations with the Nalori.

But I'm not glad that we're potentially on the brink of war, and Sonnie's so far away.

I miss her. And I'm worried about her.

Letter from Razka on Sarindar to Marig on Nalor, eleventh day of Sendrak, twenty-third year of Togh

My wife:

I write to you for the first time since arriving at this dreadful place. The reason is, I fear for my life. Since the cause of the fear still exists, I write. Before I go any further, however, I wish to make a request of you. Please kiss each of my children for me. When you do so, tell each of them that their father loves them. Even the ones who are too young to comprehend. You will understand why I ask this after you read this letter. But, please, do that first. Thank you.

Of all my wives, you are the one I dislike the least. So I wish you to have this record of my life in this place. We are building a sub-space accelerator here on Sarindar. It will allow our glorious government to harvest chimerium. That, I'm sure, means as much to you as it does to me. But they're paying me, so I won't complain.

The first thing that happened when I got here will amuse you. The foreman issued me a weapon. Me. It took three days just to figure out which was the right end to point. But the foreman insisted. He was a big man named Kejahna. He assigned me to be the aide to the project leader. That used to be Nalag. You would have liked Nalag. He was pleasant. He was also driven insane by this place. Much the same way you drive me insane, to be truthful. After he went mad, the government did something odd. They requested help from the Federation. The Federation sent a woman from Starfleet. I thought that made them madder than Nalag, at first. But Commander Gomez has been magnificent. Several here started calling her "Sañuul" because of her work. She made the load-lifters work. She brought the project back on schedule. She fixed several errors in the subspace accelerator.

She also killed a monster shii.

No, your fears have not been confirmed. I have not gone insane. I sometimes wish I had, but no. The monster shii is real. It is not just the stuff of legends. And Commander Gomez killed it after it attacked and killed several workers.

The problem with legends isn't when they turn out to be true. It's when they turn out to be *half*-true. You see, in all the stories I've heard about the monster shii, I've never heard anyone mention *two*. But there *were* two here. The second one is much bigger than the first. It killed Kejahna and took three others. Commander Gomez told me to organize a search party. She and Kejahna did that the last time a monster shii attacked. I didn't want to go with her, but she insisted. Especially with Kejahna dead. Do you know what she told me? That I was the only person she trusted now. Armed with my sonic rifle and this undeserved responsibility, I went out with her.

Sarindar is a beautiful place in the daylight. At night, it is somewhat less so. When the sunlight glints off the flora, it's like walking in a jewel. Without that light, it's like walking in a tomb. Especially when we came across the dead bodies. Houarner, Erobnos, and Caargenne, the three who were taken. Also Kejahna's body. We found their remains on the ground, ripped to pieces. Except, of course, for their heads. The monster shii presumably still had them. The one Commander Gomez had killed had taken poor Kelrek's head.

We continued to follow the trail. It led to a large cave. Commander Gomez told me that the last monster shii was in a cave. This cave was apparently much bigger. But it had the same thing in it. Skulls. Many many skulls from many many animals. Some of them looked quite old. The monster shii had obviously been killing for a long time.

Commander Gomez, for some reason, kept

saying that we had done something to provoke the monster. I explained that it didn't need provocation. It simply collected heads. Then she said that if it collected heads, it might be rational. I suppose they teach that sort of silliness in Starfleet. Most of the party thought her to be mad. Zilder, the religious Bolian pilot, summed it up best. "This is not one of Ho'nig's creatures." Ho'nig is his god. From the moment we met, he tried to convert me to worshipping Ho'nig. Unfortunately, his missionary zeal was not very convincing, and was even less so when the monster shii cut his head off.

I froze when that happened. I just stood there and watched as the monster shii leapt out of nowhere and ripped Zilder into pieces. Just two days ago, I was teasing Zilder about his conversion attempts. In fact, I joked that he should have tried to convert the monster shii. Then Commander Gomez would not have had to kill it. Instead, it killed him. Commander Gomez did not hesitate. She fired on the creature. Several others followed suit.

I did not. I just stood there. My mouth was agape. I couldn't even raise my weapon. My first thought was that I would never see my children again. That is why I asked you to kiss them earlier. I swore at that moment that the first thing I would do if I made it back alive was express my love for my children.

Not that I *expected* to get back alive. Even as most everyone else fired on the creature, it continued its rampage. The sonic rifle fire didn't even slow it down. This wasn't a total surprise, as it is about twice as big as the first one to attack. That one is a corpse, presently sitting in the camp hospital. Its fellow started killing indiscriminately. After Zilder, it decapitated D'Ren and literally sliced Eridak in two. Entorr started to run away, and G'sob ran toward it.

Still I did not move. I just stood in the cave. People were scattering around me. The shii was slicing at anything that came near it. And the only sound I heard was the whining of the rifles. Sonic rifles don't give off any kind of emission, the way a laser would. They just make that whining sound. I heard no screams, though I saw mouths move. I did not hear the sounds of flesh being rendered, though I saw it being done. But all I could hear was the sound of every rifle firing. Every rifle, save my own.

At least until Commander Gomez ordered a retreat. That I did hear. Somehow, then, I found the wherewithal to make my legs move. We ran back to the camp. I came straight to my tent and began writing this letter. I have now fulfilled my oath to myself. When the next window in the suns' interference opens, we will send many messages. The primary one will be to request of the government that the project be terminated and we be allowed to leave. This letter, however, will go as well.

If I die here, please let my children know who their father was. Tell them that I was a coward, or lie to them, it does not matter. Just tell them.

Best regards,
your husband,
Razka

First officer's log, Commander Sonya Gomez, planet Sarindar, Stardate 53283.9

I have returned with the search party. We were able to trace the "monster shii" to its lair—another cave system, about half a kilometer farther from the camp than the smaller cave where the previous shii had its lair. This cave was much larger, and contained a concomitantly larger number of skulls. I was hoping to collect some skulls for samples, for Dr. Dolahn to examine, but the opportunity did not present itself, as the shii attacked. Zilder, D'Ren, and Eridak were all killed, and several others were injured. (Tricorder recording of attack appended.)

It is after midnight, so our next quasar/pulsar window won't be until tomorrow afternoon. When that happens, I intend to send a message to the Nalori government, requesting that we receive permission to suspend the SA project until we can deal with this problem. I'm also preparing a distress signal to send to the *da Vinci*—based on Lt. Commander Duffy's last communiqué, they may not be able to respond to it, but I'd rather play it safe.

I've also instructed the remaining workers to construct a sonic barrier around the camp. The electric fence we put up didn't even slow this creature down, and we need some kind of defense. True, the sonic weapons didn't work, but that may have been because they're not powerful enough. J'Roh—who is now the foreperson, following Kejahna's death—pointed out that we'd have to cannibalize some of the sonic rifles to accomplish this, but, to my mind, it's worth it.

It's not like the weapons were doing us any good. . . .

My next task is to find a way to conduct an active scan on this planet. I need to get proper sensor readings of this area, see what it is that's attracting the shii here. I suspect that we're doing something to provoke it. Animals generally don't attack without a reason. Since it can't digest carbon-based life, it obviously isn't pursuing us for food. Besides, the specificity of the attacks indicates a possibility of intelligence. But this is all speculation until I can get this tricorder to do some actual scans.

Personal log, Commander Sonya Gomez, planet Sarindar, Stardate 53284.1

A miracle has happened. I was up all night working on it, but I finally figured out a way to adjust the tricorder so I can get at least partial sensor readings of the chimerium-laced area. The resolution is awful and the readings are spotty, but it's better than what we had before, which was nothing. I hope that I get to live long enough to share this breakthrough with Starfleet.

Razka's at my tent. . . .

Supplemental

For the second time on this expedition, Razka has asked me to perform the funeral rites for the people who were killed by the monster shii, which reminded me that I hadn't yet written condolence letters to the families of the ones who died. I already did one for Kejahna's family. I have to admit—I *hate* to admit—that I forgot about both duties in the rush of getting the workers to build the barrier and adjusting the tricorder.

I just remembered that time on the *Enterprise*—our first encounter with the Borg. I was an ensign, fresh out of the Academy, working in engineering under Geordi La Forge. The Borg cut parts of three decks out of the saucer section—with eighteen people in them. They were missing and presumed assimilated. I kept trying to focus on getting the shields back up, but I couldn't get those eighteen people out of my mind. Geordi said two things to me: "Just put it out of your head" and "We'll have time to grieve later."

But the Nalori peoples have very particular funeral rites. And I'm a part of it now, whether I like it or not.

Besides, there's not a helluva lot I can do until noon, when we send the messages.

Supplemental

The funeral was subdued. The ceremony was for everyone who died except Zilder. I think I did a better job of commending the *mazza* of the dead to the Endless Wind this time. I wish that I didn't have to keep practicing, though.

Eridak, one of the Nalori who died, only had two scars—both on his face, none on his forearms. From what I've learned, those are the basic coming-of-age scars. Every Nalori here has them, but he was the only one I remember who had *only* those two. Which meant he was very young. Too young to die.

Afterward, I checked the tent that Zilder had shared with three other workers, and it turned out that he had made up a will since arriving on Sarindar. Rather than follow any Bolian traditions, his wishes related to the death rites of the Damiani. Zilder had worshipped the Damiani god Ho'nig, and according to the *Se'rbeg*—the holy book of Ho'nig-worshippers—he was required to be buried within three days of death.

That, of course, isn't going to happen. The crystalline nature of this world makes it impossible to bury anything.

Zilder wrote his will on a piece of paper. He had made many corrections and addenda to it during his time here. He left the *Culloden* to the Nalori Republic, "as my thanks for hiring me to work for them."

He left his copy of the *Se'rbeg* to me. He had originally left it to Nalag, my predecessor, but that had been replaced with my name. The exact phrasing was, "To [Nalag, crossed out] Commander Sonya Gomez, I leave my most valued copy of the *Se'rbeg*, the holy words of Ho'nig, in the hopes that [he, crossed out] she will find the same enlightenment and glory through it that I found over the years. This is the book that changed my life for the better. I hope it can do the same for [him, crossed out] her."

I stared at the cracked leather binding of the book and shook my head. I had found Zilder's constant religious harping to be irritating from the moment he picked me up in the *Culloden* at

Starbase 96, several dozen eternities ago, but now, realizing that I would never hear him imploring me to take Ho'nig into my life again, I found I was going to miss it.

I can't even give him a proper burial.

Dammit, this whole thing is falling apart. Yesterday, we were on schedule and the one danger to the project had been killed. Now, seven more people are dead, work has ground to a halt while we try to defend ourselves against a hostile alien—and try to find out *why* it's attacking us. How the hell did this happen?

I'm going to find out.

Supplemental

I just finished my first scan of the area. So far, nothing. Razka came up to me and asked me what I was doing, and I explained to him that I was trying to determine why the shii was attacking.

Razka looked at me like I was insane. "Did you look at the skulls in the cave, Commander? This monster has been killing things on this planet for much longer than this installation has been here. Besides, what does the reason matter?"

"It hasn't just been killing, it's been decapitating and saving the skulls. It may be intelligent. We can't just kill it without finding out why."

"Perhaps you can't. And perhaps I can't." He got a funny look on his face when he said that. "But there are dozens of workers here who will do whatever is necessary to avenge their comrades.

And, regardless of your status, Commander, they
will not listen to any words you say about it possibly being intelligent or something to talk to. It is
an animal, and it has already killed seven men.
The only response that anyone here will support is
to kill it."

Transcript of message sent from Nalori
Republic Senator Moyya to Commander Sonya
Gomez on planet Sarindar, twelfth day of
Sendrak, twenty-third year of Togh

We are distressed by your absurd request to
suspend operations on the Sarindar Subspace
Accelerator Project. We had been led to believe
that the officers of the Federation Starfleet were
professionals who did not succumb to the foolish
ramblings of old women. To insult the intelligence
of this senate by suggesting that you have (again)
fallen behind in the project's timetable due to
attacks by a "monster shii" is bad enough, but to
accompany it with a "recording" of an attack that
is so obviously a forgery merely compounds the
offense. It is obvious to us that the workers you
claim were killed by this "monster" were malin-
gerers and drunks who allowed themselves to be
attacked by native fauna. It is equally obvious that
Starfleet has sent not their best, as promised, but
an incompetent and a fool. There are some voices
among the senate who believe that Starfleet sim-

ply dressed a foolish woman in a commander's uniform and sent her to us, hoping we would not notice. The only way to prove those voices wrong is to get the project back on schedule.

Therefore your request is denied. Work will continue. Any unauthorized departure from the planet Sarindar will result in the exclusion of those departing *and all other workers on Sarindar* from any and all government work for the rest of their natural lives.

First officer's log, Commander Sonya Gomez, planet Sarindar, Stardate 53285.0

In light of the Nalori Republic's refusal to accede to my request, I have ordered the workers to resume the scheduled construction of the SA. I have lodged a formal protest with the senate and with Starfleet Command over the gross inhumanity being displayed by the senate in this instance. A distress call was also sent out to Starfleet—specifically for the *da Vinci*, but sent on a general Starfleet frequency—fourteen hours prior to the reception of the senate's refusal. While it will take two days for it to reach the Federation, I have faith that someone will respond and, if necessary, evacuate the planet.

Departing is only an option if another ship arrives, as the *Culloden* is keyed to Zilder's DNA. The radical dissimilarity between Bolian DNA and that of any of the races represented on this project—not just that of the assorted Nalori races, but also of my human and Dr. Dolahn's Gallamite genetic structure—renders it impossible to "hot-wire" the *Culloden*, at least with the equipment available to me.

I have instead devoted my resources to restructuring the duty schedule in light of the reduced personnel, maintaining our defense against the shii, and attempting to improve the presently limited ability of the tricorder to scan the surrounding area despite the high concentrations of chimerium. I am hoping that Dr. Dolahn's autopsy of the first shii will give us some idea of how we can either defend against or communicate with this creature. In addition, I intend to take a bioscan of a "normal" shii, to give me a base for my readings.

I will continue to send updates and recordings of the monster shii to the Nalori senate, in the hopes that they will come to their senses.

Personal log, Commander Sonya Gomez,
planet Sarindar, Stardate 53285.2

I just finished a trip outside the encampment to take a bioreading of the shii. The normal-sized ones are roughly the size of a pony, and they move through the crystalline landscape with an impressive grace. After twice nearly being killed by the mutant versions—or whatever they are—it's nice to be reminded that the "normal" ones are quite elegant.

In fact, they're more noble than a good chunk of the sentients presently on the planet. I had to put someone on guard over the *Culloden* after four different incidents of people breaking into the ship to try to get off-planet. They didn't succeed, of course, but that's hardly the point. These are people who make their living working for the government. That same government has made it clear that any attempt to leave the planet will result in them never working again. A lot of these people have families, but they're willing to risk their livelihood to get out of here.

I, on the other hand, am willing to risk going outside the sonic barrier to get those bioscans. Luckily, I wasn't attacked by the "monster."

Not that anyone would have volunteered to come along to protect me. Nobody's called me "Sañuul" since the massacre at the cave, and I've been getting the same doleful looks that I got when I first arrived. Nobody's invited me to join them for meals, either.

The project is even more behind schedule, with much less than a day's worth of work getting done on either of the last two days. Everyone wants to leave. No one wants to work.

And I can't blame them.

But I need to find out what is causing the shii to attack us. There *has* to be a reason.

Someone's raising the alarm.

Supplemental

Another attack. Five people are dead—the guard on the *Culloden* and the latest four who had tried to commandeer it. While they were trying to break into the ship—I'd placed a coded lock on it, along with a recording device—the shii attacked. The ship is docked outside the perimeter of the sonic barrier, so the shii had a clear path to them. In fact, I'm stunned that none of the others who've attempted escape before them were similarly attacked.

All five corpses were missing their heads.

One thing I did notice on the recording is that one of the victims—G'sob, one of the Osina assigned to the tubing detail—managed to wound the shii. His weapon was set on a lower intensity, but a higher frequency than normal. I checked his weapon—the shii left it behind—and its reading indicated a different setting from what it had actually fired.

For the first time since I arrived on Sarindar, the substandard equipment is working in my favor. Thanks to G'sob's rifle being defective, we now know that we can wound the creature.

As good news goes, however, this isn't much. I suspect that things will only get worse.

**Personal log, Commander Sonya Gomez,
planet Sarindar, Stardate 53286.2**

Things have gotten worse.

Half the workers have refused to leave their
tents. The ones who still have sonic weapons—
many of them were cannibalized to make the
sonic barrier around the encampment—are
clutching them to their persons and threatening to
shoot anything that comes near them. They've all
readjusted their weapons to the setting G'sob
used.

I've tried to get them to go to work, but I have
no hold over them anymore. The senate's decree
has served to completely undercut any authority I
had with these people, even as it undercut their
own authority. No one here can possibly take seriously a body that refuses to accept the existence of
something most of us have seen with our own
eyes. And yet, the fact that they don't believe what
I tell them about the same creature has given the
workers carte blanche to ignore my orders.

Neither the tubing nor the mining mechanics

are finished, even though they should have been done by now. The delivery system is off-line, and probably will remain that way—especially since the three most talented members of that particular detail are now dead. In my next message to the senate, I intend to ask for replacements since they can't be bothered to actually shut down the project. There's no way I can complete the SA without sufficient personnel, and even if the remaining crew worked their hardest—which they most definitely won't—we couldn't finish this thing.

I've been scanning for twenty-eight hours, and I can't find a single reason why the shii is attacking. I'm half-tempted to go back to the cave and try to do a scan there, but I don't think it's worth the risk—yet. But it may come to that. I'm still awaiting Dr. Dolahn's autopsy report on the shii I killed. He said he'd get to it today, but he's said that every day since I first brought it to him.

I've also come up with an idea for how to trap the creature without killing it.

First officer's log, Commander Sonya Gomez, planet Sarindar, Stardate 53286.8

I have managed to boost worker morale slightly. The tubing was finally finished this morning, so I reassigned them to construct a trap for the shii. This was work they could actually get enthusiastic about, since they're stuck on the planet for the time being. (My numerous communiqués to the senate have met with a resounding silence. I'm hoping to get a reply from the *da Vinci* tomorrow.)

The principle of the trap is quite simple: it's a box that's divided into two halves by a set of metal bars. I had been hoping for duranium, but all that's available is a steel composite left over from the tubing. Three people stand on one side of the bars, armed. The other side is open. Based on the bioscan I took of the regular shii, there's one particular ruby-like flower that they are fond of eating. The plan is to place several of those flowers into the open end of the trap. Once the shii enters, a force field will be activated, trapping the creature inside. The three armed people then fire on the creature at the low-intensity-high-frequency setting, which should be enough to stun it, or at least to subdue it.

The detail has taken to the task with relish, and I'm hoping they'll have it done by nightfall. Kugot, Amuk, and Entorr have volunteered to serve as the executors of the trap.

Supplemental

The trap has failed. Entorr, Kugot, and Amuk are dead. One of the weapons misfired and damaged one of the bars. The shii flailed and sliced through the bar. All three missed the shii with their shots, and then were, unfortunately, prime targets once the bars went down. It is unclear why the three of them did not escape through the rear hatch, but their failure to do so resulted in their tragic deaths. Entorr was killed by decapitation. The other two were beheaded after they were killed. The creature departed with all three heads.

I doubt the creature will fall for the same trap again, and we don't have the material to reconstruct it in any case.

I am still waiting for the final autopsy report from Dr. Dolahn on the shii that I killed. Scans of the region still fail to provide any reason why the shii would be attacking us.

Personal log, Commander Sonya Gomez, planet Sarindar, Stardate 53287.0

Okay, my official log has the formal report about how exactly Entorr, Kugot, and Amuk were killed.

I need to say, however, that it was the most pathetic sight I have ever seen in my life! Much as I hate to speak ill of the dead, I really have to wonder about those three. Did they *have* a death wish?

Admittedly, part of it was the fault of the ever-substandard Nalori equipment. At least one of the rifles was on the wrong setting.

But still—how the hell can you *miss* something at *point-blank range?*

The shii took the bait we laid out. I activated the force field. The shii realized it was trapped and started making this squeaky noise. I gave the order to fire.

And they *missed*.

Worse, one of them—Entorr, whose weapon was on the wrong setting—hit one of the bars. That weakened the steel enough so that it started to buckle. The shii must have noticed this—or maybe it would have attacked the bars anyhow. Either way, it sliced through one of the bars, leaving the three Nalori vulnerable—

—especially since they panicked and started firing wildly instead of doing what they were supposed to do if something like this happened, which was *run out the back door.* I had made sure that there was a method of escape in case something like this happened, and they *didn't use it.*

I've been sending regular updates on the situation to the senate, including images of every attack of the shii. I'm really of two minds as to whether or not to send this one, as it makes all of us look like idiots.

Naturally, everyone's blaming me for the trap not working, even though it *should* have worked, if those three jackasses had done what they were *supposed* to do.

Okay, that's not fair. They panicked. It happens. But that panic got them killed.

The last batch of messages included one from the *da Vinci.* Even though it's time-stamped two days after I sent out the distress call, it makes no acknowledgment of it. I've continued to send it at each opportunity, so, with any luck, they *will* get it eventually. According to Kieran, things are going better—it turns out that there *isn't* going to be a war, and the *da Vinci* has been assigned to help the folks at Deep Space 9 put the station back together. Fabian Stevens used to be assigned to DS9, so he's probably happy about the assignment.

Right now, I *really* wish I was back with them. I

wish I could watch Fabian and Pattie crawl around a warp core with me, listen to Carol make one of her snide remarks, try to decipher Soloman's chirpy computer-speak, watch Bart write a letter on paper to Anthony, hear Captain Gold go on about his grandchildren. Hell, I wouldn't even mind listening to Corsi complain.

But most of all, I miss Kieran's smile. That dopey, aw-shucks smile that he always gets on his face when he decides to torture me by reminding me of when I spilled hot chocolate on Captain Picard.

Work on the SA has crawled to a halt. The team that put the trap together is down to one person now, and he refuses to work. Nobody's tried to steal the *Culloden*—mainly because of what happened last time—but nobody's willing to work, or talk to me, either.

I'm going to go to the camp hospital and sit on Dolahn until he gives me an autopsy report.

Partial transcript of autopsy report of sample SO19 (a.k.a. "monster shii") by Dr. Dolahn, Sarindar Medical Unit, thirteenth day of Sendrak, twenty-third year of Togh

DOLAHN: The creature also shows signs of— Ah, Commander Gomez, I was just going to summon you.

GOMEZ: I see you're actually working on the autopsy.

DOLAHN: Don't sound so surprised, Commander. I admit, I've been dilatory in getting to this, but caring for Kani and Rimlek has been difficult—I almost lost them a couple of times.

GOMEZ: I'm sorry, Doctor, I didn't realize . . .

DOLAHN: Yes, well, there was no way you could've known.

GOMEZ: Especially since you didn't tell me. If you actually gave me reports . . .

DOLAHN: [makes throat-clearing noise] Yes, well, be that as it may, I have begun the autopsy, and I've come to rather a shocking revelation.

GOMEZ: What?

DOLAHN: Whatever this creature is, it *isn't* native to Sarindar.

GOMEZ: But—

DOLAHN: It may *appear* to be a shii—and rather a mutated one at that—but it isn't. Take a look at this. Some of these match the way the internal organs of a shii are *supposed* to be arranged, but half of them aren't even actual organs. I've been studying silicon-based life-forms for most of my career, and I can't make heads nor feet out of any of th—

GOMEZ: These aren't organs.

DOLAHN: I beg your pardon?

GOMEZ: These aren't organs.

DOLAHN: What are you doing with that thing? I thought those Starfleet contraptions of yours were just glorified recording devices on this planet.

GOMEZ: I've been able to modify this one to get at least partial readings, even with the chimerium. And, according to the readings I'm getting right now, these don't behave like "proper" organs because they're biomechanical.

DOLAHN: Commander, most silicon-based life might read on a tricorder as "biomechanical" due to the nature of their—

GOMEZ: Doctor, contrary to the opinions of the Nalori government, I'm not stupid. I compensated for that. But this creature was never "alive" in the traditional sense. It's an artificial life-form. In fact . . .

DOLAHN: What is it?

GOMEZ: If I'm reading this right, some of these "organs" are actually chameleon circuits. Some people at the Daystrom Institute were working on something like this, but they were never able to make it work.

DOLAHN: For those of us who don't follow every move of the Daystrom Institute, Commander, what, exactly, is a chameleon circuit?

GOMEZ: It's something that allows a mechanism to change its outer form. You program it to alter its appearance. The problem is, the power demands to let something with an unstable molecular structure perform stable mechanical functions were always way in excess of what was practical. Whoever built this was able to solve that. This is amazing.

DOLAHN: Why would anyone build something like this?

GOMEZ: I don't know. But this changes everything. I need to study these circuits, see if I can figure out the programming.

DOLAHN: What, you're going to work *here?*

GOMEZ: Unless you have a better idea, Doctor. I won't have the space to do this in my tent, and this is the closest we have to a lab in the camp.

DOLAHN: Fine, if you must, but please stay out of my way.

First officer's log, Commander Sonya Gomez,
planet Sarindar, Stardate 53288.6

I have left Razka and J'Roh in charge of what
remains of the project—apparently, the crew
working on the mining mechanics have been
throwing themselves into their work, on the
premise that it's better than waiting for something
to kill them. Everyone else is sulking in their tents.
I, meanwhile, have spent the last twenty-eight
hours trying to figure out what makes the "monster shii" tick.

And, I'm happy to say, I think I've found it.

I've been able to extract a visual record from the
creature's "eyes"—actually, recording devices. It
took a while for me to determine how to read the
things—I finally managed it by constructing an
image translator, cannibalizing parts from Dr.
Dolahn's X-ray machine, of all things.

Some time in the past—it's impossible to be
sure *how* far, as the manner in which this mechanism tells time doesn't have an obvious analogue
to Federation or Nalori timekeeping—an expedi-

tion of aliens came to Sarindar. I can't say what they were called—the universal translator renders the references to them as simply "the owners"—but the two shii were the protectors for the expedition. Their job was to keep them safe and gather food for them.

The owners are quadrupedal beings who look, at first glance, like a hybrid between seals and dogs—but, honestly, they don't look like anything I've ever seen before. The expedition seemed to be a simple archaeological survey.

However, I noticed, as time went on, that the owners looked weaker and gaunter—and that there were fewer and fewer of them. My best guess is that they succumbed to some kind of disease. After a certain amount of time, they were gone.

If the shii—the protectors had taken on a large-scale version of the form of shii when they arrived on Sarindar—had any notion of what had happened to the owners, they gave no indication of it. They simply continued carrying out their duties.

Those duties included gathering food. The owners, I soon realized, fed on the cranial matter of animals.

This explains the hoarding of heads and the discarding of the bodies. In their minds, they're still gathering food for their masters, despite the fact that those masters are never going to return.

**Personal log, Commander Sonya Gomez,
planet Sarindar, Stardate 53288.9**

I've been working on a way to try to communicate with the "shii." I've moved to my tent, since the doleful looks from Dolahn (pardon the pun) have gotten tiresome.

The work Bart Faulwell did in upgrading the universal translators to understand Bynar speech, when they commune with computers or with each other, has turned into a boon. Most of that work was programmed into my *da Vinci*-issue tricorder, so I was able to start building a language algorithm for the shii.

Razka came by to give me a report, and asked me what I was doing. I explained it to him—including what I'd learned about our attacker.

"Why do you want to talk to it?"

"To convince it to stop. It doesn't realize that it's doing anything wrong. If we can explain to it that its masters are dead and it doesn't have to hoard food for them anymore, maybe we can get it to leave us alone."

"To what end? Commander, this is pointless. These are simple automatons. You no more 'killed' anything last week when you shot the first shii than I did when I crashed my father's hovercraft when I was a child."

"Razka, I appreciate—"

"Commander, you are an engineer. So are most of the men working here. When a piece of equipment malfunctions, you turn it off."

"No, you try to fix it. Razka, I really do understand what you mean, but I can't just condemn this thing without giving it a chance to stop. I killed the first one in self-defense—maybe if I can talk to it—"

Razka laughed. "You're even calling the creature 'it.'" Then he grew serious. "Let me put it another way, Commander. You are in charge of this project. This project has been endangered by these two creatures. Don't you owe it to the men you're responsible for to do whatever you can to safeguard them? Yes, it's true, this thing has been left without any kind of guidance, and it's simply following its programming. But Kejahna, Rimlek, Entorr, G'sob, D'Ren, and the others are all dead. You yourself commended their *mazza* to the *Shigemos*. What of them?"

I found I didn't have an answer to that.

He left.

I went back to work. Maybe he was right. But the next time I saw that thing, I *was* going to try to talk to it.

Him. Her. Whatever.

First officer's log, Commander Sonya Gomez, planet Sarindar, Stardate 53289.1

All requests to the Nalori senate have gone unanswered. There is also no reply from the *da Vinci* or anyone else from Starfleet.

The sonic barrier that we erected around the camp has failed. The sonic rifles issued to the Nalori were not designed for such sustained use. One of them had a breakdown in the control unit when the coils overheated. The fact that they even *use* coils instead of an EPS system is an indication of how substandard they are.

Unfortunately, the breakdown of one converted rifle caused a cascade reaction, and now it doesn't work. I have managed to reconstruct parts of the barrier, but that makes it all but useless. Unless the barrier is "airtight," as it were, the shii can get through with ease.

The only way to properly fix the barrier is to cannibalize the remaining sonic rifles, but—even if I could convince the workers to give them up—

that isn't a viable option. They are our only defense against the creature.

And, since the camp is no longer a safe haven, I need to take action.

The trap would have worked if the shii had actually been hit with any of the shots fired at it. One thing that did work was the lure. So I'm going to try the lure again, this time in the camp hospital. It's generally the most crowded place anyhow, so the shii would probably scope it out in any case. Meanwhile, I will move everyone to the space beneath the SA. Dolahn should be able to convert it to a makeshift hospital, and I'll put the remaining armed workers on guard.

Once that's done, I'll lure the shii with the ruby flowers and try to communicate with it. I've programmed my combadge so that its translator will render the machine language of the shii, based on what I could glean from the first one.

Letter from Razka on Sarindar to Marig on Nalor, fifteenth day of Sendrak, twenty-third year of Togh

My wife:

Yes, another letter. Because once again I have been reminded of my mortality. Once again, I ask you to kiss my children for me before reading the rest of this letter. Thank you.

Commander Gomez yesterday hit upon the idea of setting a lure for the monster shii. By the way, she has learned that this creature of legend is, in fact, a machine. It was programmed by strangers who came here on an expedition. The expedition members died, but the two shii lived on. These strangers fed on the brains of other living creatures. This is why the monster shii take the heads of men. They are gathering food for their dead masters. Tragic, in a way, especially given the number of good men who have had to die. In any case, Commander Gomez decided to lure the creature.

A previous attempt to trap the monster failed, but she did succeed in luring it with a *glemnar* flower. So she cleared out the hospital and had Dr. Dolahn and J'Roh construct a new hospital under the subspace accelerator. This was sensible, as the old hospital was the easiest place to defend. The new hospital will be even easier to defend. So all the wounded and sick, the doctor, and all the remaining healthy people were moved to the new hospital. Commander Gomez remained behind at the old hospital. She liberally spread the *glemnar* flowers and waited. She felt that the monster shii would come to the hospital. Her plan was to try to talk to it. She thought she had come up with a way to do so. At least she was not foolish enough to try this without backup. She was armed with her Starfleet sonic rifle. All she had to do was wait until the monster came. We would wait in the hospital until it was safe.

That, at least, was the theory. Unfortunately, the practice proved somewhat different. We had very few sonic rifles left. Mine, having gone completely unused since I was issued it, was one of them. Those of us who were armed stood guard at the two entrances to the hospital. One led to the dish, the other to the underground tubing. I was stationed, along with J'Roh, at the dish entrance. The other four were at the tubing entrance. This made sense. J'Roh was not a very good shot, and you know what I'm like with a weapon. It was very unlikely that the shii would come in through the dish, as it would have to climb up onto it and then slide to its center. The tubing provides a more direct access. That, therefore, had the best guard.

Not that we thought it would matter, of course. We all assumed that Commander Gomez's plan would work. Well, actually, *I* assumed that. So did J'Roh. He was the one to first call her "Sañuul" after she solved the riddle of the load-lifters. And so did some others. Most, however, thought that the plan was a foolish one. Many wanted it to work anyhow, but only so that the shii would kill Commander Gomez.

In fact, I distinctly remember that part. Querti had just said, "If we're lucky, the beast will take her bait and take that hideous head of hers off." Then he started to say something else as Anilegna started to laugh. Then the entryway buckled, making an awful, tearing noise. Then a triangle-shaped claw ripped into Anilegna's torso. As he coughed up blood, Querti lifted his rifle and made as if to fire. The claw, still stained with Anilegna's blood and encrusted with his innards, continued its arc and ripped both the rifle and Querti's hands to ribbons.

Next to me, J'Roh aimed his sonic rifle at the door. Unfortunately, there was nothing to aim at. The shii hadn't come all the way through, and the parts that had were blocked by Querti and by Anilegna's remains. Not that it would have mattered to me. As before, I froze.

Oddly, this time, I couldn't hear the rifles firing, but I could hear Querti's screams. People closer to me than he was were saying things. I think Dr. Dolahn cried out, and several people ducked under the beds, but I didn't hear that. The shii ripped through the rest of the doorway, but I didn't hear that, either. I continued to hear Querti's screams, though.

Once he had a clear shot, J'Roh fired his rifle. So did one of the other guards at the door. The second guard's rifle literally exploded in his face. *That*, I did hear, as well as his screams, intermingled with Querti's.

A hole seemed to open up in the shii's torso, but it didn't slow down. It sliced the head of the first guard clean off, while the second guard continued to scream in pain. Then it got quiet for a moment. I noticed that the shii had cut Querti's head off as well.

Suddenly, sound exploded in my ears. Dolahn telling everyone to take cover. J'Roh screaming for me to shoot. The second guard still screaming in agony. And I still couldn't move, couldn't fire my weapon, couldn't speak.

I wanted to, Marig, that's the worst thing. As loudly as J'Roh was screaming at me, I was screaming at myself. I tried to motivate myself to do *something*. But I could not budge. I told myself that the deaths of Kejahna, Kelrek, D'Ren, Entorr, and all the others had to be avenged. I told myself that others would die at any moment. I told myself that Commander Gomez had said that I was the one she trusted.

But mostly I just thought about how I was going to die. And I was so frightened of that possibility that I could do nothing but think about it. And so fear continued to grip me as the shii decapitated Kani and Rimlek. Both of them had been attacked by the other shii, which Commander Gomez had killed. Though they had survived, they had been left comatose. Now they, too, were dead.

J'Roh leapt down from our guard post at the doorway and shot the creature again. It started to bleed mercury, as the other one had. But its wounds did not seem to stem its horrific tide. With one slash, it cut J'Roh's body in two. Then Dolahn, the Gallamite doctor, ran up to it. Dolahn is not what I would consider a brave man. In fact, I would mostly consider him a fool. Like all Gallamites, he has a transparent head, so you can see his brain. Someone used to joke that he wore a hat so no one would know how small that brain truly was. The sad truth is, he wore the hat because Kejahna threatened to kill him if he didn't. In any case, Dolahn ran up to the shii. He was armed only with some kind of edged instrument. He stabbed the creature in an odd place. It was right in the creature's lower thorax. Probably where its stomach was. After the doctor did that, the shii cut his head off, too.

His head lay on the floor, the hat having fallen off. I could see his brain. It was not small. In fact, it seemed rather large.

Then the shii collected all the heads it had severed. I noticed that all the wounds that had been inflicted on it had healed. Well, almost all. The one Dolahn had inflicted continued to drip mercury, even as it collected heads. When it was done, it tucked the heads under a foreleg. Then it ran out the way it came.

Slowly, people started to come out from under the beds and tables. The floors were awash in blue from all the blood. Some red was mixed in, from the doctor.

A moment later, Commander Gomez ran in. She asked, "What happened?"

Some mad fool burst out laughing at that absurd question. It took me a moment to realize that I was that fool. I continued to laugh while someone else—I believe it was Mranol—explained that the shii had come through and killed fifteen more people. The odd thing is, I hadn't even noticed all the deaths. But I certainly wasn't going to contradict Mranol.

I am now sitting in my tent. I am not sure if I'm ever going to leave the tent again. I have now had my rifle for almost an entire year. It has gone unfired the whole time. Could I have made a difference, either in the cave or in the hospital? Probably not. But perhaps I might have helped save a life or two.

It is obvious that I am not worthy to live when so many good men, like Kejahna and Dolahn and J'Roh, have died. Tell my children that I love them, Marig. And tell them that their father is a coward and a fool.

> Best regards,
> your unworthy husband,
> Razka

Personal log, Commander Sonya Gomez, planet Sarindar, Stardate 53289.4

I'm a complete idiot.

I made the biggest mistake you can make—humanizing a machine. Well, maybe "animalizing" is more accurate. But I should have realized that my idea wasn't going to work.

The ruby-like flowers *weren't* what lured the shii to the trap in the first place, it was the three Nalori. It was looking for more food to collect for its masters. Because *it's a machine.* Machines do what they're programmed to do, and this one is programmed to kill animals and decapitate them so their masters can eat.

So, naturally, when you collect everyone in one spot, that's where it's going to go.

God, it's like I'm a green ensign back on the *Enterprise* again. And now fifteen more people are dead, and it's my fault. I'm supposed to be in charge, and all I've done is get people killed.

One of the workers—I don't even know his name—just came in and asked me to perform the funeral rites again. I was surprised at this, but he said something that surprised me even more:

"It is not your fault, Commander, it is ours. We fooled ourselves into thinking you were the sañuul, that you had lifted the curse of this miserable place. But you are, in the end, just a woman— as you yourself told us all along. You did not wish us to call you sañuul, and we should have listened. Instead, we are simply all victims of the curse of Sarindar."

With that, he left.

I wish it made me feel better, but it doesn't even come close. I've failed in my duty here. And it's past time I made up for it.

First officer's log, Commander Sonya Gomez, planet Sarindar, Stardate 53289.7

I've received a transmission from the *da Vinci*, but it's garbled. The only thing I know for sure is that the signal originated from the Trivas system, which is an unclaimed region of space near the border between Federation and Cardassian space. Unfortunately, it's not clear from the message if they were cutting short their mission to the Trivas system or if they *couldn't* cut short that mission.

I'm proceeding on the latter assumption, and plan to once again attempt to activate the *Culloden*. First, however, I must perform funeral rites for those who have most recently died at the hands of the shii.

After the service for those Nalori who died in the hospital, I checked to see what rites needed to be performed for Dolahn. According to the database, most Gallamites didn't practice any particular death rituals, but some belonged to a religion known as Ambrushroi, which requires that the body be burned within six hours of death. However, there's no evidence that Dolahn was Ambrushroi—and in any case, most non-Ambrushroi Gallamites don't care what's done to their bodies, and Razka told me that Dolahn had no family. So I ordered his body burned anyhow. Seemed the best thing to do.

It's like the Dominion War all over again—each day goes by with us all wondering who's going to die next.

No.

That's not going to happen.

I'm going to face this thing. I've assigned one of the engineers to work on the *Culloden*. As for me, I'm going to find the shii and either convince it to stop what it's doing—

—or stop it myself.

Letter from the workers on the subspace accelerator project to Commander Sonya Gomez, sixteenth day of Sendrak, twenty-third year of Togh

Commander Gomez:

By the time you receive this letter, we will be gone. We have faith in Starfleet's ability to rescue you. Nomis and Repooc were able to bypass the DNA encoding on the Bolian's ship, and we are taking it. We are willing to face the consequences of our actions. A choice between not working and dying is no choice at all.

We wish you the best of luck in your future endeavors, Commander. We apologize for placing the burden of being sañuul on you. That was our mistake, and we hope you can find it in your heart to forgive us, assuming humans have hearts like ours. We should have known that the curse of Sarindar would destroy us all.

Razka has said that he will remain behind,

and he will deliver this missive to you. Razka is a good man, and we are sure he will be helpful to you.

We are sorry that we were unable to finish the subspace accelerator, but the curse has shown us that it was not meant to be.

Regretfully,
Your former staff

Transcript of tricorder recording by Commander Sonya Gomez, outside SA project camp perimeter, planet Sarindar, Stardate 53290.1

GOMEZ: Please, wait! Don't attack! I'm not your enemy, and I'm not food.

SHII: Speak . . . you.

GOMEZ: Yes, I speak. I am sentient. I'm not an animal for you to kill for food.

SHII: Do . . . not . . . comprehend . . . "sentient." You . . . not . . . owner.

GOMEZ: No, I'm not one of the owners, but I'm very much like them.

SHII: You . . . not . . . owner. Await . . . owners.

GOMEZ: Your owners are gone.

SHII: Do . . . not . . . comprehend . . . "gone."

GOMEZ: They—they ceased to function. They died. You don't need to keep gathering food for them.

SHII: Function . . . to . . . gather . . . food . . . and . . . protect.

GOMEZ: I know that. But without the owners, that function no longer exists. You need a new function.

SHII: Do . . . not . . . comprehend . . . "new."

GOMEZ: It means that things have changed. You have to adapt to the situation.

SHII: Do . . . not . . . comprehend . . . "changed."

GOMEZ: Oh, great.

SHII: Do . . . not . . . comprehend . . . "adapt."

GOMEZ: You've been committing murder for no reason. We can't defend ourselves against you, and you have no need to attack us.

SHII: Do . . . not . . . comprehend . . . "murder." Am . . . fulfilling . . . function. Must . . . gather . . . food . . . await . . . return . . . owners.

GOMEZ: The owners are gone! They're dead! They've ceased to function!

SHII: Must . . . gather . . . food.

GOMEZ: Please, you must listen to me.

SHII: Do . . . not . . . comprehend . . . "dead."
You . . . not . . . owner. Your . . . instructions . . .
relevant . . . not. Must . . . gather . . . food.

GOMEZ: There's no need to gather food!
There's—dammit! [sonic rifle fire]

Personal log, Commander Sonya Gomez, planet Sarindar, Stardate 53290.3

The bastards took the *Culloden*.

I saw it taking off after I managed to get away from the shii. It attacked me after I tried to reason with it, but the rifle on full blast managed to at least force it to run away, though I didn't do any appreciable damage to it. For that matter, there's no sign of any other injury it's taken. Not surprising, given its chameleon circuitry—it can heal any "wound" by simply shape-changing over it.

Right after it ran off, I heard the screaming sound of impulse engines. My heart soared for a brief instant, as I thought it might be either the *Archimedes* or the *Franklin*, but I quickly realized that it wasn't a Starfleet impulse signature—and it was the sound of a ship taking off, not landing.

Then I looked up to see the *Culloden* taking off.

I ran back to the camp, only to find Razka alone. He showed me the note the workers had left for me. I asked Razka what the hell was going on.

"I should think the letter explains it all, Commander. They have left."

"So why are you still here?" I asked him.

He smiled. "My job is to assist you. You're still here, so I'm still here."

I stared at him. "What's the real reason?"

"Does there need to be another reason?"

"No, but I'm pretty sure there is one."

Razka sighed, and then he smiled at me. "All my life, I have prided myself on always doing the best job I could. I have always excelled at the tasks I have been given. Mind you, not all those tasks were especially challenging, but that wasn't the point."

He started to pace. "The other day, I was given another simple task: to help you track down the monster shii. When it attacked, I did nothing. I could not fire my weapon. I could not move. You were threatened, and I did not move. My comrades were wounded, and I did not move. Zilder was killed right in front of me, and *I did not move.*"

He looked up at me with a stricken look. I'd never seen him like this—he'd always been so easygoing and pleasant before.

"So I have stayed. Becaue it is my job to aid you, and I will not fail again."

I nodded and said, "All right, fine. It's just you and me, then. We can either wait until that thing comes and gets us, or we can stop it once and for all. It's not going to listen to reason."

"Why should it, Commander?"

I actually chuckled at that, which surprised me.

I hadn't thought I had any chuckles left in me. "You were right. I forgot the first rule of programming."

"Which is?" Razka asked.

"A machine is only as good as what's put into it—no more, no less. Garbage in, garbage out. Now, c'mon," I said, hefting my sonic rifle, "we've got to take out the garbage."

Razka and I went and used the remnants of the camp perimeter barrier and the remaining Nalori-issue sonic rifles to form a small barricade for the pair of us. We're within the confines of that barricade now, having just finished modifying my own sonic rifle. It now emits a pulse intended to immobilize the shii for several minutes. Of course, there's no way to test it until the shii attacks. . . .

We're waiting for midnight to come around. The next window in the pulsar/quasar interference will provide us with the best chance to stop it. I'm recording this log entry while we wait. We've both eaten some field rations, and we're as ready to go as we can be.

It's funny, I've been thinking back on all the life-or-death situations I've been in in my career. I mean, I spent the first three-and-a-half years of my career on the *Enterprise*, where we had life-or-death situations on what seemed to be a weekly basis, starting with the Borg. Then there was that one-year project on the *Oberth*, which was pretty sedate until all hell broke loose at the end, when the Romulans turned up out of nowhere.

Then there was the *Sentinel*. And the war.

I'm sick of people dying. I'm sick of losing people. Whether they're friends, comrades, subordinates—it doesn't matter.

It stops now.

I reached into one of the pouches on my uniform—where I'd normally keep my tricorder. I had put Zilder's copy of the *Se'rbeg* there—not entirely sure why. I'm not particularly religious. I remember what Kejahna joked when we tested the antimatter reactor: "Ho'nig helps those who help themselves." He mainly said it to tease Zilder, who didn't think that the reactor would be ready in time with only two antigrav units.

Now they're both dead. And I need to use their work to help stop the monster that is trying to destroy that work.

It's almost midnight. Time to get moving.

First officer's log, Commander Sonya Gomez,
planet Sarindar, Stardate 53290.6

At ten minutes prior to midnight, I came out from
behind the barricade, leaving Razka safe inside. I
had the feeling that the shii would attack us as soon
as it could. Its function is to collect heads for its
owners. It had targeted my particular head on three
occasions now without getting it. I don't know if it's
capable of grudge matches—in fact, I'm sure it
isn't—but I also suspect that it was programmed to
keep trying to fulfill its goals. That meant that it
would keep trying for me until it had my head.

That, at least, was my plan. It turned out to be
accurate. I waited near the concave dish that
formed the most prominent part of the SA. The
tricorder was able to detect its approach, and I
fired a shot from the sonic rifle near it to give it
pause. Then I ran toward the SA dish.

As soon as I got to the ladder that would lead
me up to the SA, I fired a shot with the rifle at the
ground behind me, then again at one of the crystal
bushes near the ladder. It wouldn't delay the shii

much, but I only needed to slow it down enough to make up the difference between its four legs and my two . . .

Excerpt from a letter from Razka on Sarindar to Marig on Nalor, sixteenth day of Sendrak, twenty-third year of Togh

. . . everything seemed fine until the barricade failed. I should have known that the curse of Sarindar wasn't finished with me just yet.

Luckily, Commander Gomez is no fool. She gave me her tricorder device. She had modified it so that it would emit a sonic pulse. The idea was that if the monster shii came for me, I should activate the pulse.

As soon as the barricade failed, I clutched the tricorder to myself for dear life. I looked at the tableau in front of me.

A fierce wind was blowing, as often happened at night. The crystalline trees and bushes made a mild tinkling noise that almost sounded musical. To the right was the massive concave dish that was the focus of so much of our labors. Commander Gomez was climbing the ladder to the dish. The monster shii was standing at the ladder's base. I somehow doubted it had ever encountered anything like this ladder before.

Then it turned to look at me. It ran for me. It happened again, Marig. I froze.

But this time, I was able to push the button. Though I could not raise or activate a

weapon, I was somehow able to make myself
activate the sonic pulse. And it worked. The
monster shii stopped dead in its tracks. Then
it went for me a second time. I pushed the
button again.

(In fact, Marig, it is truly not a button, but
a touch-sensitive control. But allow a frightened old man to wax poetic.)

Amazingly enough, it worked again. And a
third time. After that, the monster shii turned
around and ran back toward the ladder. I
looked up to see that Commander Gomez had
climbed up to the top of the dish . . .

First officer's log, supplemental

. . . as soon as I got to the edge of the dish, I
turned to see that the shii had turned its attention
to Razka. I braced my legs in the struts of the ladder, then fired a shot over the shii's head.

Since the shii was staying about three meters
away from Razka, yet facing him, I assumed that
the sonic pulse I built into the tricorder worked.
But I had no way to judge how long it would last,
and besides, I needed to get the shii up to the dish.
So I fired.

Sure enough, the shii turned around—probably
deciding that Razka's head wasn't worth all this
trouble anyhow—and ran back to the dish. It
loped over to the bottom of the ladder, then tried
to figure out how to climb up it.

I looked down and tried to figure out the same
thing. The shii had triangular "paws"—no individ-

ual claws or fingers or anything like that. Presumably the shii that the creature emulated had evolved that way as the most adequate way to navigate Sarindar's glassy surface. Unfortunately, it wasn't very useful for climbing up ladders with rounded rungs.

Of course, the whole point of the exercise was to lure the shii up the ladder to the SA dish. Something *else* I didn't think of. Latest in a series, collect 'em all.

Then the shii's paws changed shape, to something closer to a human hand. That made sense. It, and its smaller companion, had taken on the shape of a shii in order to blend in with the local fauna, and, being a machine, hadn't changed shape to anything else since then because it hadn't had reason to.

Now, though, it did. Armed with its newfound opposable thumbs, it clambered up the ladder. As soon as the shii was about three-quarters of the way up the ladder, I did some clambering of my own, onto the outer edge of the dish. The plan was to get the shii up on the edge also, then immobilize it.

It was a good plan. So, naturally, it went all to hell . . .

Excerpt from a letter from Razka on Sarindar to Marig on Nalor, sixteenth day of Sendrak, twenty-third year of Togh

. . . I watched as Commander Gomez stood on the dish's edge. The monster shii climbed the rest of the way up. She raised her weapon. The creature, however, moved faster than expected.

Actually, that is not true. The creature had been moving fast all along. It is simply so fast that it's difficult to comprehend just how fast it is. I suspect that Commander Gomez failed to anticipate this. One cannot blame her. This monster is very easy to underestimate.

The monster attacked her, knocking her weapon out of her hands. She lost her balance, and fell into the dish. The rifle, though, fell down the outside of the dish and plummeted to the ground.

This presented me with something of a dilemma, Marig. You see, Commander Gomez needed that rifle in order to stop the shii. Which meant that I needed to grab the rifle and get it to her. However, that meant getting much closer to the shii than I particularly wanted.

Besides, I knew that if I picked up the rifle, I would freeze again. I remembered Commander Gomez's words. She told me of the engineer's axiom that when garbage goes in, garbage comes out. I am like that. I hold a rifle, I freeze. It is the way of things.

But I promised Commander Gomez that I would continue to do my job. I had told her that that was why I stayed behind. Of course, that is not the real reason. The truth is that the other workers did not want me with them on the *Culloden*. They also did not want

Commander Gomez with them. While not all of them believed her to be bad luck, enough of them did. And enough of those also thought I fell into that category. That was why they waited to take off until they knew that she was away from the camp. However, I did not wish her to know that. Besides, what I told her was true. I wanted to redeem myself, to do my job. I owed her that much. I owed myself that much.

So I ran for the rifle. I picked it up. And I climbed the ladder, trying not to pay attention to the scream of pain I heard from the inner workings of the dish . . .

First officer's log, supplemental

. . . I tumbled into the inside of the dish, the duranium panels colliding with my body in a nastily bone-jarring manner. I managed to halt my descent, stopping myself at what appeared to be fifty meters down into the dish—or halfway to the center. It was about where the dish started to flatten out a bit and get less steep.

I quickly tried to get my bearings, attempting to stand up and keep my balance. The rifle was nowhere to be seen, which made my life a helluva lot more complicated. The shii was still at the perimeter of the dish. Since I was unarmed, and could barely keep my balance, I was at a distinct disadvantage.

Then it started running down the dish toward me, its "paws" having morphed back into shii form, since that was much more efficient for decapitating.

This worked in my favor, actually, as the claws—which could easily get a grip on the crystalline surface of Sarindar—couldn't grab hold of duranium. So, instead of loping gracefully down the inner surface of the dish, it slipped, slid, and tumbled down the dish, past me and toward the center.

I just needed to be able to press this advantage—unfortunately, no real opportunity to do so presented itself. Instead, I found myself facing this creature from fifty meters away, with it standing between me and my only legitimate means of escape—the center of the dish. There was a small hatch in the center that was my best bet for getting out of there—climbing up the edge of the dish wasn't going to be much of an option.

Then the creature somehow managed to get enough of a grip on the dish to take one giant leap toward me. Starfleet training kicked in, and I managed to roll with the impact as it landed on me—rolling upward at first, then tumbling back down toward the center as gravity took over from the force of impact. I took a kick at it, but before I could, it slashed at my cheek. I cried out in surprise as much as pain, then followed through on the kick.

The kick didn't do much to damage it—though it felt like it had done plenty to my foot—but it wound up being enough for the shii to lose its balance and start scrabbling around on the dish some more. Under other circumstances, I might have found it amusing, watching it try desperately to maintain some kind of grip, its arms flailing as each attempt failed.

I was standing in the middle of a concave dish at night on a crystal planet facing a creature out to kill me. I was armed with nothing more than a torn Starfleet uniform and a battered copy of someone else's religious text—and my brain, which I had always relied on in the past. However, it was failing me now. There had to be *some* way to keep the creature still long enough for me to get off the dish, but I was damned if I could think of it. I needed to get the rifle back . . .

Excerpt from a letter from Razka on Sarindar to Marig on Nalor, sixteenth day of Sendrak, twenty-third year of Togh

. . . with the rifle slung over my shoulder, I started to climb. I am grateful that my great list of weaknesses does not include a fear of heights. Climbing the ladder was not difficult. In fact, I had done it several times before, during the project. No, the fear that gripped me had solely to do with why I took the climb. But I continued to climb. And I tried not to think about the scream I had heard. I also was hearing odd scraping noises.

I got to the top of the dish and I saw that the monster was trying to attack Commander Gomez. For her part, Commander Gomez was trying to get away from it. She was bleeding from her face and her uniform was torn and ripped.

As soon as she saw me, she shouted at me to shoot the monster . . .

First officer's log, supplemental

. . . I don't think I've ever been as happy to see anyone as I was to see Razka at that moment. I screamed at him to shoot the shii. Once he did that, everything else would come into place.

He held up the rifle . . .

Excerpt from a letter from Razka on Sarindar to Marig on Nalor, sixteenth day of Sendrak, twenty-third year of Togh

. . . but once again I failed to shoot. I *was* programmed, it seemed. Nothing I could do could make me push the button. Not even the constant shouting of "Shoot it!" from Commander Gomez. Not even the monster finally being able to slash at both her face and her torso. I saw her strangely colored blood flowing from two wounds on her face now, as well as her side, and still she shouted, "Shoot it!" And still I could not pull the trigger.

Garbage in, garbage out.

I knew for sure that I was not someone who could fire a weapon. I was, however, still the aide to the head of the project. So I would do what I'd been doing. I would help her.

Commander Gomez was about seventy meters down the dish and about ten meters to my left. I could not trust my ability to throw the rifle to her. I could, however, trust gravity. I laid the rifle down on the surface of the dish and let it slide toward the center . . .

First officer's log, supplemental

. . . the pain in my side was the worst I'd felt since that *mugato* sliced me open on Neural five years ago, but I managed to crawl the twelve meters to where the rifle was going to wind up. Razka wasn't a fighter, and I respected that—I just wished he had realized it *before* that thing sliced me open.

Speaking of which, it was still trying to maintain its grip on the dish, and was hoping to use me as an anchor. It dug one claw into my boot heel as I was crawling over toward the rifle. I managed to yank my foot out of the boot, which sent the thing sprawling back down toward the center, once again trying to get some kind of footing.

The salty taste of my own blood from the two cuts on my cheeks, pain slicing through my entire torso like a phaser set on burn, I grabbed on the sonic rifle, rolled painfully onto my back, and saw the shii getting ready to pounce on me again.

It was almost funny—as it leapt through the air, I saw that my boot was still wedged in its claw.

I fired the rifle.

The shii was immobilized.

Unfortunately, its momentum was still carrying it through the air, and it landed right on top of me.

As bad as the pain in my side was before, it was a thousand times worse now. I cried out in agony.

But the good news was that the shii was just a dead weight on top of me.

A very heavy weight. I managed to push the thing off me—and it still didn't move—and tapped my combadge. "Computer, time."

The grating, atonal voice of the Nalori computer said, "The time is 0014 hours."

I had cut it close—the quasar/pulsar window would close any minute. If I didn't do this now, I wouldn't be able to for fourteen hours. "Computer, activate ACB."

I now had two minutes to get to the center of the dish before the annular confinement beam reached full power. . . .

Excerpt from a letter from Razka on Sarindar to Marig on Nalor, sixteenth day of Sendrak, twenty-third year of Togh

. . . I had thought that everything was fine. The monster was stopped as planned. Commander Gomez was activating the beam that would stop it. And now she was moving toward the center. I, too, moved toward escape. Her route would take her to the underside of the dish. Ironically, the door she was using was the same one that I had guarded at the secondary hospital. My own route was simply back the way I came.

Then I saw that the monster had started to move. And Commander Gomez hadn't reached the hatch yet. I reached for the tricorder, hoping I might be able to stop it. Unfortunately, I fumbled with the device and dropped it. It fell dozens of meters to the ground. So, instead, I called the commander's name . . .

First officer's log, supplemental

. . . and it was a good thing he did, because I was able to whirl around and fire one last time at the creature. Unfortunately, doing so seemed to rip open my wound, and I cried out.

Then I heard the steady thrum that indicated the ACB was about to come on-line. If I stayed where I was, I would be reduced to my component atoms inside about half a second.

I dove for the hatch . . .

Excerpt from a letter from Razka on Sarindar to Marig on Nalor, sixteenth day of Sendrak, twenty-third year of Togh

. . . and then I started climbing madly down the ladder. I had no idea if Commander Gomez had heard me or not. My main concern at that point was my own survival. That, and the death of the monster shii.

I heard the sound of the mighty engine that powered the dish. Forces that were intended to displace atmosphere and create a vacuum sliced through the air. The noise was deafening. The light was blinding. When we had first tested the beam, I had been standing at a safe distance. Now I was at anything but. I don't think that my ears will ever cease ringing. Nor do I believe that the spots will ever disappear from in front of my eyes.

But I have to say it was a spectacular view. The nearby crystalline trees reflected the shimmering beam, which shot into the night with such intensity that I thought it would bisect the entire galaxy.

A lifetime later, the beam finally ceased. There was no sign of either Commander Gomez or the monster shii.

Second officer's log, Lt. Commander Kieran Duffy, Shuttlecraft *Archimedes*, Stardate 53291.0

I'm on final approach to the planet Sarindar. According to the Nalori Republic representative that Captain Gold talked to when the *da Vinci* entered Nalori space two hours ago, all contact with Sarindar was lost several days ago. They had come across the transport ship, the *Culloden*, that had been assigned to the project. The Nalori had assumed that everyone else on the planet had been killed, but the testimony of the workers on the *Culloden*, combined with sensor readings the *da Vinci* took, show that the interference around the planet has gotten too heavy for even com signals to get through.

I just hope that Commander Gomez is okay.

Personal log, Lt. Commander Kieran Duffy, Shuttlecraft
Archimedes, Stardate 53291.1

I landed on Sarindar to find the remnants of a tent
system, some broken-down machinery, a very
large concave dish—

—and Commander Gomez and a Nalori getting
very drunk on Saurian brandy.

As soon as she saw me, the commander ran
toward me and leapt into my arms. Before she did,
I noticed that her uniform was torn in dozens of
places and looked (and smelled) like it hadn't been
laundered in weeks, she had two nasty cuts on her
face, and she was clutching her right side as she
ran.

Then she kissed me.

I would say that the commander is alive and
well and doing just fine.

Personal log, Commander Sonya Gomez,
U.S.S. da Vinci, Stardate 53291.5

I had been quite convinced that Razka and I were
going to get completely plastered long before anyone rescued us. But I didn't care. I was so giddy
from actually defeating the shii and knowing that
I was going to live, that the fact that we would
probably starve to death if someone didn't show
up soon wasn't something either of us wanted to
think about.

Then I saw the *Archimedes* come swooping
down out of the atmosphere. It was the most glorious sight I'd ever seen. (Razka said it was the
second-most glorious, as he gave first prize to the
ACB wiping out the shii. Sadly, I didn't get to see
that, as I was under the hatch at the time.)

Part of it was the brandy, part of it was eupho-
ria—and part of it was sheer stupidity, given my
torso wound—but a big part of why I ran into
Kieran's arms was simply because I didn't want to
ever let go of him.

I learned a lot on this mission, and found out a

lot of things about myself that I didn't like. Primary among them was that life is too damn short to let the good things get away.

What Kieran and I had on the *Enterprise* was a good thing. There are probably dozens of good reasons why we shouldn't start up our relationship again, but right now, I can't think of a single one of them.

Now we're back on the *da Vinci*. I've been in touch with Senator Moyya, and he actually apologized to me. Apparently he wasn't showing the recordings I sent along to the rest of the senate because he believed they were fakes. One of his fellow senators insisted that he look at the full communiqués from Sarindar, and suddenly the senate thought that maybe their initial reaction was a bit on the harsh side.

Unfortunately, by the time the senate had realized their mistake, all communication with Sarindar had been lost, thanks to worse interference than usual from the quasar/pulsar combination. That's also why the *da Vinci*'s com signal was so patchy. They had, in fact, dropped their mission to Trivas like a hot potato and come to rescue me.

The current plan is to assign new workers to the camp, with Razka now in charge, at my recommendation. He will follow the work schedule I laid out, and—without the two shii to terrorize the workers—the SA should finally be finished. The senate has also promised that Starfleet will be allowed to aid the team that studies and harvests the chimerium—and, best of all, they're willing to talk about allowing Starfleet safe passage through to Sector 969. Which means that the mission Captain Scott gave me back on Earth has actually been fulfilled.

This should be good news. I just wish it hadn't come at the expense of so many lives.

I was seriously tempted not to have Dr. Lense get rid of the two scars I got. Razka said that they made me look like a Nalori who'd gotten his coming-of-age scars, and, in a sense, he was right. But I decided to get rid of them anyhow. Keeping scars is an affectation, suffered mostly by people with more mental difficulties than I'm willing to put on display. I did it after Captain Gold debriefed me and I had talked to Senator Moyya.

Now I'm in my quarters, having been instructed by both Dr. Lense and Captain Gold to relax. But I can't sleep. I keep thinking about Zilder and Kejahna and J'Roh, and the score of others who died under my command.

I guess the only way I can make their deaths have any meaning to me at all is to live.

And I intend to do just that.

"Gomez to Duffy. Please report to my quarters."

End log entry.

Star Trek®: Starfleet Corps of Engineers

MINIPEDIA

by Keith R.A. DeCandido

This "minipedia" covers information from the first eight installments of *Star Trek: S.C.E.* (in other words, the stories reprinted in *Have Tech, Will Travel* and *Miracle Workers*). It follows the same format as *The Star Trek Encyclopedia: A Reference Guide to the Future* (updated and expanded edition) by Michael Okuda & Denise Okuda (1999). Some entries or parts of entries are taken or adapted from the *Encyclopedia*, for which the author humbly thanks the Okudas.

In addition to the Okudas, the author would like to thank GraceAnne A. DeCandido, Christie Golden, John J. Ordover, Terri Osborne, and Marco Palmieri for their assistance in compiling this reference.

Most references in the minipedia are to the books in the *S.C.E.* series, but there are also references to *Star Trek* television episodes, movies, novels, and comic books. Episode designations are tagged with an abbreviation referring to series:

TOS=*Star Trek*, the original series; TAS=*Star Trek*, the animated series; TNG=*Star Trek: The Next Generation*; DS9=*Star Trek: Deep Space Nine*; VOY=*Star Trek: Voyager*.

Any errors, corrections, or comments should be sent to *S.C.E.* Minipedia, Pocket Books, 1230 Avenue of the Americas, New York, NY 10020, or e-mailed to SCE@albeshiloh.com.

#

110/Soloman. Noncommissioned Starfleet engineer assigned to the *U.S.S. da Vinci* as a computer specialist. One half of a bonded **Bynar pair** with **111** (*The Belly of the Beast*). The two were assigned as civilian observers and computer experts to the **Starfleet Corps of Engineers** team on the *da Vinci* (*Fatal Error*). During the salvage of the ship known as **"the** *Beast*,**"** the **insectoid aliens** that had taken over the ship attacked the salvage team from the *da Vinci* and killed 111 in front of 110 (*The Belly of the Beast*). The loss devastated 110. Bynar tradition holds that if one of a pairing is killed, the other should return to **Bynaus** for rebonding, but 110 was unwilling to soil 111's memory by rebonding. He continued to go on missions for the S.C.E., and wound up being vital to a mission to remove a computer virus from the world-controlling computer **Ganitriul** (*Fatal Error*). He also was on the away team that investigated the **Omearan Starsearcher** called **Friend.**

When the *da Vinci* transported **Jaldark Keniria's** corpse off of Friend's bridge, 110 was trying to link with Friend's computer, and the ship's outrage at being separated from its **pilot** put him into a coma. However, that formed a link between him and Friend, and 110 was able to communicate the truth about Jaldark's death to Friend. Friend invited 110 to become his new pilot, which he found tempting but ultimately refused, deciding to remain on his own. He was no longer permitted to have a numerical designation at that point, so **Captain David Gold** nicknamed him "Soloman." Soloman joined Starfleet as a noncommissioned engineer and retained his position as the computer expert on the *da Vinci* (*Hard Crash*). When the *da Vinci* first encountered the **Androssi** on **Maeglin,** 110 and 111 were able to interface with Androssi computers, but with much difficulty. When the *da Vinci* came up against the Androssi on **Empok Nor,** Soloman found that he was unable to repeat the process, as the Androssi had upgraded their systems (*Cold Fusion*). Soloman, like all Bynars, has a belt unit that allows him to communicate directly with computer systems, so he is not required to use the voice interface, which he views as clumsy. Soloman has a computer efficiency rating of ten; the next highest person in Starfleet has an eight (*Fatal Error*). *110 is the equivalent of the number six in binary code; the name was chosen as a sort of in-joke for fans of* The Prisoner, *where the title character was Number Six, who did not fit in with the society into which he had been placed.*

111. Civilian computer specialist assigned to the **U.S.S. da Vinci** as a computer specialist. One half of a bonded **Bynar pair** with **110** (*The Belly of the Beast*). The two were assigned as civilian observers and computer experts to the **S.C.E.** team on the *da Vinci* (*Fatal Error*). When the *da Vinci* encountered the **Androssi** on **Maeglin**, 110 and 111 were able to interface with Androssi computers, but with much difficulty (*Cold Fusion*). During the salvage of the ship known as **"the Beast,"** the **insectoid aliens** that had taken over the ship attacked the salvage team from the *da Vinci* and killed 111 (*The Belly of the Beast*). 111 had a computer efficiency rating of ten; the next highest person in Starfleet has an eight (*Fatal Error*).

A

ACB. See **annular confinement beam.**

Abramowitz, Carol. Noncommissioned Starfleet personnel assigned to the **U.S.S. da Vinci** as a cultural specialist (*The Belly of the Beast*). Abramowitz theorized that the **Eerlik** had a cultural bias against computer security because all their computer systems are linked through **Ganitriul.** Because of that, their cryptography is nonexistent, and **Bart Faulwell** and **Fabian Stevens** were able to hack into the systems of the **Senbolma,** a ship that was free of Ganitriul's influence (*Fatal Error*). Abramowitz served as the liaison between the *da Vinci* crew and the **Tholians** during the S.C.E.'s salvage of the *U.S.S. Defiant* (*Interphase* Book 1). She also clandestinely monitored the Tholians' coded communiqués, and after the Tholians fired on the *da Vinci*, she enlisted Faulwell's aid in translating those coded messages (*Interphase* Book 2). Abramowitz is fond of **Sinnravian *drad* music**, particularly the recordings of **Blee Luu**. Her roommate, **P8 Blue**, objected to her constant playing of Luu's latest recording, and was only assuaged when **Lt. Commander Kieran Duffy**, acting as temporary first officer, changed their duty shifts so they wouldn't be in their quarters at the same time. As a way of making peace, Abramowitz traded her copy of Luu's music to **Lieutenant Nog** of **Deep Space 9** for an as-yet unspecified item (*Cold Fusion*).

Ambrushroi. Religion of some members of the **Gallamite** race. Followers of Ambrushroi who die are to have their bodies burned within six hours of death (*Invincible* Book 2).

Amuk. Worker assigned to the **subspace accelerator** project on **Sarindar**. Amuk was killed by the second **monster shii** when he, **Entorr**, and **Kugot** failed to properly spring a trap for it (*Invincible* Book 2).

Androssi. Civilization about which very little is known. They first appeared in the Alpha Quadrant in the Demilitarized Zone (DMZ) between Cardassian and Federation space, offering to give technological aid to the Maquis rebels in the DMZ. They have made several appearances since the **Dominion War** ended, offering to provide technological aid, but often at a high price. The Androssi have a skin tone that ranges from yellow to brown to sepia, with similarly colored hair. Androssi society has a very hierarchical structure. The **Elite** appear to be the ruling class, and they finance individual ships, with a mandate to acquire technology for their Elite sponsors. Members of the **officer class** run the ships, and members of the **worker class** do most of the work on those ships. Among the officer and worker classes, the males generally have untrimmed beards, and both genders wear their hair long and tied back. Members of the officer and worker classes generally are not particularly emotional, and focus on their work. Regard for life appears to be fairly low in Androssi society, at least when it comes to the worker class and alien life. Androssi generally communicate with each other over distances through devices in their ears. They never use visual communication. Androssi ships are rectangular in shape, and tend toward the functional rather than the aesthetic (*Cold Fusion*). *The name Androssi is a play on Andreassi, which is author Keith R.A. DeCandido's mother's side of the family, and also what the second of his middle initials stands for.*

Androssi Protocol 1. Security procedure initiated by **Lt. Commander Domenica Corsi** of the *U.S.S. da Vinci*. During the *da Vinci's* first encounter with the **Androssi** on **Maeglin**, they discovered that they could disrupt their equipment with a phaser shot at Level 2, or light stun. During their second encounter at **Empok Nor**, that protocol failed to stop an **Androssi security device**, forcing Corsi to call for **Androssi Protocol 2** (*Cold Fusion*).

Androssi Protocol 2. Security procedure initiated by **Lt. Commander Domenica Corsi** of the *U.S.S. da Vinci*. This is a fallback in case **Androssi Protocol 1** fails. It entails setting phasers on random settings and frequencies until one is found that can disrupt **Androssi** technology (*Cold Fusion*).

Androssi security device. A circular device, known among the **Androssi** as a **panshar**, that, like much Androssi technology, employs **dimensional shifts**. When activated, the device fires electrical bursts at opponents that cause damage to the central nervous system. Such damage is greater to Bolians than to humans. The device can be disrupted by phasers on a particular setting (*Cold Fusion*).

Anilegna. Worker assigned to the **subspace accelerator** project on **Sarindar**. Anilegna was killed by the second **monster shii** (*Invincible* Book 2).

annular confinement beam. A cylindrical force field used in transporters to ensure that a person being transported remains within the beam ("Power Play" [TNG]). A larger-scale version of the ACB was used on the **subspace accelerator** on **Sarindar**. This ACB was designed to clear a path of vacuum through the atmosphere. The power needs of the ACB are such that increases in size mean that its power output is increased logarithmically proportional to that size. The original design of the Sarindar ACB only increased the power exponentially, a potentially devastating error caught by **Commander Sonya Gomez** (*Invincible* Book 1). Gomez used the ACB to destroy the second **monster shii** (*Invincible* Book 2).

anprat. A delicacy on the **Androssi** homeworld that **Overseer Biron** is particularly fond of (*Cold Fusion*).

anril torpedo. Type of weapon that is capable of completely disrupting deflector shields, making it impossible to reconstitute immediately. **Overseer Biron's Androssi** ship was equipped with two anril torpedoes, one of which was used against the *U.S.S. da Vinci* at **Empok Nor** (*Cold Fusion*).

Ansed. The **First Speaker** of **Eerlik**. The head of Eerlik's government, Ansed had to guide her people when **Ganitriul**, the computer that ran all functions on Eerlik, was sabotaged by **Pevvni Purists**. Ansed found the need to walk places, to open doors manually, and to be subject to uncontrolled weather patterns to be quite a hardship. Ansed was born on **Maryllo Island**. She was killed by **Undlar,** the leader of the Purists (*Fatal Error*).

Archimedes, **Shuttlecraft.** Shuttlecraft assigned to the *U.S.S. da Vinci* (*Fatal Error*). *Named after the famed Greek mathematician.*

atonal minimalist. Subgenre of **Sinnravian** *drad* music. **Blee Luu** is one of its purveyors (*Cold Fusion*).

B

Barbanti. Chief engineer of the *U.S.S. Sugihara.* Lieutenant Barbanti thought that **Lieutenant Nog**'s plan to tow **Empok Nor** with nine ships was "categorically insane," and refused to accept any responsibility for it if **Captain Janna Demitrijian** went along with it (*Cold Fusion*).

Barnak, Jil. Chief engineer of the *U.S.S. da Vinci.* Lieutenant Barnak is an Atrean (*The Belly of the Beast*). When the **Androssi security device** was discovered to interfere with all the *da Vinci* crew's combadges, Barnak had new ones replicated for the entire crew, which worked on different frequencies and would be less affected by the interference (*Cold Fusion*).

Bashir, Julian. Chief medical officer of Station **Deep Space 9**. Bashir was second in his Starfleet Medical Academy class, behind **Dr. Elizabeth Lense** ("Explorers" [DS9]).

"Beast, the." Nickname given by the crew of the *U.S.S. da Vinci* to a large, round ship. The ship had two rings circling the outer hull—one across its equator, the other across its poles—that served as observation ports and were made of a material that is transparent from the inside. The *Beast* travelled via a **black-hole propulsion drive**. Believed to be a cruise ship originally, run by a humanoid race, it was taken over by **insectoid aliens** who were breeding in the engine core. They attacked the colony at **Blossom IV**, and were defeated by the *U.S.S. Enterprise* and examined by the *da Vinci*. More than a thousand times the size of a *Sovereign*-class ship, and with a hull resistant to sensor scans, the ship had hundreds of redundant environmental systems, energy collectors, and over a hundred airlocks. Though the original twelve aliens that had taken over the ship were killed in the fight with the *Enterprise*, their offspring attacked the **Starfleet Corps of Engineers** team from the *da Vinci* that examined the ship afterward, and killed one of them, **111**. The S.C.E. team was forced to destroy the vessel (*The Belly of the Beast*). The **Androssi** salvaged a ship similar to the *Beast* and utilized some of its technology to modify the station **Empok Nor** as part of an attempt to convert the station into a mobile weapons platform (*Cold Fusion*).

Biral. Speaker of **Eerlik**. After the death of **First Speaker Ansed**, Biral took her place as the head of Eerlik's government (*Fatal Error*).

Biron. An **overseer** for the **Androssi**. Like all members of the Androssi **officer class**, Biron's mandate is to acquire technology for his ship's **Elite** sponsor. His method of doing so is generally to exploit other races by fixing—or pretending to fix—their technological problems in exchange for new technology. Biron first encountered the *U.S.S. da Vinci* on the planet **Maeglin**. Although details are not known, Biron came away poorly from that encounter. He ordered one of his ship's **Androssi security devices** to be calibrated so that it would interfere with the specific combadges of the *da Vinci* crew if they encountered each other again. He next encountered the *da Vinci* at **Empok Nor,** where he was converting the abandoned station into a mobile weapons platform for an unnamed client, who had promised to provide holo-emitters for Biron's Elite sponsor in return. Unfortunately, he had to cannibalize some of the weapons from his own ship in order to upgrade the station to the client's specifications, which left his ship more vulnerable to an attack. The *da Vinci* succeeded in driving him off, though he was able to use a **dimensional shift** to retrieve all the upgraded components (*Cold Fusion*).

black-hole propulsion drive. Propulsion system that utilizes dozens of tiny black holes that are dropped into subspace and then returned to normal space a slight distance away, shoving the containment and thus the ship. The ship nicknamed **"the Beast"** used such a drive (*The Belly of the Beast*).

Blair, Thomas. Commanding officer of the *U.S.S. Defiant*. After investigating an attack on a Klingon colony at **Traelus II** in 2268, Captain Blair took the *Defiant* to Federation space, along with the **web generator** that was the only evidence of the **Tholian** attack on the colony. While being pursued by the Tholians, the *Defiant* fell into **interphase** and became trapped, with the crew suffering debilitating neurophysiological effects. Blair was killed by one of his crew while recording a log entry (*Interphase* Book 1).

Blossom IV. Federation colony. The farming colony was attacked by the ship known as **"the Beast."** The enemy vessel did significant damage to the colony, killing a thousand and injuring a thousand more, before it was engaged and defeated by the *U.S.S. Enterprise* (*The Belly of the Beast*).

Borg. An immensely powerful civilization of enhanced humanoids. Starfleet's first contact with the Borg was in 2365, while **Sonya Gomez** served on the *U.S.S. Enterprise* as an ensign. ("Q Who" [TNG]) In 2376, the crew of the *U.S.S. da Vinci* mistook the **Omearan pilot** named **Jaldark Keniria** for a Borg and her **Starsearcher** ship **Friend** for a Borg ship (*Hard Crash*).

Brioni Port. Spaceport on planet **Eerlik** (*Fatal Error*).

Bynar pair. Term given to two members of the **Bynar** race who are bonded. Bynar pairs do everything in tandem, including finishing each other's sentences ("11001001" [TNG]).

Bynars. Humanoid civilization from the planet **Bynaus**. The Bynars are heavily integrated with a sophisticated planetary computer network. They mostly live in bonded pairings, and have numerical binary designations for names ("11001001" [TNG]). Bynars are also able to interface directly with most computer systems (*The Belly of the Beast*). Bynars only require a few hours of downtime per day, and their skin is able to conduct electrical impulses of up to at least two hundred kilojoules. Bynars are less sensitive to bright lights than humans, nor are they as impaired as humans by certain toxic gases (*Fatal Error*). Bynars are generally bonded with another at birth, and **Bynar pairs** remain together, linked very closely ("11001001" [TNG]). Traditionally, when one member of a bonded pairing dies, the surviving member returns to Bynaus to be rebonded with another. Those that do not are removed from the central computer net and forced to relinquish their numerical designation (*Fatal Error*). Bynar brains are also better suited than humans to cybernetic links (*Hard Crash*).

Bynaus. Planet located in the Beta Magellan system, home to the **Bynars** ("11001001" [TNG]). Bynaus has a super-computer that is virtually unique in the galaxy in terms of sheer size, though the **Eerlik** computer, **Ganitriul,** is comparable (*Fatal Error*).

C

Caargenne. Worker assigned to the **subspace accelerator** project on **Sarindar**. Caargenne was killed by the second **monster shii** (*Invincible* Book 1).

Cabbi. Race that is part of the **Nalori Republic**. They have flippers (*Invincible* Book 1).

Calwei. Worker assigned to the **subspace accelerator** project on **Sarindar**. Calwei was a **Cabbi** (*Invincible* Book 1).

chameleon circuit. Device that allows a mechanism to change its outer form. Scientists at the Daystrom Institute attempted to put such circuitry to use, but the power demands to let something with an unstable molecular structure perform stable mechanical functions were in excess of what was practical. **The owners** were able to solve that problem, and constructed two servants with such circuitry. It took on the form of **shii** (*Invincible* Book 2). *The fact that this has the same name as the malfunctioning device on the TARDIS in the long-running British TV series* Doctor Who *is, of course, a complete coincidence. Really.*

chimerium. Dense mineral, a composite of magnesite and kelbonite. High concentrations of chimerium interfere with transporters and sensors. By far the largest concentration of chimerium found so far is on the planet **Sarindar** in the **Nalori Republic**. Its very nature makes it difficult to mine. The Nalori ordered the construction of a **subspace accelerator** to send the chimerium to a refinery in orbit (*Invincible* Book 1). **Commander Sonya Gomez** discovered a way to get at least minimal tricorder readings on Sarindar, despite the interference from the chimerium (*Invincible* Book 2).

Claris. Engine Master on the **Androssi** ship commanded by **Overseer Biron** (*Cold Fusion*).

Conjoined. Term used to refer to **Omearans** linking with **Starsearcher** vessels (*Hard Crash*).

Conlon, Nancy. Engineering officer assigned to the *U.S.S. da Vinci*. Conlon is an ensign (*Interphase* Book 2).

Cook, Shuttlecraft. Shuttlecraft assigned to the *U.S.S. Enterprise*. **Lt. Commander Geordi La Forge** and **Lieutenant Christine Vale** used the *Cook* to rendezvous with the *U.S.S. da Vinci* in order to investigate the ship known as **"the Beast."** When the mission was complete, Vale took the *Cook* back to the *Enterprise*, leaving La Forge to remain temporarily on the *da Vinci* (*The Belly of the Beast*).

Copper, John. Medical technician assigned to the *U.S.S. da Vinci* (*Interphase* Book 1).

Corsi, Domenica. Security chief of the *U.S.S. da Vinci*. Lt. Commander Corsi is a stickler for security details and has a fierce temper (*The Belly of the Beast*). She is referred to behind her back as

"Core-Breach" (*Fatal Error*). She is responsible for *U.S.S. Enterprise* security chief **Lieutenant Christine Vale** joining Starfleet, according to Vale, though details are unknown (*The Belly of the Beast*). Corsi took the conn when **Ensign Songmin Wong** was injured during a conflict with the **Tholians** while the *da Vinci* was attempting to salvage the *U.S.S. Defiant* from **interphase** (*Interphase* Book 1). Corsi had a surprising one-night liaison with **Fabian Stevens** on the *da Vinci*, which happened in part due to the anniversary of an incident with someone named **Dar**, though details are unknown. Though she insisted that it was a one-time thing, she continued to show subconscious interest in Stevens. Despite her attempts at secrecy, both **Bart Faulwell** and **Dr. Elizabeth Lense** (his and her roommates, respectively) learned of the brief liaison (*Cold Fusion*).

Crusher, Beverly. Chief medical officer of the *U.S.S. Enterprise.* Crusher had to deal with numerous casualties inflicted on the crew of the *Enterprise* by the ship dubbed **"the Beast,"** though, mercifully, no one on the ship was killed (*The Belly of the Beast*).

Culloden. Ship owned and operated by **Zilder,** a Bolian, and attached to the **subspace accelerator** project on the planet **Sarindar** in the **Nalori Republic**. The ship was used to bring supplies to and from the planet (*Invincible* Book 1). The ship was encoded to Zilder's DNA, and after he was killed by the **monster shii,** the rest of the SA team was initially unable to gain access to the vessel, though two engineers, **Nomis** and **Repooc**, were able to do so eventually, and most of the remaining workers escaped in the ship. Zilder left the ship to the Nalori Republic in his will (*Invincible* Book 2). *The* Culloden *was named after the famous Battle of Culloden of 1745, in which the Jacobite rebels under Bonnie Prince Charlie were defeated.*

D

da Vinci, U.S.S. Federation starship, *Saber-*class, Starfleet registry number NCC-81623. The *da Vinci* was assigned to the **Starfleet Corps of Engineers** under the command of **Captain David Gold** (*The Belly of the Beast*). The ship has a crew complement of forty-two (*Interphase* Book 1), has limited crew quarters, and no guest quarters (*The Belly of the Beast*). The *da Vinci* has two shuttle-craft, the *Franklin* and the *Archimedes* (*Fatal Error*). *The* da Vinci *was named after famous Renaissance artist/scientist Leonardo da Vinci.*

Dakota's Disease. Name given to a minor respiratory ailment discovered by a doctor named Dakota. It is relatively easy to fake the symptoms of Dakota's Disease. A group of workers on the **subspace accelerator** team on **Sarindar** pretended to have Dakota's Disease by way of a "sick-out" protest against having their duty assignments changed (*Invincible* Book 1).

Danilova, Raisa. Assistant chief engineer on the *U.S.S. Enterprise*. Danilova gained a reputation as the slowest person in the *Enterprise* engine room, but during the **Dominion War** she blossomed, turning into one of the most reliable and fastest engineers, making lieutenant during the war. **Lt. Commander Geordi La Forge** made her assistant chief engineer after the war's end (*Fatal Error*).

Data. Second officer of the *U.S.S. Enterprise* (*The Belly of the Beast*).

Deep Space 9. Space station formerly known as Terok Nor, currently under joint Federation and Bajoran administration. DS9 was attacked by renegade Jem'Hadar in 2376 (*Star Trek: Deep Space Nine: Avatar* Book 1), and subsequent events forced station commander **Colonel Kira Nerys** to eject the station's fusion core (*Star Trek: Deep Space Nine: Avatar* Book 2). Chief of operations **Lieutenant Nog** travelled to DS9's sister station, **Empok Nor,** to retrieve its fusion core, and Kira diverted the *U.S.S. da Vinci*—which was originally assigned to aid in station repairs—to assist him in this endeavor (*Cold Fusion*).

Defiant, U.S.S. Federation starship, *Constitution*-class, Starfleet registry number NCC-1764 ("The Tholian Web" [TOS]). The *Defiant* was under the command of **Captain Thomas Blair** (*Interphase* Book 1). In 2268, the ship investigated an attack that wiped out a Klingon colony on **Traelus II** and found a device that was later revealed to be a **web generator** built by the **Tholians**. While on the run from Tholian pursuit, trying to bring the web generator to Starfleet Command, the *Defiant* fell into a **spatial interphase** (*Interphase* Book 2). This interphase had an adverse effect on humanoid neurophysiology, and caused mass insanity among the crew prior to the disappearance of the ship. The *U.S.S. Enterprise* attempted to rescue the ship, but was attacked by Tholians and unable to complete the salvage before the ship was drawn completely into interphase ("The Tholian Web" [TOS]). The *Defiant* reappeared in Tholian space in 2376 and was detected by a Tholian ship commanded by **Nostrene**. The *U.S.S. da Vinci* was sent to attempt to salvage the ship. When the web generator was discovered by the *da Vinci*'s **Starfleet Corps of Engineers** team, Nostrene was ordered by the Tholian **High Magistrates** to destroy the evidence. The attack pushed the ship deeper into interphase (*Interphase* Book 1). The S.C.E. team was able to nudge the ship out of interphase with a two-second warp pulse (*Interphase* Book 2).

Defiant*, U.S.S.** Federation starship, *Defiant*-class, Starfleet registry number NX-74205. The prototype for its class, the *Defiant* was originally designed to combat the **Borg**, and was later assigned to Station **Deep Space 9** ("The Search Part 1" [DS9]). When **Fabian Stevens** was assigned to DS9, he primarily served as an engineer on the *Defiant* ("Starship Down" [DS9]). Because of that, Stevens was especially interested in the earlier ship called the *Defiant* that the **U.S.S. *da Vinci was sent to salvage (*Interphase* Book 1). The *Defiant* was destroyed during the **Dominion War** ("The Changing Face of Evil" [DS9]) and replaced with the *Sao Paolo*, which was rechristened after being assigned to DS9 ("The Dogs of War" [DS9]). When the *Defiant* and the *U.S.S. Aldebaran* were attacked by renegade Jem'Hadar, the entire Alpha Quadrant was put on yellow alert (*Star Trek: Deep Space Nine: Avatar* Book 1), which disturbed **Lt. Commander Kieran Duffy** (*Invincible* Book 1).

Demitrijian, Janna. Commanding officer of the *U.S.S. Sugihara.* Captain Demitrijian's son is dating a **Sinnravian.** She was willing to aid in the towing of **Empok Nor** from the **Trivas system** to **Deep Space 9**—against the better judgment of her chief engineer **Lieutenant Barbanti**—if **Lieutenant Nog** obtained an original recording of **Blee Luu**'s most recent recording for her son's girlfriend (*Cold Fusion*).

dimensional shifts. Technological aid used by the **Androssi.** They are able to shunt items into an alternate dimension, which can serve to disguise technology that is actually present or to dispose of it or store it for later retrieval (*Cold Fusion*).

Dlyax. Scientist serving on experimental **Tholian** vessel under the command of **Nostrene** (*Interphase* Book 1).

Dolahn. Doctor assigned to the **subspace accelerator** project on **Sarindar.** A **Gallamite**, Dolahn was an expert in **silicon-based life,** hence his being assigned to the project by the **Nalori Republic.** According to rumor, he took the job with the Nalori because no other hospital would take him. Dolahn wore a hat so that the workers would not see his transparent cranium. His hospital was primitive by twenty-fourth-century standards, and included among its equipment an X-ray machine (*Invincible* Book 1). Dolahn discovered that the **monster shii** weren't true natives of the planet, but were made to look like **shii.** He was killed by the second monster shii when it attacked the secondary hospital (*Invincible* Book 2).

Dominion War. Extended conflict between the Dominion and many of the major powers of the Alpha Quadrant. Primary combatants were the United Federation of Planets, the Klingon Empire, and the Romulan Empire against the Dominion, the Cardassian Union, and the Breen. **Sonya Gomez** served on the *U.S.S. Sentinel* during the war, and received a commendation for modulating the ship's warp field so that the Breen thought the ship to be a Cardassian freighter (*The Belly of the Beast*). She also modified an away team's phasers so that they would function in a Breen **scattering field** (*Fatal Error*). **Bart Faulwell** served as a cryptographer during the war (*Interphase* Book 2). **Elizabeth Lense** served on the *U.S.S. Lexington* as chief medical officer, where she treated large numbers of wounded, leading to her requesting a transfer to the **Starfleet Corps of Engineers** after the war (*Hard Crash*). **Salek** served on the *U.S.S. da Vinci* as first officer and head of the S.C.E. team during the war until his death (*The Belly of the Beast*). The planet **Eerlik** was able to stay out of the war (*Fatal Error*). The **Tholians** signed a nonaggression pact with the Dominion in 2373, keeping them out of the war as well ("Call to Arms" [DS9]). Tholian captain **Nostrene** felt this was wise, as he thought the Tholians would fare poorly against the Jem'Hadar (*Interphase* Book 1). The war ended in 2375 ("What You Leave Behind" [DS9]).

drad **music.** See **Sinnravian *drad* music.**

D'Ren. Worker assigned to the **subspace accelerator** project on **Sarindar**. D'Ren was an **Osina** (*Invincible* Book 1). He was killed by the second **monster shii** (*Invincible* Book 2).

Drew, Stephen. Noncommissioned Starfleet personnel assigned to the *U.S.S. da Vinci* as a security guard (*Fatal Error*). Drew was able to put together a program that would detect **Androssi security device**s even when they were using a **dimensional shift** to be rendered invisible and theoretically undetectable (*Cold Fusion*).

Duffy, Kieran. Second officer of the *U.S.S. da Vinci,* second-in-command of the ship's **Starfleet Corps of Engineers** team. Duffy was formerly assigned as an engineer on the *U.S.S. Enterprise* ("Hollow Pursuits" [TNG]). He and fellow engineer **Sonya Gomez** had a relationship during much of their time serving together (*The Belly of the Beast*). When she was promoted to full lieutenant and assigned to the *U.S.S. Oberth,* the relationship ended (*Invincible* Book 1). Duffy served on the *da Vinci* as second officer under **Commander Salek** as well (*The Belly of the Beast*). Duffy's favorite "comfort food" is macaroni and cheese (*Hard Crash*). He drinks coffee in the morning (*Cold Fusion*), and he is also fond of drinking quinine water over ice with a lime twist, particularly when he's in a pensive mood. Duffy was given temporary command of the *da Vinci* when both Gomez and **Captain David Gold** went on the away team to salvage the *U.S.S. Defiant* from **interphase**. He found himself thrust into a crisis situation when the **Tholians** opened fire on the *Defiant* and the *da Vinci* (*Interphase* Book 1). Although he had trouble dealing with command at first, he eventually was able to take charge of the situation and comported himself well, which increased his confidence (*Interphase* Book 2). When Gomez was sent on a mission to **Sarindar** (*Invincible* Book 1), Duffy temporarily served as first officer of the *da Vinci*, where he had to deal with personnel issues involving roommates **Carol Abramowitz** and **P8 Blue**, then lead an away mission to **Empok Nor** (*Cold Fusion*). That mission was cut short by a distress call from Gomez on Sarindar. By the time they got there, the crisis had passed, but Gomez, after the hardships she endured on the planet, decided to renew her and Duffy's relationship (*Invincible* Book 2). *Duffy first appeared in the episode "Hollow Pursuits" [TNG]. His first name and history with fellow* Enterprise *engineer Gomez was established in* The Belly of the Beast.

Dun. Officer assigned to the **Androssi** ship commanded by **Overseer Biron** (*Cold Fusion*).

E

Eddy, Claire. Noncommissioned Starfleet personnel assigned to the *U.S.S. da Vinci* as a security guard (*Cold Fusion*).

Eerlik. Planet, home to the **Eerlikka**. Eerlik is not a member of the Federation, but does trade with them. Eerlik has burgundy oceans and contains many rich deposits of **uridium.** All of Eerlik's planetary functions, from weather control to communications to transportation, are handled by a computer called **Ganitriul,** which was constructed on Eerlik's moon some three thousand years prior to 2376. A group of Eerlikka called the **Pevvni** colonized the ninth planet in their star system in 2326. Eerlik managed to stay out of the hostilities of the **Dominion War.** In 2376, a group of Pevvni **Purists** sabotaged Ganitriul with a computer virus that sent Eerlik into chaos, until the damage was repaired by the crew of the *U.S.S. da Vinci* (*Fatal Error*). *Eerlik was named after Max Ehrlich, the writer of the episode "The Apple" [TOS], which also featured a world-running computer.*

Eerlikka. Natives of the planet **Eerlik.** A humanoid race with teal skin, short in stature, hairless, eyelids both above and below their eyes. Their arms and legs are disproportionately short, and their blood is blue. The Eerlikka's technological evolution was geared more toward comfort than expansion, and few felt the need to travel off-planet, though they have had the technology to do so for thousands of years. In 2326, a group called the **Pevvni** decided to colonize the ninth planet, but such off-world travel remains rare. The Eerlikka are very religious, and their priests are entrusted with many spiritual duties, as well as the maintenance of **Ganitriul,** the computer that controls most of their world's functions. In 2376, seventeen priests and twenty acolytes served in the temple and performed those functions, but they were all murdered by **Undlar,** a Pevvni **Purist** who had gone undercover as a priest in order to sabotage Ganitriul and eliminate those most qualified to fix it (*Fatal Error*).

eldrak consumption rates. Component of the **overdrive** on an **Androssi** ship. **Overseer Biron** could tell simply from the feel of the bulkheads that the eldrak consumption rates on his ship were off-kilter and needed to be checked (*Cold Fusion*).

Elite. Ruling class of **Androssi** society. The Elite sponsor ships that seek out technology and other items for the Elite. The Elite are apparently the only members of Androssi who groom themselves (*Cold Fusion*).

Emarur. Owner and operator of the **Pevvni** ship the *Senbolma*. The ship was used by the **Purists** in their sabotage of **Ganitriul** (*Fatal Error*).

Emergency Medical Hologram-3. Holographic program available on some Federation starships. Unlike earlier editions of the EMH, this version is neither acerbic nor arrogant, and functions on a learning curve—instead of being a fully functional doctor, EMH-3 is more like an intern learning the ropes. The EMH on the *U.S.S. da Vinci* has been nicknamed "Emmett." Emmett made the connection between **Jaldark Keniria**'s removal from **Friend** and the latter's subsequent rampage (*Hard Crash*).

Emmett. See **Emergency Medical Hologram-3**.

Empok Nor. Cardassian space station. Empok Nor, which was abandoned by the Cardassian military in 2372, is nearly identical in original design to station Terok Nor, a.k.a. **Deep Space 9,** and was located in the **Trivas system.** A team from DS9 conducted a salvage mission to Empok Nor in 2373 to obtain abandoned Cardassian hardware ("Empok Nor" [DS9]). In 2376, after the crew of DS9 was forced to eject their fusion core (*Star Trek: Deep Space Nine: Avatar* Book 2), **Lieutenant Nog** rendezvoused with the **Starfleet Corps of Engineers** team on the *U.S.S. da Vinci* in order to salvage Empok Nor's fusion core. However, a team of **Androssi** led by **Overseer Biron** had gotten there first, and were trying to turn the station into a mobile weapons platform. The Androssi added powerful thrusters, phasers, quantum torpedoes, and a plasma energy weapon, and gave the station the capacity to travel at warp 6. Nog, the S.C.E. team, and the *da Vinci* were able to chase off the Androssi, who used their **dimensional shifts** to remove all of their modifications. However, doing so damaged the fusion core's structural integrity field to the point that towing the core would not be viable. Instead, they towed the entire station back to the Bajoran system (*Cold Fusion*). The station is now positioned around one of Bajor's moons (*Star Trek: Deep Space Nine: Section 31: Abyss*).

Endless Dream. Recording of **Sinnravian** *drad* **music** by **Blee Luu. Lieutenant Nog,** one of the few non-Sinnravians who is fond of *drad*, was listening to this while waiting to rendezvous with the **U.S.S.** *da Vinci* in the **Trivas system** (*Cold Fusion*).

Endless Wind. The afterlife in **Nalori** myth (*Invincible* Book 1).

Enforcement. The police force on the planet **Eerlik.** Enforcement was strained to its limits dealing with the crisis when **Ganitriul,** Eerlik's world-running computer, failed, and they also had to deal with the murder of virtually the entire priesthood (*Fatal Error*).

Enterprise, U.S.S. Federation starship, *Constitution*-class, registry number NCC-1701. Under the command of Captain James T. Kirk, in 2268 the *Enterprise* encountered a **Tholian** vessel while trying to rescue the **U.S.S.** *Defiant* from **interphase** ("The Tholian Web" [TOS]). It wasn't until 2376 that Starfleet learned that the *Defiant* had received intelligence about a Tholian attack on the Klingon colony at **Traelus II** (*Interphase* Book 2).

***Enterprise*, U.S.S.** Federation starship, *Galaxy*-class, registry number NCC-1701-D. **Sonya Gomez** and **Kieran Duffy** both served as engineers on the *Enterprise* under the command of **Geordi La Forge.** Gomez and Duffy also had a relationship during their time on the vessel (*The Belly of the Beast*). That relationship came to an end when Gomez was promoted to lieutenant and transferred to the *U.S.S. Oberth* (*Invincible* Book 1). In 2369, the *Enterprise* rescued **Montgomery Scott** from the *U.S.S. Jenolen*'s transporter buffer ("Relics" [TNG]), allowing him to eventually become the official liaison between the **Starfleet Corps of Engineers** and the admiralty (*The Belly of the Beast*).

***Enterprise*, U.S.S.** Federation starship, *Sovereign*-class, registry number NCC-1701-E. Commanded by **Captain Jean-Luc Picard,** the ship encountered and fought a ship dubbed **"the Beast"** and defeated it (*The Belly of the Beast*). The ship, along with the *U.S.S. Lexington,* responded to a distress call sent by the *da Vinci* at **Intar** to aid against the living ship known as **Friend** (*Hard Crash*).

Entorr. Worker assigned to the **subspace accelerator** project on **Sarindar.** Entorr smuggled some Saurian brandy into the camp, and was asked by **Kejahna** to share it after **Commander Sonya Gomez** killed the first **monster shii** (*Invincible* Book 1). Entorr was killed by the second **monster**

shii when he, **Amuk,** and **Kugot** failed to properly spring a trap for it (*Invincible* Book 2).

Eridak. Worker assigned to the **subspace accelerator** project on **Sarindar.** Eridak was killed by the second **monster shii**. He only had two scars, which meant he was very young (*Invincible* Book 2).

Erobnos. Worker assigned to the **subspace accelerator** project on **Sarindar.** Erobnos was killed by the second **monster shii** (*Invincible* Book 1).

F

Faulwell, Bartholomew "Bart." Noncommissioned Starfleet personnel assigned to the **U.S.S. da Vinci** as a linguist and cryptography specialist. Faulwell shares quarters with **Fabian Stevens** (*Hard Crash*). He served as a cryptographer during the **Dominion War,** and was one of Starfleet's best at cracking Dominion codes (*Interphase* Book 2). Faulwell drinks French roast coffee with half-and-half and sugar. He also does not maintain "normal" sleeping hours, preferring to grab naps here and there (*Fatal Error*). Faulwell is in a committed relationship with **Anthony Mark,** an officer assigned to **Starbase 92.** Faulwell regularly writes letters by hand to Mark, then dictates them and sends them via subspace—however, he always gives Mark the paper versions when they are able to get together. These letters all begin with the phrase "Just a brief note. . ." regardless of the letter's actual length. Faulwell hates first contact situations, as he's very much aware of how easy it is for them to go wrong (*Hard Crash*). Faulwell was able to hack into the computer systems of the **Senbolma** when the ship attacked the *da Vinci*, since the **Eerlik** have very primitive computer security (*Fatal Error*). He was assigned to translate the records of **Friend**, and was able to determine that it was an **Omearan Starsearcher** rather than a new type of **Borg** ship, as the *da Vinci* crew feared (*Hard Crash*). He worked with **Carol Abramowitz** to translate coded **Tholian** communiqués after a Tholian vessel fired on the *da Vinci* during its salvage of the **U.S.S. Defiant** from **interphase** (*Interphase* Book 2). Faulwell deduced that Stevens and **Lt. Commander Domenica Corsi** had a one-night liaison, and he advised Stevens to not let it distract him from work. He also suggested that the *da Vinci* use the **prefix codes** of the runabout **Rio Grande** to aid them in their battle against **Overseer Biron** of the **Androssi** at **Empok Nor** (*Cold Fusion*).

Feliciano, Diego. Noncommissioned personnel assigned to the *U.S.S. da Vinci* as transporter chief. When the **Androssi security device** on **Empok Nor** broadcast an interference pattern that affected the *da Vinci* crew's combadges, Feliciano found he could still get a lock on **Lieutenant Nog**, who is not part of the *da Vinci* crew (*Cold Fusion*).

Ferengi Rules of Acquisition. Words to live by in the Ferengi culture ("The Nagus" [DS9]). The Fifth Rule states: "Always exaggerate your estimates." When **Lieutenant Nog** quoted that Rule to **Montgomery Scott,** the latter stated that it was an engineer's axiom "long before you heathens took it on" (*Cold Fusion*).

Fifth Rule of Acquisition. See **Ferengi Rules of Acquisition.**

First Speaker. Title given to the head of the **Eerlik** government. **Ansed** was First Speaker until her death in 2376. She was succeeded by **Biral** (*Fatal Error*).

Folnar system. Star system. The *U.S.S. Enterprise* had a mission in the Folnar system following its defeat of the ship known as **"the *Beast"*** at **Blossom IV** (*The Belly of the Beast*).

Franklin, **Shuttlecraft.** Shuttlecraft assigned to the *U.S.S. da Vinci* (*Fatal Error*). *Named after famed politician and inventor Benjamin Franklin.*

Friend. Bio-mechanical **Starsearcher** vessel from **Omeara,** designated number 7445. Friend is oval in shape, with four extensions jutting out of its fore and aft sections that can serve as limbs in an atmosphere. Like all Starsearchers, Friend had a living **pilot,** in this case **Jaldark Keniria.** Jaldark died when her implants failed, and Friend crash-landed on the planet **Intar,** right in the middle of its capital city. The crash did very little damage to Friend, as its outer hull is several orders of magnitude stronger than that of most space-faring vessels. When the *U.S.S. da Vinci* removed Jaldark's corpse from Friend, Friend, not realizing that Jaldark had died, went berserk. The vessel's rampage ceased after **110** convinced it that Jaldark had died. Friend offered to make 110 its new pilot, but 110 chose to remain on the *da Vinci*. The *da Vinci* crew initially believed Friend to be a **Borg** ship (*Hard Crash*).

Friesner. Noncommissioned Starfleet personnel assigned to the *U.S.S. da Vinci* as a security guard (*Cold Fusion*).

Frnats. Noncommissioned Starfleet personnel assigned to the *U.S.S. da Vinci* as a security guard. A Bolian, Frnats was injured by an **Androssi security device** at Station **Empok Nor** (*Cold Fusion*).

G

Gallamite. Species of humanoid with transparent skulls ("The Maquis Part 1" [DS9]). **Dr. Dolahn** was a Gallamite (*Invincible* Book 1). Some

Gallamites are part of the **Ambrushroi** religion (*Invincible* Book 2).

Galloway. Starfleet personnel assigned to the *U.S.S. Lexington.* Galloway was wounded during the **Dominion War,** but refused treatment so that the more seriously injured could be cared for ahead of her. She eventually died from her wounds (*Hard Crash*).

Ganitriul. Computer system, sometimes referred to as **"the Great One."** Constructed on the moon of **Eerlik,** Ganitriul was constructed some three thousand years prior to 2376, and has been constantly upgraded since. In the 23rd century, auto-repair components were added, allowing the computer to fix itself. Ganitriul, which is programmed with a personality and located in an extensive cave system under the moon's surface, controls all functions on Eerlik, including climate controls, entertainment, communications, food distribution, transportation, and planetary defense. Approximately twenty-five percent of Eerlik's moon was excavated for Ganitriul's use, though by 2376, only ten percent of its original installation was still active, thanks to advances in miniaturization. Ganitriul's interfaces appear to be solid marble walls that only go active when touched. Those surfaces are also changeable. The main terminal has a chair that can only be used by members of the clergy. Ganitriul has several security measures—**Security Measure 7** initiates a **scattering field** that disrupts energy weapons. Other security devices include force fields, gas, and **rodinium** bulkheads. The main computer core is protected by a computer system that is independent of Ganitriul's own systems. An object of religious observance, the clergy on Eerlik are responsible for the maintenance of Ganitriul, and many Eerlikka (and offworlders) make regular pilgrimages. Ganitriul has been compared favorably to the super-computer on **Bynaus.** Several years prior to 2376, a team of Federation computer experts, including eight **Bynars,** inspected Ganitriul. When **Pevvni Purists** sabotaged Ganitriul with a computer virus, the computer—unable to contact anyone on Eerlik for help—sent a distress call to the Federation, who summoned the *U.S.S. da Vinci.* The **Starfleet Corps of Engineers** team on the *da Vinci* was able to reverse the sabotage and restore Ganitriul to full capacity, with some help from Ganitriul itself (*Fatal Error*).

garbage in, garbage out. Used generally to refer to computers and other machines only being as good as what's put into them, **Commander Sonya Gomez** used the expression to refer to **Ganitriul,** the world-running computer of **Eerlik** (*Fatal Error*). She also used the expression on **Sarindar** to refer to the **monster shii,** where she described it as the first rule of programming. **Razka** later used the expression to explain his own inability to change his habits (*Invincible* Book 2).

GIGO. See **garbage in, garbage out.**

Gilman, Rabbi Rachel. Professor at **Stern College.** Gilman is married to **Captain David Gold** of the *U.S.S. da Vinci* (*The Belly of the Beast*). An excellent cook, Gilman makes a renowned matzoh ball soup. In 2376, she was able to entertain **Captain Montgomery Scott,** after months of asking her husband to have "the legend" come over for dinner. Gilman has difficulty waking up in the morning, and often needs four cups of tea to "get going." She also insists that Gold's impatience will be the death of him (*Fatal Error*), and that he shouldn't slouch (*Cold Fusion*).

glemnar **flower.** Flora native to **Sarindar,** similar to a ruby (*Invincible* Book 2).

Gold, David. Commanding officer of the *U.S.S. da Vinci.* Gold graduated from Starfleet Academy in 2324. As a senior, he ran in the Academy marathon, but was defeated by first-year student **Jean-Luc Picard.** Captain Gold is married to **Rabbi Rachel Gilman,** a teacher at **Stern College** in New York City (*The Belly of the Beast*). Gilman makes an excellent matzoh ball soup, about which Gold has been known to dream fondly. He has several children, grandchildren, and great-grandchildren; **Ruth,** one of his grandchildren, became pregnant in 2376 (*Fatal Error*).

Ruth's fetus is a girl (*Cold Fusion*). There is a pool on the *da Vinci* as to what the child's name will be (*Invincible* Book 1). Gold participated in a rare away mission when he accompanied **Commander Sonya Gomez** on the *da Vinci*'s salvage of the *U.S.S. Defiant,* due to his experience with older ships. His task was to retrieve the captain's logs (*Interphase* Book 1). Gold's strategy to fire on the **Tholians** who had attacked the *da Vinci* and the *Defiant* helped save the day in the end (*Interphase* Book 2).

Gomez, Sonya. First officer of the *U.S.S. da Vinci,* commanding officer of the ship's **Starfleet Corps of Engineers** team. Gomez graduated from Starfleet Academy in 2365 and was assigned to the *U.S.S. Enterprise* as an engineer. Her specialty was antimatter operations. Shortly after her arrival, the *Enterprise* had its first encounter with the **Borg,** during which eighteen people were lost, an event that had a profound impact on her. She spilled hot chocolate on **Captain Jean-Luc Picard** upon first meeting him ("Q Who" [TNG]). The "hot chocolate incident" would continue to hound her for a large portion of her Starfleet career. By way of making up for the gaffe, she took to drinking Earl Grey tea, Picard's favorite drink (*Fatal Error*). She received a commendation for her work during the Borg attack, though she never understood why (*Invincible* Book 1). Gomez helped devise a means of using the *Enterprise*'s Bussard collectors to create a harmless pyrotechnic display when **Geordi La Forge** was being held captive aboard the Pakled ship, the *Mondor* ("Samaritan Snare" [TNG]). During her time on the *Enterprise*, she had a relationship with **Kieran Duffy,** a fellow engineer (*The Belly of the Beast*). Duffy refers to her as "Sonnie" (*Interphase* Book 1). She served on the *Enterprise* for three-and-a-half years before being promoted to full lieutenant and being assigned to a one-year project on the **U.S.S. Oberth,** which ended her relationship with Duffy (*Invincible* Book 1). That project ended with a life-or-death encounter with the Romulans (*Invincible* Book 2). She did not get involved with anyone else after leaving the *Enterprise* (*Hard Crash*). In 2371, she was on Neural and was wounded by a **mugato** (*Invincible* Book 2). During the **Dominion War,** she was assigned to the **U.S.S. Sentinel** as chief engineer. At one point, the *Sentinel* was damaged behind enemy lines, and Gomez managed to reconfigure the warp field so that Breen sensors would think them to be a Cardassian freighter (*The Belly of the Beast*). This bought her time to get the warp drive back on-line (*Invincible* Book 1). Also during the war, Gomez was able to modify an away team's hand phasers so they weren't affected by a Breen **scattering field,** though they were only able to attain light stun. Gomez repeated this trick in 2376 on **Eerlik**'s moon (*Fatal Error*). After the war, she was promoted to commander. While at the Academy, she wrote a paper on **subspace accelerator**s. The quality of the paper so impressed **Captain Montgomery Scott** that he recommended her to **Captain David Gold** to fill a vacancy on the *da Vinci* (*Invincible* Book 1). On the *da Vinci*, she was reunited with Duffy, and the two were not sure how to approach their personal relationship (*The Belly of the Beast*). Gomez's first mission on the *da Vinci* was an encounter with **Overseer Biron** of the **Androssi** on the planet **Maeglin** (*Cold Fusion*). Gomez was uncomfortable when La Forge was temporarily assigned to the *da Vinci*, as he was her first commanding officer out of the Academy and now she outranked him, though she got over this problem in relatively short order (*Fatal Error*). After the heart-wrenching encounter with the **Omearan Starsearcher** called **Friend,** Gomez decided to indulge in a rare hot chocolate (*Hard Crash*). She and **P8 Blue** engineered the warp pulse that got the *U.S.S. Defiant* out of **interphase** after it fell further into that interspatial phenomenon following a **Tholian** attack (*Interphase* Book 2). After dropping the *Defiant* off at Spacedock, Gomez was given a special assignment to head up a project to construct a **subspace accelerator** on the planet **Sarindar** in the **Nalori Republic**. She was not treated well on her arrival, since the Nalori view both Starfleet and women who do "men's work" with disdain, but she won some of them over after fixing the antigrav units, and more of them when she killed a **monster shii** that was threatening the project. They started referring to her as the **sañuul**, the lifter of curses, which made Gomez uncomfortable (*Invincible* Book 1). After a second monster shii attacked the camp and the death count grew, Gomez had a harder time maintaining morale. However, she did figure out a way to get partial tricorder readings on the **chimerium**-laced planet. She was also able to determine the monster shii's origin as a creation of **the owners** and communicate with it, but to little avail. The trap she constructed to stop the monster shii failed. She finally stopped the creature by catching it in the **annular confinement beam** of the SA. She received two scars that matched the coming-of-age scars in **Nalori** culture, which she had removed, though she was tempted to keep them. After that harrowing experience, she decided to renew her relationship with Duffy (*Invincible* Book 2). *Gomez first appeared in "Q Who" [TNG] and also appeared in "Samaritan Snare" [TNG]. Her relationship with Duffy was established in* The Belly of the Beast.

Great One, the. Name sometimes given to **Ganitriul,** the world-running computer on the planet **Eerlik** (*Fatal Error*).

Grelin. Officer in Starfleet Intelligence. Commander Grelin was surprised to hear that the **U.S.S. Defiant** had reportedly appeared in **Tholian** space, since the ship was supposed to be docked at **Deep Space 9**. **Montgomery Scott** corrected his assumption, pointing out that it was the *Constitution*-class *Defiant*, not the newer *Defiant*-class model assigned to DS9 (*Interphase* Book 1).

G'Sob. Worker assigned to the **subspace accelerator** project on **Sarindar.** G'Sob was an **Osina.** He was killed by the second **monster shii** (*Invincible* Book 2).

H

Hagi. One of the **Pevvni Purists** working for **Reger Undlar** to sabotage **Ganitriul** (*Fatal Error*).

Hamilton. Chief medical officer of the *U.S.S. Defiant.* In 2268, Dr. Hamilton was unable to combat the severe neurophysiological effects of **interphase.** At one point, she was attacked by one of her nurses (*Interphase* Book 1).

Hawkins, Vance. Noncommissioned Starfleet personnel assigned to the *U.S.S. da Vinci* as a security guard. Hawkins was wounded on **Eerlik's** moon while assigned to an away team that was attempting to fix **Ganitriul,** Eerlik's world-running computer (*Fatal Error*). He was wounded again by an **Androssi security device** on **Empok Nor** (*Cold Fusion*).

Hendorf Island. An island on the planet **Eerlik** (*Fatal Error*).

High Magistrates. Name for the ruling body of the **Tholians** (*Interphase* Book 1).

Ho'nig. Collective god of the **Damiani** (*Star Trek: The Next Generation: Perchance to Dream*). The holy words of Ho'nig are collected in the *Se'rbeg*. Most Damiani worship Ho'nig; the only known offworlder to worship the god is the Bolian **Zilder** (*Invincible* Book 1). Worshippers of Ho'nig are supposed to be buried within three days of their death (*Invincible* Book 2).

Houarner. Worker assigned to the **subspace accelerator** project on **Sarindar**. Houarner was killed by the second **monster shii** (*Invincible* Book 1).

Howwi. A **sub-overseer** on the **Androssi** ship run by **Overseer Biron.** Howwi trimmed his beard, which Biron deemed a frivolous affectation. Howwi also allowed himself to be defeated by the **Starfleet Corps of Engineers** team from the *U.S.S. da Vinci* on **Empok Nor** (*Cold Fusion*).

Huuk. Officer assigned to the **Androssi** ship commanded by **Overseer Biron** (*Cold Fusion*).

I

Ina Mar. Alpha-shift operations officer on the *U.S.S. da Vinci* (*The Belly of the Beast*). A native of Bajor, Ina is a devout member of the Bajoran faith (*Cold Fusion*).

insectoid aliens. Alien race. This unnamed race of telepathic hive creatures used other forms of animal life to hatch their eggs in order to reproduce. A dozen of these aliens took over a cruise ship that was nicknamed **"the Beast,"** and used the crew in that manner; they attacked the Federation colony on **Blossom IV** in an attempt to procure more bodies. The adults were killed in a retaliatory attack by the *U.S.S. Enterprise*, and the hatchlings were killed by the **Starfleet Corps of Engineers** team from the *U.S.S. da Vinci*, but not before the aliens killed one of the team members, **111** (*The Belly of the Beast*). *The aliens' proper name was never established.*

Intar. Planet, home to the **Intarians.** Intar has a monitoring station to warn them of approaching ships and allow them to transmit a greeting. Intar is known as a hospitable planet, though not as well regarded a vacation spot as Risa. They have a planetary defense system, but it is rudimentary (*Hard Crash*).

Intarians. Natives of planet **Intar.** Intarians have retractable tentacles for limbs and have multifaceted eyes. Intarians generally prefer to work in groups, and are a hospitable people who wish harm to no one. They are also famous for their friendliness. When **Friend** was discovered by **Tlaimon Kassant** to be on a collision course with the planet, the Intarians tried to communicate with it, then opened fire, neither of which did any good. They were able to evacuate their capital city, so there were no casualties when Friend crash-landed on the planet. Their leader, **Intari Makestru,** requested help from the Federation, which was sent in the form of the *U.S.S. da Vinci* (*Hard Crash*).

interphase. Time-space phenomenon in which two or more dimensional planes briefly overlap and connect. The *U.S.S. Defiant* disappeared into such a phenomenon in 2268. The interphase phenomenon also had debilitating effects on humanoid nervous systems, and apparently caused the crew of the *Defiant* to mutiny and eventually kill each other. A ship in interphase also sometimes will go through a **molecular shift** that puts it out of sync with objects from "normal" space ("The Tholian Web" [TOS]). In 2376, the *Defiant* started to reappear in "normal" space, and was observed by the **Tholian** ship commanded by **Nostrene.** The **Starfleet Corps of Engineers** sent the *U.S.S. da Vinci* to salvage it, but after they found a **web**

generator on the ship—which contained evidence of a century-old Tholian massacre of a Klingon colony on **Traelus II**—Nostrene fired on the *da Vinci* and the *Defiant*, pushing the latter ship further into interphase (*Interphase* Book 1). The S.C.E. team were able to push the *Defiant* out of interphase with a two-second warp pulse (*Interphase* Book 2).

J

J'Roh. Assistant foreperson on the **subspace accelerator** project on **Sarindar**. J'Roh was an **Osina.** After **Commander Sonya Gomez** fixed the project's antigrav units, J'Roh was the first to call her **"Sañuul"** (*Invincible* Book 1). J'Roh was killed when the second **monster shii** attacked the secondary hospital (*Invincible* Book 2).

Jenson. Starfleet personnel assigned to the *U.S.S. Lexington.* Jenson was wounded during the **Dominion War** and died while being treated by **Dr. Elizabeth Lense** (*Hard Crash*).

jiksn. Drink. Served on **Intar,** and generally served hot. **Tlaimon Kassant** was drinking *jiksn* and spilled it when he discovered **Friend** on a collision course with Intar (*Hard Crash*).

Journal of the Federation Consortium of Engineers and Technicians. Technical journal read by **P8 Blue.** It included several articles on Romulan **tight-beam tachyon pulses** as a method of communication (*Cold Fusion*).

K

Kani. Worker on the **subspace accelerator** project on **Sarindar.** Kani was attacked by the first **monster shii,** and went into a coma from blood loss (*Invincible* Book 1). He was later killed by the second **monster shii** (*Invincible* Book 2).

Kassant, Tlaimon. An **Intarian** male. Kassant worked the night shift at the Intarian monitor station. Unlike most Intarians, Kassant preferred solitude and enjoyed working alone. Kassant first discovered the approach of **Friend** when it crash-landed on **Intar** (*Hard Crash*).

Kejahna. Foreperson of the **subspace accelerator** team on **Sarindar.** Kejahna had by far more scars on his face and forearms than any other **Nalori** on the project. He resented the presence of **Commander Sonya Gomez** on the project, partly out of loyalty to her predecessor **Nalag,** partly because he didn't think a woman could do the job. Kejahna also supported the "sick-out" staged by several workers claiming to have **Da-**

kota's Disease. He was, however, won over by Gomez's skills. Kejahna's oldest son is named **Revodro,** to whom Kejahna wrote one letter before he was killed by a **monster shii** (*Invincible* Book 1).

Kelrek. Worker assigned to the **subspace accelerator** project on **Sarindar.** Kelrek was killed by the first **monster shii** (*Invincible* Book 1).

Keniria, Jaldark. An **Omearan pilot.** Jaldark was sent on a deep exploratory mission to seek out new worlds for the Omearans to colonize after their war with the **Sarimun.** She died due to some kind of fault in her implants that connected her with **Friend,** the **Starsearcher** to which she had become bonded. She altered Friend's circuitry so that it would not self-destruct on her death, as it was programmed to do. After her death, Friend crashed on **Intar** and went berserk when the crew of the *U.S.S. da Vinci* transported her corpse off the ship. The *da Vinci* crew initially mistook Jaldark's cybernetic implants for **Borg** technology (*Hard Crash*).

Kira Nerys. Commanding officer of **Deep Space 9.** After Jem'Hadar sabotage forced Colonel Kira to eject the station's fusion core (*Star Trek: Deep Space Nine: Avatar* Book 2), she requested that the **Starfleet Corps of Engineers** team on the *U.S.S. da Vinci* aid her chief operations officer

Lieutenant Nog in salvaging the fusion core from DS9's sister station **Empok Nor** (*Cold Fusion*).

kliyor. Animal life native to **Sarindar.** They travel in packs (*Invincible* Book 1).

Kugot. Worker assigned to the **subspace accelerator** project on **Sarindar.** Kugot was killed by the second **monster shii** when he, **Amuk,** and **Entorr** failed to properly spring a trap for it (*Invincible* Book 2).

Kyepas Coast. Landmass on planet **Eerlik. First Speaker Ansed** spent many summers there when she was a girl (*Fatal Error*).

L

La Forge, Geordi. Chief engineer of the *U.S.S. Enterprise.* Lt. Commander La Forge and **Lieutenant Christine Vale** were temporarily detached to the *U.S.S. da Vinci* to help salvage the ship known as **"the Beast."** La Forge engineered the cascade reaction in the **black-hole propulsion system** on the *Beast* that resulted in its explosion. When the mission was complete, La Forge stayed behind in order to aid in the cleanup (*The Belly of the Beast*). The *da Vinci* was en route to Starbase 505 to transfer La Forge back to the *Enterprise* when they were diverted by a distress call from

Eerlik. La Forge aided the *da Vinci* crew against the **Pevvni Purists** who had sabotaged Eerlik's computer **Ganitriul.** He was able to come up with a way to reconstitute the *da Vinci's* shields after they were decimated by the *Senbolma's* weapons (*Fatal Error*). La Forge also aided the *da Vinci* in its mission to **Intar,** at the end of which he was finally brought back to the *Enterprise* (*Hard Crash*).

ladrion bursts. Type of high-powered directed energy weapon. The **Androssi** ship commanded by **Overseer Biron** fired ladrion bursts (*Cold Fusion*).

Lankap mountain range. Landmass on **Eerlik** just outside the capital city (*Fatal Error*).

Lense, Elizabeth. Physician assigned to the *U.S.S. da Vinci* as Chief Medical Officer. Lense was first in her Starfleet Medical School class; **Julian Bashir** was second. She served on the *U.S.S. Lexington* prior to being assigned to the *da Vinci* ("Explorers" [DS9]). After graduation, Lense worked at Starfleet Medical for a few years before transferring to the *Lexington* (*Interphase* Book 1). Lense grew sick of treating wounded during the **Dominion War,** and after her transfer to the *da Vinci*, preferred the forensic aspects of the assignment to dealing with flesh-and-blood patients (*Hard Crash*). Lense is roommates with **Lt. Commander Domenica Corsi,** and she saw

Fabian Stevens emerging from their shared quarters one night, deducing that they had had a liaison (*Cold Fusion*). *Lense first appeared in the episode "Explorers" [DS9].*

Lexington, **U.S.S.** Federation starship, *Nebula*-class, Starfleet registry number NCC-61832 ("Explorers" [DS9]). **Dr. Elizabeth Lense** served as chief medical officer of the *Lexington* before being assigned to the **U.S.S. *da Vinci*** (*The Belly of the Beast*). Two others who served on the *Lexington* and died during the **Dominion War** were **Jenson** and **Galloway**. The *Lexington* responded to a distress call from the *da Vinci* to the planet **Intar** to aid against what was believed to be a **Borg** ship, but turned out to be the **Omearan Starsearcher** called *Friend*, so they broke off the rendezvous (*Hard Crash*).

Lipinski, Andrea. Noncommissioned Starfleet personnel assigned to the **U.S.S. *da Vinci*** as a security guard (*Cold Fusion*).

Luu, Blee. Musician from **Sinnrav**. Luu plays in the **atonal minimalist** style of **Sinnravian *drad* music.** One of her recordings is entitled *Endless Dream.* In 2376, she released a new recording, which **Carol Abramowitz** acquired, and with which she irritated her roommate **P8 Blue**. **Lieutenant Nog** took the recording off Abramowitz's hands, to Blue's relief, as part of a deal to get the **U.S.S. Sugihara** to aid in the towing of **Empok Nor** (*Cold Fusion*).

M

Maeglin. Planet. The **Starfleet Corps of Engineers** crew from the **U.S.S. *da Vinci*** aided the government of Maeglin against **Overseer Biron** of the **Androssi**. Although the *da Vinci* crew defeated Biron, the planet will take several decades to recover from what the Androssi did to their world (*Cold Fusion*).

Maeglin Law-Enforcement Bureau. Agency charged with policing the planet **Maeglin**. **Captain David Gold** told **Overseer Biron** of the **Androssi** that the bureau had deputized the **U.S.S. *da Vinci*** to apprehend Biron and his crew for crimes against Maeglin when they encountered each other at **Empok Nor**. This was a bluff on Gold's part (*Cold Fusion*).

Marig. One of **Razka's** five wives. Razka described her as the one he disliked the least (*Invincible* Book 2).

Mark, Anthony. Officer assigned to **Starbase 92**. Mark is in a committed relationship with **Bart Faulwell** of the **U.S.S. *da Vinci*** (*Hard Crash*).

Marshall. Federation diplomat. Marshall was concerned that the *U.S.S. da Vinci*'s salvage of the *U.S.S. Defiant* from **Tholian** space would damage the fragile relationship the Federation had achieved with the Tholians, deeming avoiding a war more important even than giving its long-lost crew a proper burial (*Interphase* Book 1). Marshall blamed **Lt. Commander Kieran Duffy,** temporarily in charge of the *da Vinci*, for the hostilities that erupted between the Tholians and the *da Vinci*, even though the Tholians fired first (*Interphase* Book 2).

Maryllo Island. A teardrop-shaped island on **Eerlik**. Birthplace of **First Speaker Ansed** (*Fatal Error*).

mazza. Word for the life force or soul of a **Nalori.** When a Nalori dies, his or her *mazza* must be commended to the **Endless Wind** by a person of authority, who announces the arrival of the *mazza* to the *Shigemos.* **Commander Sonya Gomez** served this function on **Sarindar** (*Invincible* Book 1).

McAllan, David. Alpha-shift tactical officer for the *U.S.S. da Vinci* (*The Belly of the Beast*).

McCoy, Leonard. Chief medical officer of the *U.S.S. Enterprise,* and later a retired admiral in the Starfleet Medical Corps. In 2268, McCoy discovered that a derivative of **theragen** mixed with alcohol could retard the debilitating neurophysiological effects of **interphase** experienced by the *Enterprise* crew when they attempted to rescue the *U.S.S. Defiant* from that interspatial phenomenon ("The Tholian Web" [TOS]). When the *Defiant* was finally salvaged in 2376, the elderly Admiral McCoy led the forensic detail that went over the ship after it was brought to Spacedock. McCoy always felt guilty that he found a cure when the *Defiant's* **Dr. Hamilton** didn't (*Interphase* Book 2).

meir. Animal life native to **Sarindar** that travels by gliding through the air (*Invincible* Book 1).

Miko. Speaker of **Eerlik** (*Fatal Error*).

Mokae. Worker on the **subspace accelerator** project on **Sarindar.** He was killed by the first **monster shii** (*Invincible* Book 1).

molecular shift. Occasional occurrence to ships in **interphase** when they fall out of sync with objects from "normal" space ("The Tholian Web" [TOS]). One such shift caused **P8 Blue** and **Dr. Elizabeth Lense** to fall through a cargo bay bulkhead on the *U.S.S. Defiant* while it was in interphase (*Interphase* Book 1).

monster shii. See **shii, monster**.

Moyya. Senator in the **Nalori Republic**. Moyya was in charge of the **subspace accelerator** project on **Sarindar**. He was not happy with **Commander Sonya Gomez**'s performance as supervisor, even though she put the project back on schedule (*Invincible* Book 1). He also did not believe her reports about the **monster shii**, and refused to curtail the project or allow the workers to evacuate. He did not show the evidence Gomez submitted to his fellow senators, and when he finally did, they reversed their position and authorized a cessation of the project until the monster shii problem could be solved. Moyya formally apologized to Gomez (*Invincible* Book 2).

Mranol. Worker assigned to the **subspace accelerator** project on **Sarindar** (*Invincible* Book 2).

mugato. Apelike carnivore with white fur and poisonous fangs. They are found on Neural ("A Private Little War" [TOS]). A mugato injured **Commander Sonya Gomez** in 2371 (*Invincible* Book 2).

Murphy's Law. Human proverb: "Whatever can go wrong, will go wrong." **Dr. Elizabeth Lense** postulated that it should be the motto of the **Starfleet Corps of Engineers** (*Interphase* Book 1).

Musgrave, U.S.S. Federation starship, *Saber*-class. The *Musgrave* was assigned to the **Starfleet Corps of Engineers** (*Interphase* Book 1).

N

Nalag. Supervisor of the **subspace accelerator** project on **Sarindar.** The multiple problems suffered by the project led Nalag to quit in disgust. He was replaced by **Commander Sonya Gomez** from the **Starfleet Corps of Engineers** (*Invincible* Book 1).

Nalori. Humanoid race, part of the **Nalori Republic.** Nalori have skin tones ranging from medium ash gray to charcoal. Their eyes are black with no pupils, and their blood is blue. Nalori males practice a form of ritual scarring of the forearms and face, which marks rites of passage like adolescence, adulthood, marriage, birth of sons, veneration of elders, and so on. Nalori count age by scars rather than years lived. Males are also generally bald, with long braided chin-beards of pale violet hair. Nalori are polygamous, and the accumulation of wives is often seen as a symbol of status (*Invincible* Book 1).

Nalori Republic. Government consisting of several planets near **Sector 969.** Among the member races of the republic are the **Nalori,** the **Osina,**

and the **Cabbi.** Traditional Nalori culture practices polygamy, and women have a much lower place in the social strata than men. The Federation and the Nalori had a border clash some time in the 2100s. The Nalori refused to allow any Federation passage through their space, and relations were strained until 2376, when they requested help from Starfleet in constructing a **subspace accelerator** on the planet **Sarindar.** The **Starfleet Corps of Engineers** sent **Commander Sonya Gomez,** on the recommendation of **Montgomery Scott.** The Nalori government is made up of **senators,** and government contracts, such as working on the SA project, are among the most lucrative. The government also has the power to keep someone from working, not only on government contracts, but any others as well (*Invincible* Book 1).

Nasats. Insectoid race. Nasats have eight limbs and a chitinous outer armor ("Jihad" [TAS]). Nasats make assorted tinkling noises to indicate emotion that many non-Nasats have trouble distinguishing, although many of **P8 Blue**'s shipmates on the *U.S.S. da Vinci* are able to differentiate them (*Cold Fusion*). *Nasats were first seen in "Jihad," in the form of the character Em/3/Green. The name for the race was first given in* The Belly of the Beast.

Nemar. Language with similarities to the **Omearan** tongue (*Hard Crash*).

Nevari. A race that builds viewships that include observation areas that work on the same principle as the rings on the ship nicknamed **"the *Beast*"** (*The Belly of the Beast*).

Nog. Chief operations officer of Station **Deep Space 9.** Nog lost his left leg in the **Dominion War** ("The Siege at AR-558" [DS9]). It was replaced by a biosynthetic leg ("It's Only a Paper Moon" [DS9]), which sometimes gets a psychosomatic itch in times of stress (*Cold Fusion*). After **Colonel Kira Nerys** was forced to eject DS9's fusion core (*Star Trek: Deep Space Nine: Avatar* Book 2), Nog thought of retrieving a new one from DS9's abandoned sister station **Empok Nor.** He took the runabout ***Rio Grande*** to the **Trivas system** to rendezvous with the **Starfleet Corps of Engineers** team on the *U.S.S. da Vinci* to aid in the salvage (*Cold Fusion*). Nog was not happy about returning to the station where he was almost killed twice, once by a Cardassian booby trap ("Empok Nor" [DS9]), once by Jem'Hadar ("The Magnificent Ferengi" [DS9]). He was equally unhappy with the condescending attitude the S.C.E. took toward him, though that attitude changed after he proved his mettle, both in engineering terms and against the **Androssi** pirates who had beaten them to the station. After Nog and the *da Vinci* crew drove off the Androssi, they discovered that the fusion core could not be towed back to the station; Nog instead came up with the plan to tow the entire station back to the

Bajoran system. He also had to convince nine Starfleet captains to lend their ships to the massive towing effort. Most were willing, though he had to bribe **Captain Jenna Demitrijian** of the *U.S.S. Sugihara* with a recording of **Sinnravian drad music**, which he obtained from **Carol Abramowitz** for an as-yet-undetermined price (*Cold Fusion*). Nog led the convoy back to DS9 and placed Empok Nor in orbit around one of Bajor's moons once the fusion core transfer was complete (*Star Trek: Deep Space Nine: Section 31: Abyss*).

Nomis. Worker assigned to the **subspace accelerator** project on **Sarindar**. Nomis and **Repooc** were able to "hot-wire" the *Culloden*, allowing the surviving workers to escape Sarindar after the second **monster shii** started attacking (*Invincible* Book 2).

Nostrene. Commander of an experimental **Tholian** vessel that was testing a new propulsion system. Nostrene thought that the Tholians' nonagression pact with the Dominion that kept them out of the **Dominion War** was wise, as he felt the Tholians would fare poorly against the Jem'Hadar. Nostrene was surprised when the Tholian **High Magistrates** gave the order for him to fire on the *U.S.S. da Vinci* and the *U.S.S. Defiant* when a crew from the former salvaged the latter and unwittingly uncovered evidence of a century-old atrocity committed by the Tholians

(*Interphase* Book 1). Initially driven off by the *da Vinci*, Nostrene returned with five other ships to finish it and the *Defiant* off with a newer version of the infamous **Tholian web.** The Starfleet ships were able to break the web, however (*Interphase* Book 2).

Nyn. Science officer on the *U.S.S. Defiant.* In 2268, Nyn was the first to theorize that the *Defiant* fell into **interphase** (*Interphase* Book 1).

O

Oberth, U.S.S. Federation starship, *Oberth*-class ("Hero Worship" [TNG]). **Sonya Gomez** transferred to the *Oberth* for a project after she made full lieutenant (*Invincible* Book 1). The project lasted one year, and ended in a confrontation with the Romulans (*Invincible* Book 2). *The* Oberth *class was established in "Hero Worship," although the* Grissom *from* Star Trek III: The Search for Spock *was also of this class. One assumes there's a ship that the class is named after.*

O'Brien, Miles Edward. Instructor at Starfleet Academy, former transporter chief of the *U.S.S. Enterprise,* former chief of operations for Station **Deep Space 9.** O'Brien supervised **Fabian Stevens** on DS9 ("Starship Down" [DS9]), and worked with **Lt. Commander Duffy** on the *Enterprise* ("Hollow Pursuits" [TNG]).

officer class. Subsection of **Androssi** society that is in charge of their ships. Ranks are indicated by the number of nose rings worn by the officer. The highest rank is **overseer** (five nose rings), followed by **sub-overseer** (four nose rings) (*Cold Fusion*).

Olisu. Language with similarities to the **Omearan** tongue (*Hard Crash*).

Omearan pilot. See **pilot**.

Omearans. Race of humanoids. Omearans have extended ribcages and longer fingers than humans. They also have two hearts and several organs that neither **Dr. Elizabeth Lense** nor **Emmett** could identify when they did their autopsy of **Jaldark Keniria**. Their language is a branch of the **Taklathi** language, with some grammatical elements of **Nemar, Olisu, Xlatitigu,** and **Pe.** The Omearans fought a brutal war with the **Sarimun** some time prior to 2376, and that left them short of **pilots** for their **Starsearcher** ships. After the war, the Starsearchers were sent out to seek out new worlds for the Omearans to colonize. The *U.S.S. da Vinci*'s encounter with the Starsearcher **Friend** led to relations with the Federation (*Hard Crash*).

Osina. Insectoid race, part of the **Nalori Republic** (*Invincible* Book 1).

overdrive. Name given to the warp drive on an **Androssi** ship (*Cold Fusion*).

overseer. Rank in **Androssi** society given to one who runs a ship (*Cold Fusion*).

owners, the. Name given to quadrupedal beings who made an archaeological expedition to **Sarindar.** They brought two mechanical servants with **chameleon circuits** that allowed them to assume the shape of local flora. Those servants took on the form of **shii.** Since the owners fed on the cranial matter of animals, the servants would decapitate animal life they came across as a means of gathering food. The owners died off, apparently of a disease, but the servants remained-ed, and their actions mirrored those of the legendary **monster shii** out of **Nalori** myth (*Invincible* Book 2). *The exact name of the owners' race was never given.*

P

P-38. Designation for Starfleet equipment used to open doors and hatches. The **Starfleet Corps of Engineers** team on the *U.S.S. da Vinci* used P-38s to open hatches on a Pakled ship that had suffered systems failure after installing a faulty cloaking device sold to them by the Ferengi. The Pakleds were impressed with the crew's ability to "make things open" (*Interphase* Book 2).

P8 Blue. Noncommissioned Starfleet engineer assigned to the *U.S.S. da Vinci* as a structural systems specialist. "Pattie" is a member of the **Nasat** race, an insectoid with eight limbs (*The Belly of the Beast*). She also has larvae, which can apparently eat anything (*Cold Fusion*). She can contort herself into a ball-shaped object that only leaves her chitinous armor exposed (*The Belly of the Beast*). She has a specially designed chair in the *da Vinci* conference lounge to accommodate her (*Fatal Error*). Blue's armor is protection against vacuum (*Interphase* Book 1). She and **Commander Sonya Gomez** engineered the warp pulse that got the *U.S.S. Defiant* out of **interphase** after it fell further into that interspatial phenomenon following a **Tholian** attack (*Interphase* Book 2). She intensely dislikes **Sinnravian** *drad* music; her roommate **Carol Abramowitz** is fond of that type of music, particularly a recording by **Blee Luu.** Her complaining to temporary first officer **Lt. Commander Kieran Duffy** got her shift rotation changed so she and Abramowitz no longer were on duty at the same time. When **Lieutenant Nog** played a Luu recording in her presence, she threatened bodily harm, but Nog was able to engineer a deal that took the Luu recording off Abramowitz's hands, thus making Blue much happier (*Cold Fusion*).

panshar. See **Androssi security device**.

Pe. Language with similarities to the **Omearan** tongue (*Hard Crash*).

Pevvni. A group of **Eerlikka** who colonized the ninth planet in their system in 2326. They were the first Eerlikka to travel offworld, and approval for their colony was only granted after much debate by the **Speakers of Eerlik.** A group of radical terrorists known as **Purists** led by **Reger Undlar** sabotaged Eerlik's world-running computer, **Ganitriul,** throwing the planet into chaos in 2376. They were stopped by the **Starfleet Corps of Engineers** team from the *U.S.S. da Vinci,* with help from Ganitriul itself (*Fatal Error*). *The Pevvni were named for Joseph Pevney, who directed both "The Apple" and "Return of the Archons," TOS episodes that featured world-running computers.*

photonic grenade. Starfleet weapon. Photonic grenades do no physical damage, but do let off an intense light that can blind most species. **Domenica Corsi** used a photonic grenade on **Eerlik's** moon in order to distract a group of **Pevvni Purists** and get away from them. The **Eerlikka,** with their wide eyes, were particularly susceptible to the grenade (*Fatal Error*).

Picard, Jean-Luc. Commanding officer of the *U.S.S. Enterprise* and one of the most prominent figures in Starfleet. Picard won the Starfleet Academy Marathon in his first year there in 2324 ("The Best of Both Worlds" Part 2). **Captain David Gold** was a fourth-year student that year, and was one of the upper-class students whom Picard beat (*The Belly of the Beast*). **Sonya Gomez** served under Picard on the *Enterprise* as an ensign; when they first met after she was assigned in 2365, she spilled hot chocolate all over him ("Q Who" [TNG]). After leading the *Enterprise* in battle against a large ship dubbed **"the Beast"** in 2376, Captain Picard lent his chief engineer, **Lt. Commander Geordi La Forge,** and his security chief, **Lieutenant Christine Vale,** to the *U.S.S. da Vinci* to aid in the salvage of the ship (*The Belly of the Beast*). The *Enterprise*, as well as the *Lexington,* also responded to the *da Vinci*'s distress call at **Intar** to aid against what was believed to be a type of **Borg** ship, but which turned out to be the **Omearan Starsearcher** known as **Friend.** Hostilities with Friend ended, but the *Enterprise* rendezvoused with the *da Vinci* anyhow in order to bring La Forge back (*Hard Crash*).

pilot. Omearans who are modified from infancy to accommodate the links to the bio-mechanical **Starsearcher** ships. Their arms are altered to allow the arm sheaths to be attached, with their heads altered to accommodate cybernetic cranial implants. Only one in ten thousand **Omearans**

can accept the modifications. **Jaldark Keniria** was a pilot who passed the rejection window, but her modifications failed anyway and she died, unable to process nutrients from her Starsearcher, **Friend** (*Hard Crash*).

Piotrowski. Gamma shift tactical officer on the *U.S.S. da Vinci* (*Cold Fusion*).

"Pompous Windbag." Nickname given by **Anthony Mark** to his supervisor at **Starbase 92** (*Hard Crash*).

prefix code. In a Federation starship's computer systems, the prefix code is a security passcode prepensed to computer commands to prevent unauthorized activation or control of key systems (*Star Trek II: The Wrath of Khan*). The **Starfleet Corps of Engineers** team from the *U.S.S. da Vinci* used the prefix code of the *U.S.S. Defiant* in order to gain access to the ship's logs (*Interphase* Book 1). The *da Vinci* also was able to take control of the *Rio Grande* when combatting an **Androssi** ship at **Empok Nor** by using the runabout's prefix code (*Cold Fusion*).

Purists. Radical group of **Pevvni** who believe that the **Eerlikka** had become too dependent on their world-running computer, **Ganitriul,** and so sabotaged the computer, sending **Eerlik** into chaos. Led by **Reger Undlar,** they were stopped by the

Starfleet Corps of Engineers team on the *U.S.S. da Vinci* (*Fatal Error*).

"PW." See **"Pompous Windbag."**

Q

Querti. Member of the **subspace accelerator** team on **Sarindar.** Querti was killed by the second **monster shii** (*Invincible* Book 2).

R

Razka. Assistant to the supervisor of the **subspace accelerator** team on **Sarindar.** Razka has five wives, none of whom he likes, and seventeen children (*Invincible* Book 1). The wife he detests least is **Marig,** and she is the one he wrote to when things went badly on Sarindar (*Invincible* Book 2). Razka was the first person to tell **Commander Sonya Gomez** about the **monster shii,** and he also shared his secret stash of Saurian brandy with her (*Invincible* Book 1). Although he was issued a sonic rifle upon his arrival on Sarindar, he never fired it because he was afraid (*Invincible* Book 2).

Reger. Title given to priests on **Eerlik** (*Fatal Error*).

Repooc. Worker assigned to the **subspace accelerator** project on **Sarindar.** Repooc and **Nomis** were able to "hot-wire" the *Culloden,* allowing the surviving workers to escape Sarindar after the second **monster shii** started attacking (*Invincible* Book 2).

Riker, William T. First officer of the *U.S.S. Enterprise* (*The Belly of the Beast*).

Rimlek. Worker on the **subspace accelerator** project on **Sarindar.** Rimlek was one of the first to be attacked by the first **monster shii.** Though he survived the encounter, he did fall into shock afterward (*Invincible* Book 1). He was later killed by the second **monster shii** (*Invincible* Book 2).

Rio Grande. Runabout assigned to **Deep Space 9. Lieutenant Nog** took the *Rio Grande* to **Empok Nor,** where he rendezvoused with the *U.S.S. da Vinci* in order to salvage the station's fusion core for DS9's use. During the subsequent firefight between the *da Vinci* and **Overseer Biron's Androssi** ship, the *da Vinci* used the **prefix codes** of the *Rio Grande* in order to remotely control it during the battle (*Cold Fusion*). The *Rio Grande* then led the convoy that towed Empok Nor to the Bajoran system (*Star Trek: Deep Space Nine: Section 31: Abyss*).

Robins. Noncommissioned Starfleet personnel assigned to the *U.S.S. da Vinci* as a security guard (*Cold Fusion*).

rodinium. One of the hardest substances known to Federation science ("Balance of Terror" [TOS]). The security bulkheads used by **Ganitriul** were made of rodinium (*Fatal Error*).

Ross, William. Starfleet admiral ("A Time to Stand" [DS9]). Ross appointed **Montgomery Scott** to serve as the liaison between the **Starfleet Corps of Engineers** and the admiralty. Ross led the meeting with Scott, **Marshall** and **Commander Grelin** about the rediscovery of the *U.S.S. Defiant.* (*Interphase* Book 1). Ross was also present when the *U.S.S. da Vinci* towed the *Defiant* into Spacedock (*Interphase* Book 2).

Ruth. Granddaughter of **Captain David Gold** and **Rabbi Rachel Gilman**. In 2376, Ruth became pregnant (*Fatal Error*). The child will be a girl (*Cold Fusion*). There is a betting pool on the *U.S.S. da Vinci* as to what the girl's name will be. (*Invincible* Book 1). *Ruth's last name has yet to be established.*

S

SA. See **subspace accelerator.**

S.C.E. See **Starfleet Corps of Engineers.**

Saber-class ship. Type of Federation starship. With a crew complement of approximately forty, the *Saber*-class ships are 190 meters long and are equipped with two shuttlecraft. Top speed is warp 9.7 for twelve hours. Many *Saber*-class ships have been assigned to the **Starfleet Corps of Engineers** (*The Belly of the Beast*). *Saber*-class ships in service include the *U.S.S. Yeager* (*Star Trek: First Contact*), the **U.S.S. da Vinci** (*The Belly of the Beast*), the **U.S.S. Musgrave** (*Interphase* Book 1), the *U.S.S. Marco Polo,* and the *U.S.S. Mercury* (*Star Trek: The Next Generation: Gateways* Book 3: *Doors Into Chaos*). *The* Saber-*class was first seen in* Star Trek: First Contact *in the form of the* Yeager, *which was part of the armada that faced the Borg. It was chosen for the S.C.E. due to its small size and maneuverability.*

Salek. First officer of the **U.S.S. da Vinci,** commanding officer of the ship's **Starfleet Corps of Engineers** team. A Vulcan, Commander Salek served on the *da Vinci* during the **Dominion War.** He was killed on a mission, and replaced by **Commander Sonya Gomez** (*The Belly of the Beast*).

sañuul. Word for "curse-lifter" in the **Nalori** language. Some members of the **subspace accelerator** team on **Sarindar** started referring to **Commander Sonya Gomez** as "Sañuul" after she fixed the antigrav units and then later killed a **monster shii,** despite her attempts to discourage it (*Invincible* Book 1). When a second monster shii appeared and began killing more and more members of the team, they stopped calling her that (*Invincible* Book 2).

Saolgud. Worker on the **subspace accelerator** project on **Sarindar.** He was killed by the first **monster shii** (*Invincible* Book 1).

Sarimun. Alien race. The Sarimun and the **Omearans** fought a war that the Omearans won, but which left them devastated, leading to their sending **Starsearchers** on exploratory missions (*Hard Crash*).

Sarindar. Planet in the **Nalori Republic.** Sarindar is a world with heavy concentrations of **chimerium.** The high concentration of this mineral also makes it nigh unto impossible to use transporters or sensors. In addition, Sarindar's sun puts out interference that renders stratospheric electromagnetic activity null except for once every fourteen hours. The planet is crystalline in nature, and the planet is populated by **silicon-based life.** The clouds are reddish-purple, and the sky is orange. Among the native animal life forms are **shii, meir,** and **kliyor.** The plant life is photosynthetic living crystal, and the ground is made up of similar substances, ranging from diamonds to quartz to topaz to amethyst. This topography makes the use of light-based energy weapons tantamount to suicide. In 2375, the Nalori started a project to construct a **subspace accelerator** on Sarindar that would allow them to mine the chimerium (*Invincible* Book 1). An alien race known only as **"the owners"** travelled to Sarindar some time in the past to conduct an archaeological expedition. They died out, apparently of an illness, but two machines equipped with **chameleon circuits** that they brought along to gather food for them remained. These machines took on the form of shii. Since the owners ate the cranial matter of other animals, the faux shii killed any visitors to Sarindar by decapitation, an eerie similarity to the Nalori legends of the **monster shii.** The creatures were killed by **Commander Sonya Gomez,** thus allowing the construction of the SA to continue (*Invincible* Book 2).

scattering field. Energy field that disrupts phasers and other energy-based weapons. During the **Dominion War, Sonya Gomez** found a way to minimize the effects of a Breen scattering field on Starfleet hand phasers, and was able to repeat the trick on **Eerlik**'s moon against a similar field generated by **Ganitriul** (*Fatal Error*).

Scott, Montgomery. Also known as "Scotty."
Former chief engineer of the *U.S.S. Enterprise,*
current chief liaison officer for the **Starfleet
Corps of Engineers.** Scotty was on his way to
retire at the Norpin colony on the *U.S.S. Jenolen* in
2294 when it crashed into a Dyson Sphere. Scotty
was able to save himself as a regenerating transporter pattern until he was rescued by the *U.S.S.
Enterprise* in 2369 ("Relics" [TNG]). During the
latter days of the **Dominion War,** Scotty, who
retains the rank of captain, was appointed the liaison between the S.C.E. and the admiralty, with the
task of giving assignments to the S.C.E.'s personnel (*The Belly of the Beast*). He was appointed to
that position by **Admiral William Ross** (*Interphase* Book 1). Scotty recommended **Commander
Sonya Gomez** for the position of first officer on
the *U.S.S. da Vinci* following the death of
Commander Salek, in part due to her Academy
paper on **subspace accelerator**s (*Invincible* Book
1). After much cajoling, Scotty had dinner with
Rabbi Rachel Gilman, wife of **Captain David
Gold** of the *da Vinci* (*Fatal Error*). In 2268, Scotty
served on the *Enterprise* when it attempted to rescue the *U.S.S. Defiant* from **interphase** ("The
Tholian Web" [TOS]). When the *Defiant* reappeared in "normal" space in 2376, Scotty sent
the *da Vinci* to perform the salvage (*Interphase*
Book 1). After the **Tholians,** who first rediscov-
ered the *Defiant,* fired on the *da Vinci,* Scotty
bought **Lt. Commander Kieran Duffy** the time
he needed to complete the rescue operation,
despite resistance from Starfleet Command and

the Diplomatic Corps (*Interphase* Book 2). After the *Defiant* salvage, Scotty assigned Gomez to take over the subspace accelerator project on **Sarindar** (*Invincible* Book 1). Scotty was able to round up nine Starfleet ships to tow **Empok Nor** from the **Trivas system** to **Deep Space 9,** though he left it to **Lieutenant Nog** to convince the ship's captains to perform the operation (*Cold Fusion*).

Sector 969. Area of space. The most direct route from the Federation to this sector is through the **Nalori Repubic,** but the government refuses to allow Starfleet vessels safe passage. Going around the republic would be prohibitive (*Invincible* Book 1). In 2376, aid given by **Commander Sonya Gomez** to a project on the planet **Sarindar** led the Nalori to reconsider this ban on Starfleet vessels, opening up the possibility of exploring the region (*Invincible* Book 2).

Security Measure 7. Security protocol observed by **Ganitriul,** the world-running computer on **Eerlik.** This protocol activates a **scattering field** that affects most energy-based weapons (*Fatal Error*).

Senbolma. Interplanetary spaceship. Designed by the **Pevvni** to be completely independent of **Ganitriul,** the world-running computer of **Eerlik,** it was used by the **Purists** to sabotage Ganitriul, leaving it as the only functioning spacefaring ship in **Eerlikka** space. The ship is owned and operated by **Emarur.** The *Senbolma's* weaponry is capable of eliminating the shields on a **Saber-class ship** with one shot. However, because the *Senbolma* had no real safeguards on their computer system, the **Starfleet Corps of Engineers** crew on the *U.S.S. da Vinci* were able to take over the ship's systems, rendering them defenseless (*Fatal Error*).

Sendrak. Month in the **Nalori** calendar (*Invincible* Book 1).

Sentinel, U.S.S. Federation starship, *Akira*-class (*Invincible* Book 1). **Sonya Gomez** served as chief engineer on the *Sentinel* during the **Dominion War.** When the ship was trapped behind enemy lines, she reconfigured the warp field so that a Breen ship thought it was a Cardassian freighter (*The Belly of the Beast*). This bought her time to get the warp drive on-line. She received a commendation for the action (*Invincible* Book 1).

Se'rbeg. The holy words of **Ho'nig,** the god of the **Damiani. Zilder,** a worshipper of Ho'nig, despite being a Bolian, carried a cracked, leather-bound copy of the *Se'rbeg* with him on **Sarindar** (*Invincible* Book 1). After he was killed by the **monster shii,** he left the book to **Commander Sonya Gomez** (*Invincible* Book 2).

Shigemos. The keepers of the dead in **Nalori** culture. When Nalori die, their *mazza,* or souls, must be commended to the **Endless Wind** by a person of authority, who announces this to the *Shigemos.* **Commander Sonya Gomez** performed this function on **Sarindar** (*Invincible* Book 1).

shii. Animal native to **Sarindar.** A silicon-based life-form, and a predator, a shii has four legs that end in triangle-shaped paws with razor-sharp points. Their heads are also triangle-shaped. The mechanical servants brought to Sarindar by **the owners** took on the form of shii, and were at first believed to be mutated shii (*Invincible* Book 1).

shii, monster. A creature from **Nalori** myth that hunts and beheads those who would try to tame the planet **Sarindar.** The mechanical servants brought to Sarindar by **the owners** took on the form of shii (*Invincible* Book 1). The owners eat the cranial matter of animals for food, so the "monster shii" would decapitate any living being they encountered, thus unintentionally fulfilling the role in the legend (*Invincible* Book 2). They horded the skulls of their kills in caves, presumably awaiting their consumption by the owners. The first monster shii was killed by **Commander Sonya Gomez** in self-defense (*Invincible* Book 1). Gomez tried to reason with the second one, but it was unable to break its programming and stop killing, so Gomez was forced to destroy it as well (*Invincible* Book 2).

silicon-based life. Biological forms whose organic chemistry is based on the element silicon, rather than the more common element, carbon ("The Devil in the Dark" [TOS]). Life forms native to **Sarindar** are silicon-based (*Invincible* Book 1).

Sinnrav. Planet. A type of music pioneered on Sinnrav is **Sinnravian** *drad* **music,** though it is not universally popular (*Cold Fusion*).

Sinnravian *drad* **music.** Style of music from planet **Sinnrav.** One of its subgenres is **atonal minimalism,** and one of that subgenre's purveyors is **Blee Luu.** Most nonSinnravians, and many from Sinnrav, find *drad* music unlistenable, but both **Carol Abramowitz** and **Lieutenant Nog** are fond of it. Abramowitz's roommate **P8 Blue** most assuredly is not (*Cold Fusion*).

Sinnravian. Native of the planet **Sinnrav.** The son of **Captain Janna Demitrijian** of the *U.S.S. Sugihara* is dating a Sinnravian (*Cold Fusion*).

Soloman. See **110/Soloman.**

sonic weapons. Sound-based weapons. On **Sarindar,** the planet's crystalline nature made using more traditional light-based energy weapons like phasers impractical, so the **subspace acceler-**

ator team from the **Nalori Republic** used sonic weapons instead. When the **monster shii** started to attack the team, **Commander Sonya Gomez** cannibalized some of the sonic weapons in order to make a sonic barrier to deter the creature (*Invincible* Book 1).

spatial interphase. See **interphase.**

Speakers. Name given to the administrators of government on **Eerlik** (*Fatal Error*).

Starbase 42. Federation starbase. Prior to the salvage of the *U.S.S. Defiant,* the last time **Kieran Duffy** was left in command of the *U.S.S. da Vinci* was when **Captain David Gold** and **Commander Sonya Gomez** had a meeting at this starbase (*Interphase* Book 1).

Starbase 92. Federation starbase. **Anthony Mark** is assigned to Starbase 92 (*Hard Crash*).

Starbase 96. Federation starbase under the supervision of Commander Ju'les L'ullho (*Star Trek: Deep Space Nine: Gateways* Book 4: *Demons of Air and Darkness*). **Captain Janna Demitrijian** was unimpressed by **Lieutenant Nog's** offer of shore leave on **Deep Space 9** and Bajor, as all the facilities there could be matched at Starbase 96 (*Cold Fusion*). The *U.S.S. da Vinci* dropped

Commander Sonya Gomez at Starbase 96, where she was picked up by the **Culloden** and taken to the planet **Sarindar** (*Invincible* Book 1).

Starbase 505. Federation starbase. The **U.S.S. da Vinci** was on its way to Starbase 505 to drop off **Geordi La Forge** and **110,** but was diverted to **Eerlik** instead (*Fatal Error*). They resumed their route there, but were once again diverted to **Intar** (*Hard Crash*).

Starfleet Corps of Engineers (S.C.E.). Division of Starfleet. The S.C.E. was responsible for the construction of Dr. Carol Marcus's underground laboratory at the asteroid Regula, at which the second phase of Project Genesis was conducted (*Star Trek II: The Wrath of Khan*). Near the end of the **Dominion War**, **Captain Montgomery Scott** was assigned to serve as the chief liaison between the S.C.E. and the admiralty. The S.C.E. has numerous ships assigned to it, including several **Saber**-class ships. One of the ships assigned is the **U.S.S. da Vinci** under the command of **Captain David Gold**, with first officer **Commander Sonya Gomez** commanding the ship's S.C.E. team. S.C.E. teams traditionally include a variety of technical specialists, as well as cultural specialists and linguists (*The Belly of the Beast*). Another S.C.E. ship is the *U.S.S. Musgrave* (*Interphase* Book 1).

Starfleet Quarantine Regulation #471946A, Paragraph 9, Subsection C. Wholly fictional regulation made up by **Commander Sonya Gomez** on **Sarindar** in order to end the "sick-out" protest by a group of workers on the **subspace accelerator** team who objected to a change in their duty assignments by pretending to have **Dakota's Disease** (*Invincible* Book 1).

Starsearcher. Name given to bio-mechanical **Omearan** exploration ships. Starsearchers bond permanently with a **pilot.** Several were sent out after a brutal war with the **Sarimun** some time prior to 2376 in order to seek out new worlds for the Omearans to colonize. If the pilot dies, the ships are supposed to auto-destruct. However, when the pilot **Jaldark Keniria** discovered that she was dying, she reprogrammed her ship, **Friend,** to continue to survive after her death (*Hard Crash*).

Starsearcher 7445. See **Friend.**

Stern College. Institute of higher learning located in New York on Earth. **Rabbi Rachel Gilman** is a professor there (*The Belly of the Beast*).

Stevens, Fabian. Noncommissioned Starfleet engineer assigned to the *U.S.S. da Vinci* as a tactical systems specialist. Stevens was formerly assigned to **Deep Space 9** and the *U.S.S. Defiant* ("Starship Down" [DS9]). Stevens' parents operate a shuttle service in the **Rigel**

Colonies (*Cold Fusion*). Stevens found a planet in the **Eerlik** system with an atmosphere that would render the *da Vinci* undetectable by sensors if they went into a low orbit; this proved a useful hiding place while the *da Vinci* effected repairs from an attack by the **Senbolma**. He later wrote a program based on **Bart Faulwell**'s design to take over the computer systems on the *Senbolma* (*Fatal Error*). Faulwell is also Stevens's roommate (*Hard Crash*). Stevens took a particular interest in the salvage of the *Constitution*-class **U.S.S. Defiant** when the *da Vinci* was assigned to salvage it from **interphase,** since he had served on one of that ship's successors. When the **Tholians** fired on the *da Vinci* while salvaging the *Defiant*, Stevens took the tactical station (*Interphase* Book 1). Afterward, he took the science station while waiting to see if the Tholians would attack again. His attempt to prematurely reopen the rift into interphase with the *da Vinci*'s deflector dish did not succeed (*Interphase* Book 2). Stevens was surprised when he was approached for a one-night liaison by **Lt. Commander Domenica Corsi** on the *da Vinci*, though he was less surprised when she assured him it would not be an ongoing thing. He was equally surprised to learn that **Nog,** whom he had last seen as a cadet on **Deep Space 9,** was now a junior-grade lieutenant and DS9's chief operations officer (*Cold Fusion*). *Stevens first appeared in "Starship Down" [DS9]. He was given a first name in* The Belly of the Beast.

sub-overseer. Rank in **Androssi** society given to the second-in-command of a ship (*Cold Fusion*).

subspace accelerator. Device that can be used to shunt objects into orbit from a planet's surface using a brief warp pulse. **Commander Sonya Gomez** did a paper on SAs when she was at the Academy. The SA constructed on planet **Sarindar** was a two-hundred-meter-in-diameter concave dish through which **chimerium** could be fed via a tubing system. The dish would then generate an **annular confinement beam** that would clear a path of vacuum through the planet's atmosphere, through which payloads would be sent via an eight-nanosecond high-warp pulse. The team that constructed the device consisted of various member races of the **Nalori Republic,** as well as some Federation races (*Invincible* Book 1).

Sugihara, **U.S.S.** Federation starship under the command of **Captain Janna Demitrijian** (*Cold Fusion*). The *Sugihara* was in the area of **Eerlik** and responded to a distress call from a Talarian freighter whose warp core went critical. Because of this, they were unable to immediately aid the **U.S.S.** *da Vinci* when they came under attack by the *Senbolma.* By the time they did arrive, the crisis was ended (*Fatal Error*). Over the objections of chief engineer **Lieutenant Barbanti,** Demitrijian agreed to have the *Sugihara* be part of the convoy that towed **Empok Nor** to the Bajoran system, but only if **Lieutenant Nog** acquired a recording of

Blee Luu's music for her son (*Cold Fusion*). *The* Sugihara *was named after Chiune Sugihara, a Japanese diplomat in Lithuania who issued visas that helped more than two thousand Lithuanian Jews to freedom during World War II. The name was suggested to author Keith R.A. DeCandido by* Enterprise Logs *editor Carol Greenburg.*

T

Taghrex. Second in command of the **Tholian** vessel commanded by **Nostrene** (*Interphase* Book 1).

Talu. Speaker of **Eerlik**. Talu had a reputation as being the voice of reason among the Speakers (*Fatal Error*).

theragen. Biochemical weapon used by the Klingon military; a nerve gas that is instantly lethal if used in pure form. **Dr. Leonard McCoy** prepared a diluted form of theragen mixed with alcohol to deaden certain nerve inputs to the brain in an effort to prevent madness in the crew of the *U.S.S. Enterprise* caused by exposure to **interphase** in 2268 ("The Tholian Web" [TOS]). In 2376, **Dr. Elizabeth Lense** of the *U.S.S. da Vinci* used the same theragen derivative to stave off the effects of interphase on the team sent to the *Defiant* to salvage it (*Interphase* Book 1), though repeated inoculations resulted in the team members developing an immunity to it and needing booster shots more often than anticipated (*Interphase* Book 2).

Tholian web. Energy field used by the **Tholians** in 2268 to entrap a disabled enemy spacecraft. A tractor field is spun by two Tholian ships that remain outside of weapons range, encircling the target, destroying the ship within ("The Tholian Web" [TOS]). By 2376, the Tholians had upgraded their web to be "pre-spun" by at least six ships, and to work on the same principle as a butterfly net, ensnaring a foe in a web-shaped energy field at least a thousand meters in diameter (*Interphase* Book 2).

Tholians. Civilization known for its punctuality and highly territorial nature. In 2268, the Tholians accused the *U.S.S. Enterprise* of violating a territorial annex of the Tholian Assembly while on a rescue mission when the *U.S.S. Defiant* was trapped in **interphase** ("The Tholian Web" [TOS]). In 2376, a Tholian ship commanded by **Nostrene** came across the *Defiant* as it came back into this universe through interphase, and reluctantly invited Starfleet to salvage the ship. The *U.S.S. da Vinci* was sent to perform the salvage. When the *da Vinci* unwittingly found evidence that the Tholians were responsible for a massacre on the Klingon colony at **Taelus II** in 2268, the Tholian **High Magistrates** ordered Nostrene to destroy the *da Vinci* and the *Defiant* (*Interphase* Book 1). They were unsuccessful, and Nostrene retreated and regrouped, returning with five other ships and the newest version of the famed **Tholian web**. However, the combined forces of the *da Vinci* and the *Defiant* were able to defeat them (*Interphase* Book 2).

tight-beam tachyon pulses. Method of communication used by the Romulans. This method is not affected by interference in subspace. The Romulans shared intelligence on this shortly before the end of the **Dominion War,** and it was written up in the *Journal of the Federation Consortium of Engineers and Technicians.* **P8 Blue** suggested it as a way for the various ships towing **Empok Nor** at warp to keep in contact despite the massive subspace distortions necessitated by such a tow (*Cold Fusion*).

Togh. A timeframe in the **Nalori** calendar. The year 2376 in the Earth calendar is the twenty-third year of Togh in Nalori (*Invincible* Book 1).

Torin. Speaker of **Eerlik** (*Fatal Error*).

Traelus II. Klingon agricultural colony. The colony was wiped out by a **Tholian web generator** in 2268. Evidence of the massacre was found by the *U.S.S. Defiant,* but the ship fell into **interphase** before it could report these findings. In

2376, when the *U.S.S. da Vinci* salvaged the *Defiant*, Tholian commander **Nostrene** was ordered to destroy the evidence of the attack on the colony in order to minimize damage to Tholian relations with the Klingon Empire (*Interphase* Book 1).

triovar field. An **Androssi** security device that, like most of their technology, employs **dimensional shifts**. When an item is surrounded by a triovar field, the field remains in an alternate dimension until someone or something comes in proximity to it, at which point a net-like force field surrounds the item (*Cold Fusion*).

Trivas system. Planetary system ("Empok Nor" [DS9]). Located in unclaimed space between the Federation and Cardassian borders, the system is the location of abandoned station **Empok Nor**. The system is not strategically useful, which is why the Cardassians abandoned it in 2372 (*Cold Fusion*).

Troi, Deanna. Ship's counselor on the *U.S.S. Enterprise* (*The Belly of the Beast*).

U

Undlar. Priest of **Eerlik**. Though he did take the vows of the priesthood, Undlar was in fact a

Pevvni Purist who masterminded the sabotage of **Ganitriul,** the computer that ran Eerlik. He murdered the remaining priests and acolytes, and also killed **First Speaker Ansed**. He also paid to have the *Senbolma* installed with non-Ganitriul parts. Through the actions of the crew of the *U.S.S. da Vinci,* the sabotage was undone and Undlar was taken into custody by **Enforcement** to answer for his crimes (*Fatal Error*).

uridium. Mineral substance. Uridium has been found on several planets, including **Eerlik** (*Fatal Error*).

Utaka. One of the **Pevvni Purists** working for **Reger Undlar** to sabotage **Ganitriul** (*Fatal Error*).

V

Valandriw Hall. Meeting place for the **Speakers** of Eerlik (*Fatal Error*).

Vale, Christine. Security chief of the *U.S.S. Enterprise*. Lieutenant Vale accompanied **Lt. Commander Geordi La Forge** on his mission to the *U.S.S. da Vinci* to salvage the ship known as *"the Beast."* Vale has an as-yet unexplained past acquaintance with **Lt. Commander Domenica Corsi,** the *da Vinci*'s security chief—Vale cites

Corsi as the reason why she joined Starfleet. Vale took the **Shuttlecraft Cook** back to the *Enterprise* without La Forge after the *Beast* was salvaged (*The Belly of the Beast*).

vixpril. A delicacy from the **Nalori** homeworld (*Invincible* Book 1).

Vlugta system. Star system near Cardassian space ("Rivals" [DS9]). **Overseer Biron** of the **Androssi** cut short a planned rendezvous with his unnamed client in the Vlugta system when the **Starfleet Corps of Engineers** crew from the **U.S.S. da Vinci** penetrated the security he had placed on Station **Empok Nor** (*Cold Fusion*).

W

web generator. A prototype **Tholian** weapon. The web generator was intended to be land-based, designed to capture the inhabitants of a planetary installation without harm to them or their structures (*Interphase* Book 1). In 2268, the Tholians tested the weapon on a Klingon agricultural colony on **Traelus II,** and it wiped the entire colony out. The **U.S.S. Defiant** investigated the destruction of Traelus and found the web generator. They were on their way to deliver it to Starfleet Command when they fell into **interphase** and were trapped between universes

(*Interphase* Book 2). In 2376, the **U.S.S. da Vinci** found the web generator on the *Defiant*, and its discovery prompted the Tholians to try to destroy the evidence of their long-ago act of violence against the Klingon Empire (*Interphase* Book 1).

Wetzel, Sandy. Nurse assigned to the **U.S.S. da Vinci** (*Interphase* Book 1). Wetzel gave the crew of the *da Vinci* **theragen** boosters while they were in proximity to **interphase** (*Interphase* Book 2).

Wong, Songmin. Alpha-shift conn officer for the **U.S.S. da Vinci** (*The Belly of the Beast*). Wong was badly injured when the *da Vinci* was attacked by the **Tholians** during the salvage of the **U.S.S. Defiant** from **interphase** (*Interphase* Book 1).

Worf. Federation Ambassador to the Klingon Empire. In 2376, Ambassador Worf pushed for smooth negotiations among the **Tholians,** the Federation, and the Klingon Empire when the 2268 Tholian massacre of the Klingon colony on **Traelus II** came to light (*Interphase* Book 2).

worker class. Subsection of **Androssi** society that does the work on their ships. Members of the worker class are considered interchangable and expendable in Androssi society, existing only to carry out the orders of the **officer class.** They are generally not even deemed worthy of eye contact.

It is acceptable protocol for a member of the officer class to kill a member of the worker class if the latter is deemed to be giving a poor performance of duty (*Cold Fusion*).

X

Xlatitigu. Language with similarities to the **Omearan** tongue (*Hard Crash*).

Y

Yanasa. One of the **Pevvni Purists** working for **Reger Undlar** to sabotage **Ganitriul** (*Fatal Error*).

Yarnallian architectural style. A type of architecture found on the planet **Eerlik**. By 2376, the style had fallen out of fashion, though some temples retain the design (*Fatal Error*).

Z

Zilder. Bolian pilot, owner and operator of the *Culloden*. Zilder was a worshipper of **Ho'nig**, the god of the **Damiani**. **Commander Sonya Gomez** wondered if he was the first non-Damiani to worship Ho'nig. Zilder was hired in 2376 by the **Nalori Republic** to provide services for the **sub-**

space accelerator project on the planet **Sarindar** (*Invincible* Book 1). He was killed by the second **monster shii.** After his death, he left his copy of the *Se'rbeg,* the holy words of Ho'nig, to Gomez and his ship to the Nalori Republic (*Invincible* Book 2).

ABOUT THE AUTHORS

Born, raised, educated, and still residing in the Bronx, **Keith R.A. DeCandido** is the co-developer of *Star Trek: S.C.E.* with John J. Ordover, and he has written or co-written several eBooks in the series. Besides *Fatal Error*, *Cold Fusion*, and *Invincible*, he has also written *Here There Be Monsters*, and more of his *S.C.E.* scribblings will be available in electronic form in 2002 and 2003 (some also in collaboration with David Mack). Keith's other *Star Trek* work includes the novels *Star Trek: The Next Generation: Diplomatic Implausibility*, *Star Trek: Deep Space Nine: Demons of Air and Darkness*, and the two-book cross-series tale *Star Trek: The Brave & the Bold* (coming in 2002), and the comic book *Star Trek: The Next Generation: Perchance to Dream* (reprinted in the trade paperback *Enemy Unseen*). He has also written best-selling novels, short stories, and nonfiction books in the worlds of *Buffy the Vampire Slayer*, *Doctor Who*, *Farscape*, Marvel Comics, and *Xena*, and is the editor of the forthcoming anthology of original science fiction *Imaginings*. Learn more than you ever really needed to know about Keith on his Web site at the easy-to-remember URL of DeCandido.net.

Kevin Dilmore counts himself as very thankful for the person who tipped him off at age nine, to the fact that *Star Trek* was a live-action television show before it was a Saturday morning cartoon. A graduate of the University of Kansas, he works as news editor and "cops and courts" reporter for a twice-weekly newspaper in Paola, Kansas. Kevin also covers "nonfiction" aspects of the *Star Trek* universe as a contributing writer for *Star Trek Communicator* magazine, as well as the Internet site StarTrek.com. He is looking forward to his next writing project with Dayton Ward, the *S.C.E.* trilogy *Foundations*, to be published in 2002. Kevin always will be proud that the formula for transparent aluminum was devised by the user of a Macintosh computer.

David Mack is a writer whose work for *Star Trek* spans multiple media. With writing partner John J. Ordover, he co-wrote the *Star Trek: Deep Space Nine* episode "Starship Down" and the story treatment for the *Star Trek: Deep Space Nine* episode "It's only a Paper Moon." David and John also penned the four-issue *Star Trek: Deep Space Nine/Star Trek: The Next Generation* crossover comic-book miniseries *Divided We Fall*. David's solo writing for *Star Trek* includes the *Star Trek: New Frontier Minipedia* and the forthcoming *Starfleet Survival Guide,* as well as behind-the-scenes contributions to several *Star Trek* CD-ROM products. He and Keith R.A. DeCandido are working on another *S.C.E.* eBook as well.

Dayton Ward has been a fan of *Star Trek* since conception (his, not the show's). After serving for eleven years in the U.S. Marine Corps, he discovered the private sector and the piles of cash to be made there as a software engineer. His start in professional writing came as a result of placing stories in each of the first three *Star Trek: Strange New Worlds* anthologies. In addition to co-writing *Interphase*, Dayton is also the author of the *Star Trek* Original Series novel, *In the Name of Honor*. He and Kevin Dilmore are also writing the forthcoming *S.C.E.* trilogy *Foundations*, to be published in eBook form in the summer of 2002. Though he currently lives in Kansas City with his wife, Michi, he is a Florida native and still maintains a torrid long-distance romance with his beloved Tampa Bay Buccaneers. Feel free to contact Dayton anytime via e-mail at DWardKC@aol.com.

Star Trek: The Next Generation®

Star Trek: Deep Space Nine®

Star Trek: Klingon • Dean Wesley Smith & Kristine Kathryn Rusch
Trials and Tribble-ations • Diane Carey
Far Beyond the Stars • Steve Barnes
What You Leave Behind • Diane Carey

Enterprise™

Star Trek®: New Frontier

Star Trek®: Starfleet Corps of Engineers (eBooks)

STAR TREK
SECTION 31

BASHIR
Never heard of it.

SLOAN
We keep a low profile....
We search out and identify
potential dangers to the
Federation.

BASHIR
And Starfleet sanctions
what you're doing?

SLOAN
We're an autonomous
department.

BASHIR
Authorized by whom?

SLOAN
Section Thirty-One was
part of the original
Starfleet Charter.

BASHIR
That was two hundred years
ago. Are you telling me
you've been on your own
ever since? Without specific
orders? Accountable to
nobody but yourselves?

SLOAN
You make it sound so
ominous.

BASHIR
Isn't it?

No law. No conscience. No stopping them.
A four book, all <u>Star Trek</u> series beginning in June.

Excerpt adapted from *Star Trek:Deep Space Nine*®
"Inquisition" written by Bradley Thompson & David Weddle.

2161